Case Studies in Contemporary Criticism

HENRY JAMES

The Turn of the Screw

Case Studies in Contemporary Criticism
SERIES EDITOR: Ross C Murfin

Jane Austen, *Emma*
EDITED BY Alistair M. Duckworth, University of Florida

Charlotte Brontë, *Jane Eyre*
EDITED BY Beth Newman, Southern Methodist University

Emily Brontë, *Wuthering Heights,* Second Edition
EDITED BY Linda H. Peterson, Yale University

Geoffrey Chaucer, *The Wife of Bath*
EDITED BY Peter G. Beidler, Lehigh University

Kate Chopin, *The Awakening,* Second Edition
EDITED BY Nancy A. Walker, Vanderbilt University

Samuel Taylor Coleridge, *The Rime of the Ancient Mariner*
EDITED BY Paul H. Fry, Yale University

Joseph Conrad, *Heart of Darkness,* Second Edition
EDITED BY Ross C Murfin, Southern Methodist University

Joseph Conrad, *The Secret Sharer*
EDITED BY Daniel R. Schwarz, Cornell University

Charles Dickens, *Great Expectations*
EDITED BY Janice Carlisle, Tulane University

E. M. Forster, *Howards End*
EDITED BY Alistair M. Duckworth, University of Florida

Thomas Hardy, *Tess of the d'Urbervilles*
EDITED BY John Paul Riquelme, Boston University

Nathaniel Hawthorne, *The Scarlet Letter*
EDITED BY Ross C Murfin, Southern Methodist University

Henry James, *The Turn of the Screw,* Second Edition
EDITED BY Peter G. Beidler, Lehigh University

James Joyce, *The Dead*
EDITED BY Daniel R. Schwarz, Cornell University

James Joyce, *A Portrait of the Artist as a Young Man*
EDITED BY R. B. Kershner, University of Florida

A Companion to James Joyce's Ulysses
EDITED BY Margot Norris, University of California, Irvine

Thomas Mann, *Death in Venice*
EDITED BY Naomi Ritter, University of Missouri

William Shakespeare, *Hamlet*
EDITED BY Susanne L. Wofford, University of Wisconsin — Madison

Mary Shelley, *Frankenstein,* Second Edition
EDITED BY Johanna M. Smith, University of Texas at Arlington

Bram Stoker, *Dracula*
EDITED BY John Paul Riquelme, Boston University

Jonathan Swift, *Gulliver's Travels*
EDITED BY Christopher Fox, University of Notre Dame

Edith Wharton, *The House of Mirth*
EDITED BY Shari Benstock, University of Miami

Case Studies in Contemporary Criticism

SERIES EDITOR: Ross C Murfin, *Southern Methodist University*

HENRY JAMES
The Turn of the Screw

Complete, Authoritative Text with
Biographical, Historical, and Cultural Contexts,
Critical History, and Essays from
Contemporary Critical Perspectives

SECOND EDITION

EDITED BY

Peter G. Beidler
Lehigh University

Bedford/St. Martin's
BOSTON ♦ NEW YORK

For Bedford / St. Martin's

Executive Editor: Stephen A. Scipione
Editorial Assistant: Anne Noyes
Associate Editor, Publishing Services: Maria Teresa Burwell
Senior Production Supervisor: Dennis J. Conroy
Production Associate: Christie Gross
Senior Marketing Manager: Jenna Bookin Barry
Project Management: Publisher's Studio/Stratford Publishing Services
Cover Design: Donna Lee Dennison
Cover Art: Claude Monet, *A Corner of the Apartment* © Archivo Iconografico, S.A./CORBIS
Composition: Stratford Publishing Services, Inc.
Printing and Binding: Haddon Craftsmen, an RR Donnelley & Sons Company

President: Joan E. Feinberg
Editorial Director: Denise B. Wydra
Director of Marketing: Karen Melton Soeltz
Director of Editing, Design, and Production: Marcia Cohen
Manager, Publishing Services: Emily Berleth

Library of Congress Control Number: 2003108632

For information, write: Bedford / St. Martin's,
75 Arlington Street, Boston, MA 02116   (617-399-4000)

ISBN-13: 978-0-312-40691-2   ISBN-10: 0-312-40691-6

Published and distributed outside North America by:
PALGRAVE MACMILLAN
Houndmills, Basingstoke, Hampshire RG21 2XS and London
Companies and representatives throughout the world.
ISBN: 1-4039-3235-2
A catalogue record for this book is available from the British Library.

Acknowledgments

"'Red hair, very red, close-curling': Sexual Hysteria, Physiognomical Bogeymen, and the 'Ghosts' in *The Turn of the Screw*" by Stanley Renner was originally published in *Nineteenth-Century Literature* 43 (1988). Reprinted, revised, with permission of the editors of that journal.

About the Series

Volumes in the *Case Studies in Contemporary Criticism* series introduce college students to the current critical and theoretical ferment in literary studies. Each volume reprints the complete text of a significant literary work, together with critical essays that approach the work from different theoretical perspectives and editorial matter that introduces both the literary work and the critics' theoretical perspectives.

The volume editor of each *Case Study* has selected and prepared an authoritative text of a classic work, written introductions (sometimes supplemented by cultural documents) that place the work in biographical and historical context, and surveyed the critical responses to the work since its original publication. Thus situated biographically, historically, and critically, the work is subsequently examined in several critical essays that have been prepared especially for students. The essays show theory in practice; whether written by established scholars or exceptional young critics, they demonstrate how current theoretical approaches can generate compelling readings of great literature.

As series editor, I have prepared introductions to the critical essays and to the theoretical approaches they entail. The introductions, accompanied by bibliographies, explain and historicize the principal concepts, major figures, and key works of particular theoretical approaches as a prelude to discussing how they pertain to the critical essays that follow. It is my hope that the introductions will reveal to students that effective criticism — including their own — is informed by a set of coherent assumptions that can be not only articulated but also modified and extended through comparison of different theoretical approaches.

Finally, I have included a glossary of key terms that recur in these volumes and in the discourse of contemporary theory and criticism.

I hope that the *Case Studies in Contemporary Criticism* series will reaffirm the richness of its literary works, even as it presents invigorating new ways to mine their apparently inexhaustible wealth.

I would like to thank Supryia M. Ray, with whom I wrote *The Bedford Glossary of Critical and Literary Terms*, for her invaluable help in revising introductions to the critical approaches represented in this volume.

Ross C Murfin
Provost, Southern Methodist University
Series Editor

About This Volume

In Part One of this volume I present the complete text of the New York Edition of Henry James's *The Turn of the Screw* as well as a number of cultural documents and illustrations that will help modern readers understand the story in its historical context.

Henry James wrote *The Turn of the Screw* at the invitation of Robert J. Collier. Collier had just taken over his father's magazine and hoped to improve the quality and sales of *Collier's Weekly* by publishing a serial story by Henry James, who was already making a name for himself as a writer of serious fiction. James worked on the story in the fall of 1897, finishing it by the end of November. The serialized version was published in twelve weekly installments in *Collier's Weekly* between January 27 and April 16, 1898.

From the start Henry James intended to bring out *The Turn of the Screw* in book form, and by October of 1898 it was printed in two separate editions, one by Heinemann in England and one by Macmillan in the United States. The title of both the English and the American books was *The Two Magics;* it contained both *The Turn of the Screw* and another long story by James, *Covering End.*

Ten years later Henry James supervised the publication of what has come to be called the "New York Edition" of his works. In volume 12 of that edition, published by Charles Scribner's Sons in 1908, were included four of James's tales: two long stories or "novellas," *The Aspern Papers* and *The Turn of the Screw,* and two short stories, "The Liar" and "The Two Faces."

James made some changes for the New York Edition, but that edition is not really much different from the earlier versions. To give just one example, at the end of chapter V the governess discovers that the man she has just described to Mrs. Grose was named Peter Quint and that Peter Quint had died. In an intense moment the puzzled and frightened governess asks, "'Died?'" James wrote for the *Collier's* version that Mrs. Grose planted her feet firmly to "articulate" her answer to the governess, "'Yes. Yes. Quint is dead.'" In the book version that year he changed "articulate" to "utter" and changed Mrs. Grose's speech to "'Yes. Mr. Quint is dead.'" In the New York Edition ten years later he changed "utter" to "express" and changed Mrs. Grose's speech to "'Yes. Mr. Quint's dead.'" The changes, in other words, were minor.

At no point did James undertake a rewriting of any portion of the story, and the few changes he did make were generally "tinkering" ones of punctuation, diction, and style. The only change that might be considered major was that after the *Collier's* edition James raised the age of Flora from six to eight years. Even though most of James's changes were minor, we follow here his final wishes — even his now obsolete practice of separating the elements of two-syllable contractions of negatives: "did n't," "has n't," and "is n't" rather than the more modern "didn't," "hasn't," and "isn't." The most important feature of the New York Edition is Henry James's Preface to it — his retrospective account of his writing of and others' reactions to *The Turn of the Screw.* I am pleased to reprint relevant portions of the Preface at the end of the Cultural Documents and Illustrations section in this volume.

The Turn of the Screw has been to critics a chameleon text, taking on a coloring that lets it blend in with almost any way of reading it. Depending on who is reading it, the story can be a gothic tale in the tradition of Poe, a romantic tale in the tradition of Hawthorne, or a realistic tale in the tradition of Howells. It can be a Freudian tale of sexual repression, an allegory of good and evil, a detective story about murder and deception, a call for better treatment of children, or a reflection of hidden truths about its author. It can demonstrate its author's knowledge of scientific research on ghosts, his rejection of that knowledge, his accord with the social structures of his time or his rejection of those structures. It can be read as a Marxist statement, a feminist statement, or a homosexual statement. So frequent and wide-ranging have been the published interpretations of *The Turn of the Screw* that critics do not even feel the need to identify either the author or the name of the story in the title of essays. A title like "The Mysteries at Bly" is sufficient to reveal to most readers that that article is about Henry James's *The Turn of the Screw.*

In Part Two of this volume I present, in addition to my essay summarizing the critical history of *The Turn of the Screw* and Ross Murfin's five introductory essays laying the groundwork for contemporary critical approaches, five essays by eminent critics. Wayne Booth has written an essay discussing "reader-response" criticism and how something he calls "ethical criticism" works in this story. Stanley Renner has written a paper with a psychoanalytic slant, defending and extending the work of earlier Freudian critics. Priscilla Walton has written a gender-based essay in which she shows how feminist and gay readings can work in *The Turn of the Screw*. Bruce Robbins shows us what a Marxist reading makes of the story by having us pay attention to the various social classes represented at Bly. Finally, Sheila Teahan uses several of these and other approaches to discuss the variety of readings *of* the story as well as the role of reading *in* the story. Taken together, these five essays, following my summary of the critical history of *The Turn of the Screw,* show the richness and the complexity of one of the most widely discussed pieces of fiction ever written.

Readers of these essays will not finish them knowing *the* answer to the questions about the governess, the ghosts, or the children, or *the* answer to the question of what this story means, but they will know something about the amazing variety of questions that a literary work can inspire and about the amazing variety of answers that readers can find to those questions. Armed with such knowledge, they will be better prepared to frame their own questions and answers and to understand what literary criticism is all about.

New to This Edition

This second Bedford edition of *The Turn of the Screw* has several improvements on the successful first edition. Most important is the Cultural Documents and Illustrations section, which will help readers to locate the story in the period in which it is set — the 1840s — and the period in which it was written and published — the late 1890s. This section reveals some of the Victorian attitudes toward servants and the damage they can do to young children in their care; toward governesses and their precarious social position as impoverished women caught, with few choices, between classes that they were not quite a part of; and toward ghosts and possessing spirits. In this section I also bring together excerpts from several early reactions to the story and from Henry James's own letters in which he responded to readers who wrote to him about *The Turn of the Screw*. I am pleased to be able to bring together the four Eric Pape illustrations that appeared in the original *Collier's Weekly* serialized edition of the story. I publish here two new essays not in the first volume: Priscilla Walton's gendered reading of the story and Sheila Teahan's combined-approach essay. I have also updated the biographical and historical contexts for the story, particularly to reflect the views of certain scholars about the likelihood that James was gay. And of course my history of the rich variety of critical opinion of the story has been extended to reflect important new work done in the past decade. I have particularly expanded my list of quotations that show students the wide variety of ways that readers and writers of various critical and creative orientations have understood Miles's death at the very end of the novel, when the governess tells us that Miles's "little heart, dispossessed, had stopped."

Throughout the essays, page references are to the text in this edition of *The Turn of the Screw*.

Acknowledgments

I offer thanks, first of all, to the critics who agreed to write new essays or let me reprint essays already published. Their patience with editorial promptings and their speed and cooperation in meeting deadlines have been most gratifying. I offer thanks also to several people who were of particular help to me in my part of the project: my son Paul for helping to collect the many essays I read for the critical history essay; my former colleague Jim Frakes; Suzi Naiburg of Harvard University and Cheryl Torsney of West Virginia University for reviewing parts of the manuscript; and four former students, Sandra Hordis, Jian "Stan" Shi, Patricia A. Engle, and Robert A. Wilson, for checking quotations for me. At Bedford/St. Martin's Steve Scipione has been an encouraging and efficient contact, and Emily Berleth and Maria Burwell saw the volume through production with great patience and attention to detail. I also thank Charles Christensen, Joan Feinberg, Elizabeth Schaaf, and Anne Noyes. As for series editor Ross Murfin—well, who can help being grateful for his good humor, his grace, and his toughness in all matters relating to a project like this? Finally, I thank Anne for understanding once more why at certain times in the past year or so I have had to close the door of my study and crouch low over my desk.

Peter G. Beidler
Lehigh University

Contents

About the Series   v

About This Volume   vii

PART TWO

The Turn of the Screw:

A Case Study in Contemporary Criticism

PART ONE

The Turn of the Screw: The Complete Text in Cultural Context

Introduction:
Biographical and
Historical Contexts

On April 15, 1843, Henry James was born into what was to be one of the most intellectually powerful families in the United States. The original James emigrated from Ireland shortly after the American Revolution. He married three times (his first two wives died relatively young) and fathered thirteen children, among them a son named Henry, born and reared in Albany, New York. That Henry, usually referred to now as Henry Sr. because of his more famous son of the same name, eventually settled in New York City with his wife, Mary. There they had five children: William (1842–1910), Henry Jr. (1843–1916), Garth Wilkinson (1845–1883), Robertson (1846–1910), and Alice (1848–1892). Henry Jr., the author of *The Turn of the Screw,* is the subject of this sketch, but to understand his life we need to know something about the siblings with whom he grew up and with whom he corresponded for most of their lives.[1]

William James was to become one of the most famous Americans of his day. An ambitious youth, he did well in school and showed early promise in both science and the arts. William was also the pupil of the well-known painter William Morris Hunt in Newport, Rhode Island,

---

[1]For more information about the James family than I can include here, see R. W. B. Lewis, *The Jameses: A Family Narrative* (New York: Farrar, 1991).

but in the end he turned away from art, perhaps because of the difficulty he foresaw in trying to make a living as a painter. He studied science next and finally enrolled in Harvard Medical School. When, some
years later, he was offered the chance to teach physiology at Harvard,
he accepted the post. He was to spend the rest of his professional life at
Harvard, eventually shifting from physiology to the new science of psychology. Before long his name and ideas were known on both sides of
the Atlantic. His two-volume *Principles of Psychology* (1890) was *the*
standard book on the subject, and the shorter, one-volume *Psychology*,
published in 1892, remained for years the standard college textbook.
By this time William had long since married and had fathered five children. Public lectures made him even more famous. His *Varieties of
Religious Experience* (1902) won him both respect and admiration.
William died of heart failure in August 1910 at age sixty-eight.

The younger brothers, Garth and Robertson, fought bravely in losing battles but on the winning side in the Civil War. Both were assigned
to help lead the first black regiments, and both were wounded in battle.
After the war they tried to make a go of agricultural enterprises in
Florida by buying cheap land and by hiring the newly freed black labor-
ers, but the farms failed and the two lived and died in the shadow of
their older brothers. "Wilky" died in his late thirties, of various physical
afflictions stemming from war wounds, kidney disease, a weak heart,
and distress at his financial insolvency. His younger brother, "Bob,"
struggled with alcoholism most of his life. He had some small success as
a writer, but his alcoholism and the financial security that came with
marriage into a wealthy family kept him from serious work. He died in
his early sixties of heart failure. His obituary in the Boston *Evening
Transcript* for July 9, 1910 — just weeks before his brother William
died — referred to him as the "youngest brother of Henry and William
James, with talents as brilliant as theirs, had they been as steadily exercised" (Lewis 582).

Alice, the youngest James and only daughter, lived in precarious
psychological and physical health, and she often contemplated suicide.
She never married or had children. She spent the last decade of her life
in Europe, never very far from her favorite brother Henry and her best
friend, Katharine Peabody Loring. There has been some speculation,
based in part on the brilliant journal she kept, that her fondness for
Katharine had lesbian overtones. Alice died of cancer in 1892 in her
mid-forties, leaving behind the journal, which her more literary brothers later had published.

This was a remarkable family indeed. The two younger brothers, while never famous, served heroically in America's most important war. The two older brothers became, in turn, America's foremost psychologist and America's foremost man of letters. The sister, though afflicted with bad health, kept a journal that has given her a prominent place in the study of the history of women and the psychology of depression and mental distress. If the family was remarkable, so was their father. The senior Henry James came to reject the Presbyterian faith of his own father and to espouse instead the ideas of Emanuel Swedenborg, the Swedish Christian mystic (1688–1772) who was to have so large an influence on Ralph Waldo Emerson and other nineteenth-century thinkers. Because of an inheritance from his father, he was able to live comfortably and, with his wife, Mary Walsh James (the daughter of a well-to-do Irish-American manufacturer), to provide his family with unusual educational experiences. Henry Sr. made friends with many famous intellectuals and writers, and entertained several of them in his home: Emerson, Henry David Thoreau, Margaret Fuller, Washington Irving, and William Makepeace Thackeray. He and his wife reared their children in no particular religion or set of beliefs but gave them books to read, introduced them to interesting people, enrolled them in many different schools, and traveled with them to fascinating places — particularly Europe in 1855.

Henry Jr. was twelve at the time of that journey. The trip was to last three years — with long stays in Geneva, London, and Paris, where young Henry became fluent in French. Although he returned home to New York and later moved with his family to Cambridge, Massachusetts, that long trip to the Old World was young Henry's introduction to the Europe that was to be his home for most of his life and the place where he did most of his writing.

Henry James Jr. — hereafter to be called simply "Henry James" or "James" — appears to have wanted, almost from the beginning, to be a writer of fiction. Certainly he got an early start and early encouragement in writing. In the February 1864 issue of the *Continental Monthly,* when he was not yet twenty-one, James published his first story, "A Tragedy of Error," about a woman who tries to have her husband murdered but, through a misunderstanding, has her lover murdered instead. Another story, published four years later, showed James's early interest in ghostly materials. "The Romance of Certain Old Clothes" ends with the ghost of a former wife murdering her husband's second wife. Melodramatic as these early stories were, they showed that James was serious, inventive, and motivated and that he had a sense of what would please the reading public. Because of the confidence of his early start and the steady conviction with which he pursued his art, he achieved an output exceeding that of any other great American writer: twenty novels and well over a hundred novellas and stories — not to mention criticism, plays, travel pieces, journals, sketches, reviews, and letters. Before he died he had met or corresponded with the most important literary artists of England and America: Ralph Waldo Emerson, Ivan Turgenev, Gustave Flaubert, Robert Browning, Rudyard Kipling, Guy de Maupassant, Walter Pater, Matthew Arnold, Lord Tennyson, William Dean Howells, Oscar Wilde, Robert Louis Stevenson, Henry Adams, Edith Wharton, James Russell Lowell, George Eliot, George Meredith, Constance Fenimore Woolson, Anthony Trollope, Sarah Orne Jewett, H. G. Wells. Few scholars will deny that James was at least the equal of any of them.

Both England and America claim Henry James as their own. We cannot know exactly why someone from so profoundly an American family came to feel more at home in Europe. Perhaps he wanted to assert his independence from his father and older brother. Perhaps in America, where other young men tended to be hustling — building and buying and selling things — he was made to feel ineffectual or lazy, or as if writing were an unmanly profession. Perhaps America had for him little culture, little literary history, little history at all in comparison with Europe. Europe had the "Eternal City" of Rome and a rich Renaissance heritage still visible in the houses and churches of almost every major city; what did America have except new towns and new wealth? Whatever the reasons, James became an artistic expatriate, living in France, Switzerland, Italy, and, especially, England for most of his adult life. He wrote home frequently, sailed home occasionally, and received many visits from American friends and family members, but he was in fact a citizen of Europe. Not long before his death at age seventy-three on February 28, 1916, James became a British subject. He changed citizenship in part to show his support for the British in what came to be called World War I, in part to make official what must have been as obvious to him as to others: that after living most of his life in England, he had become in most ways an Englishman.

FRATERNAL RIVALRY

Between Henry James and his brother William there was always a cautious friendship. Reared almost as twins, the two could scarcely help competing with one another. William showed earlier promise and seemed destined to make a more lasting intellectual contribution. He taught at Harvard, married and fathered five children, and was soon on his way to a reputation as a psychologist, researcher, writer, and lecturer. Henry, on the other hand, was a quiet and sensitive young man and was aware that as a bachelor he had chosen a more questionable — certainly a less conventional — lifeway.

To judge by the caustic tone of some of his letters, however, William felt he had reason to be jealous. His younger brother chose his profession and left home first (William was still single and living at home until he was thirty-seven), wrote and published much earlier than William did, and achieved fame first. To William, Henry's life must have looked enviably free, independent, creative, and exciting. William's writing was interrupted by the obligations of teaching and family. When he traveled, he did so encumbered by children. William never quite understood why his sister, Alice, seemed to prefer Henry's company to his own, or why their father named faraway Henry executor of his will rather than the nearby William.

For his part, Henry seemed always to stand in awe of his brother's accomplishments. He traveled in some circles where his brother came to be widely respected, and he must have been somewhat envious of William's scientific fame, occupational stability, and domestic normalcy. Although Henry became one of the most celebrated men of his day, he struggled to earn a living by his pen, knew many low periods and disappointments, and never married. To Henry, William must have looked enviably steady and respectable. Even their writing was so different that the two brothers must have felt at times like rival authors. William wrote psychology so clearly that it reads almost like fiction, whereas Henry wrote fiction so complexly that it reads almost like psychology.

Rather than emphasize the jealousies between the two brothers, however, let us remind ourselves that these two men remained friends and supportive correspondents all their lives and that their friendship far outweighed any small rivalries they may have felt. Both men had a large and warm circle of friends, and both were at the very top of their professions. If one brother can be said to have established the science of psychology as a legitimate subject of study, the other can be said to have altered the direction of fiction and literary criticism in ways that we are still learning to appreciate.

Although Henry James appeared to lead a private and sedentary life, the standard biography of his life runs to five volumes and kept its author, Leon Edel, busy for more than twenty years. A short biographical sketch like this cannot do justice to such a deep and subtly layered existence, but in what follows I will introduce a few of the issues most helpful to an understanding of the circumstances leading to James's writing of *The Turn of the Screw*.[2]

JAMES'S SEXUALITY

No one who comes to know Henry James through his writings can avoid seeking in those writings an answer to the question of why he never married. It used to be assumed that James was "married to his art" and did not want to take time away from his writing for domestic concerns. James lived in a time when men were the wage-earners, and if he had had the expense and time commitments of courting a wife and then rearing a family, he might not have been able to be a writer at all.

That early hypothesis about James's reason for not marrying, however, has been replaced with an alternative one: that James was homosexual. There is little that can be called proof, but there is some circumstantial evidence. Henry James's sensibility has struck more than a few readers as "feminine." A friend of James's, an American diplomat named Ehrman Nadal, described James in these words: "He seemed to look at women rather as women looked at them. Women looked at women as persons; men look at them as women. The quality of sex in women, which is their first and chief attraction to most men, was not their chief attraction to James" (Edel 234). Nadal's assessment may tell us less about James's sexuality than about his ability to write empathetic, perceptive fiction, but it is difficult not to see hints of possible homoerotic attraction in some of James's fiction — between Pemberton and Morgan Moreen in James's story "The Pupil," for example.[3]

And James's letters suggest that he was attracted, on some level, to a series of men, most of them younger than he. In 1890, for example, he met in Europe a young American journalist named Morton Fullerton and began a long friendship with him. In letters he refers to him as "my dear boy" and "my dearest boy" (Kaplan 407), and in 1900 he used these words to invite Fullerton for a visit: "You are beautiful; you

---

[2]For readers who want to know more about Henry James but are not ready to tackle five heavy volumes, I recommend Leon Edel's one-volume condensation, *Henry James: A Life* (New York: Harper, 1985). My quotations from Edel are from this shorter version.

[3]For a useful discussion of the possible hints of homosexuality in "The Pupil" see Philip Horne, "Henry James: The Master and the 'Queer Affair' of 'The Pupil,'" *Critical Quarterly* 37.3 (Autumn 1995): 75–92.

are more than tactful, you are tenderly, magically *tactile*. . . . I'm alone
& think of you. . . . I'd meet you at Dover — I'd do anything for you"
(Kaplan 409).[4] Is this innocent friendship or homoerotic love? Certainly James knew about homosexuality, but he also knew the dangers
of revealing it. In 1885 the British Parliament had passed what was
known as the Criminal Law Amendment Act, article 11 of which read:

> Any male person who, in public or private, commits, or is a party
> to the commission of, or procures or attempts to procure the
> commission by any male person of, any act of gross indecency with
> another male person, shall be guilty of a misdemeanor, and being
> convicted thereof shall be liable at the discretion of the court to be
> imprisoned for any term not exceeding two years, with or without
> hard labor.[5]

Ten years later, in 1895, the playwright Oscar Wilde was convicted
under this law of "gross indecency with another male person" and
given the maximum sentence of two years at hard labor. Henry James
knew Wilde, knew his plays, and followed this case with great interest.
He wrote to a friend about the case. He found it "hideously, atrociously
dramatic and really interesting" but also characterized by a "sickening
horribility" (Edel 437). He wrote to his brother William that Wilde's
"fall is hideously tragic — and the squalid violence of it gives him an
interest (of misery) that he never had for me — in any degree —
before" (Edel 439). Can there be any wonder that James, if he were
homosexual, would have worked hard to conceal that fact? To reveal it
would not merely have been an embarrassment to him and his friends,
but it might also have led to a jail sentence. It is perhaps entirely coincidental that not long after Wilde was released from prison in 1897,
James set to work on *The Turn of the Screw*. Or it may not be so coincidental. I shall have more to say about gendered readings of the story in
my Critical History of the story in Part Two of this volume.

---

[4]For a recent gathering of such letters, see Susan E. Gunter and Steven H. Jobe,
Dearly Beloved Friends: Henry James's Letters to Younger Men (Ann Arbor: U of Michigan
P, 2001). The editors admit that the letters, while showing James's affection for the four
recipients, "will not resolve for most readers which, if any, of the commonly heard labels
should be applied to James: homosocial male, homoerotic male, homosexual, repressed
homosexual, gay-inflected author, exemplar of 'male homosexual panic,' nonheterosex-
ual" (3).

[5]The full text of the act is conveniently available in *The Statues*, 3rd ed. rev., vol. 11
(London: Her Majesty's Stationery Office, 1950), 129–34. I quote from page 133.

The speculation about Henry James's sexuality continues. Sheldon M. Novick finds that James's "feelings are amply on display in his work":

> He is a good friend to strong women, but a trifle callous and misogynist to woman in general. He does not care for the miscellaneous company of heterosexual men, but can be intensely fond of young men who suit his fancy. He has love affairs, apparently only with men, but disapproves of promiscuity and of open homosexuality, and possibly even of buggery. The image of James petting a young man may stand for what we know of the sexuality in James's feelings and attractions. . . . It seems plain that we would now describe James as a closeted gay man.[6]

Wendy Graham also connects James's sexuality to his work, but reaches different conclusions. Rather than finding in James's work a reflection of his own sexuality, she finds that his sexuality was all his life "thwarted" by various personal, psychological, and social forces, and that his artistic work was what he had *instead* of physical sexuality. She is rightly skeptical of what she calls the "capon theory" of James's sexual incapacity — the notion, that is, that a wound to his genital region when he was eighteen made him incapable of sexual performance in the usual sense of that term. Rather than finding him "neutered" or sexually "dormant," she finds that James:

> practiced sexual abstinence both to forestall nervous collapse and to conserve energy for work. . . . In the thirty-year interval between his first novel and his last, James became deeply depressed about his lifelong celibacy. . . . For the bulk of his career, Henry James struggled to forge an erotic economy of artistic production, seeking to relieve the strain caused by smothered passion in the sublimation provided by art. . . . [H]is sexual escapades probably emphasized forepleasure and belonged to the regions of the mind where fantasies evolve.[7]

---

[6]From Sheldon M. Novick's introduction to *Henry James and Homo-Erotic Desire*, ed. John R. Bradley (New York: St. Martin's: 1999), 10–11. Compare Bradley's *Henry James's Permanent Adolescence* (New York: Palgrave, 2000): James was "confidently aware of his homosexuality from his adolescence" (11) and Hugh Stevens, *Henry James and Sexuality* (Cambridge: Cambridge UP, 1998): "Within his own circle, James was increasingly daring in the way he constituted himself as a sexual and desiring subject, and acknowledged freely — indeed, with pleasure — that his desires were for (young and attractive) men" (167).

[7]From the introduction to Wendy Graham's *Henry James's Thwarted Love* (Stanford: Stanford UP, 1999), 1–2, 12.

In fact, however, we know very little about Henry James's sexuality, and perhaps it is wisest to focus more on his texts than on his closets. James had many close men and women friends. He refrained from writing much about the physical aspects of any human passion, and he was either puzzled or annoyed when others wrote about such subjects. In 1888 James read *Mensonges* by his friend the novelist Paul Bourget. He did not much like the novel and wrote Bourget to tell him why:

> Your out-and-out eroticism displeases me as well as this exposition of dirty linens and dirty towels. In a word, all this is far from being life as I feel it, as I see it, as I know it, as I wish to know it. . . . It would never occur to me to want to know what goes on in their bedroom, in their bed, between a man and a woman. (Edel 378–79)

It may, of course, be the explicit discussion of man-woman sex that James found so offensive, but it is just as likely that James shared the Victorian view that such matters were out of place in serious fiction.

The issue of Henry James's sexuality is, of course, of only marginal interest for readers of *The Turn of the Screw*. There has been some speculation about possible gay and lesbian readings of the story. Are there hints of a homosexual relationship between Douglas and the narrator in the prologue to the story, or between Peter Quint and Miles, or even between the uncle in Harley Street and his valet, Peter Quint? Might there be possible lesbian overtones in the relationship between Jessel and Flora, or even between Mrs. Grose and the governess? Perhaps so. But even if there is something to those hints, James's own sexuality can tell us little about them, or about how far to let them guide our reading of the story. See "A Critical History of *The Turn of the Screw*" (pp. 202–03 in this volume) for scholars who have published about possible homoerotic connections in the story.

FIVE TROUBLED YEARS

The Turn of the Screw is somewhat atypical of the work James was doing at the turn of the century. It is about ghosts — or what the governess thinks are ghosts; it shows the darker side of human nature; it is full of danger and melodrama. To understand what may have prompted Henry James to write this story at the end of 1897, we need to understand something about his life in the earlier part of that decade. His sister, Alice, died after a lingering illness in March 1892. James was with her in London during most of the long hours of her dying and wrote for her a final telegram to their brother William in Cambridge: "Tenderest love to all. Farewell. Am going soon. Alice" (Edel 370). A year later, Henry James turned fifty and was struck with a painful and temporarily crippling gout. Mortality and aging seemed suddenly closer. He wrote to a friend that he was "moody, misanthropic, melancholy, morbid, morose" (Edel 430).

An event that caused Henry James particular distress was the 1894 death, perhaps by suicide, of a writer named Constance Fenimore Woolson. A grandniece of James Fenimore Cooper, Woolson had come to Europe in 1880 to write. Unmarried and alone, Woolson had read about Europe in Henry James's writings, and she had hoped to meet him. Meet him she did in Florence. She wrote to a friend that Florence had "taken me pretty well off my feet! Perhaps I ought to add Henry James. He has been perfectly charming to me for the last three weeks" (Edel 256). The encounter was apparently charming for James as well. James was one of many who admired Woolson's work, and he later wrote a section on her in his *Partial Portraits* (1888). We gather that James enjoyed his new friend's company. James wrote to his aunt that his new friend was "old-maidish, deaf and 'intense,' but a good little woman, and a perfect lady" (Edel 256).

James and Woolson seem never to have had a full-blown romance, but they stayed friends for many years. One recent commentator puts it this way: "She was a woman he could admire without feeling threatened, a woman he could love without loving her as a woman" (Kaplan 313). In any case, they lived in different European cities for most of their friendship. They saw each other from time to time, but they kept their friendship alive mostly through letters and more letters. In January of 1894 Woolson fell or leaped from the window of her apartment in Venice. When James, then in London, learned of the circumstances of her death, he could not bring himself to go to Italy for the funeral. He put it this way to a friend: "I have utterly collapsed. I have let everything go. . . . Miss Woolson was so valued and close a friend of mine and had been for so many years that I feel an intense nearness of participation in every circumstance of her tragic end" (Edel 391). Despite his grief and possible sense of guilt, James later helped Woolson's relatives sort out her things in Venice, and it seems likely that at that time he recovered — and destroyed — all of his letters to her.[8]

---

[8]For more on Woolson, see Cheryl B. Torsney, *Constance Fenimore Woolson: The Grief of Artistry* (Athens: U of Georgia P, 1989).

In addition to physical and emotional pain, the 1890s brought professional pain as well. James's books were not selling well, and he entered the 1890s with a sense of financial failure. Aware that writers were making a lot of money writing for the stage, he determined to try his hand as a playwright. He wrote to Robert Louis Stevenson in 1891 that "Chastening necessity has laid its brutal hand on me and I have had to try to make somehow or other the money I don't make by literature. My books don't sell, and it looks as if my plays might. Therefore I am going with a brazen front to write half a dozen" (Edel 364). As it turned out, the plays did not do well either. Companies were reluctant to produce his "talky" plays, and when they did, audiences found them too "refined" — that is, too cerebral.

As he continued to work on his own fledgling plays, James glanced nervously over his shoulder at the successful dramatic productions of Oscar Wilde and Henrik Ibsen. Only a few of James's plays were produced, and they played only short runs to unenthusiastic audiences. After several years, sensing that he might not be destined to succeed as a playwright, James decided to give the theater one more chance. He wrote to his brother William on December 29, 1893:

> I mean to wage this war ferociously for one year more — 1894 — and then (unless the victory and the spoils have not by that become more proportionate than hitherto to the humiliations and vulgarities and disgusts, all the dishonor and chronic insult incurred) to "chuck" the whole intolerable experiment and return to more elevated and more independent courses. (Edel 389)

That year he put his efforts and his hopes into a promising new play, *Guy Domville*, which would star a then famous actor named George Alexander. The play was about a young man who wants to become a Benedictine monk but is forced, by the death of his only brother, to marry so that he can produce children to carry on the family name.

Opening night for *Guy Domville* was January 5, 1895. The audience was strangely mixed. On the one hand were sophisticated intellectuals who liked James's work and wanted to see his play (among them three reviewers who were to make names for themselves in the literary world: George Bernard Shaw, H. G. Wells, and Arnold Bennett). On the other hand were unsophisticated Londoners who did not know James's other work but wanted to be entertained by George Alexander. The first group liked the play; the second hated it. After the final curtain there was applause, mostly for Alexander's performance. James's friends called for the author to come out for applause, and Henry obligingly joined Alexander in front of the curtain. When the gallery folk saw him, they jeered and hissed, while those downstairs, in the more expensive seats, applauded. James was later to put it this way in a letter to William: "All the forces of civilization in the house waged a battle of the most gallant, prolonged and sustained applause with the hoots and jeers and catcalls of the roughs, whose roars (like those of a cage of beasts at some infernal zoo) were only exacerbated by the conflict" (Edel 420). James quickly retreated backstage, and George Alexander stayed in front to apologize and to say that they would try to do better in the future. A voice from the gallery said, "T'aint your fault, gov'nor, it's a rotten play."

Guy Domville went on to a month of respectable performances, but James had gotten the message. Seeing that he could not be true to his art *and* please the "cage of beasts," he made his choice: he would be true to his art and leave the beasts to their own theatricals. Two weeks later, on January 23, 1895, James wrote in his notebook: "I take up my *own* pen again — the pen of all my old unforgettable efforts and sacred struggles. To myself — today — I need say no more. Large and full and high the future still opens. It is now indeed that I may do the work of my life. And I will" (*Notebooks* 179).

One of the first fruits of his *own* pen was *The Turn of the Screw,* which shows the effects of the difficult years he had recently endured. It is about unreturned love, death, neglect, virtue unappreciated, innocence corrupted, the evil forces in human existence. The story is also one of James's most theatrical: it has a single setting in a mysterious mansion, pale faces at windows, strange figures appearing and disappearing, dramatic scenes and dialogue, a melodramatic interplay of innocence with the haunting forces of darkness. James mined his past five years of death, sickness, and failure to produce one of his most popular and successful works.

THE GERM OF THE STORY

Five days after the humiliating opening night of *Guy Domville,* James was invited to tea at the home of his friend Edward White Benson, Archbishop of Canterbury, at Addington, just outside London. He and Benson started talking about ghosts. Soon after that visit, in a January 12, 1895, entry in his notebook, James described in some detail the outlines of a ghost narrative told him by Benson:

Note here the ghost-story told me at Addington (evening of Thursday 10th), by the Archbishop of Canterbury: the mere vague, undetailed, faint sketch of it — being all he had been told (very badly and imperfectly), by a lady who had no art of relation, and no clearness: the story of the young children (indefinite number and age) left to the care of servants in an old country-house, through the death, presumably, of parents. The servants, wicked and depraved, corrupt and deprave the children; the children are bad, full of evil, to a sinister degree. The servants *die* (the story vague about the way of it) and their apparitions, figures, return to haunt the house *and* children, to whom they seem to beckon, whom they invite and solicit, from across dangerous places, the deep ditch of a sunk fence, etc. — so that the children may destroy themselves, lose themselves, by responding, by getting into their power. So long as the children are kept from them, they are not lost; but they try and try and try, these evil presences, to get hold of them. It is a question of the children "coming over to where they are." It is all obscure and imperfect, the picture, the story, but there is a suggestion of strangely gruesome effect in it. The story to be told   tolerably obviously — by an outside spectator, observer. *(Notebooks* 178–79)

That notebook entry, of course, was the germ of *The Turn of the Screw,* though James did not get around to expanding it into a full narrative until almost three years later.

 The Turn of the Screw was James's response to an invitation from the editor of *Collier's Weekly,* the illustrated magazine published in New York, to write a twelve-part ghost story by the end of 1897. James was pleased to supply the request. He had just signed a twenty-one-year lease on Lamb House, in Rye, East Sussex, and he was concerned about the upheaval that the permanent move from London would entail. The offer from *Collier's* would give him added money for the move and, moreover, would guarantee him a wider and more popular readership than most of his fiction had earned. Besides, still conveniently at hand was that old sketch of a ghost story, based on the experiences of a woman E. W. Benson had known.

MODERN SPIRITUALISM AND THE GHOST STORY

Why would James contract to write a ghost story? That question has bothered many readers, some of whom conclude that *The Turn of the Screw* must be something *other* than a ghost story. Other readers say, well, why *wouldn't* James write a ghost story? Writers as great as Shakespeare had created literary ghosts, and James himself had written other stories in which the spirits of the dead appeared as characters. Having ghosts in *The Turn of the Screw* would be no real departure, except insofar as *these* ghosts would be more evil than others he had described.

Actually, Henry James can scarcely have avoided being interested in ghosts. His father had been fascinated by the various forms of spiritualism and possession by spirits. His brother William was an active researcher of spiritual phenomena. Indeed, in the last quarter of the nineteenth century, spirits of the dead were taken seriously as subjects for both scientific discussion and literary portrayal. Modern spiritualism can be said to have begun in 1848, when, not far from Henry James's birthplace in New York, the two daughters of a man named Fox, one aged twelve and the other fifteen, heard strange rappings in their bedroom. They began to ask the mysterious rapper questions and heard measured raps in reply. Investigators found the Fox sisters to be reliable witnesses who appeared really to have been in communication with the spirit of a dead person. The case attracted a lot of publicity, and overnight the Fox sisters became notorious.[9]

That same year Catherine Crowe published a book titled *The Night Side of Nature; or, Ghosts and Ghost Seers,* a serious report of what was then known about the science of ghosts. The book was a sensation and went through several editions and many printings. It even helped to inspire the Cambridge Ghost Club in 1851 at Trinity College, at Cambridge University in England. The purpose of the group was to conduct scientific investigations of reported cases of ghostly appearances and other supernatural phenomena. In 1882 the group was transmuted into the Society for Psychical Research under the leadership of Henry Sidgwick, a Cambridge professor of moral philosophy. Other founding members of the Society for Psychical Research were Frederic W. H. Myers and Edmund Gurney. Gurney was soon to publish (with help from Myers and Frank Podmore, another psychical researcher) a book called *Phantasms of the Living* (1886), important for its detailed discussion of some 800 reported paranormal cases.

What does all this information about psychical research have to do with Henry James and *The Turn of the Screw*? The early founders of the

---

[9]For further information about these matters, see Alan Gauld's *The Founders of Psychical Research* (London: Routledge, 1968).

Society for Psychical Research had praised Henry James's father as an early and reliable observer of spiritual phenomena. Henry James's brother William had a lifelong interest in spiritual phenomena, was a guiding light of the American branch of the Society for Psychical Research, was a member of the British parent society almost since its inception, and was its president from 1894 to 1896 — the period just before Henry James wrote *The Turn of the Screw.* (See p. 122 for a photograph of Henry and William James taken at Rye a few years after James wrote the story.) Henry James was personally acquainted with Sidgwick, Myers, and Gurney. He also, as we have seen, talked about ghosts with Archbishop Benson, a Trinity man deeply interested in ghostly phenomena. Although he was never himself a member of the Society for Psychical Research, Henry James attended at least one meeting of the Society in London, the minutes of which show that he read aloud, on behalf of his absent brother William, a scientific report about a woman named Mrs. Piper, a spirit medium whose body and voice seemed at times to be used by the spirit of a man long dead. We also know from his correspondence that Henry James purchased a copy of Gurney's *Phantasms of the Living* in 1886. James unquestionably knew about ghosts and spirit possession, and he was aware that some of the best scientists of his time, including his own brother, took such phenomena seriously.

As an example of the ghost cases investigated and reported by James's friend Edmund Gurney, here are two passages from the published account of a woman identified only as "Mrs. G." or "Birdie." After her husband's death Mrs. G. rented a lovely village house for herself, her daughters Edith, age nine, and Florence, age ten, and a maid named Anne. Gurney, who visited Mrs. G. several times as part of his investigation of this case, tells us that in his opinion she was "an excellent witness. I have never received an account in which the words and manner of telling were less suggestive of exaggeration or superstition." I give in my "Cultural Documents and Illustrations" section (see pp. 157–61) a much more complete account of Mrs. G.'s narrative as published in the 1889 *Proceedings of the Society for Psychical Research,* but it will be instructive to say here just a little more about it. One day Mrs. G.'s daughter Edith sees a man's white face peering around the door. Her sister Florence had seen nothing. Puzzled and concerned, Mrs. G. investigates and learns from some neighbors that an earlier tenant in the house had had "a wicked servant . . . a very wicked servant." Mrs. G. can get them to tell her nothing more of the servant, "but of course I imagined this very wicked servant had done something, and felt very uneasy." Later the skeptical Florence sees the face also:

> The next morning, as Florence was passing the room on the stairs, she saw a man standing by the window staring fixedly; blue eyes, dark brown hair, and freckles. She rushed up to me, looking very white and frightened; the house was searched at once, and nothing seen.

There is also a female ghost, dressed in black:

> One day, when I was out, the children were playing with Anne in the room downstairs; they all distinctly heard a very heavy footfall walk across the drawing-room, play two notes on the piano, and walk out. I came in shortly after, astonished to see them, candle in hand, looking under the beds. It was a dreadful time. . . . I then had an interview with Miss M., the former tenant, who told me she had gone through precisely what I had, but had said very little about it, for fear of being laughed at. I was far too angry to take notice whether any one laughed or not. Miss M. said one afternoon between four and five she was in very good spirits, and was playing the piano, and as she crossed the room a figure enveloped in black, with a very white face, and such a forlorn look, stood before her, and then it faded away.

After five months of these strange experiences, which terrify and sicken her children, Mrs. G. breaks the lease and leaves: "All is quite true that I have stated, whether mortal or immortal I know not. I am glad to say my children are recovering, though Edith is still very weak." A later investigation revealed that ten years earlier a forty-two-year-old woman had committed suicide by hanging herself by a skip rope from a peg in one of the bedrooms in the house.

Thousands of such narrative reports were published in the quarter-century before James wrote *The Turn of the Screw*.[10] The characters Peter Quint and Miss Jessel are both described to be in appearance like many of the ghosts reported in these scientific investigations, and it is interesting to note that James describes Douglas, in the prologue of *The Turn of the Screw*, as a *Trinity* College student when he first meets the governess and learns of her experiences at Bly. As James well knew,

---

[10]For many more examples of such narratives and an extended discussion of their possible importance to an understanding of *The Turn of the Screw*, see my *Ghosts, Demons, and Henry James* (Columbia: U of Missouri P, 1989).

Trinity College was the center of psychical research in his time, and it is significant that the man who vouches for the governess and who has her manuscript is associated with that college.

It is important to remember, then, that James launched *The Turn of the Screw* into a world that seriously investigated ghostly phenomena. We don't know whether Henry James personally believed in ghosts, but he was undoubtedly interested in them, knew about scientific research into reports about them, and was acquainted with the men most directly involved in such research. And there is no question that when James was invited to write a "ghost story" for *Collier's*, he had a wealth of information about "real" ghost cases to draw on.

THE COMPOSITION OF THE STORY

Modern readers might want to remember two facts about the composition of *The Turn of the Screw*. First, James wrote this story for publication in installments in a popular weekly magazine, *Collier's*. The first publication had, to be sure, the prologue and the twenty-four continuously numbered chapters of the current edition, but it also had the twelve groups of chapters and five larger parts. These are all indicated in the notes to the edition in this volume. The point here is that many people who read that first serialized version might have been barely able to remember the main events from previous installments, let alone the details. Unless they saved the earlier installments and read the twelve issues all at once, their reading would have been a more discontinuous experience than it is for us who read the story as James later presented it in the 1908 New York edition — the edition used for this Bedford volume.

And, second, strictly speaking, James did not "write" *The Turn of the Screw* at all. By his mid-fifties James's lifetime of writing with a pen had all but ruined his wrist. We would now call this painful phenomenon carpal tunnel syndrome. To continue to ply his trade James had to buy a typewriter — a recent invention in the 1890s. He never learned to type, but he hired others to type for him. As you read *The Turn of the Screw*, do not imagine Henry James writing the story longhand but imagine him, rather, dictating to his secretary, William MacAlpine, who typed as James spoke. Initially, then, the story of the governess and Miles and Flora was an oral tale told very much in the tradition of the ghost story recounted in front of the fire of a Christmas evening.

James made his deadline. In December of 1897 he wrote to his sister-in-law: "I *have*, at last, finished my little book" (Edel 462–63). The little book he spoke of was *The Turn of the Screw*. It appeared in *Collier's* from January to April 1898. Thus was launched the work that was to become Henry James's most widely read — and most controversial — piece of fiction. In a reminiscence written just after James's death, Yale professor William Lyon Phelps called James "the best example of the psychological realist that we have in American literature" (788) and *The Turn of the Screw* "the most powerful, the most nerve-shattering ghost story I have ever read. . . . This story made my blood chill, my spine curl, and every individual hair to stand on end." When Phelps described his reaction to Henry James, his friend replied, "I meant to scare the whole world with that story; and you had precisely the emotion that I hoped to arouse in everybody" (Phelps 794).

But not everybody, particularly in the last fifty years, has had the reaction Phelps described. Indeed, so divergent have been the reactions to James's "little book" that *The Turn of the Screw* has become as famous for the critical controversies as for the emotions it has aroused. These controversies are the subject of my essay "A Critical History of *The Turn of the Screw*," which opens Part Two of this book, following the story itself.

WORKS CITED

Beidler, Peter G. *Ghosts, Demons, and Henry James: "The Turn of the Screw" at the Turn of the Century*. Columbia: U of Missouri P, 1989.

Bradley, John R. *Henry James's Permanent Adolescence*. New York: Palgrave, 2000.

"Criminal Law Amendment Act" [1885]. *The Statutes*. 3rd ed. rev. London: Her Majesty's Stationery Office, 1950. Vol. 11, 129–34.

Crowe, Catherine Stevens. *The Night Side of Nature; or, Ghosts and Ghost Seers*. London: T. C. Newby, 1848.

Edel, Leon. *Henry James: A Life*. New York: Harper, 1985.

Gauld, Alan. *The Founders of Psychical Research*. London: Routledge, 1968.

Graham, Wendy. *Henry James's Thwarted Love*. Stanford: Stanford UP, 1999.

Gunter, Susan E., and Steven H. Jobe. *Dearly Beloved Friends: Henry James's Letters to Younger Men*. Ann Arbor: U of Michigan P, 2001.

Gurney, Edmund, Frederic W. H. Myers, and Frank Podmore. *Phantasms of the Living.* 2 vols. London: Trubner, 1886.

Horne, Philip. "Henry James: The Master and the 'Queer Affair' of 'The Pupil.'" *Critical Quarterly* 37.3 (Autumn 1995): 75–92.

James, Alice. *The Diary of Alice James.* Ed. Leon Edel. New York: Dodd, Mead, 1964.

James, William. *The Principles of Psychology.* 2 vols. New York: Holt, 1890.

———. *Psychology.* New York: Holt, 1892.

Kaplan, Fred. *Henry James: The Imagination of Genius.* New York: Morrow, 1992.

Lewis, R. W. B. *The Jameses: A Family Narrative.* New York: Farrar, 1991.

Matthiessen, F. O., and Kenneth B. Murdock, eds. *The Notebooks of Henry James.* New York: Braziller, 1955.

Novick, Sheldon M. "Introduction" to *Henry James and Homo-Erotic Desire.* Ed. John R. Bradley. New York: St. Martin's, 1999.

Phelps, William Lyon. "Henry James." *Yale Review* 5 (1916): 783–97.

Stevens, Hugh. *Henry James and Sexuality.* Cambridge: Cambridge UP, 1998.

Torsney, Cheryl B. *Constance Fenimore Woolson: The Grief of Artistry.* Athens: U of Georgia P, 1989.

The Turn of the Screw°

The story° had held us, round the fire, sufficiently breathless, but except the obvious remark that it was gruesome, as on Christmas Eve in an old house a strange tale should essentially be, I remember no comment uttered till somebody happened to note it as the only case° he had met in which such a visitation had fallen on a child. The case, I may mention, was that of an apparition° in just such an old house as had gathered us for the occasion — an appearance, of a dreadful kind, to a little boy sleeping in the room with his mother and waking her up in the terror of it; waking her not to dissipate his dread and soothe him to sleep again, but to encounter also herself, before she had succeeded in doing so, the same sight that had shocked him. It was this observation

---

The Turn of the Screw: In the original *Collier's Weekly* publication, *The Turn of the Screw* was divided into five "parts" and twelve installments in addition to the prologue and twenty-four roman-numeraled chapters of the New York Edition. *Part First* and the first weekly installment started here. The various parts and installments were deleted in the book edition, but for readers who want some sense of the pace of the periodical version, these notes indicate where the five parts and twelve installments began.   *story:* This term refers to the tale told by Griffin, one of the men gathered around the fire. It was traditional in James's time to tell ghost stories on Christmas Eve. Griffin's story had been about the appearance of a ghost to a little boy and his mother.   *case:* The term *case* indicates that Griffin's "story" was not a fictional narrative but rather a factual one, one that we are to suppose actually happened or that was reported by someone who studied actual cases in which apparitions appeared to the living. Note that the term is used again in the second sentence.   *apparition:* A more technical term for ghost or visible spirit.

that drew from Douglas — not immediately, but later in the evening — a reply that had the interesting consequence to which I call attention. Some one else told a story not particularly effective, which I saw he was not following. This I took for a sign that he had himself something to produce and that we should only have to wait. We waited in fact till two nights later; but that same evening, before we scattered, he brought out what was in his mind.

"I quite agree — in regard to Griffin's ghost, or whatever it was — that its appearing first to the little boy, at so tender an age, adds a particular touch. But it's not the first occurrence of its charming kind that I know to have been concerned with a child. If the child gives the effect another turn of the screw, what do you say to *two* children — ?"

"We say of course," somebody exclaimed, "that two children give two turns! Also that we want to hear about them."

I can see Douglas there before the fire, to which he had got up to present his back, looking down at this converser with his hands in his pockets. "Nobody but me, till now, has ever heard. It's quite too horrible." This was naturally declared by several voices to give the thing the utmost price, and our friend, with quiet art, prepared his triumph by turning his eyes over the rest of us and going on: "It's beyond everything. Nothing at all that I know touches it."

"For sheer terror?" I remember asking.

He seemed to say it was n't so simple as that; to be really at a loss how to qualify it. He passed his hand over his eyes, made a little wincing grimace. "For dreadful — dreadfulness!"

"Oh how delicious!" cried one of the women.

He took no notice of her; he looked at me, but as if, instead of me, he saw what he spoke of. "For general uncanny ugliness and horror and pain."

"Well then," I said, "just sit right down and begin."

He turned round to the fire, gave a kick to a log, watched it an instant. Then as he faced us again: "I can't begin. I shall have to send to town."° There was a unanimous groan at this, and much reproach; after which, in his preoccupied way, he explained. "The story's written. It's in a locked drawer — it has not been out for years. I could write to my man and enclose the key; he could send down the packet as he finds it." It was to me in particular that he appeared to propound this — appeared almost to appeal for aid not to hesitate. He had broken a

---

town: London. The guests are visitors at a country estate not far from London, which would have been accessible by coach.

thickness of ice, the formation of many a winter; had had his reasons for a long silence. The others resented postponement, but it was just his scruples that charmed me. I adjured° him to write by the first post and to agree with us for an early hearing; then I asked him if the experience in question had been his own. To this his answer was prompt. "Oh thank God, no!"

"And is the record yours? You took the thing down?"

"Nothing but the impression. I took that *here*" — he tapped his heart. "I've never lost it."

"Then your manuscript — ?"

"Is in old faded ink and in the most beautiful hand." He hung fire° again. "A woman's. She has been dead these twenty years. She sent me the pages in question before she died." They were all listening now, and of course there was somebody to be arch,° or at any rate to draw the inference. But if he put the inference by without a smile it was also without irritation. "She was a most charming person, but she was ten years older than I. She was my sister's governess," he quietly said. "She was the most agreeable woman I've ever known in her position; she'd have been worthy of any whatever. It was long ago, and this episode was long before. I was at Trinity,° and I found her at home on my coming down the second summer. I was much there that year — it was a beautiful one; and we had, in her off-hours, some strolls and talks in the garden — talks in which she struck me as awfully clever and nice. Oh yes; don't grin: I liked her extremely and am glad to this day to think she liked me too. If she had n't she would n't have told me. She had never told any one. It was n't simply that she said so, but that I knew she had n't. I was sure; I could see. You'll easily judge why when you hear."

"Because the thing had been such a scare?"

He continued to fix° me. "You'll easily judge," he repeated: "*you* will."

I fixed him too. "I see. She was in love."

He laughed for the first time. "You *are* acute. Yes, she was in love. That is she *had* been. That came out — she could n't tell her story without its coming out. I saw it, and she saw I saw it; but neither of us spoke of it. I remember the time and the place — the corner of the

---

adjured: Begged, strongly encouraged.   *hung fire:* Paused.   *arch:* Mischievous, suspicious. Apparently someone raised an eyebrow at the hint that Douglas may have had some relationship with the woman.   *Trinity:* Trinity College, Cambridge. Several of the faculty and students at Trinity were among the earliest serious scientific researchers into ghostly and other psychical or paranormal phenomena.   *fix:* Stare at, gaze "fixedly" at.

lawn, the shade of the great beeches and the long hot summer afternoon. It was n't a scene for a shudder; but oh — !" He quitted the fire and dropped back into his chair.

"You'll receive the packet Thursday morning?" I said.

"Probably not till the second post."

"Well then; after dinner — "

"You'll all meet me here?" He looked us round again. "Is n't anybody going?" It was almost the tone of hope.

"Everybody will stay!"

"*I* will — and *I* will!" cried the ladies whose departure had been fixed.° Mrs. Griffin, however, expressed the need for a little more light. "Who was it she was in love with?"

"The story will tell," I took upon myself to reply.

"Oh I can't wait for the story!"

"The story *won't* tell," said Douglas; "not in any literal vulgar way."

"More's the pity then. That's the only way I ever understand."

"Won't *you* tell, Douglas?" somebody else enquired.

He sprang to his feet again. "Yes — to morrow. Now I must go to bed. Good-night." And, quickly catching up a candlestick, he left us slightly bewildered. From our end of the great brown hall we heard his step on the stair; whereupon Mrs. Griffin spoke. "Well, if I don't know who she was in love with I know who *he* was."

"She was ten years older," said her husband.

"*Raison de plus*° — at that age! But it's rather nice, his long reticence."

"Forty years!" Griffin put in.

"With this outbreak at last."

"The outbreak," I returned, "will make a tremendous occasion of Thursday night"; and every one so agreed with me that in the light of it we lost all attention for everything else. The last story, however incomplete and like the mere opening of a serial, had been told; we handshook and "candlestuck,"° as somebody said, and went to bed.

I knew the next day that a letter containing the key had, by the first post, gone off to his London apartments; but in spite of — or perhaps just on account of — the eventual diffusion of this knowledge we quite let him alone till after dinner, till such an hour of the evening in fact as might best accord with the kind of emotion on which our hopes were

---

fixed: Settled, arranged. ***Raison de plus:*** French for "all the more reason." ***candlestuck:*** Lit their candles by touching them to one another so they could find their way to their chambers for the night.

fixed. Then he became as communicative as we could desire, and indeed gave us his best reason for being so. We had it from him again before the fire in the hall, as we had had our mild wonders of the previous night. It appeared that the narrative he had promised to read us really required for a proper intelligence a few words of prologue. Let me say here distinctly, to have done with it, that this narrative, from an exact transcript of my own made much later, is what I shall presently give. Poor Douglas, before his death — when it was in sight — committed to me the manuscript that reached him on the third of these days and that, on the same spot, with immense effect, he began to read to our hushed little circle on the night of the fourth. The departing ladies who had said they would stay did n't, of course, thank heaven, stay: they departed, in consequence of arrangements made, in a rage of curiosity, as they professed, produced by the touches with which he had already worked us up. But that only made his little final auditory° more compact and select, kept it, round the hearth, subject to a common thrill.

The first of these touches conveyed that the written statement took up the tale at a point after it had, in a manner, begun. The fact to be in possession of was therefore that his old friend, the youngest of several daughters of a poor country parson, had at the age of twenty, on taking service for the first time in the schoolroom, come up to London, in trepidation, to answer in person an advertisement that had already placed her in brief correspondence with the advertiser. This person proved, on her presenting herself for judgement at a house in Harley Street° that impressed her as vast and imposing — this prospective patron proved a gentleman, a bachelor in the prime of life, such a figure as had never risen, save in a dream or an old novel, before a fluttered anxious girl out of a Hampshire° vicarage. One could easily fix his type; it never, happily, dies out. He was handsome and bold and pleasant, offhand and gay and kind. He struck her, inevitably, as gallant and splendid, but what took her most of all and gave her the courage she afterwards showed was that he put the whole thing to her as a favour, an obligation he should gratefully incur. She figured him as rich, but as fearfully extravagant — saw him all in a glow of high fashion, of good looks, of expensive habits, of charming ways with women. He had for

---

auditory: Group of listeners.   **Harley Street:** A fashionable street in London, not yet associated with the medical profession. It is perhaps coincidental that about the time when the story is set, the Governesses' Benevolent Society, a charitable organization established to help unemployed or elderly governesses, was established and set up in a house in Harley Street.   **Hampshire:** A county southwest of London.

his town residence a big house filled with the spoils of travel° and the trophies of the chase; but it was to his country home, an old family place in Essex,° that he wished her immediately to proceed.

He had been left, by the death of his parents in India,° guardian to a small nephew and a small niece, children of a younger, a military brother whom he had lost two years before. These children were, by the strangest of chances for a man in his position — a lone man without the right sort of experience or a grain of patience — very heavy on his hands. It had all been a great worry and, on his own part doubtless, a series of blunders, but he immensely pitied the poor chicks and had done all he could; had in particular sent them down to his other house, the proper place for them being of course the country, and kept them there from the first with the best people he could find to look after them, parting even with his own servants to wait on them and going down himself, whenever he might, to see how they were doing. The awkward thing was that they had practically no other relations and that his own affairs took up all his time. He had put them in possession of Bly,° which was healthy and secure, and had placed at the head of their little establishment — but belowstairs only — an excellent woman, Mrs. Grose,° whom he was sure his visitor would like and who had formerly been maid to his mother. She was now housekeeper and was also acting for the time as superintendent to the little girl, of whom, without children of her own, she was by good luck extremely fond. There were plenty of people to help, but of course the young lady who should go down as governess would be in supreme authority. She would also have, in holidays, to look after the small boy, who had been for a term at school — young as he was to be sent, but what else could be done? — and who, as the holidays were about to begin, would be back from one day to the other. There had been for the two children at first a young lady whom they had had the misfortune to lose. She had done for them

---

spoils of travel: The goods and souvenirs he had acquired on his many trips abroad. **Essex:** A county northeast of London.   **the death of his parents in India:** In the original *Collier's Weekly* edition, James had written "the death of their parents in India." It is not entirely clear why James made the change to having the children orphaned by the death of their grandparents rather than their parents. India, of course, was an important part of the British empire and the reference may have suggested, if only indirectly, the imperialism of the ruling class. One effect of the change is that in the new version we are no longer explicitly told that the mother of the children dies.   **Bly:** The name of the uncle's country estate in Essex, possibly an allusion to the Bly family in Cotton Mather's account of the witchcraft trial of Bridget Bishop.   **Grose:** Possibly an allusion to the antiquarian Francis Grose (d. 1791), who wrote about ghosts and was commemorated in some of Robert Burns's poems.

quite beautifully — she was a most respectable person — till her death, the great awkwardness of which had, precisely, left no alternative but the school for little Miles. Mrs. Grose, since then, in the way of manners and things, had done as she could for Flora; and there were, further, a cook, a housemaid, a dairywoman, an old pony, an old groom and an old gardener, all likewise thoroughly respectable.

So far had Douglas presented his picture when some one put a question. "And what did the former governess die of? Of so much respectability?"

Our friend's answer was prompt. "That will come out. I don't anticipate."

"Pardon me — I thought that was just what you *are* doing."

"In her successor's place," I suggested, "I should have wished to learn if the office brought with it —"

"Necessary danger to life?" Douglas completed my thought. "She did wish to learn, and she did learn. You shall hear to-morrow what she learnt. Meanwhile of course the prospect struck her as slightly grim. She was young, untried, nervous: it was a vision of serious duties and little company, of really great loneliness. She hesitated — took a couple of days to consult and consider. But the salary offered much exceeded her modest measure, and on a second interview she faced the music, she engaged." And Douglas, with this, made a pause that, for the benefit of the company, moved me to throw in —

"The moral of which was of course the seduction exercised by the splendid young man. She succumbed to it."

He got up and, as he had done the night before, went to the fire, gave a stir to a log with his foot, then stood a moment with his back to us. "She saw him only twice."

"Yes, but that's just the beauty of her passion."

A little to my surprise, on this, Douglas turned round to me. "It *was* the beauty of it. There were others," he went on, "who had n't succumbed. He told her frankly all his difficulty — that for several applicants the conditions had been prohibitive. They were somehow simply afraid. It sounded dull — it sounded strange; and all the more so because of his main condition."

"Which was — ?"

"That she should never trouble him — but never, never: neither appeal nor complain nor write about anything; only meet all questions herself, receive all moneys from his solicitor, take the whole thing over and let him alone. She promised to do this, and she mentioned to me that when, for a moment, disburdened, delighted, he held her hand, thanking her for the sacrifice, she already felt rewarded."

"But was that all her reward?" one of the ladies asked.

"She never saw him again."

"Oh!" said the lady; which, as our friend immediately again left us, was the only other word of importance contributed to the subject till, the next night, by the corner of the hearth, in the best chair, he opened the faded red cover of a thin old-fashioned gilt-edged album. The whole thing took indeed more nights than one, but on the first occasion the same lady put another question. "What's your title?"

"I have n't one."

"Oh *I* have!" I said. But Douglas, without heeding me, had begun to read with a fine clearness that was like a rendering to the ear of the beauty of his author's hand.

I°

I remember the whole beginning as a succession of flights and drops, a little see-saw of the right throbs and the wrong. After rising, in town, to meet his appeal I had at all events a couple of very bad days — found all my doubts bristle again, felt indeed sure I had made a mistake. In this state of mind I spent the long hours of bumping swinging coach that carried me to the stopping-place at which I was to be met by a ve-hicle from the house. This convenience, I was told, had been ordered, and I found, toward the close of the June afternoon, a commodious fly° in waiting for me. Driving at that hour, on a lovely day, through a coun-try the summer sweetness of which served as a friendly welcome, my fortitude revived and, as we turned into the avenue,° took a flight that was probably but a proof of the point to which it had sunk. I suppose I had expected, or had dreaded, something so dreary that what greeted me was a good surprise. I remember as a thoroughly pleasant impres-sion the broad clear front, its open windows and fresh curtains and the pair of maids looking out; I remember the lawn and the bright flowers and the crunch of my wheels on the gravel and the clustered tree-tops over which the rooks° circled and cawed in the golden sky. The scene had a greatness that made it a different affair from my own scant home, and there immediately appeared at the door, with a little girl in her

---

I: The second weekly *Collier's* installment began here. drawn carriage. **avenue:** Lane leading to the house. ***commodious fly:*** Large horse- ***rooks:*** Black crows.

hand, a civil person who dropped me as decent a curtsey as if I had been
the mistress or a distinguished visitor. I had received in Harley Street a
narrower notion of the place, and that, as I recalled it, made me think
the proprietor still more of a gentleman, suggested that what I was to
enjoy might be a matter beyond his promise.

I had no drop again till the next day, for I was carried triumphantly
through the following hours by my introduction to the younger of my
pupils. The little girl who accompanied Mrs. Grose affected me on the
spot as a creature too charming not to make it a great fortune to have to
do with her. She was the most beautiful child I had ever seen, and I
afterwards wondered why my employer had n't made more of a point
to me of this. I slept little that night — I was too much excited; and this
astonished me too, I recollect, remained with me, adding to my sense
of the liberality with which I was treated. The large impressive room,
one of the best in the house, the great state bed, as I almost felt it, the
figured full draperies, the long glasses° in which, for the first time, I
could see myself from head to foot, all struck me — like the wonderful
appeal of my small charge — as so many things thrown in. It was
thrown in as well, from the first moment, that I should get on with Mrs.
Grose in a relation over which, on my way, in the coach, I fear I had
rather brooded. The one appearance indeed that in this early outlook
might have made me shrink again was that of her being so inordinately
glad to see me. I felt within half an hour that she was so glad — stout
simple plain clean wholesome woman — as to be positively on her
guard against showing it too much. I wondered even then a little why
she should wish *not* to show it, and that, with reflexion, with suspicion,
might of course have made me uneasy.

But it was a comfort that there could be no uneasiness in a connexion with anything so beatific as the radiant image of my little girl, the
vision of whose angelic beauty had probably more than anything else to
do with the restlessness that, before morning, made me several times
rise and wander about my room to take in the whole picture and
prospect; to watch from my open window the faint summer dawn, to
look at such stretches of the rest of the house as I could catch, and to
listen, while in the fading dusk the first birds began to twitter, for the
possible recurrence of a sound or two, less natural and not without but
within, that I had fancied I heard. There had been a moment when I
believed I recognised, faint and far, the cry of a child; there had been

glasses: Mirrors.

another when I found myself just consciously starting as at the passage, before my door, of a light footstep. But these fancies were not marked enough not to be thrown off, and it is only in the light, or the gloom, I should rather say, of other and subsequent matters that they now come back to me. To watch, teach, "form" little Flora would too evidently be the making of a happy and useful life. It had been agreed between us downstairs that after this first occasion I should have her as a matter of course at night, her small white bed being already arranged, to that end, in my room. What I had undertaken was the whole care of her, and she had remained just this last time with Mrs. Grose only as an effect of our consideration for my inevitable strangeness and her natural timidity. In spite of this timidity — which the child herself, in the oddest way in the world, had been perfectly frank and brave about, allowing it, without a sign of uncomfortable consciousness, with the deep sweet serenity indeed of one of Raphael's holy infants,° to be discussed, to be imputed to her, and to determine us — I felt quite sure she would presently like me. It was part of what I already liked Mrs. Grose herself for, the pleasure I could see her feel in my admiration and wonder as I sat at supper with four tall candles and with my pupil, in a high chair and a bib, brightly facing me between them over bread and milk. There were naturally things that in Flora's presence could pass between us only as prodigious and gratified looks, obscure and roundabout allusions.

"And the little boy — does he look like her? Is he too so very remarkable?"

One would n't, it was already conveyed between us, too grossly flatter a child. "Oh Miss, *most* remarkable. If you think well of this one!" — and she stood there with a plate in her hand, beaming at our companion, who looked from one of us to the other with placid heavenly eyes that contained nothing to check us.

"Yes; if I do — ?"

"You *will* be carried away by the little gentleman!"

"Well, that, I think, is what I came for — to be carried away. I'm afraid, however," I remember feeling the impulse to add, "I'm rather easily carried away. I was carried away in London!"

I can still see Mrs. Grose's broad face as she took this in. "In Harley Street?"

"In Harley Street."

Raphael's holy infants: Angelic children in paintings by the Italian artist Raphael (1483–1520).

"Well, Miss, you're not the first — and you won't be the last."

"Oh I've no pretensions," I could laugh, "to being the only one. My other pupil, at any rate, as I understand, comes back to-morrow?"

"Not to-morrow — Friday, Miss. He arrives, as you did, by the coach, under care of the guard,° and is to be met by the same carriage."

I forthwith wanted to know if the proper as well as the pleasant and friendly thing would n't therefore be that on the arrival of the public conveyance I should await him with his little sister; a proposition to which Mrs. Grose assented so heartily that I somehow took her manner as a kind of comforting pledge — never falsified, thank heaven! — that we should on every question be quite at one. Oh she was glad I was there!

What I felt the next day was, I suppose, nothing that could be fairly called a reaction from the cheer of my arrival; it was probably at the most only a slight oppression produced by a fuller measure of the scale, as I walked round them, gazed up at them, took them in, of my new circumstances. They had, as it were, an extent and mass for which I had not been prepared and in the presence of which I found myself, freshly, a little scared not less than a little proud. Regular lessons, in this agitation, certainly suffered some wrong; I reflected that my first duty was, by the gentlest arts I could contrive, to win the child into the sense of knowing me. I spent the day with her out of doors; I arranged with her, to her great satisfaction, that it should be she, she only, who might show me the place. She showed it step by step and room by room and secret by secret, with droll delightful childish talk about it and with the result, in half an hour, of our becoming tremendous friends. Young as she was I was struck, throughout our little tour, with her confidence and courage, with the way, in empty chambers and dull corridors, on crooked staircases that made me pause and even on the summit of an old machicolated° square tower that made me dizzy, her morning music, her disposition to tell me so many more things than she asked, rang out and led me on. I have not seen Bly since the day I left it, and I dare say that to my present older and more informed eyes it would show a very reduced importance. But as my little conductress, with her hair of gold and her frock of blue, danced before me round corners and pattered down passages, I had the view of a castle of romance inhabited by a rosy sprite, such a place as would somehow, for diversion of the young idea, take all colour out of story-books and fairy-tales. Was n't it

---

guard: Man who rides with the coach to protect mail and passengers.   *machicolated:* Provided with holes through which the defenders of a castle might drop rocks, coals, or hot liquids on attackers below.

just a story-book over which I had fallen a-doze and a-dream? No; it was a big ugly antique but convenient house, embodying a few features of a building still older, half-displaced and half-utilised, in which I had the fancy of our being almost as lost as a handful of passengers in a great drifting ship. Well, I was strangely at the helm!

II

This came home to me when, two days later, I drove over with Flora to meet, as Mrs. Grose said, the little gentleman; and all the more for an incident that, presenting itself the second evening, had deeply disconcerted me. The first day had been, on the whole, as I have expressed, reassuring; but I was to see it wind up to a change of note. The postbag that evening — it came late — contained a letter for me which, however, in the hand of my employer, I found to be composed but of a few words enclosing another, addressed to himself, with a seal still unbroken. "This, I recognise, is from the head-master, and the head-master's an awful bore. Read him, please; deal with him; but mind you don't report. Not a word. I'm off!" I broke the seal with a great effort — so great a one that I was a long time coming to it; took the unopened missive at last up to my room and only attacked it just before going to bed. I had better have let it wait till morning, for it gave me a second sleepless night. With no counsel to take, the next day, I was full of distress; and it finally got so the better of me that I determined to open myself at least to Mrs. Grose.

"What does it mean? The child's dismissed his school."°

She gave me a look that I remarked at the moment; then, visibly, with a quick blankness, seemed to try to take it back. "But are n't they all — ?"

"Sent home — yes. But only for the holidays. Miles may never go back at all."

Consciously, under my attention, she reddened. "They won't take him?"

"They absolutely decline."

At this she raised her eyes, which she had turned from me; I saw them fill with good tears. "What has he done?"

I cast about; then I judged best simply to hand her my document — which, however, had the effect of making her, without taking it, simply

---

dismissed his school: Been expelled from the boarding school he has been attending.

put her hands behind her. She shook her head sadly. "Such things are
not for me, Miss."

My counsellor could n't read! I winced at my mistake, which I
attenuated as I could, and opened the letter again to repeat it to her;
then, faltering in the act and folding it up once more, I put it back in
my pocket. "Is he really *bad*?"

The tears were still in her eyes. "Do the gentlemen say so?"

"They go into no particulars. They simply express their regret that
it should be impossible to keep him. That can have but one meaning."
Mrs. Grose listened with dumb emotion; she forbore to ask me what
this meaning might be; so that, presently, to put the thing with some
coherence and with the mere aid of her presence to my own mind, I
went on: "That he's an injury to the others."

At this, with one of the quick turns of simple folk, she suddenly
flamed up. "Master Miles! — *him* an injury?"

There was such a flood of good faith in it that, though I had not yet
seen the child, my very fears made me jump to the absurdity of the idea.
I found myself, to meet my friend the better, offering it, on the spot,
sarcastically. "To his poor little innocent mates!"

"It's too dreadful," cried Mrs. Grose, "to say such cruel things!
Why he's scarce ten years old."

"Yes, yes; it would be incredible."

She was evidently grateful for such a profession. "See him, Miss,
first. *Then* believe it!" I felt forthwith a new impatience to see him; it
was the beginning of a curiosity that, all the next hours, was to deepen
almost to pain. Mrs. Grose was aware, I could judge, of what she had
produced in me, and she followed it up with assurance. "You might
as well believe it of the little lady. Bless her," she added the next moment — "*look* at her!"

I turned and saw that Flora, whom, ten minutes before, I had established in the schoolroom with a sheet of white paper, a pencil and a
copy of nice "round O's,"° now presented herself to view at the open
door. She expressed in her little way an extraordinary detachment from
disagreeable duties, looking at me, however, with a great childish light
that seemed to offer it as a mere result of the affection she had conceived for my person, which had rendered necessary that she should follow me. I needed nothing more than this to feel the full force of Mrs.

"round O's": The governess had set Flora the task of practicing her penmanship in antic-
ipation of learning to read and write.

Grose's comparison, and, catching my pupil in my arms, covered her with kisses in which there was a sob of atonement.

None the less, the rest of the day, I watched for further occasion to approach my colleague, especially as, toward evening, I began to fancy she rather sought to avoid me. I overtook her, I remember, on the staircase; we went down together and at the bottom I detained her, holding her there with a hand on her arm. "I take what you said to me at noon as a declaration that *you've* never known him to be bad."

She threw back her head; she had clearly by this time, and very honestly, adopted an attitude. "Oh never known him — I don't pretend *that*!"

I was upset again. "Then you *have* known him — ?"

"Yes indeed, Miss, thank God!"

On reflexion I accepted this. "You mean that a boy who never is — ?"

"Is no boy for *me*!"

I held her tighter. "You like them with the spirit to be naughty?" Then, keeping pace with her answer, "So do I!" I eagerly brought out. "But not to the degree to contaminate —"

"To contaminate?" — my big word left her at a loss.

I explained it. "To corrupt."

She stared, taking my meaning in; but it produced in her an odd laugh. "Are you afraid he'll corrupt *you*?" She put the question with such a fine bold humour that with a laugh, a little silly doubtless, to match her own, I gave way for the time to the apprehension of ridicule.

But the next day, as the hour for my drive approached, I cropped up in another place. "What was the lady who was here before?"

"The last governess? She was also young and pretty — almost as young and almost as pretty, Miss, even as you."

"Ah then I hope her youth and her beauty helped her!" I recollect throwing off. "He seems to like us young and pretty!"

"Oh he *did*," Mrs. Grose assented: "it was the way he liked every one!" She had no sooner spoken indeed than she caught herself up. "I mean that's *his* way — the master's."

I was struck. "But of whom did you speak first?"

She looked blank, but she coloured. "Why of *him*."

"Of the master?"

"Of who else?"

There was so obviously no one else that the next moment I had lost my impression of her having accidentally said more than she meant; and I merely asked what I wanted to know. "Did *she* see anything in the boy — ?"

"That was n't right? She never told me."

I had a scruple, but I overcame it. "Was she careful — particular?"

Mrs. Grose appeared to try to be conscientious. "About some things — yes."

"But not about all?"

Again she considered. "Well, Miss — she's gone. I won't tell tales."

"I quite understand your feeling," I hastened to reply; but I thought it after an instant not opposed to this concession to pursue: "Did she die here?"

"No — she went off."

I don't know what there was in this brevity of Mrs. Grose's that struck me as ambiguous. "Went off to die?" Mrs. Grose looked straight out of the window, but I felt that, hypothetically, I had a right to know what young persons engaged for Bly were expected to do. "She was taken ill, you mean, and went home?"

"She was not taken ill, so far as appeared, in this house. She left it, at the end of the year, to go home, as she said, for a short holiday, to which the time she had put in had certainly given her a right. We had then a young woman — a nursemaid who had stayed on and who was a good girl and clever; and *she* took the children altogether for the interval. But our young lady never came back, and at the very moment I was expecting her I heard from the master that she was dead."

I turned this over. "But of what?"

"He never told me! But please, Miss," said Mrs. Grose, "I must get to my work."

III°

Her thus turning her back on me was fortunately not, for my just preoccupations, a snub that could check the growth of our mutual esteem. We met, after I had brought home little Miles, more intimately than ever on the ground of my stupefaction, my general emotion: so monstrous was I then ready to pronounce it that such a child as had now been revealed to me should be under an interdict.° I was a little late on the scene of his arrival, and I felt, as he stood wistfully looking out for me before the door of the inn at which the coach had put him down, that I had seen him on the instant, without and within, in the great glow of freshness, the same positive fragrance of purity, in which I

III: The third weekly *Collier's* installment began here.   ***interdict:*** Excommunication or expulsion from school.

had from the first moment seen his little sister. He was incredibly beautiful, and Mrs. Grose had put her finger on it: everything but a sort of
passion of tenderness for him was swept away by his presence. What I
then and there took him to my heart for was something divine that I
have never found to the same degree in any child — his indescribable
little air of knowing nothing in the world but love. It would have been
impossible to carry a bad name with a greater sweetness of innocence,
and by the time I had got back to Bly with him I remained merely
bewildered — so far, that is, as I was not outraged — by the sense of
the horrible letter locked up in one of the drawers of my room. As soon
as I could compass a private word with Mrs. Grose I declared to her
that it was grotesque.

She promptly understood me. "You mean the cruel charge — ?"

"It does n't live an instant. My dear woman, *look* at him!"

She smiled at my pretension to have discovered his charm. "I assure
you, Miss, I do nothing else! What will you say then?" she immediately
added.

"In answer to the letter?" I had made up my mind. "Nothing at all."

"And to his uncle?"

I was incisive. "Nothing at all."

"And to the boy himself?"

I was wonderful. "Nothing at all."

She gave with her apron a great wipe to her mouth. "Then I'll stand
by you. We'll see it out."

"We'll see it out!" I ardently echoed, giving her my hand to make it
a vow.

She held me there a moment, then whisked up her apron again with
her detached hand. "Would you mind, Miss, if I used the freedom —"

"To kiss me? No!" I took the good creature in my arms and after we
had embraced like sisters felt still more fortified and indignant.

This at all events was for the time: a time so full that as I recall the
way it went it reminds me of all the art I now need to make it a little distinct. What I look back at with amazement is the situation I accepted. I
had undertaken, with my companion, to see it out, and I was under a
charm apparently that could smooth away the extent and the far and
difficult connexions of such an effort. I was lifted aloft on a great wave
of infatuation and pity. I found it simple, in my ignorance, my confusion, and perhaps my conceit, to assume that I could deal with a boy
whose education for the world was all on the point of beginning. I am
unable even to remember at this day what proposal I framed for the end
of his holidays and the resumption of his studies. Lessons with me

indeed, that charming summer, we all had a theory that he was to have; but I now feel that for weeks the lessons must have been rather my own. I learnt something — at first certainly — that had not been one of the teachings of my small smothered life; learnt to be amused, and even amusing, and not to think for the morrow. It was the first time, in a manner, that I had known space and air and freedom, all the music of summer and all the mystery of nature. And then there was consideration — and consideration was sweet. Oh it was a trap — not designed but deep — to my imagination, to my delicacy, perhaps to my vanity; to whatever in me was most excitable. The best way to picture it all is to say that I was off my guard. They gave me so little trouble — they were of a gentleness so extraordinary. I used to speculate — but even this with a dim disconnectedness — as to how the rough future (for all futures are rough!) would handle them and might bruise them. They had the bloom of health and happiness; and yet, as if I had been in charge of a pair of little grandees,° of princes of the blood,° for whom everything, to be right, would have to be fenced about and ordered and arranged, the only form that in my fancy the after-years could take for them was that of a romantic, a really royal extension of the garden and the park. It may be of course above all that what suddenly broke into this gives the previous time a charm of stillness — that hush in which something gathers or crouches. The change was actually like the spring of a beast.

In the first weeks the days were long; they often, at their finest, gave me what I used to call my own hour, the hour when, for my pupils, tea-time and bed-time having come and gone, I had before my final retire-ment a small interval alone. Much as I liked my companions this hour was the thing in the day I liked most; and I liked it best of all when, as the light faded — or rather, I should say, the day lingered and the last calls of the last birds sounded, in a flushed sky, from the old trees — I could take a turn into the grounds and enjoy, almost with a sense of property that amused and flattered me, the beauty and dignity of the place. It was a pleasure at these moments to feel myself tranquil and jus-tified; doubtless perhaps also to reflect that by my discretion, my quiet good sense and general high propriety, I was giving pleasure — if he ever thought of it! — to the person to whose pressure I had yielded. What I was doing was what he had earnestly hoped and directly asked of me, and that I *could,* after all, do it proved even a greater joy than I

---

grandees: Persons of high nobility or importance.   *princes of the blood:* Members of the royal family.

had expected. I dare say I fancied myself in short a remarkable young woman and took comfort in the faith that this would more publicly appear. Well, I needed to be remarkable to offer a front to the remarkable things that presently gave their first sign.

It was plump, one afternoon, in the middle of my very hour: the children were tucked away and I had come out for my stroll. One of the thoughts that, as I don't in the least shrink now from noting, used to be with me in these wanderings was that it would be as charming as a charming story suddenly to meet some one. Some one would appear there at the turn of a path and would stand before me and smile and approve. I did n't ask more than that — I only asked that he should *know;* and the only way to be sure he knew would be to see it, and the kind light of it, in his handsome face. That was exactly present to me — by which I mean the face was — when, on the first of these occasions, at the end of a long June day, I stopped short on emerging from one of the plantations° and coming into view of the house. What arrested me on the spot — and with a shock much greater than any vision had allowed for — was the sense that my imagination had, in a flash, turned real. He did stand there! — but high up, beyond the lawn and at the very top of the tower to which, on that first morning, little Flora had conducted me. This tower was one of a pair — square incongruous crenellated° structures — that were distinguished, for some reason, though I could see little difference, as the new and the old. They flanked opposite ends of the house and were probably architectural absurdities, redeemed in a measure indeed by not being wholly disengaged nor of a height too pretentious, dating, in their gingerbread antiquity, from a romantic revival that was already a respectable past. I admired them, had fancies about them, for we could all profit in a degree, especially when they loomed through the dusk, by the grandeur of their actual battlements;° yet it was not at such an elevation that the figure I had so often invoked seemed most in place.

It produced in me, this figure, in the clear twilight, I remember, two distinct gasps of emotion, which were, sharply, the shock of my first and that of my second surprise. My second was a violent perception of the mistake of my first: the man who met my eyes was not the person I had precipitately supposed. There came to me thus a bewilderment of vision of which, after these years, there is no living view that I can hope

---

plantations: Groves or gardens.   *crenellated:* Notched as on an old castle wall to provide protection for archers and other defenders.   *battlements:* Fortifications atop a tower wall, usually with open spaces for shooting.

to give. An unknown man in a lonely place is a permitted object of fear
to a young woman privately bred; and the figure that faced me was — a
few more seconds assured me — as little any one else I knew as it was
the image that had been in my mind. I had not seen it in Harley
Street — I had not seen it anywhere. The place moreover, in the
strangest way in the world, had on the instant and by the very fact of its
appearance become a solitude. To me at least, making my statement
here with a deliberation with which I have never made it, the whole
feeling of the moment returns. It was as if, while I took in, what I did
take in, all the rest of the scene had been stricken with death. I can hear
again, as I write, the intense hush in which the sounds of evening
dropped. The rooks stopped cawing in the golden sky and the friendly
hour lost for the unspeakable minute all its voice. But there was no
other change in nature, unless indeed it were a change that I saw with a
stranger sharpness. The gold was still in the sky, the clearness in the air,
and the man who looked at me over the battlements was as definite as a
picture in a frame. That's how I thought, with extraordinary quickness,
of each person he might have been and that he was n't. We were confronted across our distance quite long enough for me to ask myself with
intensity who then he was and to feel, as an effect of my inability to say,
a wonder that in a few seconds more became intense.

The great question,° or one of these, is afterwards, I know, with
regard to certain matters, the question of how long they have lasted.
Well, this matter of mine, think what you will of it, lasted while I caught
at a dozen possibilities, none of which made a difference for the better,
that I could see, in there having been in the house — and for how long,
above all? — a person of whom I was in ignorance. It lasted while I just
bridled a little with the sense of how my office seemed to require that
there should be no such ignorance and no such person. It lasted while
this visitant, at all events — and there was a touch of the strange freedom, as I remember, in the sign of familiarity of his wearing no hat —
seemed to fix me, from his position, with just the question, just the
scrutiny through the fading light, that his own presence provoked. We
were too far apart to call to each other, but there was a moment at
which, at shorter range, some challenge between us, breaking the hush,
would have been the right result of our straight mutual stare. He was in
one of the angles, the one away from the house, very erect, as it struck

The great question: Probably a reference to one of the standard questions asked by psychical researchers of people who claimed to have seen a ghost: "How long did the apparition remain there?"

me, and with both hands on the ledge. So I saw him as I see the letters I form on this page; then, exactly, after a minute, as if to add to the spectacle, he slowly changed his place — passed, looking at me hard all the while, to the opposite corner of the platform. Yes, it was intense to me that during this transit he never took his eyes from me, and I can see at this moment the way his hand, as he went, moved from one of the crenellations to the next. He stopped at the other corner, but less long, and even as he turned away still markedly fixed me. He turned away; that was all I knew.

IV°

It was not that I did n't wait, on this occasion, for more, since I was as deeply rooted as shaken. Was there a "secret" at Bly — a mystery of Udolpho° or an insane, an unmentionable relative° kept in unsuspected confinement? I can't say how long I turned it over, or how long, in a confusion of curiosity and dread, I remained where I had had my collision; I only recall that when I re-entered the house darkness had quite closed in. Agitation, in the interval, certainly had held me and driven me, for I must, in circling about the place, have walked three miles; but I was to be later on so much more overwhelmed that this mere dawn of alarm was a comparatively human chill. The most singular part of it in fact — singular as the rest had been — was the part I became, in the hall, aware of in meeting Mrs. Grose. This picture comes back to me in the general train — the impression, as I received it on my return, of the wide white panelled space, bright in the lamplight and with its portraits and red carpet, and of the good surprised look of my friend, which immediately told me she had missed me. It came to me straightway, under her contact, that, with plain heartiness, mere relieved anxiety at my appearance, she knew nothing whatever that could bear upon the incident I had there ready for her. I had not suspected in advance that her comfortable face would pull me up, and I somehow measured the importance of what I had seen by my thus finding myself hesitate to mention it. Scarce anything in the whole history seems to me so odd as this fact that my real beginning of fear was one, as I may say, with the

---

IV: The fourth weekly *Collier's* installment and *Part Second* began here.   ***mystery of Udolpho:*** An allusion to Ann Radcliffe's famous gothic novel *The Mysteries of Udolpho* (1794), in which the heroine is carried away to a gloomy castle.   ***an unmentionable relative:*** Almost certainly an allusion to Bertha, Rochester's insane wife, hidden upstairs in Charlotte Brontë's *Jane Eyre* (1847).

instinct of sparing my companion. On the spot, accordingly, in the pleasant hall and with her eyes on me, I, for a reason that I could n't then have phrased, achieved an inward revolution — offered a vague pretext for my lateness and, with the plea of the beauty of the night and of the heavy dew and wet feet, went as soon as possible to my room.

Here it was another affair; here, for many days after, it was a queer affair enough. There were hours, from day to day — or at least there were moments, snatched even from clear duties — when I had to shut myself up to think. It was n't so much yet that I was more nervous than I could bear to be as that I was remarkably afraid of becoming so; for the truth I had now to turn over was simply and clearly the truth that I could arrive at no account whatever of the visitor with whom I had been so inexplicably and yet, as it seemed to me, so intimately concerned. It took me little time to see that I might easily sound, without forms of enquiry and without exciting remark, any domestic complication. The shock I had suffered must have sharpened all my senses; I felt sure, at the end of three days and as the result of mere closer attention, that I had not been practiced upon by the servants nor made the object of any "game." Of whatever it was that I knew nothing was known around me. There was but one sane inference: some one had taken a liberty rather monstrous. That was what, repeatedly, I dipped into my room and locked the door to say to myself. We had been, collectively, subject to an intrusion; some unscrupulous traveller, curious in old houses, had made his way in unobserved, enjoyed the prospect from the best point of view and then stolen out as he came. If he had given me such a bold hard stare, that was but a part of his indiscretion. The good thing, after all, was that we should surely see no more of him.

This was not so good a thing, I admit, as not to leave me to judge that what, essentially, made nothing else much signify was simply my charming work. My charming work was just my life with Miles and Flora, and through nothing could I so like it as through feeling that to throw myself into it was to throw myself out of my trouble. The attraction of my small charges was a constant joy, leading me to wonder afresh at the vanity of my original fears, the distaste I had begun by entertaining for the probable grey prose of my office. There was to be no grey prose, it appeared, and no long grind; so how could work not be charming that presented itself as daily beauty? It was all the romance of the nursery and the poetry of the schoolroom. I don't mean by this of course that we studied only fiction and verse; I mean that I can express no otherwise the sort of interest my companions inspired. How

can I describe that except by saying that instead of growing deadly used
to them — and it's a marvel for a governess: I call the sisterhood to witness! — I made constant fresh discoveries. There was one direction,
assuredly, in which these discoveries stopped: deep obscurity continued
to cover the region of the boy's conduct at school. It had been
promptly given me, I have noted, to face that mystery without a pang.
Perhaps even it would be nearer the truth to say that — without a
word — he himself had cleared it up. He had made the whole charge
absurd. My conclusion bloomed there with the real rose-flush of his
innocence: he was only too fine and fair for the little horrid unclean
school-world, and he had paid a price for it. I reflected acutely that the
sense of such individual differences, such superiorities of quality, always,
on the part of the majority — which could include even stupid sordid
head-masters — turns infallibly to the vindictive.

Both the children had a gentleness — it was their only fault, and it
never made Miles a muff° — that kept them (how shall I express it?)
almost impersonal and certainly quite unpunishable. They were like
those cherubs of the anecdote who had — morally at any rate — nothing to whack!° I remember feeling with Miles in especial as if he had
had, as it were, nothing to call even an infinitesimal history. We expect
of a small child scant enough "antecedents," but there was in this beautiful little boy something extraordinarily sensitive, yet extraordinarily
happy, that, more than in any creature of his age I have seen, struck me
as beginning anew each day. He had never for a second suffered. I took
this as a direct disproof of his having really been chastised. If he had
been wicked he would have "caught" it, and I should have caught it by
the rebound — I should have found the trace, should have felt the
wound and the dishonour. I could reconstitute nothing at all, and he
was therefore an angel. He never spoke of his school, never mentioned
a comrade or a master; and I, for my part, was quite too much disgusted
to allude to them. Of course I was under the spell, and the wonderful
part is that, even at the time, I perfectly knew I was. But I gave myself
up to it; it was an antidote to any pain, and I had more pains than one. I
was in receipt in these days of disturbing letters from home,° where

muff: A sissy; an unmanly boy.   *nothing to whack:* A humorous reference to angels so
immaterial that they have no bottoms to spank and so good that there could be nothing
to spank them for.   *letters from home:* Letters from her parson father at the vicarage
reporting problems, perhaps financial or medical problems. Many young women became
governesses because there were problems at home. Often they had to send money home
to help their families survive.

things were not going well. But with this joy of my children what things in the world mattered? That was the question I used to put to my scrappy retirements. I was dazzled by their loveliness.

There was a Sunday — to get on — when it rained with such force and for so many hours that there could be no procession to church; in consequence of which, as the day declined, I had arranged with Mrs. Grose that, should the evening show improvement, we would attend together the late service. The rain happily stopped, and I prepared for our walk, which, through the park and by the good road to the village, would be a matter of twenty minutes. Coming downstairs to meet my colleague in the hall, I remembered a pair of gloves that had required three stitches and that had received them — with a publicity perhaps not edifying — while I sat with the children at their tea, served on Sundays, by exception, in that cold clean temple of mahogany and brass, the "grown-up" dining-room. The gloves had been dropped there, and I turned in to recover them. The day was grey enough, but the afternoon light still lingered, and it enabled me, on crossing the threshold, not only to recognise, on a chair near the wide window, then closed, the articles I wanted, but to become aware of a person on the other side of the window and looking straight in. One step into the room had sufficed; my vision was instantaneous; it was all there. The person looking straight in was the person who had already appeared to me. He appeared thus again with I won't say greater distinctness, for that was impossible, but with a nearness that represented a forward stride in our intercourse° and made me, as I met him, catch my breath and turn cold. He was the same — he was the same, and seen, this time, as he had been seen before, from the waist up, the window, though the dining-room was on the ground floor, not going down to the terrace on which he stood. His face was close to the glass, yet the effect of this better view was, strangely, just to show me how intense the former had been. He remained but a few seconds — long enough to convince me he also saw and recognised; but it was as if I had been looking at him for years and had known him always. Something, however, happened this time that had not happened before; his stare into my face, through the glass and across the room, was as deep and hard as then, but it quitted me for a moment during which I could still watch it, see it fix successively several other things. On the spot there came to me the added shock of a certitude that it was not for me he had come. He had come for some one else.

intercourse: Dealings or communications between persons or groups; interchange of thoughts and feelings. The word had not yet come to carry overtones of "sexual intercourse."

The flash of this knowledge — for it was knowledge in the midst of dread — produced in me the most extraordinary effect, starting, as I stood there, a sudden vibration of duty and courage. I say courage because I was beyond all doubt already far gone. I bounded straight out of the door again, reached that of the house, got in an instant upon the drive and, passing along the terrace as fast as I could rush, turned a corner and came full in sight. But it was in sight of nothing now — my visitor had vanished. I stopped, almost dropped, with the real relief of this; but I took in the whole scene — I gave him time to reappear. I call it time, but how long was it? I can't speak to the purpose to-day of the duration of these things. That kind of measure must have left me: they could n't have lasted as they actually appeared to me to last. The terrace and the whole place, the lawn and the garden beyond it, all I could see of the park, were empty with a great emptiness. There were shrubberies and big trees, but I remember the clear assurance I felt that none of them concealed him. He was there or was not there: not there if I did n't see him. I got hold of this; then, instinctively, instead of returning as I had come, went to the window. It was confusedly present to me that I ought to place myself where he had stood. I did so; I applied my face to the pane and looked, as he had looked, into the room. As if, at this moment, to show me exactly what his range had been, Mrs. Grose, as I had done for himself just before, came in from the hall. With this I had the full image of a repetition of what had already occurred. She saw me as I had seen my own visitant; she pulled up short as I had done; I gave her something of the shock that I had received. She turned white, and this made me ask myself if I had blanched as much. She stared, in short, and retreated just on *my* lines, and I knew she had then passed out and come round to me and that I should presently meet her. I remained where I was, and while I waited I thought of more things than one. But there's only one I take space to mention. I wondered why *she* should be scared.

                                      V

Oh she let me know as soon as, round the corner of the house, she loomed again into view. "What in the name of goodness is the matter — ?" She was now flushed and out of breath.

I said nothing till she came quite near. "With me?" I must have made a wonderful face. "Do I show it?"

"You're as white as a sheet. You look awful."

I considered; I could meet on this, without scruple, any degree of innocence. My need to respect the bloom of Mrs. Grose's had dropped, without a rustle, from my shoulders, and if I wavered for the instant it was not with what I kept back. I put out my hand to her and she took it; I held her hard a little, liking to feel her close to me. There was a kind of support in the shy heave of her surprise. "You came for me for church, of course, but I can't go."

"Has anything happened?"

"Yes. You must know now. Did I look very queer?"

"Through this window? Dreadful!"

"Well," I said, "I've been frightened." Mrs. Grose's eyes expressed plainly that *she* had no wish to be, yet also that she knew too well her place not to be ready to share with me any marked inconvenience. Oh it was quite settled that she *must* share! "Just what you saw from the dining-room a minute ago was the effect of that. What *I* saw — just before — was much worse."

Her hand tightened. "What was it?"

"An extraordinary man. Looking in."

"What extraordinary man?"

"I have n't the least idea."

Mrs. Grose gazed round us in vain. "Then where is he gone?"

"I know still less."

"Have you seen him before?"

"Yes — once. On the old tower."

She could only look at me harder. "Do you mean he's a stranger?"

"Oh very much!"

"Yet you did n't tell me?"

"No — for reasons. But now that you've guessed — "

Mrs. Grose's round eyes encountered this charge. "Ah I have n't guessed!" she said very simply. "How can I if *you* don't imagine?"

"I don't in the very least."

"You've seen him nowhere but on the tower?"

"And on this spot just now."

Mrs. Grose looked round again. "What was he doing on the tower?"

"Only standing there and looking down at me."

She thought a minute. "Was he a gentleman?"

I found I had no need to think. "No." She gazed in deeper wonder. "No."

"Then nobody about the place? Nobody from the village?"

"Nobody — nobody. I did n't tell you, but I made sure."

She breathed a vague relief: this was, oddly, so much to the good. It only went indeed a little way. "But if he is n't a gentleman — "

"What *is* he? He's a horror."

"A horror?"

"He's — God help me if I know *what* he is!"

Mrs. Grose looked round once more; she fixed her eyes on the duskier distance and then, pulling herself together, turned to me with full inconsequence. "It's time we should be at church."

"Oh I'm not fit for church!"

"Won't it do you good?"

"It won't do *them* — !" I nodded at the house.

"The children?"

"I can't leave them now."

"You're afraid — ?"

I spoke boldly. "I'm afraid of *him*."

Mrs. Grose's large face showed me, at this, for the first time, the far-away faint glimmer of a consciousness more acute: I somehow made out in it the delayed dawn of an idea I myself had not given her and that was as yet quite obscure to me. It comes back to me that I thought instantly of this as something I could get from her; and I felt it to be connected with the desire she presently showed to know more. "When was it — on the tower?"

"About the middle of the month. At this same hour."

"Almost at dark," said Mrs. Grose.

"Oh no, not nearly. I saw him as I see you."

"Then how did he get in?"

"And how did he get out?"° I laughed. "I had no opportunity to ask him! This evening, you see," I pursued, "he has not been able to get in."

"He only peeps?"

"I hope it will be confined to that!" She had now let go my hand; she turned away a little. I waited an instant; then I brought out: "Go to church. Good-bye. I must watch."

Slowly she faced me again. "Do you fear for them?"

We met in another long look. "Don't *you*?" Instead of answering

---

Then how . . . did he get out? This exchange echoes a line in the ghost narrative of Mrs. Vatas-Simpson, published a dozen years before James wrote his story: "Now, then, how did that man get in? — or rather, how did he get *out*?" The full account, with citation, is given on pp. 151–55.

she came nearer to the window and, for a minute, applied her face to the glass. "You see how he could see," I meanwhile went on.

She did n't move. "How long was he here?"

"Till I came out. I came to meet him."

Mrs. Grose at last turned round, and there was still more in her face. "*I* could n't have come out."

"Neither could I!" I laughed again. "But I did come. I've my duty."

"So have I mine," she replied; after which she added: "What's he like?"

"I've been dying to tell you. But he's like nobody."

"Nobody?" she echoed.

"He has no hat."° Then seeing in her face that she already, in this, with a deeper dismay, found a touch of picture, I quickly added stroke to stroke. "He has red hair, very red, close-curling, and a pale face, long in shape, with straight good features and little rather queer whiskers that are as red as his hair. His eyebrows are somehow darker; they look particularly arched and as if they might move a good deal. His eyes are sharp, strange — awfully; but I only know clearly that they're rather small and very fixed. His mouth's wide, and his lips are thin, and except for his little whiskers he's quite clean-shaven. He gives me a sort of sense of looking like an actor."

"An actor!" It was impossible to resemble one less, at least, than Mrs. Grose at that moment.

"I've never seen one, but so I suppose them. He's tall, active, erect," I continued, "but never — no, never! — a gentleman."

My companion's face had blanched as I went on; her round eyes started and her mild mouth gaped. "A gentleman?" she gasped, confounded, stupefied: "a gentleman *he*?"

"You know him then?"

She visibly tried to hold herself. "But he *is* handsome?"

I saw the way to help her. "Remarkably!"

"And dressed — ?"

"In somebody's clothes. They're smart, but they're not his own."

She broke into a breathless affirmative groan. "They're the master's!"

I caught it up. "You *do* know him?"

She faltered but a second. "Quint!" she cried.

"Quint?"

---

no hat: That he wears no hat would have suggested to a Victorian audience that he was not a gentleman. The governess had first noticed the absence of the hat in the last paragraph of chapter III (p. 40).

"Peter Quint° — his own man, his valet, when he was here!"

"When the master was?"

Gaping still, but meeting me, she pieced it all together. "He never wore his hat, but he did wear — well, there were waistcoats missed! They were both here — last year. Then the master went, and Quint was alone."

I followed, but halting a little. "Alone?"

"Alone with *us*." Then as from a deeper depth, "In charge," she added.

"And what became of him?"

She hung fire so long that I was still more mystified. "He went too," she brought out at last.

"Went where?"

Her expression, at this, became extraordinary. "God knows where! He died."

"Died?" I almost shrieked.

She seemed fairly to square herself, plant herself more firmly to express the wonder of it. "Yes Mr. Quint's dead."

VI°

It took of course more than that particular passage to place us together in presence of what we had now to live with as we could, my dreadful liability° to impressions of the order so vividly exemplified, and my companion's knowledge henceforth — a knowledge half consternation and half compassion — of that liability. There had been this evening, after the revelation that left me for an hour so prostrate — there had been for either of us no attendance on any service but a little service of tears and vows, of prayers and promises, a climax to the series of mutual challenges and pledges that had straightway ensued on our retreating together to the schoolroom and shutting ourselves up there to have everything out. The result of our having everything out was simply to reduce our situation to the last rigour of its elements. She herself had seen nothing, not the shadow of a shadow, and nobody in the

---

Peter Quint: Perhaps an allusion to Peter Quince in Shakespeare's *A Midsummer Night's Dream?*   *VI:* The fifth weekly *Collier's* installment began here.   *dreadful liability:* Unwanted ability to see the visible presence of a spirit. Just below in this paragraph the governess refers to her "plight" in being the only one to see the ghost of Peter Quint. It was a common feature of ghost cases that only one or two people had the power to see apparitions that to others remained invisible.

house but the governess was in the governess's plight; yet she accepted without directly impugning my sanity the truth as I gave it to her, and ended by showing me on this ground an awestricken tenderness, a deference to my more than questionable privilege,° of which the very breath has remained with me as that of the sweetest of human charities.

What was settled between us accordingly that night was that we thought we might bear things together; and I was not even sure that in spite of her exemption° it was she who had the best of the burden. I knew at this hour, I think, as well as I knew later, what I was capable of meeting to shelter my pupils; but it took me some time to be wholly sure of what my honest comrade was prepared for to keep terms with so stiff an agreement. I was queer company enough — quite as queer as the company I received; but as I trace over what we went through I see how much common ground we must have found in the one idea that, by good fortune, *could* steady us. It was the idea, the second movement, that led me straight out, as I may say, of the inner chamber of my dread. I could take the air in the court, at least, and there Mrs. Grose could join me. Perfectly can I recall now the particular way strength came to me before we separated for the night. We had gone over and over every feature of what I had seen.

"He was looking for some one else, you say — some one who was not you?"

"He was looking for little Miles." A portentous clearness now possessed me. "*That's* whom he was looking for."

"But how do you know?"

"I know, I know, I know!" My exaltation grew. "And you know, my dear!"

She did n't deny this, but I required, I felt, not even so much telling as that. She took it up again in a moment. "What if *he* should see him?"

"Little Miles? That's what he wants!"

She looked immensely scared again. "The child?"

"Heaven forbid! The man. He wants to appear to *them*." That he might was an awful conception, and yet somehow I could keep it at bay; which moreover, as we lingered there, was what I succeeded in practically proving. I had an absolute certainty that I should see again what I had already seen, but something within me said that by offering myself

---

privilege: The ability to see apparitions. In the second paragraph of the first chapter of Charles Dickens's *David Copperfield* (1850), David speaks of a nurse who predicted before his actual birth that he would be "priviledged to see ghosts and spirits." **exemption:** Inability to see the ghost.

bravely as the sole subject of such experience, by accepting, by inviting, by surmounting it all, I should serve as an expiatory victim and guard the tranquillity of the rest of the household. The children in especial I should thus fence about and absolutely save. I recall one of the last things I said that night to Mrs. Grose.

"It does strike me that my pupils have never mentioned — !"

She looked at me hard as I musingly pulled up. "His having been here and the time they were with him?"

"The time they were with him, and his name, his presence, his history, in any way. They've never alluded to it."

"Oh the little lady does n't remember. She never heard or knew."

"The circumstances of his death?" I thought with some intensity. "Perhaps not. But Miles would remember — Miles would know."

"Ah don't try him!" broke from Mrs. Grose.

I returned her the look she had given me. "Don't be afraid." I continued to think. "It *is* rather odd."

"That he has never spoken of him?"

"Never by the least reference. And you tell me they were 'great friends.'"

"Oh it was n't *him*!" Mrs. Grose with emphasis declared. "It was Quint's own fancy. To play with him, I mean — to spoil him." She paused a moment; then she added: "Quint was much too free."

This gave me, straight from my vision of his face — *such* a face! — a sudden sickness of disgust. "Too free with *my* boy?"

"Too free with every one!"

I forbore for the moment to analyse this description further than by the reflexion that a part of it applied to several of the members of the household, of the half-dozen maids and men who were still of our small colony. But there was everything, for our apprehension, in the lucky fact that no discomfortable legend, no perturbation of scullions,° had ever, within any one's memory, attached to the kind old place. It had neither bad name nor ill fame, and Mrs. Grose, most apparently, only desired to cling to me and to quake in silence. I even put her, the very last thing of all, to the test. It was when, at midnight, she had her hand on the schoolroom door to take leave. "I *have* it from you then — for it's of great importance — that he was definitely and admittedly bad?"

"Oh not admittedly. *I* knew it — but the master did n't."

"And you never told him?"

"Well, he did n't like tale-bearing — he hated complaints. He was

scullions: Unskilled kitchen workers.

terribly short with anything of that kind, and if people were all right to
him — "

"He would n't be bothered with more?" This squared well enough
with my impression of him: he was not a trouble-loving gentleman, nor
so very particular perhaps about some of the company he himself kept.
All the same, I pressed my informant. "I promise you *I* would have
told!"

She felt my discrimination. "I dare say I was wrong. But really I was
afraid."

"Afraid of what?"

"Of things that man could do. Quint was so clever — he was so
deep."

I took this in still more than I probably showed. "You were n't
afraid of anything else? Not of his effect — ?"

"His effect?" she repeated with a face of anguish and waiting while I
faltered.

"On innocent little precious lives. They were in your charge."

"No, they were n't in mine!" she roundly and distressfully returned.
"The master believed in him and placed him here because he was supposed not to be quite in health and the country air so good for him. So
he had everything to say. Yes" — she let me have it — "even about
them."

"Them — that creature?" I had to smother a kind of howl. "And
you could bear it?"

"No. I could n't — and I can't now!" And the poor woman burst
into tears.

A rigid control, from the next day, was, as I have said, to follow
them; yet how often and how passionately, for a week, we came back
together to the subject! Much as we had discussed it that Sunday night,
I was, in the immediate later hours in especial — for it may be imagined
whether I slept — still haunted with the shadow of something she had
not told me. I myself had kept back nothing, but there was a word Mrs.
Grose had kept back. I was sure moreover by morning that this was not
from a failure of frankness, but because on every side there were fears. It
seems to me indeed, in raking it all over, that by the time the morrow's
sun was high I had restlessly read into the facts before us almost all the
meaning they were to receive from subsequent and more cruel occurrences. What they gave me above all was just the sinister figure of the
living man — the dead one would keep a while! — and of the months
he had continuously passed at Bly, which, added up, made a formidable
stretch. The limit of this evil time had arrived only when, on the dawn

of a winter's morning, Peter Quint was found, by a labourer going to early work, stone dead on the road from the village: a catastrophe explained — superficially at least — by a visible wound to his head; such a wound as might have been produced (and as, on the final evidence, *had* been) by a fatal slip, in the dark and after leaving the public-house, on the steepish icy slope, a wrong path altogether, at the bottom of which he lay. The icy slope, the turn mistaken at night and in liquor, accounted for much — practically, in the end and after the inquest and boundless chatter, for everything; but there had been matters in his life, strange passages and perils, secret disorders, vices more than suspected, that would have accounted for a good deal more.

I scarce know how to put my story into words that shall be a credible picture of my state of mind; but I was in these days literally able to find a joy in the extraordinary flight of heroism the occasion demanded of me. I now saw that I had been asked for a service admirable and difficult; and there would be a greatness in letting it be seen — oh in the right quarter! — that I could succeed where many another girl might have failed. It was an immense help to me — I confess I rather applaud myself as I look back! — that I saw my response so strongly and so simply. I was there to protect and defend the little creatures in the world the most bereaved and the most loveable, the appeal of whose helplessness had suddenly become only too explicit, a deep constant ache of one's own engaged affection. We were cut off, really, together; we were united in our danger. They had nothing but me, and I — well, I had *them*. It was in short a magnificent chance. This chance presented itself to me in an image richly material. I was a screen° — I was to stand before them. The more I saw the less they would. I began to watch them in a stifled suspense, a disguised tension, that might well, had it continued too long, have turned to something like madness. What saved me, as I now see, was that it turned to another matter altogether. It did n't last as suspense — it was superseded by horrible proofs. Proofs, I say, yes — from the moment I really took hold.

This moment dated from an afternoon hour that I happened to spend in the grounds with the younger of my pupils alone. We had left Miles indoors, on the red cushion of a deep window-seat; he had wished to finish a book, and I had been glad to encourage a purpose so laudable in a young man whose only defect was a certain ingenuity of restlessness. His sister, on the contrary, had been alert to come out, and

---

I was a screen: The governess believes that her seeing and confronting the ghost of Peter Quint will let her act as a barrier between him and the children.

I strolled with her half an hour, seeking the shade, for the sun was still
high and the day exceptionally warm. I was aware afresh with her, as we
went, of how, like her brother, she contrived — it was the charming
thing in both children — to let me alone without appearing to drop me
and to accompany me without appearing to oppress. They were never
importunate and yet never listless. My attention to them all really went
to seeing them amuse themselves immensely without me: this was a
spectacle they seemed actively to prepare and that employed me as an
active admirer. I walked in a world of their invention — they had no
occasion whatever to draw upon mine; so that my time was taken only
with being for them some remarkable person or thing that the game of
the moment required and that was merely, thanks to my superior, my
exalted stamp, a happy and highly distinguished sinecure. I forget what
I was on the present occasion; I only remember that I was something
very important and very quiet and that Flora was playing very hard. We
were on the edge of the lake, and, as we had lately begun geography,
the lake was the Sea of Azof.°

Suddenly, amid these elements, I became aware that on the other
side of the Sea of Azof we had an interested spectator. The way this
knowledge gathered in me was the strangest thing in the world — the
strangest, that is, except the very much stranger in which it quickly
merged itself. I had sat down with a piece of work° — for I was something or other that could sit — on the old stone bench which overlooked the pond; and in this position I began to take in with certitude
and yet without direct vision the presence, a good way off, of a third
person. The old trees, the thick shrubbery, made a great and pleasant
shade, but it was all suffused with the brightness of the hot still hour.
There was no ambiguity in anything; none whatever at least in the conviction I from one moment to another found myself forming as to what
I should see straight before me and across the lake as a consequence of
raising my eyes. They were attached at this juncture to the stitching in
which I was engaged, and I can feel once more the spasm of my effort
not to move them till I should so have steadied myself as to be able to
make up my mind what to do. There was an alien object in view — a
figure whose right of presence I instantly and passionately questioned. I
recollect counting over perfectly the possibilities, reminding myself that
nothing was more natural for instance than the appearance of one of

Sea of Azof: An inland sea (now often spelled Azov) on the north or Russian side of the
Black Sea. The governess is having Flora learn a bit of geography by having her imagine
that the pond at Bly is this sea.   *a piece of work:* A bit of knitting.

the men about the place, or even of a messenger, a postman or a trades-
man's boy, from the village. That reminder had as little effect on my
practical certitude as I was conscious — still even without looking — of
its having upon the character and attitude of our visitor. Nothing was
more natural than that these things should be the other things they
absolutely were not.

Of the positive identity of the apparition I would assure myself as
soon as the small clock of my courage should have ticked out the right
second; meanwhile, with an effort that was already sharp enough, I
transferred my eyes straight to little Flora, who, at the moment, was
about ten yards away. My heart had stood still for an instant with the
wonder and terror of the question whether she too would see; and I
held my breath while I waited for what a cry from her, what some sudden innocent sign either of interest or of alarm, would tell me. I waited,
but nothing came; then in the first place — and there is something
more dire in this, I feel, than in anything I have to relate — I was determined by a sense that within a minute all spontaneous sounds from her
had dropped; and in the second by the circumstance that also within
the minute she had, in her play, turned her back to the water. This was
her attitude when I at last looked at her — looked with the confirmed
conviction that we were still, together, under direct personal notice.
She had picked up a small flat piece of wood which happened to have in
it a little hole that had evidently suggested to her the idea of sticking
in another fragment that might figure as a mast and make the thing a
boat. This second morsel, as I watched her, she was very markedly and
intently attempting to tighten in its place. My apprehension of what she
was doing sustained me so that after some seconds I felt I was ready for
more. Then I again shifted my eyes — I faced what I had to face.

VII

I got hold of Mrs. Grose as soon after this as I could; and I can give
no intelligible account of how I fought out the interval. Yet I still hear
myself cry as I fairly threw myself into her arms: "They *know* — it's too
monstrous: they know, they know!"

"And what on earth — ?" I felt her incredulity as she held me.

"Why all that *we* know — and heaven knows what more besides!"
Then as she released me I made it out to her, made it out perhaps only
now with full coherency even to myself. "Two hours ago, in the garden" — I could scarce articulate — "Flora *saw*!"

Mrs. Grose took it as she might have taken a blow in the stomach. "She has told you?" she panted.

"Not a word — that's the horror. She kept it to herself! The child of eight,° *that* child!" Unutterable still for me was the stupefaction of it.

Mrs. Grose of course could only gape the wider. "Then how do you know?"

"I was there — I saw with my eyes: saw she was perfectly aware."

"Do you mean aware of *him*?"

"No — of *her*." I was conscious as I spoke that I looked prodigious things, for I got the slow reflexion of them in my companion's face. "Another person — this time; but a figure of quite as unmistakeable horror and evil: a woman in black, pale and dreadful — with such an air also, and such a face! — on the other side of the lake. I was there with the child — quiet for the hour; and in the midst of it she came."

"Came how — from where?"

"From where they come from! She just appeared and stood there — but not so near."

"And without coming nearer?"

"Oh for the effect and the feeling she might have been as close as you!"

My friend, with an odd impulse, fell back a step. "Was she some one you've never seen?"

"Never. But some one the child has. Some one *you* have." Then to show how I had thought it all out: "My predecessor — the one who died."

"Miss Jessel?"

"Miss Jessel. You don't believe me?" I pressed.

She turned right and left in her distress. "How can you be sure?"

This drew from me, in the state of my nerves, a flash of impatience. "Then ask Flora — *she's* sure!" But I had no sooner spoken than I caught myself up. "No, for God's sake *don't*! She'll say she is n't — she'll lie!"

Mrs. Grose was not too bewildered instinctively to protest. "Ah how *can* you?"

"Because I'm clear. Flora does n't want me to know."

"It's only then to spare you."

---

child of eight: In the original version published in *Collier's* James had written "child of six." In the first chapter she is said to sit in a high chair and to wear a bib and she is referred to elsewhere as both an "infant" and a "baby." Perhaps because a reader had suggested that at times Flora acts and talks like an older girl, James changed her age to eight in the book version.

"No, no — there are depths, depths! The more I go over it the more I see in it, and the more I see in it the more I fear. I don't know what I *don't* see, what I *don't* fear!"

Mrs. Grose tried to keep up with me. "You mean you're afraid of seeing her again?"

"Oh no; that's nothing — now!" Then I explained. "It's of *not* seeing her."

But my companion only looked wan. "I don't understand."

"Why, it's that the child may keep it up — and that the child assuredly *will* — without my knowing it."

At the image of this possibility Mrs. Grose for a moment collapsed, yet presently to pull herself together again as from the positive force of the sense of what, should we yield an inch, there would really be to give way to. "Dear, dear — we must keep our heads! And after all, if she does n't mind it — !" She even tried a grim joke. "Perhaps she likes it!"

"Like *such* things — a scrap of an infant!"

"Isn't it just a proof of her blest innocence?" my friend bravely enquired.

She brought me, for the instant, almost round. "Oh we must clutch at *that* — we must cling to it! If it is n't a proof of what you say, it's a proof of — God knows what! For the woman's a horror of horrors."

Mrs. Grose, at this, fixed her eyes a minute on the ground; then at last raising them, "Tell me how you know," she said.

"Then you admit it's what she was?" I cried.

"Tell me how you know," my friend simply repeated.

"Know? By seeing her! By the way she looked."

"At you, do you mean — so wickedly?"

"Dear me, no — I could have borne that. She gave me never a glance. She only fixed the child."

Mrs. Grose tried to see it. "Fixed her?"

"Ah with such awful eyes!"

She stared at mine as if they might really have resembled them. "Do you mean of dislike?"

"God help us, no. Of something much worse."

"Worse than dislike?" — this left her indeed at a loss.

"With a determination — indescribable. With a kind of fury of intention."

I made her turn pale. "Intention?"

"To get hold of her." Mrs. Grose — her eyes just lingering on mine — gave a shudder and walked to the window; and while she stood there looking out I completed my statement. "*That's* what Flora knows."

After a little she turned round. "The person was in black, you say?"

"In mourning° — rather poor, almost shabby. But — yes — with extraordinary beauty." I now recognised to what I had at last, stroke by stroke, brought the victim of my confidence, for she quite visibly weighed this. "Oh handsome — very, very," I insisted; "wonderfully handsome. But infamous."°

She slowly came back to me. "Miss Jessel — *was* infamous." She once more took my hand in both her own, holding it as tight as if to fortify me against the increase of alarm I might draw from this disclosure. "They were both infamous," she finally said.

So for a little we faced it once more together; and I found absolutely a degree of help in seeing it now so straight. "I appreciate," I said, "the great decency of your not having hitherto spoken; but the time has certainly come to give me the whole thing." She appeared to assent to this, but still only in silence; seeing which I went on: "I must have it now. Of what did she die? Come, there was something between them."

"There was everything."

"In spite of the difference — ?"

"Oh of their rank, their condition" — she brought it woefully out. "*She* was a lady."

I turned it over; I again saw. "Yes — she was a lady."

"And he so dreadfully below," said Mrs. Grose.

I felt that I doubtless need n't press too hard, in such company, on the place of a servant in the scale; but there was nothing to prevent an acceptance of my companion's own measure of my predecessor's abasement. There was a way to deal with that, and I dealt; the more readily for my full vision — on the evidence — of our employer's late clever good-looking "own" man; impudent, assured, spoiled, depraved. "The fellow was a hound."°

Mrs. Grose considered as if it were perhaps a little a case for a sense of shades. "I've never seen one like him. He did what he wished."

"With *her*?"

"With them all."

It was as if now in my friend's own eyes Miss Jessel had again appeared. I seemed at any rate for an instant to trace their evocation of

---

In mourning: We are never told precisely whose death Miss Jessel may be mourning, but there are hints that it may be her own baby's. We are made to understand that she left Bly because she was pregnant with Quint's child, and there is "the cry of a child" (p. 30) that the governess hears when she first comes to Bly.   *infamous:* Loathsome, detestable, grossly shocking.   *a hound:* Sexually indiscriminate man.

her as distinctly as I had seen her by the pond; and I brought out with decision: "It must have been also what *she* wished!"

Mrs. Grose's face signified that it had been indeed, but she said at the same time: "Poor woman — she paid for it!"

"Then you do know what she died of?" I asked.

"No — I know nothing. I wanted not to know; I was glad enough I did n't; and I thanked heaven she was well out of this!"

"Yet you had then your idea — "

"Of her real reason for leaving?° Oh yes — as to that. She could n't have stayed. Fancy it here — for a governess! And afterwards I imagined — and I still imagine. And what I imagine is dreadful."

"Not so dreadful as what *I* do," I replied; on which I must have shown her — as I was indeed but too conscious — a front of miserable defeat. It brought out again all her compassion for me, and at the renewed touch of her kindness my power to resist broke down. I burst, as I had the other time made her burst, into tears; she took me to her motherly breast, where my lamentation overflowed. "I don't do it!" I sobbed in despair; "I don't save or shield them! It's far worse than I dreamed. They're lost!"°

VIII°

What I had said to Mrs. Grose was true enough: there were in the matter I had put before her depths and possibilities that I lacked resolution to sound; so that when we met once more in the wonder of it we were of a common mind about the duty of resistance to extravagant fancies. We were to keep our heads if we should keep nothing else — difficult indeed as that might be in the face of all that, in our prodigious experience, seemed least to be questioned. Late that night, while the house slept, we had another talk in my room; when she went all the way with me as to its being beyond doubt that I had seen exactly what I had seen. I found that to keep her thoroughly in the grip of this I had only to ask her how, if I had "made it up," I came to be able to give, of each of the persons appearing to me, a picture disclosing, to the last detail, their special marks — a portrait on the exhibition of which she had

---

her real reason for leaving: The implication is that Miss Jessel left because she was pregnant. Her appearance beside the pond may be a hint that she drowned herself, possibly in despair or grief over the death of her child. James never specifies the details of Miss Jessel's history.   *lost:* Damned, given over to the devil.   *VIII:* The sixth weekly *Collier's* installment and *Part Third* began here.

instantly recognised and named them. She wished, of course — small blame to her! — to sink the whole subject; and I was quick to assure her that my own interest in it had now violently taken the form of a search for the way to escape from it. I closed with her cordially on the article of the likelihood that with recurrence — for recurrence we took for granted — I should get used to my danger; distinctly professing that my personal exposure had suddenly become the least of my discomforts. It was my new suspicion that was intolerable; and yet even to this complication the later hours of the day had brought a little ease.

On leaving her, after my first outbreak, I had of course returned to my pupils, associating the right remedy for my dismay with that sense of their charm which I had already recognised as a resource I could positively cultivate and which had never failed me yet. I had simply, in other words, plunged afresh into Flora's special society and there become aware — it was almost a luxury! — that she could put her little conscious hand straight upon the spot that ached. She had looked at me in sweet speculation and then had accused me to my face of having "cried." I had supposed the ugly signs of it brushed away; but I could literally — for the time at all events — rejoice, under this fathomless charity, that they had not entirely disappeared. To gaze into the depths of blue of the child's eyes and pronounce their loveliness a trick of premature cunning was to be guilty of a cynicism in preference to which I naturally preferred to abjure° my judgement and, so far as might be, my agitation. I could n't abjure for merely wanting to, but I could repeat to Mrs. Grose — as I did there, over and over, in the small hours — that with our small friends' voices in the air, their pressure on one's heart and their fragrant faces against one's cheek, everything fell to the ground but their incapacity and their beauty. It was a pity that, somehow, to settle this once for all, I had equally to re-enumerate the signs of subtlety that, in the afternoon, by the lake, had made a miracle of my show of self-possession. It was a pity to be obliged to re-investigate the certitude of the moment itself and repeat how it had come to me as a revelation that the inconceivable communion I then surprised must have been for both parties a matter of habit. It was a pity I should have had to quaver out again the reasons for my not having, in my delusion, so much as questioned that the little girl saw our visitant even as I actually saw Mrs. Grose herself, and that she wanted, by just so much as she did thus see, to make me suppose she did n't, and at the same time,

---

abjure: Give up, retract. She would rather recant her suspicions of Flora than imagine evil in one whose blue eyes seem to signal such innocence.

without showing anything, arrive at a guess as to whether I myself did! It was a pity I needed to recapitulate the portentous little activities by which she sought to divert my attention — the perceptible increase of movement, the greater intensity of play, the singing, the gabbling of nonsense and the invitation to romp.

Yet if I had not indulged, to prove there was nothing in it, in this review, I should have missed the two or three dim elements of comfort that still remained to me. I should n't for instance have been able to asseverate° to my friend that I was certain — which was so much to the good — that *I* at least had not betrayed myself. I should n't have been prompted, by stress of need, by desperation of mind — I scarce know what to call it — to invoke such further aid to intelligence as might spring from pushing my colleague fairly to the wall. She had told me, bit by bit, under pressure, a great deal; but a small shifty spot on the wrong side of it all still sometimes brushed my brow like the wing of a bat; and I remember how on this occasion — for the sleeping house and the concentration alike of our danger and our watch seemed to help — I felt the importance of giving the last jerk to the curtain. "I don't believe anything so horrible," I recollect saying; "no, let us put it definitely, my dear, that I don't. But if I did, you know, there's a thing I should require now, just without sparing you the least bit more — oh not a scrap, come! — to get out of you. What was it you had in mind when, in our distress, before Miles came back, over the letter from his school, you said, under my insistence, that you did n't pretend for him he had n't literally *ever* been 'bad'? He has *not,* truly, 'ever,' in these weeks that I myself have lived with him and so closely watched him; he has been an imperturbable little prodigy of delightful loveable goodness. Therefore you might perfectly have made the claim for him if you had not, as it happened, seen an exception to take. What was your exception, and to what passage in your personal observation of him did you refer?"

It was a straight question enough, but levity was not our note, and in any case I had before the grey dawn admonished us to separate got my answer. What my friend had had in mind proved immensely to the purpose. It was neither more nor less than the particular fact that for a period of several months Quint and the boy had been perpetually together. It was indeed the very appropriate item of evidence of her having ventured to criticise the propriety, to hint at the incongruity, of so close an alliance, and even to go so far on the subject as a frank overture to Miss Jessel would take her. Miss Jessel had, with a very high

asseverate: Assert, proclaim.

manner about it, requested her to mind her business, and the good woman had on this directly approached little Miles. What she had said to him, since I pressed, was that *she* liked to see young gentlemen not forget their station.

I pressed again, of course, the closer for that. "You reminded him that Quint was only a base menial?"°

"As you might say! And it was his answer, for one thing, that was bad."

"And for another thing?" I waited. "He repeated your words to Quint?"

"No, not that. It's just what he *would n't*!" she could still impress on me. "I was sure, at any rate," she added, "that he did n't. But he denied certain occasions."

"What occasions?"

"When they had been about together quite as if Quint were his tutor — and a very grand one — and Miss Jessel only for the little lady. When he had gone off with the fellow, I mean, and spent hours with him."

"He then prevaricated about it — he said he had n't?" Her assent was clear enough to cause me to add in a moment: "I see. He lied."

"Oh!" Mrs. Grose mumbled. This was a suggestion that it did n't matter; which indeed she backed up by a further remark. "You see, after all, Miss Jessel did n't mind. She did n't forbid him."

I considered. "Did he put that to you as a justification?"

At this she dropped again. "No, he never spoke of it."

"Never mentioned her in connexion with Quint?"

She saw, visibly flushing, where I was coming out. "Well, he did n't show anything. He denied," she repeated; "he denied."

Lord, how I pressed her now! "So that you could see he knew what was between the two wretches?"

"I don't know — I don't know!" the poor woman wailed.

"You do know, you dear thing," I replied; "only you have n't my dreadful boldness of mind, and you keep back, out of timidity and modesty and delicacy, even the impression that in the past, when you had, without my aid, to flounder about in silence, most of all made you miserable. But I shall get it out of you yet! There was something in the boy that suggested to you," I continued, "his covering and concealing their relation."

"Oh he could n't prevent — "

base menial: Lowly servant, lackey.

"Your learning the truth? I dare say! But, heavens," I fell, with vehemence, a-thinking, "what it shows that they must, to that extent, have succeeded in making of him!"

"Ah nothing that's not nice *now*!" Mrs. Grose lugubriously° pleaded.

"I don't wonder you looked queer," I persisted, "when I mentioned to you the letter from his school!"

"I doubt if I looked as queer as you!" she retorted with homely force. "And if he was so bad then as that comes to, how is he such an angel now?"

"Yes indeed — and if he was a fiend at school! How, how, how? Well," I said in my torment, "you must put it to me again, though I shall not be able to tell you for some days. Only put it to me again!" I cried in a way that made my friend stare. "There are directions in which I must n't for the present let myself go." Meanwhile I returned to her first example — the one to which she had just previously referred — of the boy's happy capacity for an occasional slip. "If Quint — on your remonstrance at the time you speak of — was a base menial, one of the things Miles said to you, I find myself guessing, was that you were another." Again her admission was so adequate that I continued: "And you forgave him that?"

"Wouldn't *you*?"

"Oh yes!" And we exchanged there, in the stillness, a sound of the oddest amusement. Then I went on: "At all events, while he was with the man — "

"Miss Flora was with the woman. It suited them all!"

It suited me too, I felt, only too well; by which I mean that it suited exactly the particular deadly view I was in the very act of forbidding myself to entertain. But I so far succeeded in checking the expression of this view that I will throw, just here, no further light on it than may be offered by the mention of my final observation to Mrs. Grose. "His having lied and been impudent are, I confess, less engaging specimens than I had hoped to have from you of the outbreak in him of the little natural man.° Still," I mused, "they must do, for they make me feel more than ever that I must watch."

It made me blush, the next minute, to see in my friend's face how much more unreservedly she had forgiven him than her anecdote

---

lugubriously: Mournfully.   *natural man:* In his famous sermon "Sinners in the Hands of an Angry God," first published in 1741 and in print throughout the nineteenth century, Jonathan Edwards describes "natural men" as those who are unsaved, who have not yet had the saving experience of God's grace. The governess's point here is that none of what Mrs. Grose has told her about Miles makes him sound particularly evil.

struck me as pointing out to my own tenderness any way to do. This was marked when, at the schoolroom door, she quitted me. "Surely you don't accuse *him* — "

"Of carrying on an intercourse that he conceals from me? Ah remember that, until further evidence, I now accuse nobody." Then before shutting her out to go by another passage to her own place, "I must just wait," I wound up.

IX

I waited and waited, and the days took as they elapsed something from my consternation. A very few of them, in fact, passing, in constant sight of my pupils, without a fresh incident, sufficed to give to grievous fancies and even to odious memories a kind of brush of the sponge. I have spoken of the surrender to their extraordinary childish grace as a thing I could actively promote in myself, and it may be imagined if I neglected now to apply at this source for whatever balm it would yield. Stranger than I can express, certainly, was the effort to struggle against my new lights. It would doubtless have been a greater tension still, however, had it not been so frequently successful. I used to wonder how my little charges could help guessing that I thought strange things about them; and the circumstance that these things only made them more interesting was not by itself a direct aid to keeping them in the dark. I trembled lest they should see that they *were* so immensely more interesting. Putting things at the worst, at all events, as in meditation I so often did, any clouding of their innocence could only be — blameless and foredoomed as they were — a reason the more for taking risks. There were moments when I knew myself to catch them up by an irresistible impulse and press them to my heart. As soon as I had done so I used to wonder — "What will they think of that? Doesn't it betray too much?" It would have been easy to get into a sad wild tangle about how much I might betray; but the real account, I feel, of the hours of peace I could still enjoy was that the immediate charm of my companions was a beguilement still effective even under the shadow of the possibility that it was studied. For if it occurred to me that I might occasionally excite suspicion by the little outbreaks of my sharper passion for them, so too I remember asking if I might n't see a queerness in the traceable increase of their own demonstrations.

They were at this period extravagantly and preternaturally fond of me; which, after all, I could reflect, was no more than a graceful response in children perpetually bowed down over and hugged. The homage of which they were so lavish succeeded in truth for my nerves quite as well as if I never appeared to myself, as I may say, literally to catch them at a purpose in it. They had never, I think, wanted to do so many things for their poor protectress; I mean — though they got their lessons better and better, which was naturally what would please her most — in the way of diverting, entertaining, surprising her; reading her passages, telling her stories, acting her charades, pouncing out at her, in disguises, as animals and historical characters, and above all astonishing her by the "pieces" they had secretly got by heart° and could interminably recite. I should never get to the bottom — were I to let myself go even now — of the prodigious private commentary, all under still more private correction, with which I in these days over-scored their full hours. They had shown me from the first a facility for everything, a general faculty which, taking a fresh start, achieved remarkable flights. They got their little tasks as if they loved them; they indulged, from the mere exuberance of the gift, in the most unimposed little miracles of memory. They not only popped out at me as tigers and as Romans, but as Shakespeareans, astronomers, and navigators. This was so singularly the case that it had presumably much to do with the fact as to which, at the present day, I am at a loss for a different explana-tion: I allude to my unnatural composure on the subject of another school for Miles. What I remember is that I was content for the time not to open the question, and that contentment must have sprung from the sense of his perpetually striking show of cleverness. He was too clever for a bad governess, for a parson's daughter, to spoil; and the strangest if not the brightest thread in the pensive embroidery I just spoke of was the impression I might have got, if I had dared to work it out, that he was under some influence operating in his small intellectual life as a tremendous incitement.

If it was easy to reflect, however, that such a boy could postpone school, it was at least as marked that for such a boy to have been "kicked out" by a schoolmaster was a mystification without end. Let me add that in their company now — and I was careful almost never to be out of it — I could follow no scent very far. We lived in a cloud of music and affection and success and private theatricals. The musical sense in each of the children was of the quickest, but the elder in especial had a marvellous knack of catching and repeating. The schoolroom piano

---

got by heart: Memorized. The governess is describing here the amazing feats of recitation and acting that the two children engaged in to impress — and possibly distract — her.

broke into all gruesome fancies; and when that failed there were con-
fabulations in corners, with a sequel of one of them going out in the
highest spirits in order to "come in" as something new. I had had
brothers° myself, and it was no revelation to me that little girls could be
slavish idolaters of little boys. What surpassed everything was that there
was a little boy in the world who could have for the inferior age, sex,
and intelligence so fine a consideration. They were extraordinarily at
one, and to say that they never either quarrelled or complained is to
make the note of praise coarse for their quality of sweetness. Sometimes
perhaps indeed (when I dropped into coarseness) I came across traces
of little understandings between them by which one of them should
keep me occupied while the other slipped away. There is a naïf side, I
suppose, in all diplomacy; but if my pupils practiced upon me it was
surely with the minimum of grossness. It was all in the other quarter
that, after a lull, the grossness broke out.

    I find that I really hang back; but I must take my horrid plunge. In
going on with the record of what was hideous at Bly I not only challenge the most liberal faith — for which I little care; but (and this is
another matter) I renew what I myself suffered, I again push my dreadful way through it to the end. There came suddenly an hour after
which, as I look back, the business seems to me to have been all pure
suffering; but I have at least reached the heart of it, and the straightest
road out is doubtless to advance. One evening — with nothing to lead
up or prepare it — I felt the cold touch of the impression that had
breathed on me the night of my arrival and which, much lighter then as
I have mentioned, I should probably have made little of in memory had
my subsequent sojourn been less agitated. I had not gone to bed; I sat
reading by a couple of candles. There was a roomful of old books at
Bly — last-century fiction some of it, which, to the extent of a distinctly
deprecated renown, but never to so much as that of a stray specimen,
had reached the sequestered home and appealed to the unavowed
curiosity of my youth. I remember that the book I had in my hand was
Fielding's "Amelia";° also that I was wholly awake. I recall further both

---

brothers: Douglas had referred to her in the prologue as "the youngest of several daughters of a poor country parson" (p. 26), so the appearance of brothers here is surprising.
Later she refers to "my brothers and sisters" (p. 79).   **Fielding's "Amelia":** A novel
by Henry Fielding (1707–1754) published in 1751. *Amelia* is about an unfailingly good
and faithful heroine pursued by an assortment of men. It is interesting that Fielding's sister Sarah had published in 1749 a short novel called *The Governess, or Little Female Academy,* an imaginative but realistic account of the life of a young governess teaching in a
girl's school.

a general conviction that it was horribly late and a particular objection to looking at my watch. I figure finally that the white curtain draping, in the fashion of those days, the head of Flora's little bed, shrouded, as I had assured myself long before, the perfection of childish rest. I recollect in short that though I was deeply interested in my author I found myself, at the turn of a page and with his spell all scattered, looking straight up from him and hard at the door of my room. There was a moment during which I listened, reminded of the faint sense I had had, the first night,° of there being something undefinably astir in the house, and noted the soft breath of the open casement just move the half-drawn blind. Then, with all the marks of a deliberation that must have seemed magnificent had there been any one to admire it, I laid down my book, rose to my feet and, taking a candle, went straight out of the room and, from the passage, on which my light made little impression, noiselessly closed and locked the door.

I can say now neither what determined nor what guided me, but I went straight along the lobby, holding my candle high, till I came within sight of the tall window that presided over the great turn of the staircase. At this point I precipitately found myself aware of three things. They were practically simultaneous, yet they had flashes of succession. My candle, under a bold flourish, went out, and I perceived, by the uncovered window, that the yielding dusk of earliest morning rendered it unnecessary. Without it, the next instant, I knew that there was a figure on the stair. I speak of sequences, but I required no lapse of seconds to stiffen myself for a third encounter with Quint. The apparition had reached the landing half-way up and was therefore on the spot nearest the window, where, at sight of me, it stopped short and fixed me exactly as it had fixed me from the tower and from the garden. He knew me as well as I knew him; and so, in the cold faint twilight, with a glimmer in the high glass and another on the polish of the oak stair below, we faced each other in our common intensity. He was absolutely, on this occasion, a living detestable dangerous presence. But that was not the wonder of wonders; I reserve this distinction for quite another circumstance: the circumstance that dread had unmistakeably quitted me and that there was nothing in me unable to meet and measure him.

I had plenty of anguish after that extraordinary moment, but I had, thank God, no terror. And he knew I had n't — I found myself at the end of an instant magnificently aware of this. I felt, in a fierce rigour of

---

the first night: She refers here to her first night at Bly when she "fancied" she heard the sound of a child crying and "a light footstep" outside her door (pp. 30–31).

confidence, that if I stood my ground a minute I should cease — for the time at least — to have him to reckon with; and during the minute, accordingly, the thing was as human and hideous as a real interview: hideous just because it *was* human, as human as to have met alone, in the small hours, in a sleeping house, some enemy, some adventurer, some criminal. It was the dead silence of our long gaze at such close quarters that gave the whole horror, huge as it was, its only note of the unnatural. If I had met a murderer in such a place and at such an hour we still at least would have spoken. Something would have passed, in life, between us; if nothing had passed one of us would have moved. The moment was so prolonged that it would have taken but little more to make me doubt if even *I* were in life. I can't express what followed it save by saying that the silence itself — which was indeed in a manner an attestation of my strength — became the element into which I saw the figure disappear; in which I definitely saw it turn, as I might have seen the low wretch to which it had once belonged turn on receipt of an order, and pass, with my eyes on the villainous back that no hunch could have more disfigured, straight down the staircase and into the darkness in which the next bend was lost.

X°

I remained a while at the top of the stair, but with the effect presently of understanding that when my visitor had gone, he had gone; then I returned to my room. The foremost thing I saw there by the light of the candle I had left burning was that Flora's little bed was empty; and on this I caught my breath with all the terror that, five minutes before, I had been able to resist. I dashed at the place in which I had left her lying and over which — for the small silk counterpane and the sheets were disarranged — the white curtains had been deceivingly pulled forward; then my step, to my unutterable relief, produced an answering sound: I noticed an agitation of the window-blind, and the child, ducking down, emerged rosily from the other side of it. She stood there in so much of her candour and so little of her night-gown, with her pink bare feet and the golden glow of her curls. She looked intensely grave, and I had never had such a sense of losing an advantage acquired (the thrill of which had just been so prodigious) as on my con-

---

X: The seventh weekly *Collier's* installment began here.

sciousness that she addressed me with a reproach — "You naughty: where *have* you been?" Instead of challenging her own irregularity I found myself arraigned and explaining. She herself explained, for that matter, with the loveliest eagerest simplicity. She had known suddenly, as she lay there, that I was out of the room, and had jumped up to see what had become of me. I had dropped, with the joy of her reappearance, back into my chair — feeling then, and then only, a little faint; and she had pattered straight over to me, thrown herself upon my knee, given herself to be held with the flame of the candle full in the wonderful little face that was still flushed with sleep. I remember closing my eyes an instant, yieldingly, consciously, as before the excess of something beautiful that shone out of the blue of her own. "You were looking for me out of the window?" I said. "You thought I might be walking in the grounds?"

"Well, you know, I thought some one was" — she never blanched as she smiled out that at me.

Oh how I looked at her now! "And did you see any one?"

"Ah *no!*" she returned almost (with the full privilege of childish inconsequence) resentfully, though with a long sweetness in her little drawl of the negative.

At that moment, in the state of my nerves, I absolutely believed she lied; and if I once more closed my eyes it was before the dazzle of the three or four possible ways in which I might take this up. One of these for a moment tempted me with such singular force that, to resist it, I must have gripped my little girl with a spasm that, wonderfully, she submitted to without a cry or a sign of fright. Why not break out at her on the spot and have it all over? — give it to her straight in her lovely little lighted face? "You see, you see, you *know* that you do and that you already quite suspect I believe it; therefore why not frankly confess it to me, so that we may at least live with it together and learn perhaps, in the strangeness of our fate, where we are and what it means?" This solicitation dropped, alas, as it came: if I could immediately have succumbed to it I might have spared myself — well, you'll see what. Instead of succumbing I sprang again to my feet, looked at her bed and took a helpless middle way. "Why did you pull the curtain over the place to make me think you were still there?"

Flora luminously considered; after which, with her little divine smile: "Because I don't like to frighten you!"

"But if I had, by your idea, gone out — ?"

She absolutely declined to be puzzled; she turned her eyes to the flame of the candle as if the question were as irrelevant, or at any rate as impersonal, as Mrs. Marcet° or nine-times-nine. "Oh but you know," she quite adequately answered, "that you might come back, you dear, and that you *have!*" And after a little, when she had got into bed, I had, a long time, by almost sitting on her for the retention of her hand, to show how I recognised the pertinence of my return.

You may imagine the general complexion, from that moment, of my nights. I repeatedly sat up till I did n't know when; I selected moments when my room-mate unmistakeably slept, and, stealing out, took noiseless turns in the passage. I even pushed as far as to where I had last met Quint. But I never met him there again, and I may as well say at once that I on no other occasion saw him in the house. I just missed, on the staircase, nevertheless, a different adventure. Looking down it from the top I once recognised the presence of a woman seated on one of the lower steps with her back presented to me, her body half-bowed and her head, in an attitude of woe, in her hands. I had been there but an instant, however, when she vanished without looking round at me. I knew, for all that, exactly what dreadful face she had to show; and I wondered whether, if instead of being above I had been below, I should have had the same nerve for going up that I had lately shown Quint. Well, there continued to be plenty of call for nerve. On the eleventh night after my latest encounter with that gentleman — they were all numbered now — I had an alarm that perilously skirted it and that indeed, from the particular quality of its unexpectedness, proved quite my sharpest shock. It was precisely the first night during this series that, weary with vigils, I had conceived I might again without laxity lay myself down at my old hour. I slept immediately and, as I afterwards knew, till about one o'clock; but when I woke it was to sit straight up, as completely roused as if a hand had shaken me. I had left a light burning, but it was now out, and I felt an instant certainty that Flora had extinguished it. This brought me to my feet and straight, in the darkness, to her bed, which I found she had left. A glance at the window enlightened me further, and the striking of a match completed the picture.

The child had again got up — this time blowing out the taper, and had again, for some purpose of observation or response, squeezed in behind the blind and was peering out into the night. That she now saw — as she had not, I had satisfied myself, the previous time — was proved to me by the fact that she was disturbed neither by my reillumi-

---

Mrs. Marcet: Jane Marcet (1769–1858), a writer of children's books.

nation nor by the haste I made to get into slippers and into a wrap. Hidden, protected, absorbed, she evidently rested on the sill — the casement opened forward — and gave herself up. There was a great still moon to help her, and this fact had counted in my quick decision. She was face to face with the apparition we had met at the lake, and could now communicate with it as she had not then been able to do. What I, on my side, had to care for was, without disturbing her, to reach, from the corridor, some other window turned to the same quarter. I got to the door without her hearing me; I got out of it, closed it and listened, from the other side, for some sound from her. While I stood in the passage I had my eyes on her brother's door, which was but ten steps off and which, indescribably, produced in me a renewal of the strange impulse that I lately spoke of as my temptation.° What if I should go straight in and march to *his* window? — what if, by risking to his boyish bewilderment a revelation of my motive, I should throw across the rest of the mystery the long halter of my boldness?

This thought held me sufficiently to make me cross to his threshold and pause again. I preternaturally° listened; I figured to myself what might portentously be; I wondered if his bed were also empty and he also secretly at watch. It was a deep soundless minute, at the end of which my impulse failed. He was quiet; he might be innocent; the risk was hideous; I turned away. There was a figure in the grounds — a figure prowling for a sight, the visitor with whom Flora was engaged; but it was n't the visitor most concerned with my boy. I hesitated afresh, but on other grounds and only a few seconds; then I had made my choice. There were empty rooms enough at Bly, and it was only a question of choosing the right one. The right one suddenly presented itself to me as the lower one — though high above the gardens — in the solid corner of the house that I have spoken of as the old tower. This was a large square chamber, arranged with some state as a bedroom, the extravagant size of which made it so inconvenient that it had not for years, though kept by Mrs. Grose in exemplary order, been occupied. I had often admired it and I knew my way about in it; I had only, after just faltering at the first chill gloom of its disuse, to pass across it and unbolt in all quietness one of the shutters. Achieving this transit I uncovered the glass without a sound and, applying my face to the pane,

---

my temptation: She is speaking of the impulse that "tempted" her (p. 69) to question Flora directly about whether she has seen the ghost of Miss Jessel. She had not "succumbed" to the temptation then, any more than she does now to the temptation to rush into Miles's bedroom and speak directly to him about whether he has seen the ghost of Quint.   *preternaturally:* Unusually, exceptionally.

was able, the darkness without being much less than within, to see that
I commanded the right direction. Then I saw something more. The
moon made the night extraordinarily penetrable and showed me on the
lawn a person, diminished by distance, who stood there motionless and
as if fascinated, looking up to where I had appeared — looking, that is,
not so much straight at me as at something that was apparently above
me. There was clearly another person above me — there was a person
on the tower; but the presence on the lawn was not in the least what I
had conceived and had confidently hurried to meet. The presence on
the lawn — I felt sick as I made it out — was poor little Miles himself.

XI

It was not till late next day that I spoke to Mrs. Grose; the rigour
with which I kept my pupils in sight making it often difficult to meet
her privately: the more as we each felt the importance of not pro-
voking — on the part of the servants quite as much as on that of the
children — any suspicion of a secret flurry or of a discussion of mysteries. I drew a great security in this particular from her mere smooth
aspect. There was nothing in her fresh face to pass on to others the least
of my horrible confidences. She believed me, I was sure, absolutely: if
she had n't I don't know what would have become of me, for I
could n't have borne the strain alone. But she was a magnificent monu-
ment to the blessing of a want of imagination, and if she could see in
our little charges nothing but their beauty and amiability, their happiness and cleverness, she had no direct communication with the sources
of my trouble. If they had been at all visibly blighted or battered she
would doubtless have grown, on tracing it back, haggard enough to
match them; as matters stood, however, I could feel her, when she surveyed them with her large white arms folded and the habit of serenity in
all her look, thank the Lord's mercy that if they were ruined the pieces
would still serve. Flights of fancy gave place, in her mind, to a steady
fireside glow, and I had already begun to perceive how, with the development of the conviction that — as time went on without a public accident — our young things could, after all, look out for themselves, she
addressed her greatest solicitude to the sad case presented by their
deputy-guardian. That, for myself, was a sound simplification: I could
engage that, to the world, my face should tell no tales, but it would
have been, in the conditions, an immense added worry to find myself
anxious about hers.

At the hour I now speak of she had joined me, under pressure, on the terrace, where, with the lapse of the season, the afternoon sun was now agreeable; and we sat there together while before us and at a distance, yet within call if we wished, the children strolled to and fro in one of their most manageable moods. They moved slowly, in unison, below us, over the lawn, the boy, as they went, reading aloud from a story-book and passing his arm round his sister to keep her quite in touch. Mrs. Grose watched them with positive placidity; then I caught the suppressed intellectual creak with which she conscientiously turned to take from me a view of the back of the tapestry. I had made her a receptacle of lurid things, but there was an odd recognition of my superiority — my accomplishments and my function — in her patience under my pain. She offered her mind to my disclosures as, had I wished to mix a witch's broth and proposed it with assurance, she would have held out a large clean saucepan. This had become thoroughly her attitude by the time that, in my recital of the events of the night, I reached the point of what Miles had said to me when, after seeing him, at such a monstrous hour, almost on the very spot where he happened now to be, I had gone down to bring him in; choosing then, at the window, with a concentrated need of not alarming the house, rather that method than any noisier process. I had left her meanwhile in little doubt of my small hope of representing with success even to her actual sympathy my sense of the real splendour of the little inspiration with which, after I had got him into the house, the boy met my final articulate challenge. As soon as I appeared in the moonlight on the terrace he had come to me as straight as possible; on which I had taken his hand without a word and led him, through the dark spaces, up the staircase where Quint had so hungrily hovered for him, along the lobby where I had listened and trembled, and so to his forsaken room.

Not a sound, on the way, had passed between us, and I had wondered — oh *how* I had wondered! — if he were groping about in his dreadful little mind for something plausible and not too grotesque. It would tax his invention certainly, and I felt, this time, over his real embarrassment, a curious thrill of triumph. It was a sharp trap for any game hitherto successful. He could play no longer at perfect propriety, nor could he pretend to it; so how the deuce would he get out of the scrape? There beat in me indeed, with the passionate throb of this question, an equal dumb appeal as to how the deuce *I* should. I was confronted at last, as never yet, with all the risk attached even now to sounding my own horrid note. I remember in fact that as we pushed into his little chamber, where the bed had not been slept in at all and the window, uncovered to the moonlight, made the place so clear that there was no need of striking a match — I remember how I suddenly dropped, sank upon the edge of the bed from the force of the idea that he must know how he really, as they say, "had" me. He could do what he liked, with all his cleverness to help him, so long as I should continue to defer to the old tradition° of the criminality of those caretakers of the young who minister to superstitions and fears. He "had" me indeed, and in a cleft stick; for who would ever absolve me, who would consent that I should go unhung, if, by the faintest tremor of an overture, I were the first to introduce into our perfect intercourse an element so dire? No, no: it was useless to attempt to convey to Mrs. Grose, just as it is scarcely less so to attempt to suggest here, how, during our short stiff brush there in the dark, he fairly shook me with admiration. I was of course thoroughly kind and merciful; never, never yet had I placed on his small shoulders hands of such tenderness as those with which, while I rested against the bed, I held him there well under fire. I had no alternative but, in form at least, to put it to him.

"You must tell me now — and all the truth. What did you go out for? What were you doing there?"

I can still see his wonderful smile, the whites of his beautiful eyes and the uncovering of his clear teeth, shine to me in the dusk. "If I tell you why, will you understand?" My heart, at this, leaped into my mouth. *Would* he tell me why? I found no sound on my lips to press it, and I was aware of answering only with a vague repeated grimacing nod. He was gentleness itself, and while I wagged my head at him he stood there more than ever a little fairy prince. It was his brightness

---

the old tradition: The governess is concerned here that it was traditionally considered a criminal act for guardians of the young to frighten their charges or play on their superstitions. She explains here her reluctance to speak to Miles directly about Quint. She speaks in the next sentence about the likelihood that she might be hanged if she were the first to raise the subject of Quint and his possible reappearance. She later refers to "Forbidden ground . . . the question of the return of the dead" (p. 79). See section 138 of John Locke's influential *Some Thoughts Concerning Education* (1705): "be sure to preserve [a child's] tender Mind from all Impressions and Notions of *Spirits* and *Goblings*. . . . Such *Bug-bear* Thoughts once got into the tender Minds of Children, and being set on with a strong impression, from the Dread that accompanies such Apprehensions, sink deep, and fasten themselves so as not easily, if ever, to be got out again." See also *The Spectator,* number 12 (March 14, 1711), where Addison speaks of the dangers of speaking with children about ghosts. He mentions particularly a little boy who is so frightened by a ghost story that he thenceforth refuses to go to bed alone. "Were I a Father," Addison says, "I should take particular Care to preserve my Children from these little Horrours of Imagination, which they are apt to contract when they are young and are not able to shake off when they are in Years."

indeed that gave me a respite. Would it be so great if he were really going to tell me? "Well," he said at last, "just exactly in order that you should do this."

"Do what?"

"Think me — for a change — *bad*!" I shall never forget the sweetness and gaiety with which he brought out the word, nor how, on top of it, he bent forward and kissed me. It was practically the end of everything. I met his kiss and I had to make, while I folded him for a minute in my arms, the most stupendous effort not to cry. He had given exactly the account of himself that permitted least my going behind it, and it was only with the effect of confirming my acceptance of it that, as I presently glanced about the room, I could say —

"Then you did n't undress at all?"

He fairly glittered in the gloom. "Not at all. I sat up and read."

"And when did you go down?"

"At midnight. When I'm bad I *am* bad!"

"I see, I see — it's charming. But how could you be sure I should know it?"

"Oh I arranged that with Flora." His answers rang out with a readiness! "She was to get up and look out."

"Which is what she did do." It was I who fell into the trap!

"So she disturbed you, and, to see what she was looking at, you also looked — you saw."

"While you," I concurred, "caught your death in the night air!"

He literally bloomed so from this exploit that he could afford radiantly to assent. "How otherwise should I have been bad enough?" he asked. Then, after another embrace, the incident and our interview closed on my recognition of all the reserves of goodness that, for his joke, he had been able to draw upon.

XII

The particular impression I had received proved in the morning light, I repeat, not quite successfully presentable to Mrs. Grose, though I re-enforced it with the mention of still another remark that he had made before we separated. "It all lies in half a dozen words," I said to her, "words that really settle the matter. 'Think, you know, what I *might* do!' He threw that off to show me how good he is. He knows down to the ground what he 'might do.' That's what he gave them a taste of at school."

"Lord, you do change!" cried my friend.

"I don't change — I simply make it out. The four, depend upon it, perpetually meet. If on either of these last nights you had been with either child you'd clearly have understood. The more I've watched and waited the more I've felt that if there were nothing else to make it sure it would be made so by the systematic silence of each. *Never,* by a slip of the tongue, have they so much as alluded to either of their old friends, any more than Miles has alluded to his expulsion. Oh yes, we may sit here and look at them, and they may show off to us there to their fill; but even while they pretend to be lost in their fairy-tale they're steeped in their vision of the dead restored to them. He's not reading to her," I declared; "they're talking of *them* — they're talking horrors! I go on, I know, as if I were crazy; and it's a wonder I'm not. What I've seen would have made *you* so; but it has only made me more lucid, made me get hold of still other things."

My lucidity must have seemed awful, but the charming creatures who were victims of it, passing and repassing in their interlocked sweetness, gave my colleague something to hold on by; and I felt how tight she held as, without stirring in the breath of my passion, she covered them still with her eyes. "Of what other things have you got hold?"

"Why of the very things that have delighted, fascinated, and yet, at bottom, as I now so strangely see, mystified and troubled me. Their more than earthly beauty, their absolutely unnatural goodness. It's a game," I went on; "it's a policy and a fraud!"

"On the part of little darlings — ?"

"As yet mere lovely babies? Yes, mad as that seems!" The very act of bringing it out really helped me to trace it — follow it all up and piece it all together. "They have n't been good — they've only been absent. It has been easy to live with them because they're simply leading a life of their own. They're not mine — they're not ours. They're his and they're hers!"

"Quint's and that woman's?"

"Quint's and that woman's. They want to get to them."

Oh how, at this, poor Mrs. Grose appeared to study them! "But for what?"

"For the love of all the evil that, in those dreadful days, the pair put into them. And to ply them with that evil still, to keep up the work of demons, is what brings the others back."

"Laws!" said my friend under her breath. The exclamation was homely, but it revealed a real acceptance of my further proof of what, in the bad time — for there had been a worse even than this! — must have occurred. There could have been no such justification for me as the plain assent of her experience to whatever depth of depravity I found credible in our brace of scoundrels. It was in obvious submission of memory that she brought out after a moment: "They *were* rascals! But what can they now do?" she pursued.

"Do?" I echoed so loud that Miles and Flora, as they passed at their distance, paused an instant in their walk and looked at us. "Don't they do enough?" I demanded in a lower tone, while the children, having smiled and nodded and kissed hands to us, resumed their exhibition. We were held by it a minute; then I answered: "They can destroy them!" At this my companion did turn, but the appeal she launched was a silent one, the effect of which was to make me more explicit. "They don't know as yet quite how — but they're trying hard. They're seen only across, as it were, and beyond — in strange places and on high places, the top of towers, the roof of houses, the outside of windows, the further edge of pools; but there's a deep design, on either side, to shorten the distance and overcome the obstacle: so the success of the tempters is only a question of time. They've only to keep to their suggestions of danger."

"For the children to come?"

"And perish in the attempt!" Mrs. Grose slowly got up, and I scrupulously added: "Unless, of course, we can prevent!"

Standing there before me while I kept my seat she visibly turned things over. "Their uncle must do the preventing. He must take them away."

"And who's to make him?"

She had been scanning the distance, but she now dropped on me a foolish face. "You, Miss."

"By writing to him that his house is poisoned and his little nephew and niece mad?"

"But if they *are*, Miss?"

"And if I am myself, you mean? That's charming news to be sent him by a person enjoying his confidence and whose prime undertaking was to give him no worry."

Mrs. Grose considered, following the children again. "Yes, he do hate worry. That was the great reason — "

"Why those fiends took him in so long? No doubt, though his indifference must have been awful. As I'm not a fiend, at any rate, I shouldn't take him in."

My companion, after an instant and for all answer, sat down again and grasped my arm. "Make him at any rate come to you."

I stared. "To *me*?" I had a sudden fear of what she might do. " 'Him'?"

"He ought to *be* here — he ought to help."

I quickly rose and I think I must have shown her a queerer face than ever yet. "You see me asking him for a visit?" No, with her eyes on my face she evidently could n't. Instead of it even — as a woman reads another — she could see what I myself saw: his derision, his amusement, his contempt for the breakdown of my resignation at being left alone and for the fine machinery I had set in motion to attract his attention to my slighted charms. She did n't know — no one knew — how proud I had been to serve him and to stick to our terms; yet she none the less took the measure, I think, of the warning I now gave her. "If you should so lose your head as to appeal to him for me — "

She was really frightened. "Yes, Miss?"

"I would leave, on the spot, both him and you."

XIII°

It was all very well to join them, but speaking to them proved quite as much as ever an effort beyond my strength — offered, in close quarters, difficulties as insurmountable as before. This situation continued a month, and with new aggravations and particular notes, the note above all, sharper and sharper, of the small ironic consciousness on the part of my pupils. It was not, I am as sure to-day as I was sure then, my mere infernal imagination: it was absolutely traceable that they were aware of my predicament and that this strange relation made, in a manner, for a long time, the air in which we moved. I don't mean that they had their tongues in their cheeks or did anything vulgar, for that was not one of their dangers: I do mean, on the other hand, that the element of the unnamed and untouched became, between us, greater than any other, and that so much avoidance could n't have been made successful without a great deal of tacit arrangement. It was as if, at moments, we were perpetually coming into sight of subjects before which we must stop short, turning suddenly out of alleys that we perceived to be blind, closing with a little bang that made us look at each other — for, like all bangs, it was something louder than we had intended — the doors we had indiscreetly opened. All roads lead to Rome, and there were times when it might have struck us that almost every branch of study or sub-

---

XIII: The eighth weekly *Collier's* installment and *Part Fourth* began here.

ject of conversation skirted forbidden ground. Forbidden ground was the question of the return of the dead in general and of whatever, in especial, might survive, for memory, of the friends little children had lost. There were days when I could have sworn that one of them had, with a small invisible nudge, said to the other: "She thinks she'll do it this time — but she *won't!*" To "do it" would have been to indulge for instance — and for once in a way — in some direct reference to the lady who had prepared them for my discipline. They had a delightful endless appetite for passages in my own history to which I had again and again treated them; they were in possession of everything that had ever happened to me, had had, with every circumstance, the story of my smallest adventures and of those of my brothers and sisters and of the cat and the dog at home, as well as many particulars of the whimsical bent of my father, of the furniture and arrangement of our house and of the conversation of the old women of our village. There were things enough, taking one with another, to chatter about, if one went very fast and knew by instinct when to go round. They pulled with an art of their own the strings of my invention and my memory; and nothing else perhaps, when I thought of such occasions afterwards, gave me so the suspicion of being watched from under cover. It was in any case over *my* life, *my* past, and *my* friends alone that we could take anything like our ease; a state of affairs that led them sometimes without the least pertinence to break out into sociable reminders. I was invited — with no visible connexion — to repeat afresh Goody Gosling's celebrated *mot*°or to confirm the details already supplied as to the cleverness of the vicarage pony.

It was partly at such junctures as these and partly at quite different ones that, with the turn my matters had now taken, my predicament, as I have called it, grew most sensible. The fact that the days passed for me without another encounter ought, it would have appeared, to have done something toward soothing my nerves. Since the light brush, that second night on the upper landing, of the presence of a woman at the foot of the stair, I had seen nothing, whether in or out of the house, that one had better not have seen. There was many a corner round

---

mot: French for "word." Goody (that is, Goodwife) Gosling is one of the "old women of our village" referred to earlier in this paragraph. She had apparently made some clever retort that Miles and Flora ask the governess to tell them about yet once again. The point is not what Goody Gosling said but that the children are keeping the governess occupied telling them stories about her home and family. Her use of this foreign word suggests that the governess is teaching the children elementary French — one of the standard duties of English governesses.

which I expected to come upon Quint, and many a situation that, in a
merely sinister way, would have favoured the appearance of Miss Jessel.
The summer had turned, the summer had gone; the autumn had
dropped upon Bly and had blown out half our lights. The place, with its
grey sky and withered garlands, its bared spaces and scattered dead
leaves, was like a theatre° after the performance — all strewn with
crumpled playbills. There were exactly states of the air, conditions of
sound and of stillness, unspeakable impressions of the *kind* of minister-
ing moment, that brought back to me, long enough to catch it, the
feeling of the medium in which, that June evening out of doors, I had
had my first sight of Quint, and in which too, at those other instants, I
had, after seeing him through the window, looked for him in vain in the
circle of shrubbery. I recognised the signs, the portents — I recognised
the moment, the spot. But they remained unaccompanied and empty,
and I continued unmolested; if unmolested one could call a young
woman whose sensibility had, in the most extraordinary fashion, not
declined but deepened. I had said in my talk with Mrs. Grose on that
horrid scene of Flora's by the lake — and had perplexed her by so saying — that it would from that moment distress me much more to lose
my power than to keep it. I had then expressed what was vividly in my
mind: the truth that, whether the children really saw or not — since,
that is, it was not yet definitely proved — I greatly preferred, as a safe-
guard, the fulness of my own exposure. I was ready to know the very
worst that was to be known. What I had then had an ugly glimpse of
was that my eyes might be sealed just while theirs were most opened.
Well, my eyes *were* sealed,° it appeared, at present — a consummation
for which it seemed blasphemous not to thank God. There was, alas, a
difficulty about that: I would have thanked him with all my soul had I
not had in a proportionate measure this conviction of the secret of my
pupils.

How can I retrace to-day the strange steps of my obsession? There
were times of our being together when I would have been ready to
swear that, literally, in my presence, but with my direct sense of it
closed, they had visitors who were known and were welcome. Then it

---

like a theatre: The governess's simile about playbills strewn around a theater after a performance seems curious in view of her statement earlier that she had "never seen" an
actor (p. 48). Perhaps we should recall, however, that at age 20, when the events take
place, she had never yet been to a play, whereas she apparently has by "now," many years
later, when she writes the story down.   *my eyes* were *sealed:* Because she has not seen
either Peter Quint or Miss Jessel for some time, she wonders whether she has lost the ability she once had. In chapter XV, when she sees Miss Jessel in the classroom, she finds, "in
a flash, my eyes unsealed" (p. 88).

was that, had I not been deterred by the very chance that such an injury might prove greater than the injury to be averted, my exaltation would have broken out. "They're here, they're here, you little wretches," I would have cried, "and you can't deny it now!" The little wretches denied it with all the added volume of their sociability and their tenderness, just in the crystal depths of which — like the flash of a fish in a stream — the mockery of their advantage peeped up. The shock had in truth sunk into me still deeper than I knew on the night when, looking out either for Quint or for Miss Jessel under the stars, I had seen there the boy over whose rest I watched and who had immediately brought in with him — had straightway there turned on me — the lovely upward look with which, from the battlements above us, the hideous apparition of Quint had played. If it was a question of a scare my discovery on this occasion had scared me more than any other, and it was essentially in the scared state that I drew my actual conclusions. They harassed me so that sometimes, at odd moments, I shut myself up audibly to rehearse — it was at once a fantastic relief and a renewed despair — the manner in which I might come to the point. I approached it from one side and the other while, in my room, I flung myself about, but I always broke down in the monstrous utterance of names. As they died away on my lips I said to myself that I should indeed help them to represent something infamous if by pronouncing them I should violate as rare a little case of instinctive delicacy as any schoolroom probably had ever known. When I said to myself: "*They* have the manners to be silent, and you, trusted as you are, the baseness to speak!" I felt myself crimson and covered my face with my hands. After these secret scenes I chattered more than ever, going on volubly enough till one of our prodigious palpable hushes occurred — I can call them nothing else — the strange dizzy lift or swim (I try for terms!) into a stillness, a pause of all life, that had nothing to do with the more or less noise we at the moment might be engaged in making and that I could hear through any intensified mirth or quickened recitation or louder strum of the piano. Then it was that the others, the outsiders, were there. Though they were not angels they "passed," as the French say, causing me, while they stayed, to tremble with the fear of their addressing to their younger victims some yet more infernal message or more vivid image than they had thought good enough for myself.

What it was least possible to get rid of was the cruel idea that, whatever I had seen, Miles and Flora saw *more* — things terrible and unguessable and that sprang from dreadful passages of intercourse in the past. Such things naturally left on the surface, for the time, a chill that we vociferously denied we felt; and we had all three, with repetition, got into such splendid training that we went, each time, to mark the close of the incident, almost automatically through the very same movements. It was striking of the children at all events to kiss me inveterately with a wild irrelevance and never to fail — one or the other — of the precious question that had helped us through many a peril. "When do you think he *will* come? Don't you think we *ought* to write?" — there was nothing like that enquiry, we found by experience, for carrying off an awkwardness. "He" of course was their uncle in Harley Street; and we lived in much profusion of theory that he might at any moment arrive to mingle in our circle. It was impossible to have given less encouragement than he had administered to such a doctrine, but if we had not had the doctrine to fall back upon we should have deprived each other of some of our finest exhibitions. He never wrote to them — that may have been selfish, but it was a part of the flattery of his trust of myself; for the way in which a man pays his highest tribute to a woman is apt to be but by the more festal celebration of one of the sacred laws of his comfort. So I held that I carried out the spirit of the pledge given not to appeal to him when I let our young friends understand that their own letters were but charming literary exercises. They were too beautiful to be posted; I kept them myself; I have them all to this hour. This was a rule indeed which only added to the satiric effect of my being plied with the supposition that he might at any moment be among us. It was exactly as if our young friends knew how almost more awkward than anything else that might be for me. There appears to me moreover as I look back no note in all this more extraordinary than the mere fact that, in spite of my tension and of their triumph, I never lost patience with them. Adorable they must in truth have been, I now feel, since I did n't in these days hate them! Would exasperation, however, if relief had longer been postponed, finally have betrayed me? It little matters, for relief arrived. I call it relief though it was only the relief that a snap brings to a strain or the burst of a thunderstorm to a day of suffocation. It was at least change, and it came with a rush.

XIV

Walking to church a certain Sunday morning, I had little Miles at my side and his sister, in advance of us and at Mrs. Grose's, well in sight. It was a crisp clear day, the first of its order for some time; the night had brought a touch of frost and the autumn air, bright and sharp, made the church-bells almost gay. It was an odd accident of thought that I should have happened at such a moment to be particularly and very gratefully struck with the obedience of my little charges. Why did they never resent my inexorable, my perpetual society? Something or other had brought nearer home to me that I had all but pinned the boy to my shawl, and that in the way our companions were marshalled before me I might have appeared to provide against some danger of rebellion. I was like a gaoler° with an eye to possible surprises and escapes. But all this belonged — I mean their magnificent little surrender — just to the special array of the facts that were most abysmal. Turned out for Sunday by his uncle's tailor, who had had a free hand and a notion of pretty waistcoats and of his grand little air, Miles's whole title to independence, the rights of his sex and situation, were so stamped upon him that if he had suddenly struck for freedom I should have had nothing to say. I was by the strangest of chances wondering how I should meet him when the revolution unmistakeably occurred. I call it a revolution because I now see how, with the word he spoke, the curtain rose on the last act of my dreadful drama and the catastrophe was precipitated. "Look here, my dear, you know," he charmingly said, "when in the world, please, am I going back to school?"

Transcribed here the speech sounds harmless enough, particularly as uttered in the sweet, high, casual pipe° with which, at all interlocutors,° but above all at his eternal governess, he threw off intonations as if he were tossing roses. There was something in them that always made one "catch," and I caught at any rate now so effectually that I stopped as short as if one of the trees of the park had fallen across the road. There was something new, on the spot, between us, and he was perfectly aware I recognised it, though to enable me to do so he had no need to look a whit less candid and charming than usual. I could feel in him how he already, from my at first finding nothing to reply, perceived the advantage he had gained. I was so slow to find anything that he had plenty of time, after a minute, to continue with his suggestive but inconclusive smile: "You know, my dear, that for a fellow to be with a lady *always* — !" His "my dear" was constantly on his lips for me, and nothing could have expressed more the exact shade of the sentiment with which I desired to inspire my pupils than its fond familiarity. It was so respectfully easy.

But oh how I felt that at present I must pick my own phrases! I

---

gaoler: British spelling for "jailer."   *pipe:* Singing voice.   *interlocutors:* Partners in dialogue.

remember that, to gain time, I tried to laugh, and I seemed to see in the beautiful face with which he watched me how ugly and queer I looked. "And always with the same lady?" I returned.

He neither blenched nor winked.° The whole thing was virtually out between us. "Ah of course she's a jolly 'perfect' lady; but after all I'm a fellow, don't you see? who's — well, getting on."

I lingered there with him an instant ever so kindly. "Yes, you're getting on." Oh but I felt helpless!

I have kept to this day the heartbreaking little idea of how he seemed to know that and to play with it. "And you can't say I've not been awfully good, can you?"

I laid my hand on his shoulder, for though I felt how much better it would have been to walk on I was not yet quite able. "No, I can't say that, Miles."

"Except just that one night, you know — !"

"That one night?" I could n't look as straight as he.

"Why when I went down — went out of the house."

"Oh yes. But I forget what you did it for."

"You forget?" — he spoke with the sweet extravagance of childish reproach. "Why it was just to show you I could!"

"Oh yes — you could."

"And I can again."

I felt I might perhaps after all succeed in keeping my wits about me. "Certainly. But you won't."

"No, not *that* again. It was nothing."

"It was nothing," I said. "But we must go on."

He resumed our walk with me, passing his hand into my arm. "Then when *am* I going back?"

I wore, in turning it over, my most responsible air. "Were you very happy at school?"

He just considered. "Oh I'm happy enough anywhere!"

"Well then," I quavered, "if you're just as happy here — !"

"Ah but that is n't everything! Of course *you* know a lot — "

"But you hint that you know almost as much?" I risked as he paused.

"Not half I want to!" Miles honestly professed. "But it is n't so much that."

"What is it then?"

---

blenched nor winked: Blanched (grew pale) nor blinked.

"Well — I want to see more life."

"I see; I see." We had arrived within sight of the church and of various persons, including several of the household of Bly, on their way to it and clustered about the door to see us go in. I quickened our step; I wanted to get there before the question between us opened up much further; I reflected hungrily that he would have for more than an hour to be silent; and I thought with envy of the comparative dusk of the pew and of the almost spiritual help of the hassock on which I might bend my knees. I seemed literally to be running a race with some confusion to which he was about to reduce me, but I felt he had got in first when, before we had even entered the churchyard, he threw out —

"I want my own sort!"

It literally made me bound forward. "There are n't many of your own sort, Miles!" I laughed. "Unless perhaps dear little Flora!"

"You really compare me to a baby girl?"

This found me singularly weak. "Don't you then *love* our sweet Flora?"

"If I did n't — and you too; if I did n't — !" he repeated as if retreating for a jump, yet leaving his thought so unfinished that, after we had come into the gate, another stop, which he imposed on me by the pressure of his arm, had become inevitable. Mrs. Grose and Flora had passed into the church, the other worshippers had followed and we were, for the minute, alone among the old thick graves. We had paused, on the path from the gate, by a low oblong table-like tomb.

"Yes, if you did n't — ?"

He looked, while I waited, about at the graves. "Well, you know what!" But he did n't move, and he presently produced something that made me drop straight down on the stone slab as if suddenly to rest. "Does my uncle think what *you* think?"

I markedly rested. "How do you know what I think?"

"Ah well, of course I don't; for it strikes me you never tell me. But I mean does *he* know?"

"Know what, Miles?"

"Why,° the way I'm going on."

I recognised quickly enough that I could make, to this enquiry, no answer that would n't involve something of a sacrifice of my employer.

Why: The commas after "why" in this line, in the ninth line below, and in the next-to-last line in chapter XVII (p. 95) are not in the New York edition, but they were in the earlier *Collier's* edition. These three commas are reinserted for clarification.

Yet it struck me that we were all, at Bly, sufficiently sacrificed to make that venial.° "I don't think your uncle much cares."

Miles, on this, stood looking at me. "Then don't you think he can be made to?"

"In what way?"

"Why, by his coming down."

"But who'll get him to come down?"

"*I* will!" the boy said with extraordinary brightness and emphasis. He gave me another look charged with that expression and then marched off alone into church.

XV

The business was practically settled from the moment I never followed him. It was a pitiful surrender to agitation, but my being aware of this had somehow no power to restore me. I only sat there on my tomb and read into what our young friend had said to me the fulness of its meaning; by the time I had grasped the whole of which I had also embraced, for absence, the pretext that I was ashamed to offer my pupils and the rest of the congregation such an example of delay. What I said to myself above all was that Miles had got something out of me and that the gage of it for him would be just this awkward collapse. He had got out of me that there was something I was much afraid of, and that he should probably be able to make use of my fear to gain, for his own purpose, more freedom. My fear was of having to deal with the intolerable question of the grounds of his dismissal from school, since that was really but the question of the horrors gathered behind. That his uncle should arrive to treat with me of these things was a solution that, strictly speaking, I ought now to have desired to bring on; but I could so little face the ugliness and the pain of it that I simply procrastinated and lived from hand to mouth. The boy, to my deep discomposure, was immensely in the right, was in a position to say to me: "Either you clear up with my guardian the mystery of this interruption of my studies, or you cease to expect me to lead with you a life that's so unnatural for a boy." What was so unnatural for the particular boy I was concerned with was this sudden revelation of a consciousness and a plan.

---

venial: A venial sin, as opposed to a mortal sin, is one that can be readily forgiven. The governess here states her opinion that since they had all paid the price for the uncle's refusing to come to Bly, it was a small enough "sacrifice," easily forgiven, to say something negative about him to his nephew.

That was what really overcame me, what prevented my going in. I walked round the church, hesitating, hovering; I reflected that I had already, with him, hurt myself beyond repair. Therefore I could patch up nothing and it was too extreme an effort to squeeze beside him into the pew: he would be so much more sure than ever to pass his arm into mine and make me sit there for an hour in close mute contact with his commentary on our talk. For the first minute since his arrival I wanted to get away from him. As I paused beneath the high east window and listened to the sounds of worship I was taken with an impulse that might master me, I felt, and completely, should I give it the least encouragement. I might easily put an end to my ordeal by getting away altogether. Here was my chance; there was no one to stop me; I could give the whole thing up — turn my back and bolt. It was only a question of hurrying again, for a few preparations, to the house which the attendance at church of so many of the servants would practically have left unoccupied. No one, in short, could blame me if I should just drive desperately off. What was it to get away if I should get away only till dinner? That would be in a couple of hours, at the end of which — I had the acute prevision — my little pupils would play at innocent wonder about my non-appearance in their train.

"What *did* you do, you naughty bad thing? Why in the world, to worry us so — and take our thoughts off too, don't you know? — did you desert us at the very door?" I could n't meet such questions nor, as they asked them, their false little lovely eyes; yet it was all so exactly what I should have to meet that, as the prospect grew sharp to me, I at last let myself go.

I got, so far as the immediate moment was concerned, away; I came straight out of the churchyard and, thinking hard, retraced my steps through the park. It seemed to me that by the time I reached the house I had made up my mind to cynical flight. The Sunday stillness both of the approaches and of the interior, in which I met no one, fairly stirred me with a sense of opportunity. Were I to get off quickly this way I should get off without a scene, without a word. My quickness would have to be remarkable, however, and the question of a conveyance was the great one to settle. Tormented, in the hall, with difficulties and obstacles, I remember sinking down at the foot of the staircase — suddenly collapsing there on the lowest step and then, with a revulsion, recalling that it was exactly where, more than a month before, in the darkness of night and just so bowed with evil things, I had seen the spectre of the most horrible of women. At this I was able to straighten myself; I went the rest of the way up; I made, in my turmoil, for the schoolroom, where there were objects belonging to me that I should have to take. But I opened the door to find again, in a flash, my eyes unsealed. In the presence of what I saw I reeled straight back upon resistance.

Seated at my own table in the clear noonday light I saw a person whom, without my previous experience, I should have taken at the first blush for some housemaid who might have stayed at home to look after the place and who, availing herself of rare relief from observation and of the schoolroom table and my pens, ink, and paper, had applied herself to the considerable effort of a letter to her sweetheart. There was an effort in the way that, while her arms rested on the table, her hands, with evident weariness, supported her head; but at the moment I took this in I had already become aware that, in spite of my entrance, her attitude strangely persisted. Then it was — with the very act of its announcing itself — that her identity flared up in a change of posture. She rose, not as if she had heard me, but with an indescribable grand melancholy of indifference and detachment, and, within a dozen feet of me, stood there as my vile predecessor. Dishonoured and tragic, she was all before me; but even as I fixed and, for memory, secured it, the awful image passed away. Dark as midnight in her black dress, her haggard beauty and her unutterable woe, she had looked at me long enough to appear to say that her right to sit at my table was as good as mine to sit at hers. While these instants lasted indeed I had the extraordinary chill of a feeling that it was I who was the intruder. It was as a wild protest against it that, actually addressing her — "You terrible miserable woman!" — I heard myself break into a sound that, by the open door, rang through the long passage and the empty house. She looked at me as if she heard me, but I had recovered myself and cleared the air. There was nothing in the room the next minute but the sunshine and the sense that I must stay.

XVI°

I had so perfectly expected the return of the others to be marked by a demonstration that I was freshly upset at having to find them merely dumb and discreet about my desertion. Instead of gaily denouncing and caressing me they made no allusion to my having failed them, and I was left, for the time, on perceiving that she too said nothing, to study Mrs. Grose's odd face. I did this to such purpose that I made sure they

XVI: The ninth weekly *Collier's* installment began here.

had in some way bribed her to silence; a silence that, however, I would engage to break down on the first private opportunity. This opportunity came before tea: I secured five minutes with her in the housekeeper's room, where, in the twilight, amid a smell of lately-baked bread, but with the place all swept and garnished, I found her sitting in pained placidity before the fire. So I see her still, so I see her best: facing the flame from her straight chair in the dusky shining room, a large clean picture of the "put away" — of drawers closed and locked and rest without a remedy.°

"Oh yes, they asked me to say nothing; and to please them — so long as they were there — of course I promised. But what had happened to you?"

"I only went with you for the walk," I said. "I had then to come back to meet a friend."

She showed her surprise. "A friend — *you*?"

"Oh yes, I've a couple!" I laughed. "But did the children give you a reason?"

"For not alluding to your leaving us? Yes; they said you'd like it better. *Do* you like it better?"

My face had made her rueful. "No, I like it worse!" But after an instant I added: "Did they say why I should like it better?"

"No; Master Miles only said 'We must do nothing but what she likes!'"

"I wish indeed he would! And what did Flora say?"

"Miss Flora was too sweet. She said 'Oh of course, of course!' — and I said the same."

I thought a moment. "You were too sweet too — I can hear you all. But none the less, between Miles and me, it's now all out."

"All out?" My companion stared. "But what, Miss?"

"Everything. It does n't matter. I've made up my mind. I came home, my dear," I went on, "for a talk with Miss Jessel."°

---

of drawers closed and locked and rest without a remedy: This phrasing is confusing since it is not clear why "rest" would need a "remedy." The idea seems to be that the governess remembers Mrs. Grose, with her housekeeping work done, resting in front of the fire. In the original *Collier's* publication, James had written "of cupboards closed and diligence vaguely baffled."   *a talk with Miss Jessel:* This is a puzzling passage, since the governess had come back to pack her things, not to talk with Miss Jessel. Perhaps the discrepancy is explained by the following sentence, where the governess says that she likes to have the unimaginative Mrs. Grose "literally well in hand" before she mentions her encounters with Quint and Jessel. Of course, in effect the governess does talk to, if not "with," Miss Jessel when she speaks directly to her predecessor: "'You terrible miserable woman!'" (p. 88).

I had by this time formed the habit of having Mrs. Grose literally well in hand in advance of my sounding that note; so that even now, as she bravely blinked under the signal of my word, I could keep her comparatively firm. "A talk! Do you mean she spoke?"

"It came to that.° I found her, on my return, in the schoolroom."

"And what did she say?" I can hear the good woman still, and the candour of her stupefaction.

"That she suffers the torments — !"

It was this, of a truth, that made her, as she filled out my picture, gape. "Do you mean," she faltered " — of the lost?"

"Of the lost. Of the damned.° And that's why, to share them — " I faltered myself with the horror of it.

But my companion, with less imagination, kept me up. "To share them — ?"

"She wants Flora." Mrs. Grose might, as I gave it to her, fairly have fallen away from me had I not been prepared. I still held her there, to show I was. "As I've told you, however, it does n't matter."

"Because you've made up your mind? But to what?"

"To everything."

"And what do you call 'everything'?"

"Why to sending for their uncle."

"Oh Miss, in pity do," my friend broke out.

"Ah but I will, I *will*! I see it's the only way. What's 'out,' as I told you, with Miles is that if he thinks I'm afraid to — and has ideas of what he gains by that — he shall see he's mistaken. Yes, yes; his uncle shall have it here from me on the spot (and before the boy himself if necessary) that if I'm to be reproached with having done nothing again about more school — "

"Yes, Miss — " my companion pressed me.

"Well, there's that awful reason."

It came to that: The governess's reply to Mrs Grose's query about whether Miss Jessel spoke is also puzzling. It is apparently meant as a further qualification of her comment that she had a talk with Miss Jessel. She replies, in effect, "Well, not really, but it amounted to that" or "we might as well have." We recall that to the governess, who has certain intuitions, Miss Jessel really did "appear to say that her right to sit at my table was as good as mine to sit at hers" (p. 88).   *Of the damned:* Another difficult passage, since Miss Jessell had not actually said anything, let alone anything so specific. One way to make sense of the statement is that the new governess has an intuitional understanding of Miss Jessel's loneliness and woe, but needs to invent Miss Jessel's speech as a way of translating her intuition into actual words for the more literal Mrs. Grose. There are alternative readings of this scene that suggest that the governess has herself become unhinged by the pressures and tensions of her position, or that she is a pathological liar.

There were now clearly so many of these for my poor colleague that she was excusable for being vague. "But — a — which?"

"Why the letter from his old place."

"You'll show it to the master?"

"I ought to have done so on the instant."

"Oh no!" said Mrs. Grose with decision.

"I'll put it before him," I went on inexorably, "that I can't undertake to work the question on behalf of a child who has been expelled — "

"For we've never in the least known what!" Mrs. Grose declared.

"For wickedness. For what else — when he's so clever and beautiful and perfect? Is he stupid? Is he untidy? Is he infirm? Is he ill-natured? He's exquisite — so it can be only *that;* and that would open up the whole thing. After all," I said, "it's their uncle's fault. If he left here such people — !"

"He did n't really in the least know them. The fault's mine." She had turned quite pale.

"Well, you shan't suffer," I answered.

"The children shan't!" she emphatically returned.

I was silent a while; we looked at each other. "Then what am I to tell him?"

"You need n't tell him anything. *I'll* tell him."

I measured this. "Do you mean you'll write — ?" Remembering she could n't, I caught myself up. "How do you communicate?"

"I tell the bailiff.° *He* writes."

"And should you like him to write our story?"

My question had a sarcastic force that I had not fully intended, and it made her after a moment inconsequently break down. The tears were again in her eyes. "Ah Miss, *you* write!"

"Well — to-night," I at last returned; and on this we separated.

XVII

I went so far, in the evening, as to make a beginning. The weather had changed back, a great wind was abroad, and beneath the lamp, in my room, with Flora at peace beside me, I sat for a long time before a blank sheet of paper and listened to the lash of the rain and the batter of the gusts. Finally I went out, taking a candle; I crossed the passage and listened a minute at Miles's door. What, under my endless obsession, I

bailiff: An administrative official or magistrate.

had been impelled to listen for was some betrayal of his not being at rest, and I presently caught one, but not in the form I had expected. His voice tinkled out. "I say, you there — come in." It was gaiety in the gloom!

I went in with my light and found him in bed, very wide awake but very much at his ease. "Well, what are *you* up to?" he asked with a grace of sociability in which it occurred to me that Mrs. Grose, had she been present, might have looked in vain for proof that anything was "out."

I stood over him with my candle. "How did you know I was there?"

"Why of course I heard you. Did you fancy you made no noise? You're like a troop of cavalry!" he beautifully laughed.

"Then you were n't asleep?"

"Not much! I lie awake and think."

I had put my candle, designedly, a short way off, and then, as he held out his friendly old hand to me, had sat down on the edge of his bed. "What is it," I asked, "that you think of?"

"What in the world, my dear, but *you?*"

"Ah the pride I take in your appreciation does n't insist on that! I had so far rather you slept."

"Well, I think also, you know, of this queer business of ours."

I marked the coolness of his firm little hand. "Of what queer business, Miles?"

"Why the way you bring me up. And all the rest!"

I fairly held my breath a minute, and even from my glimmering taper there was light enough to show how he smiled up at me from his pillow. "What do you mean by all the rest?"

"Oh you know, you know!"

I could say nothing for a minute, though I felt as I held his hand and our eyes continued to meet that my silence had all the air of admitting his charge and that nothing in the whole world of reality was perhaps at that moment so fabulous° as our actual relation. "Certainly you shall go back to school," I said, "if it be that that troubles you. But not to the old place — we must find another, a better. How could I know it did trouble you, this question, when you never told me so, never spoke of it at all?" His clear listening face, framed in its smooth whiteness, made him for the minute as appealing as some wistful patient in a children's hospital; and I would have given, as the resemblance came to me, all I possessed on earth really to be the nurse or the sister of charity who might have helped to cure him. Well, even as it was I perhaps

---

fabulous: Strange, unreal, fable-like.

might help! "Do you know you've never said a word to me about your school — I mean the old one; never mentioned it in any way?"

He seemed to wonder; he smiled with the same loveliness. But he clearly gained time; he waited, he called for guidance. "Haven't I?" It was n't for *me* to help him — it was for the thing° I had met!

Something in his tone and the expression of his face, as I got this from him, set my heart aching with such a pang as it had never yet known; so unutterably touching was it to see his little brain puzzled and his little resources taxed to play, under the spell laid on him, a part of innocence and consistency. "No, never — from the hour you came back. You've never mentioned to me one of your masters, one of your comrades, nor the least little thing that ever happened to you at school. Never, little Miles — no never — have you given me an inkling of anything that *may* have happened there. Therefore you can fancy how much I'm in the dark. Until you came out, that way, this morning, you had since the first hour I saw you scarce even made a reference to anything in your previous life. You seemed so perfectly to accept the present." It was extraordinary how my absolute conviction of his secret precocity — or whatever I might call the poison of an influence that I dared but half-phrase — made him, in spite of the faint breath of his inward trouble, appear as accessible as an older person, forced me to treat him as an intelligent equal. "I thought you wanted to go on as you are."

It struck me that at this he just faintly coloured. He gave, at any rate, like a convalescent slightly fatigued, a languid shake of his head. "I don't — I don't. I want to get away."

"You're tired of Bly?"

"Oh no, I like Bly."

"Well then — ?"

"Oh *you* know what a boy wants!"

I felt I did n't know so well as Miles, and I took temporary refuge. "You want to go to your uncle?"

Again, at this, with his sweet ironic face, he made a movement on the pillow. "Ah you can't get off with that!"

I was silent a little, and it was I now, I think, who changed colour. "My dear, I don't want to get off!"

"You can't even if you do. You can't, you can't!" — he lay beautifully staring. "My uncle must come down and you must completely settle things."

the thing: The apparition of Peter Quint.

"If we do," I returned with some spirit, "you may be sure it will be to take you quite away."

"Well, don't you understand that that's exactly what I'm working for? You'll have to *tell* him — about the way you've let it all drop: you'll have to tell him a tremendous lot!"

The exultation with which he uttered this helped me somehow for the instant to meet him rather more. "And how much will *you*, Miles, have to tell him? There are things he'll ask you!"

He turned it over. "Very likely. But what things?"

"The things you've never told me. To make up his mind what to do with you. He can't send you back — "

"I don't want to go back!" he broke in. "I want a new field."

He said it with admirable serenity, with positive unimpeachable gaiety; and doubtless it was that very note that most evoked for me the poignancy, the unnatural childish tragedy, of his probable reappearance at the end of three months with all this bravado and still more dishonour. It overwhelmed me now that I should never be able to bear that, and it made me let myself go. I threw myself upon him and in the tenderness of my pity I embraced him. "Dear little Miles, dear little Miles — !"

My face was close to his, and he let me kiss him, simply taking it with indulgent good humour. "Well, old lady?"

"Is there nothing — nothing at all that you want to tell me?"

He turned off a little, facing round toward the wall and holding up his hand to look at as one had seen sick children look. "I've told you — I told you this morning."

Oh I was sorry for him! "That you just want me not to worry you?"

He looked round at me now as if in recognition of my understanding him; then ever so gently, "To let me alone," he replied.

There was even a strange little dignity in it, something that made me release him, yet, when I had slowly risen, linger beside him. God knows *I* never wished to harass him, but I felt that merely, at this, to turn my back on him was to abandon or, to put it more truly, lose him. "I've just begun a letter to your uncle," I said.

"Well then, finish it!"

I waited a minute. "What happened before?"

He gazed up at me again. "Before what?"

"Before you came back. And before you went away."

For some time he was silent, but he continued to meet my eyes. "What happened?"

It made me, the sound of the words, in which it seemed to me I caught for the very first time a small faint quaver of consenting consciousness — it made me drop on my knees beside the bed and seize once more the chance of possessing him. "Dear little Miles, dear little Miles, if you *knew* how I want to help you! It's only that, it's nothing but that, and I'd rather die than give you a pain or do you a wrong — I'd rather die than hurt a hair of you. Dear little Miles" — oh I brought it out now even if I *should* go too far — "I just want you to help me to save you!"° But I knew in a moment after this that I had gone too far. The answer to my appeal was instantaneous, but it came in the form of an extraordinary blast and chill, a gust of frozen air and a shake of the room as great as if, in the wild wind, the casement had crashed in. The boy gave a loud high shriek which, lost in the rest of the shock of sound, might have seemed, indistinctly, though I was so close to him, a note either of jubilation or of terror. I jumped to my feet again and was conscious of darkness. So for a moment we remained, while I stared about me and saw the drawn curtains unstirred and the window still tight. "Why, the candle's out!" I then cried.

"It was I who blew it,° dear!" said Miles.

XVIII

The next day, after lessons, Mrs. Grose found a moment to say to me quietly: "Have you written, Miss?"

"Yes — I've written." But I did n't add — for the hour — that my letter, sealed and directed, was still in my pocket. There would be time enough to send it before the messenger should go to the village. Meanwhile there had been on the part of my pupils no more brilliant, more exemplary morning. It was exactly as if they had both had at heart to gloss over any recent little friction. They performed the dizziest feats of arithmetic, soaring quite out of *my* feeble range, and perpetrated, in higher spirits than ever, geographical and historical jokes. It was conspicuous of course in Miles in particular that he appeared to wish to show how easily he could let me down. This child, to my memory, really lives in a setting of beauty and misery that no words can translate;

---

to save you: In this context, "save" suggests saving his soul from damnation. Compare the end of chapter XXI: "If he confesses he's saved" (p. 110).   **It was I who blew it:** A common feature of the ghost narratives reported by psychic researchers of the time was the extinguishing of candles. Ghosts apparently did not like lights. Miles says he blew it out but gives no motive for doing so and offers no explanation for the gust of frozen air, the shake of the room, or his own shriek. This scene recalls the earlier scene, with Quint on the stairs, when the governess's candle is unaccountably blown out "under a bold flourish" (p. 67).

there was a distinction all his own in every impulse he revealed; never was a small natural creature, to the uninformed eye all frankness and freedom, a more ingenious, a more extraordinary little gentleman. I had perpetually to guard against the wonder of contemplation into which my initiated view betrayed me; to check the irrelevant gaze and discouraged sigh in which I constantly both attacked and renounced the enigma of what such a little gentleman could have done that deserved a penalty. Say that, by the dark prodigy I knew, the imagination of all evil *had* been opened up to him: all the justice within me ached for the proof that it could ever have flowered into an act.

He had never at any rate been such a little gentleman as when, after our early dinner on this dreadful day, he came round to me and asked if I should n't like him for half an hour to play to me. David playing to Saul° could never have shown a finer sense of the occasion. It was literally a charming exhibition of tact, of magnanimity, and quite tantamount to his saying outright: "The true knights we love to read about never push an advantage too far. I know what you mean now: you mean that — to be let alone yourself and not followed up — you'll cease to worry and spy upon me, won't keep me so close to you, will let me go and come. Well, I 'come,' you see — but I don't go! There'll be plenty of time for that. I do really delight in your society and I only want to show you that I contended for a principle." It may be imagined whether I resisted this appeal or failed to accompany him again, hand in hand, to the schoolroom. He sat down at the old piano and played as he had never played; and if there are those who think he had better have been kicking a football I can only say that I wholly agree with them. For at the end of a time that under his influence I had quite ceased to measure I started up with a strange sense of having literally slept at my post. It was after luncheon, and by the schoolroom fire, and yet I had n't really in the least slept; I had only done something much worse — I had forgotten. Where all this time was Flora? When I put the question to Miles he played on a minute before answering, and then could only say: "Why, my dear, how do *I* know?" — breaking moreover into a happy laugh which immediately after, as if it were a vocal accompaniment, he prolonged into incoherent extravagant song.

I went straight to my room, but his sister was not there; then, before going downstairs, I looked into several others. As she was nowhere about she would surely be with Mrs. Grose, whom in the comfort of that theory I accordingly proceeded in quest of. I found her where I had found her the evening before, but she met my quick challenge with blank scared ignorance. She had only supposed that, after the repast, I had carried off both the children; as to which she was quite in her right, for it was the very first time I had allowed the little girl out of my sight without some special provision. Of course now indeed she might be with the maids, so that the immediate thing was to look for her without an air of alarm. This we promptly arranged between us; but when, ten minutes later and in pursuance of our arrangement, we met in the hall, it was only to report on either side that after guarded enquiries we had altogether failed to trace her. For a minute there, apart from observation, we exchanged mute alarms, and I could feel with what high interest my friend returned me all those I had from the first given her.

"She'll be above," she presently said — "in one of the rooms you have n't searched."

"No; she's at a distance." I had made up my mind. "She has gone out."

Mrs. Grose stared. "Without a hat?"

I naturally also looked volumes. "Isn't that woman always without one?"

"She's with *her*?"

"She's with *her*!" I declared. "We must find them."

My hand was on my friend's arm, but she failed for the moment, confronted with such an account of the matter, to respond to my pressure. She communed, on the contrary, where she stood, with her uneasiness. "And where's Master Miles?"

"Oh *he's* with Quint. They'll be in the schoolroom."

"Lord, Miss!" My view, I was myself aware — and therefore I suppose my tone — had never yet reached so calm an assurance.

"The trick's played," I went on; "they've successfully worked their plan. He found the most divine little way to keep me quiet while she went off."

"'Divine'?" Mrs. Grose bewilderedly echoed.

"Infernal then!" I almost cheerfully rejoined. "He has provided for himself as well. But come!"

She had helplessly gloomed at the upper regions. "You leave him — ?"

"So long with Quint? Yes — I don't mind that now."

She always ended at these moments by getting possession of my hand, and in this manner she could at present still stay me. But after

gasping an instant at my sudden resignation, "Because of your letter?"
she eagerly brought out.

I quickly, by way of answer, felt for my letter, drew it forth, held it
up, and then, freeing myself, went and laid it on the great hall-table.
"Luke will take it," I said as I came back. I reached the house-door and
opened it; I was already on the steps.

My companion still demurred: the storm of the night and the early
morning had dropped, but the afternoon was damp and grey. I came
down to the drive while she stood in the doorway. "You go with nothing on?"

"What do I care when the child has nothing? I can't wait to dress,"
I cried, "and if you must do so I leave you. Try meanwhile yourself
upstairs."

"With *them*?" Oh on this the poor woman promptly joined me!

XIX°

We went straight to the lake, as it was called at Bly, and I dare say
rightly called, though it may have been a sheet of water less remarkable
than my untravelled eyes supposed it. My acquaintance with sheets of
water was small, and the pool of Bly, at all events on the few occasions
of my consenting, under the protection of my pupils, to affront its surface in the old flat-bottomed boat moored there for our use, had
impressed me both with its extent and its agitation. The usual place of
embarkation was half a mile from the house, but I had an intimate conviction that, wherever Flora might be, she was not near home. She had
not given me the slip for any small adventure, and, since the day of the
very great one that I had shared with her by the pond, I had been
aware, in our walks, of the quarter to which she most inclined. This was
why I had now given to Mrs. Grose's steps so marked a direction — a
direction making her, when she perceived it, oppose a resistance that
showed me she was freshly mystified. "You're going to the water,
Miss? — you think she's *in* — ?"

"She may be, though the depth is, I believe, nowhere very great.
But what I judge most likely is that she's on the spot from which, the
other day, we saw together what I told you."

"When she pretended not to see — ?"

"With that astounding self-possession! I've always been sure she
wanted to go back alone. And now her brother has managed it for her."

XIX: The tenth weekly *Collier's* installment and *Part Fifth* began here.

Mrs. Grose still stood where she had stopped. "You suppose they really *talk* of them?"

I could meet this with an assurance! "They say things that, if we heard them, would simply appal us."

"And if she *is* there — ?"

"Yes?"

"Then Miss Jessel is?"

"Beyond a doubt. You shall see."

"Oh thank you!" my friend cried, planted so firm that, taking it in, I went straight on without her. By the time I reached the pool, however, she was close behind me, and I knew that, whatever, to her apprehension, might befall me, the exposure of sticking to me struck her as her least danger. She exhaled a moan of relief as we at last came in sight of the greater part of the water without a sight of the child. There was no trace of Flora on that nearer side of the bank where my observation of her had been most startling, and none on the opposite edge, where, save for a margin of some twenty yards, a thick copse came down to the pond. This expanse, oblong in shape, was so narrow compared to its length that, with its ends out of view, it might have been taken for a scant river. We looked at the empty stretch, and then I felt the suggestion in my friend's eyes. I knew what she meant and I replied with a negative headshake.

"No, no; wait! She has taken the boat."

My companion stared at the vacant mooring-place and then again across the lake. "Then where is it?"

"Our not seeing it is the strongest of proofs. She has used it to go over, and then has managed to hide it."

"All alone — that child?"

"She's not alone, and at such times she's not a child: she's an old, old woman." I scanned all the visible shore while Mrs. Grose took again, into the queer element I offered her, one of her plunges of sub-mission; then I pointed out that the boat might perfectly be in a small refuge formed by one of the recesses of the pool, an indentation masked, for the hither side, by a projection of the bank and by a clump of trees growing close to the water.

"But if the boat's there, where on earth's *she*?" my colleague anxiously asked.

"That's exactly what we must learn." And I started to walk further.

"By going all the way round?"

"Certainly, far as it is. It will take us but ten minutes, yet it's far enough to have made the child prefer not to walk. She went straight over."

"Laws!" cried my friend again: the chain of my logic was ever too strong for her. It dragged her at my heels even now, and when we had got halfway round — a devious tiresome process, on ground much broken and by a path choked with overgrowth — I paused to give her breath. I sustained her with a grateful arm, assuring her that she might hugely help me; and this started us afresh, so that in the course of but few minutes more we reached a point from which we found the boat to be where I had supposed it. It had been intentionally left as much as possible out of sight and was tied to one of the stakes of a fence that came, just there, down to the brink and that had been an assistance to disembarking. I recognised, as I looked at the pair of short thick oars, quite safely drawn up, the prodigious character of the feat for a little girl; but I had by this time lived too long among wonders and had panted to too many livelier measures. There was a gate in the fence, through which we passed, and that brought us after a trifling interval more into the open. Then "There she is!" we both exclaimed at once.

Flora, a short way off, stood before us on the grass and smiled as if her performance had now become complete. The next thing she did, however, was to stoop straight down and pluck — quite as if it were all she was there for — a big ugly spray of withered fern. I at once felt sure she had just come out of the copse. She waited for us, not herself taking a step, and I was conscious of the rare solemnity with which we presently approached her. She smiled and smiled, and we met; but it was all done in a silence by this time flagrantly ominous. Mrs. Grose was the first to break the spell: she threw herself on her knees and, drawing the child to her breast, clasped in a long embrace the little tender yielding body. While this dumb convulsion lasted I could only watch it — which I did the more intently when I saw Flora's face peep at me over our companion's shoulder. It was serious now — the flicker had left it; but it strengthened the pang with which I at that moment envied Mrs. Grose the simplicity of *her* relation. Still, all this while, nothing more passed between us save that Flora had let her foolish fern again drop to the ground. What she and I had virtually said to each other was that pretexts were useless now. When Mrs. Grose finally got up she kept the child's hand, so that the two were still before me; and the singular reticence of our communion was even more marked in the frank look she addressed me. "I'll be hanged," it said, "if *I'll* speak!"

It was Flora who, gazing all over me in candid wonder, was the first. She was struck with our bare-headed aspect. "Why where are your things?"

"Where yours are, my dear!" I promptly returned.

She had already got back her gaiety and appeared to take this as an answer quite sufficient. "And where's Miles?" she went on.

There was something in the small valour of it that quite finished me: these three words from her were in a flash like the glitter of a drawn blade,° the jostle of the cup that my hand for weeks and weeks had held high and full to the brim and that now, even before speaking, I felt overflow in a deluge. "I'll tell you if you'll tell *me* — " I heard myself say, then heard the tremor in which it broke.

"Well, what?"

Mrs. Grose's suspense blazed at me, but it was too late now, and I brought the thing out handsomely. "Where, my pet, is Miss Jessel?"

XX

Just as in the churchyard with Miles, the whole thing was upon us. Much as I had made of the fact that this name had never once, between us, been sounded, the quick smitten glare with which the child's face now received it fairly likened my breach of the silence to the smash of a pane of glass. It added to the interposing cry, as if to stay the blow, that Mrs. Grose at the same instant uttered over my violence — the shriek of a creature scared, or rather wounded, which, in turn, within a few seconds, was completed by a gasp of my own. I seized my colleague's arm. "She's there, she's there!"

Miss Jessel stood before us on the opposite bank exactly as she had stood the other time, and I remember, strangely, as the first feeling now produced in me, my thrill of joy at having brought on a proof. She was there, so I was justified; she was there, so I was neither cruel nor mad. She was there for poor scared Mrs. Grose, but she was there most for Flora; and no moment of my monstrous time was perhaps so extraordinary as that in which I consciously threw out to her — with the sense that, pale and ravenous demon as she was, she would catch and understand it — an inarticulate message of gratitude. She rose erect on the spot my friend and I had lately quitted, and there n't in all the long reach of her desire an inch of her evil that fell short. This first vividness of vision and emotion were things of a few seconds, during which Mrs. Grose's dazed blink across to where I pointed struck me as showing that she too at last saw, just as it carried my own eyes precipitately to the child. The revelation then of the manner in which Flora was affected

---

blade: The New York Edition does not have the comma after "blade," but the *Collier's* version does. I have restored it to clarify the sense of the sentence.

startled me in truth far more than it would have done to find her also merely agitated, for direct dismay was of course not what I had expected. Prepared and on her guard as our pursuit had actually made her, she would repress every betrayal; and I was therefore at once shaken by my first glimpse of the particular one for which I had not allowed. To see her, without a convulsion of her small pink face, not even feign to glance in the direction of the prodigy I announced, but only, instead of that, turn at *me* an expression of hard still gravity, an expression absolutely new and unprecedented and that appeared to read and accuse and judge me — this was a stroke that somehow converted the little girl herself into a figure portentous. I gaped at her coolness even though my certitude of her thoroughly seeing was never greater than at that instant, and then, in the immediate need to defend myself, I called her passionately to witness. "She's there, you little unhappy thing — there, there, *there,* and you know it as well as you know me!" I had said shortly before to Mrs. Grose that she was not at these times a child, but an old, old woman, and my description of her could n't have been more strikingly confirmed than in the way in which, for all notice of this, she simply showed me, without an expressional concession or admission, a countenance of deeper and deeper, of indeed suddenly quite fixed reprobation. I was by this time — if I can put the whole thing at all together — more appalled at what I may properly call her manner than at anything else, though it was quite simultaneously that I became aware of having Mrs. Grose also, and very formidably, to reckon with. My elder companion, the next moment, at any rate, blotted out everything but her own flushed face and her loud shocked protest, a burst of high disapproval. "What a dreadful turn, to be sure, Miss! Where on earth do you see anything?"

I could only grasp her more quickly yet, for even while she spoke the hideous plain presence stood undimmed and undaunted. It had already lasted a minute, and it lasted while I continued, seizing my colleague, quite thrusting her at it and presenting her to it, to insist with my pointing hand. "You don't see her exactly as *we* see? — you mean to say you don't now — *now?* She's as big as a blazing fire! Only look, dearest woman, *look* — !" She looked, just as I did, and gave me, with her deep groan of negation, repulsion, compassion — the mixture with her pity of her relief at her exemption° — a sense, touching to me even then, that she would have backed me up if she had been able. I might

---

relief at her exemption: Mrs. Grose is relieved to be "exempt" from seeing the ghost (see note to second paragraph of chapter VI on page 50).

well have needed that, for with this hard blow of the proof that her eyes were hopelessly sealed I felt my own situation horribly crumble, I felt — I *saw* — my livid predecessor press, from her position, on my defeat, and I took the measure, more than all, of what I should have from this instant to deal with in the astounding little attitude of Flora. Into this attitude Mrs. Grose immediately and violently entered, breaking, even while there pierced through my sense of ruin a prodigious private triumph, into breathless reassurance.

"She is n't there, little lady, and nobody's there — and you never see nothing, my sweet! How can poor Miss Jessel — when poor Miss Jessel's dead and buried? *We* know, don't we, love?" — and she appealed, blundering in, to the child. "It's all a mere mistake and a worry and a joke — and we'll go home as fast as we can!"

Our companion, on this, had responded with a strange quick primness of propriety, and they were again, with Mrs. Grose on her feet, united, as it were, in shocked opposition to me. Flora continued to fix me with her small mask of disaffection, and even at that minute I prayed God to forgive me for seeming to see that, as she stood there holding tight to our friend's dress, her incomparable childish beauty had suddenly failed, had quite vanished. I've said it already — she was literally, she was hideously hard; she had turned common and almost ugly. "I don't know what you mean. I see nobody. I see nothing. I never *have*, I think you're cruel. I don't like you!" Then, after this deliverance, which might have been that of a vulgarly pert little girl in the street, she hugged Mrs. Grose more closely and buried in her skirts the dreadful little face. In this position she launched an almost furious wail. "Take me away, take me away — oh take me away from *her*!"

"From *me*?" I panted.

"From you — from you!" she cried.

Even Mrs. Grose looked across at me dismayed; while I had nothing to do but communicate again with the figure that, on the opposite bank, without a movement, as rigidly still as if catching, beyond the interval, our voices, was as vividly there for my disaster as it was not there for my service. The wretched child had spoken exactly as if she had got from some outside source° each of her stabbing little words, and I could therefore, in the full despair of all I had to accept, but sadly

---

from some outside source: This phrase may be a clue that Flora is "possessed" — that is, that her body is temporarily occupied by the spirit of Miss Jessel. The concept of possession was well-known in James's time. Note the word "dispossessed" in the last line of the story.

shake my head at her. "If I had ever doubted all my doubt would at present have gone. I've been living with the miserable truth, and now it has only too much closed round me. Of course I've lost you: I've interfered, and you've seen, under *her* dictation" — with which I faced, over the pool again, our infernal witness — "the easy and perfect way to meet it. I've done my best, but I've lost you. Good-bye." For Mrs. Grose I had an imperative, an almost frantic "Go, go!" before which, in infinite distress, but mutely possessed of the little girl and clearly convinced, in spite of her blindness, that something awful had occurred and some collapse engulfed us, she retreated, by the way we had come, as fast as she could move.

Of what first happened when I was left alone I had no subsequent memory. I only knew that at the end of, I suppose, a quarter of an hour, an odorous dampness and roughness, chilling and piercing my trouble, had made me understand that I must have thrown myself, on my face, to the ground and given way to a wildness of grief. I must have lain there long and cried and wailed, for when I raised my head the day was almost done. I got up and looked a moment, through the twilight, at the grey pool and its blank haunted edge, and then I took, back to the house, my dreary and difficult course. When I reached the gate in the fence the boat, to my surprise, was gone, so that I had a fresh reflexion to make on Flora's extraordinary command of the situation. She passed that night, by the most tacit and, I should add, were not the word so grotesque a false note, the happiest of arrangements, with Mrs. Grose. I saw neither of them on my return, but on the other hand I saw, as by an ambiguous compensation, a great deal of Miles. I saw — I can use no other phrase — so much of him that it fairly measured more than it had ever measured. No evening I had passed at Bly was to have had the portentous quality of this one; in spite of which — and in spite also of the deeper depths of consternation that had opened beneath my feet — there was literally, in the ebbing actual, an extraordinarily sweet sadness. On reaching the house I had never so much as looked for the boy; I had simply gone straight to my room to change what I was wearing and to take in, at a glance, much material testimony to Flora's rupture. Her little belongings had all been removed. When later, by the schoolroom fire, I was served with tea by the usual maid, I indulged, on the article of my other pupil, in no enquiry whatever. He had his freedom now — he might have it to the end! Well, he did have it; and it consisted — in part at least — of his coming in at about eight o'clock and sitting down with me in silence. On the removal of the tea-things I had blown out the candles and drawn my chair closer: I was conscious of a mortal coldness and felt as if I should never again be warm. So when he appeared I was sitting in the glow with my thoughts. He paused a moment by the door as if to look at me; then — as if to share them — came to the other side of the hearth and sank into a chair. We sat there in absolute stillness; yet he wanted, I felt, to be with me.

XXI°

Before a new day, in my room, had fully broken, my eyes opened to Mrs. Grose, who had come to my bedside with worse news. Flora was so markedly feverish that an illness was perhaps at hand; she had passed a night of extreme unrest, a night agitated above all by fears that had for their subject not in the least her former but wholly her present governess. It was not against the possible re-entrance of Miss Jessel on the scene that she protested — it was conspicuously and passionately against mine. I was at once on my feet, and with an immense deal to ask; the more that my friend had discernibly now girded her loins to meet me afresh. This I felt as soon as I had put to her the question of her sense of the child's sincerity as against my own. "She persists in denying to you that she saw, or has ever seen, anything?"

My visitor's trouble truly was great. "Ah Miss, it is n't a matter on which I can push her! Yet it is n't either, I must say, as if I much needed to. It has made her, every inch of her, quite old."

"Oh I see her perfectly from here. She resents, for all the world like some high little personage, the imputation on her truthfulness° and, as it were, her respectability. 'Miss Jessel indeed — *she*!' Ah she's 're-spectable,' the chit! The impression she gave me there yesterday was, I assure you, the very strangest of all: it was quite beyond any of the others. I *did* put my foot in it! She'll never speak to me again."

Hideous and obscure as it all was, it held Mrs. Grose briefly silent; then she granted my point with a frankness which, I made sure, had more behind it. "I think indeed, Miss, she never will. She do have a grand manner about it!"

"And that manner" — I summed it up — "is practically what's the matter with her now."

Oh that manner, I could see in my visitor's face, and not a little else besides! "She asks me every three minutes if I think you're coming in."

"I see — I see." I too, on my side, had so much more than worked it out. "Has she said to you since yesterday — except to repudiate her familiarity with anything so dreadful — a single other word about Miss Jessel?"

"Not one, Miss. And of course, you know," my friend added, "I took it from her by the lake that just then and there at least there *was* nobody."

"Rather! And naturally you take it from her still."

"I don't contradict her. What else can I do?"

"Nothing in the world! You've the cleverest little person to deal with. They've made them — their two friends, I mean — still cleverer even than nature did; for it was wondrous material to play on! Flora has now her grievance, and she'll work it to the end."

"Yes, Miss; but to *what* end?"

"Why that of dealing with me to her uncle. She'll make me out to him the lowest creature — !"

I winced at the fair show of the scene in Mrs. Grose's face; she looked for a minute as if she sharply saw them together. "And him who thinks so well of you!"

"He has an odd way — it comes over me now," I laughed, " — of proving it! But that does n't matter. What Flora wants of course is to get rid of me."

My companion bravely concurred. "Never again to so much as look at you."

"So that what you've come to me now for," I asked, "is to speed me on my way?" Before she had time to reply, however, I had her in check. "I've a better idea — the result of my reflexions. My going *would* seem the right thing, and on Sunday I was terribly near it. Yet that won't do. It's *you* who must go. You must take Flora."

My visitor, at this, did speculate. "But where in the world — ?"

"Away from here. Away from *them*. Away, even most of all, now, from me. Straight to her uncle."

"Only to tell on you — ?"

"No, not 'only'! To leave me, in addition, with my remedy."

She was still vague. "And what *is* your remedy?"

"Your loyalty, to begin with. And then Miles's."

She looked at me hard. "Do you think he — ?"

"Won't, if he has the chance, turn on me? Yes, I venture still to think it. At all events I want to try. Get off with his sister as soon as possible and leave me with him alone." I was amazed, myself, at the spirit I had still in reserve, and therefore perhaps a trifle the more disconcerted at the way in which, in spite of this fine example of it, she hesitated.

"There's one thing, of course," I went on: "they must n't, before she goes, see each other for three seconds." Then it came over me that, in spite of Flora's presumable sequestration° from the instant of her return from the pool, it might already be too late. "Do you mean," I anxiously asked, "that they *have* met?"

At this she quite flushed. "Ah, Miss, I 'm not such a fool as that! If I've been obliged to leave her three or four times, it has been each time with one of the maids, and at present, though she's alone, she's locked in safe. And yet — and yet!" There were too many things.

"And yet what?"

"Well, are you so sure of the little gentleman?"

"I'm not sure of anything but *you*. But I have, since last evening, a new hope. I think he wants to give me an opening. I do believe that — poor little exquisite wretch! — he wants to speak. Last evening, in the firelight and the silence, he sat with me for two hours as if it were just coming."

Mrs. Grose looked hard through the window at the grey gathering day. "And did it come?"

"No, though I waited and waited I confess it did n't, and it was without a breach of the silence, or so much as a faint allusion to his sister's condition and absence, that we at last kissed for good-night. All the same," I continued, "I can't, if her uncle sees her, consent to his seeing her brother without my having given the boy — and most of all because things have got so bad — a little more time."

My friend appeared on this ground more reluctant than I could quite understand. "What do you mean by more time?"

"Well, a day or two — really to bring it out. He'll then be on *my* side — of which you see the importance. If nothing comes I shall only fail, and you at the worst have helped me by doing on your arrival in town whatever you may have found possible." So I put it before her, but she continued for a little so lost in other reasons that I came again to her aid. "Unless indeed," I wound up, "you really want *not* to go."

I could see it, in her face, at last clear itself: she put out her hand to me as a pledge. "I'll go — I'll go. I'll go this morning."

I wanted to be very just. "If you *should* wish still to wait I'd engage she should n't see me."

"No, no: it's the place itself. She must leave it." She held me a moment with heavy eyes, then brought out the rest. "Your idea's the right one. I myself, Miss — "

sequestration: Seclusion, separation.

"Well?"

"I can't stay."

The look she gave me with it made me jump at possibilities. "You mean that, since yesterday, you *have* seen — ?"

She shook her head with dignity. "I've *heard* — !"

"Heard?"

"From that child — horrors! There!" she sighed with tragic relief. "On my honour, Miss, she says things — !" But at this evocation she broke down; she dropped with a sudden cry upon my sofa and, as I had seen her do before, gave way to all the anguish of it.

It was quite in another manner that I for my part let myself go. "Oh thank God!"

She sprang up again at this, drying her eyes with a groan. " 'Thank God'?"

"It so justifies me!"

"It does that, Miss!"

I could n't have desired more emphasis, but I just waited. "She's so horrible?"

I saw my colleague scarce knew how to put it. "Really shocking."

"And about me?"

"About you, Miss — since you must have it. It's beyond everything, for a young lady; and I can't think wherever she must have picked up — "

"The appalling language she applies to me? I can then!" I broke in with a laugh that was doubtless significant enough.

It only in truth left my friend still more grave. "Well, perhaps I ought to also — since I've heard some of it before!° Yet I can't bear it," the poor woman went on while with the same movement she glanced, on my dressing-table, at the face of my watch. "But I must go back."

I kept her, however. "Ah if you can't bear it — !"

"How can I stop with her, you mean? Why just *for* that: to get her away. Far from this," she pursued, "far from *them* — "

"She may be different? she may be free?" I seized her almost with joy. "Then in spite of yesterday you *believe* — "

"In such doings?" Her simple description of them required, in the light of her expression, to be carried no further, and she gave me the whole thing as she had never done. "I believe."

Yes, it was a joy, and we were still shoulder to shoulder: if I might

---

heard some of it before: She had presumably heard some of Flora's appalling language from Jessel and Quint before their deaths.

continue sure of that I should care but little what else happened. My support in the presence of disaster would be the same as it had been in my early need of confidence, and if my friend would answer for my honesty I would answer for all the rest. On the point of taking leave of her, none the less, I was to some extent embarrassed. "There's one thing of course — it occurs to me — to remember. My letter giving the alarm will have reached town before you."

I now felt still more how she had been beating about the bush and how weary at last it had made her. "Your letter won't have got there. Your letter never went."

"What then became of it?"

"Goodness knows! Master Miles — "

"Do you mean *he* took it?" I gasped.

She hung fire, but she overcame her reluctance. "I mean that I saw yesterday, when I came back with Miss Flora, that it was n't where you had put it. Later in the evening I had the chance to question Luke, and he declared that he had neither noticed nor touched it." We could only exchange, on this, one of our deeper mutual soundings, and it was Mrs. Grose who first brought up the plumb° with an almost elate "You see!"

"Yes, I see that if Miles took it instead he probably will have read it and destroyed it."

"And don't you see anything else?"

I faced her a moment with a sad smile. "It strikes me that by this time your eyes are open even wider than mine."

They proved to be so indeed, but she could still almost blush to show it. "I make out now what he must have done at school." And she gave, in her simple sharpness, an almost droll disillusioned nod. "He stole!"

I turned it over — I tried to be more judicial. "Well — perhaps."

She looked as if she found me unexpectedly calm. "He stole *letters!*"

She could n't know my reasons for a calmness after all pretty shallow; so I showed them off as I might. "I hope then it was to more purpose than in this case! The note, at all events, that I put on the table yesterday," I pursued, "will have given him so scant an advantage — for it contained only the bare demand for an interview — that he's already

---

brought up the plumb: A "plumb" is a piece of lead on the end of the cord used to measure the depth of or to "sound" a body of water. This expression picks up the image of the "deeper mutual soundings" of the previous line and extends the nautical imagery found elsewhere in the story, for example, at the very end of chapter I, where the governess is "strangely at the helm" of "a great drifting ship" (p. 33).

much ashamed of having gone so far for so little, and that what he had on his mind last evening was precisely the need of confession." I seemed to myself for the instant to have mastered it, to see it all. "Leave us, leave us" — I was already, at the door, hurrying her off. "I'll get it out of him. He'll meet me. He'll confess. If he confesses he's saved. And if he's saved — "

"Then *you* are?" The dear woman kissed me on this, and I took her farewell. "I'll save you without him!" she cried as she went.

XXII

Yet it was when she had got off — and I missed her on the spot — that the great pinch really came. If I had counted on what it would give me to find myself alone with Miles I quickly recognised that it would give me at least a measure. No hour of my stay in fact was so assailed with apprehensions as that of my coming down to learn that the carriage containing Mrs. Grose and my younger pupil had already rolled out of the gates. Now I *was,* I said to myself, face to face with the elements, and for much of the rest of the day, while I fought my weakness, I could consider that I had been supremely rash. It was a tighter place still than I had yet turned round in; all the more that, for the first time, I could see in the aspect of others a confused reflexion of the crisis. What had happened naturally caused them all to stare; there was too little of the explained, throw out whatever we might, in the suddenness of my colleague's act. The maids and the men looked blank; the effect of which on my nerves was an aggravation until I saw the necessity of making it a positive aid. It was in short by just clutching the helm that I avoided total wreck; and I dare say that, to bear up at all, I became that morning very grand and very dry. I welcomed the consciousness that I was charged with much to do, and I caused it to be known as well that, left thus to myself, I was quite remarkably firm. I wandered with that manner, for the next hour or two, all over the place and looked, I have no doubt, as if I were ready for any onset. So, for the benefit of whom it might concern, I paraded with a sick heart.

The person it appeared least to concern proved to be, till dinner, little Miles himself. My perambulations had given me meanwhile no glimpse of him, but they had tended to make more public the change taking place in our relation as a consequence of his having at the piano, the day before, kept me, in Flora's interest, so beguiled and befooled. The stamp of publicity had of course been fully given by her confinement and departure, and the change itself was now ushered in by our non-observance of the regular custom of the schoolroom. He had already disappeared when, on my way down, I pushed open his door, and I learned below that he had breakfasted — in the presence of a couple of the maids — with Mrs. Grose and his sister. He had then gone out, as he said, for a stroll; than which nothing, I reflected, could better have expressed his frank view of the abrupt transformation of my office. What he would now permit this office to consist of was yet to be settled: there was at the least a queer relief — I mean for myself in especial — in the renouncement of one pretension. If so much had sprung to the surface I scarce put it too strongly in saying that what had perhaps sprung highest was the absurdity of our prolonging the fiction that I had anything more to teach him. It sufficiently stuck out that, by tacit little tricks in which even more than myself he carried out the care for my dignity, I had had to appeal to him to let me off straining to meet him on the ground of his true capacity. He had at any rate his freedom now; I was never to touch it again: as I had amply shown, moreover, when, on his joining me in the schoolroom the previous night, I uttered, in reference to the interval just concluded, neither challenge nor hint. I had too much, from this moment, my other ideas. Yet when he at last arrived the difficulty of applying them, the accumulations of my problem, were brought straight home to me by the beautiful little presence on which what had occurred had as yet, for the eye, dropped neither stain nor shadow.

To mark, for the house, the high state I cultivated I decreed that my meals with the boy should be served, as we called it, downstairs; so that I had been awaiting him in the ponderous pomp of the room° outside the window of which I had had from Mrs. Grose, that first scared Sunday, my flash of something it would scarce have done to call light. Here at present I felt afresh — for I had felt it again and again — how my equilibrium depended on the success of my rigid will, the will to shut my eyes as tight as possible to the truth that what I had to deal with was revoltingly, against nature. I could only get on at all by taking "nature" into my confidence and my account, by treating my monstrous ordeal as a push in a direction unusual, of course, and unpleasant, but demanding after all, for a fair front, only another turn of the screw of ordinary human virtue. No attempt, none the less, could well require more tact than just this attempt to supply, one's self, *all* the nature. How

the room: The "grown-up" dining room referred to in chapter IV, from which she had earlier seen Peter Quint outside the window.

could I put even a little of that article into a suppression of reference to what had occurred? How on the other hand could I make a reference without a new plunge into the hideous obscure? Well, a sort of answer, after a time, had come to me, and it was so far confirmed as that I was met, incontestably, by the quickened vision of what was rare in my little companion. It was indeed as if he had found even now — as he had so often found at lessons — still some other delicate way to ease me off. Wasn't there light in the fact which, as we shared our solitude, broke out with a specious glitter it had never yet quite worn? — the fact that (opportunity aiding, precious opportunity which had now come) it would be preposterous, with a child so endowed, to forego the help one might wrest from absolute intelligence? What had his intelligence been given him for but to save him? Might n't one, to reach his mind, risk the stretch of a stiff arm across his character? It was as if, when we were face to face in the dining-room, he had literally shown me the way. The roast mutton was on the table and I had dispensed with attendance.° Miles, before he sat down, stood a moment with his hands in his pockets and looked at the joint,° on which he seemed on the point of passing some humorous judgement. But what he presently produced was: "I say, my dear, is she really very awfully ill?"

"Little Flora? Not so bad but that she'll presently be better. London will set her up. Bly had ceased to agree with her. Come here and take your mutton."

He alertly obeyed me, carried the plate carefully to his seat and, when he was established, went on. "Did Bly disagree with her so terribly all at once?"

"Not so suddenly as you might think. One had seen it coming on."

"Then why did n't you get her off before?"

"Before what?"

"Before she became too ill to travel."

I found myself prompt. "She's *not* too ill to travel; she only might have become so if she had stayed. This was just the moment to seize. The journey will dissipate the influence" — oh I was grand! — "and carry it off."

"I see, I see" — Miles, for that matter, was grand too. He settled to his repast with the charming little "table manner" that, from the day of his arrival, had relieved me of all grossness of admonition.° Whatever he had been expelled from school for, it was n't for ugly feeding. He was

---

dispensed with attendance: Dismissed the servants.   *the joint:* The mutton roast.
grossness of admonition: The need to correct or criticize him for bad table manners.

irreproachable, as always, today; but was unmistakeably more conscious. He was discernibly trying to take for granted more things than
he found, without assistance, quite easy; and he dropped into peaceful
silence while he felt his situation. Our meal was of the briefest — mine a
vain presence, and I had the things immediately removed. While this
was done Miles stood again with his hands in his little pockets and his
back to me — stood and looked out of the wide window through
which, that other day, I had seen what pulled me up. We continued
silent while the maid was with us — as silent, it whimsically occurred to
me, as some young couple who, on their wedding-journey, at the inn,
feel shy in the presence of the waiter. He turned round only when the
waiter had left us. "Well — so we're alone!"

XXIII°

"Oh more or less." I imagine my smile was pale. "Not absolutely.
We should n't like that!" I went on.

"No — I suppose we should n't. Of course we've the others."

"We've the others — we've indeed the others," I concurred.

"Yet even though we have them," he returned, still with his hands
in his pockets and planted there in front of me, "they don't much
count, do they?"

I made the best of it, but I felt wan. "It depends on what you call
'much'!"

"Yes" — with all accommodation — "everything depends!" On
this, however, he faced to the window again and presently reached it
with his vague restless cogitating step. He remained there a while with
his forehead against the glass, in contemplation of the stupid shrubs I
knew and the dull things of November.° I had always my hypocrisy of
"work,"° behind which I now gained° the sofa. Steadying myself with it
there as I had repeatedly done at those moments of torment that I have
described as the moments of my knowing the children to be given to
something from which I was barred, I sufficiently obeyed my habit of
being prepared for the worst. But an extraordinary impression dropped
on me as I extracted a meaning from the boy's embarrassed back — none
other than the impression that I was not barred now. This inference

---

XXIII: The twelfth and last weekly *Collier's* installment began here.   *November:* The
governess came to Bly in June, so she has been there about five months.   *hypocrisy of
"work":* The pretense that she had knitting to do.   *gained:* Moved to, sat down on.

grew in a few minutes to sharp intensity and seemed bound up with the direct perception that it was positively *he* who was.° The frames and squares of the great window were a kind of image, for him, of a kind of failure. I felt that I saw him, in any case, shut in or shut out. He was admirable but not comfortable: I took it in with a throb of hope. Was n't he looking through the haunted pane for something he could n't see? — and was n't it the first time in the whole business that he had known such a lapse? The first, the very first: I found it a splendid portent. It made him anxious, though he watched himself; he had been anxious all day and, even while in his usual sweet little manner he sat at table, had needed all his small strange genius to give it a gloss. When he at last turned round to meet me it was almost as if this genius had succumbed. "Well, I think I'm glad Bly agrees with *me!*"

"You'd certainly seem to have seen, these twenty-four hours, a good deal more of it than for some time before. I hope," I went on bravely, "that you've been enjoying yourself."

"Oh yes, I've been ever so far; all round about — miles and miles away. I've never been so free."

He had really a manner of his own, and I could only try to keep up with him. "Well, do you like it?"

He stood there smiling; then at last he put into two words — "Do *you?*" — more discrimination° than I had ever heard two words contain. Before I had time to deal with that, however, he continued as if with the sense that this was an impertinence to be softened. "Nothing could be more charming than the way you take it, for of course if we're alone together now it's you that are alone most. But I hope," he threw in, "you don't particularly mind!"

"Having to do with you?" I asked. "My dear child, how can I help minding? Though I've renounced all claim to your company — you're so beyond me — I at least greatly enjoy it. What else should I stay on for?"

He looked at me more directly, and the expression of his face, graver now, struck me as the most beautiful I had ever found in it. "You stay on just for *that?*"

"Certainly. I stay on as your friend and from the tremendous interest I take in you till something can be done for you that may be more worth your while. That need n't surprise you." My voice trembled so

---

he *who was:* The governess comes to see that Miles, rather than she herself, is now "barred" from something, "shut out" from some perception, presumably about the existence of Quint.   ***more discrimination:*** More discernment of meaning.

that I felt it impossible to suppress the shake. "Don't you remember how I told you, when I came and sat on your bed the night of the storm, that there was nothing in the world I would n't do for you?"

"Yes, yes!" He, on his side, more and more visibly nervous, had a tone to master; but he was so much more successful than I that, laughing out through his gravity, he could pretend we were pleasantly jesting. "Only that, I think, was to get me to do something for *you*!"

"It was partly to get you to do something," I conceded. "But, you know, you did n't do it."

"Oh yes," he said with the brightest superficial eagerness, "you wanted me to tell you something."

"That's it. Out, straight out. What you have on your mind, you know."

"Ah then is *that* what you've stayed over for?"

He spoke with a gaiety through which I could still catch the finest little quiver of resentful passion; but I can't begin to express the effect upon me of an implication of surrender even so faint. It was as if what I had yearned for had come at last only to astonish me. "Well, yes — I may as well make a clean breast of it. It was precisely for that."

He waited so long that I supposed it for the purpose of repudiating the assumption on which my action had been founded; but what he finally said was. "Do you mean now — here?"

"There could n't be a better place or time." He looked round him uneasily, and I had the rare — oh the queer! — impression of the very first symptom I had seen in him of the approach of immediate fear. It was as if he were suddenly afraid of me — which struck me indeed as perhaps the best thing to make him. Yet in the very pang of the effort I felt it vain to try sternness, and I heard myself the next instant so gentle as to be almost grotesque. "You want so to go out again?"

"Awfully!" He smiled at me heroically, and the touching little bravery of it was enhanced by his actually flushing with pain. He had picked up his hat, which he had brought in, and stood twirling it in a way that gave me, even as I was just nearly reaching port, a perverse horror of what I was doing. To do it in *any* way was an act of violence, for what did it consist of but the obtrusion of the idea of grossness and guilt on a small helpless creature who had been for me a revelation of the possibilities of beautiful intercourse? Was n't it base to create for a being so exquisite a mere alien awkwardness? I suppose I now read into our situation a clearness it could n't have had at the time, for I seem to see our poor eyes already lighted with some spark of a prevision of the anguish that was to come. So we circled about with terrors and scruples, fighters not daring to close. But it was for each other we feared! That kept us a little longer suspended and unbruised. "I'll tell you everything," Miles said — "I mean I'll tell you anything you like. You'll stay on with me, and we shall both be all right, and I *will* tell you — I *will*. But not now."

"Why not now?"

My insistence turned him from me and kept him once more at his window in a silence during which, between us, you might have heard a pin drop. Then he was before me again with the air of a person for whom, outside, some one who had frankly to be reckoned with was waiting. "I have to see Luke."

I had not yet reduced him to quite so vulgar a lie, and I felt proportionately ashamed. But, horrible as it was, his lies made up my truth. I achieved thoughtfully a few loops of my knitting. "Well then go to Luke, and I'll wait for what you promise. Only in return for that satisfy, before you leave me, one very much smaller request."

He looked as if he felt he had succeeded enough to be able still a little to bargain. "Very much smaller — ?"

"Yes, a mere fraction of the whole. Tell me" — oh my work preoccupied me, and I was off-hand! — "if, yesterday afternoon, from the table in the hall, you took, you know, my letter."

XXIV

My grasp of how he received this suffered for a minute from something that I can describe only as a fierce split of my attention — a stroke that at first, as I sprang straight up, reduced me to the mere blind movement of getting hold of him, drawing him close and, while I just fell for support against the nearest piece of furniture, instinctively keeping him with his back to the window. The appearance was full upon us that I had already had to deal with here: Peter Quint had come into view like a sentinel before a prison. The next thing I saw was that, from outside, he had reached the window, and then I knew that, close to the glass and glaring in through it, he offered once more to the room his white face of damnation. It represents but grossly what took place within me at the sight to say that on the second my decision was made; yet I believe that no woman so overwhelmed ever in so short a time recovered her command of the *act*. It came to me in the very horror of the immediate presence that the act would be, seeing and facing what I saw and faced, to keep the boy himself unaware. The inspiration — I can call it by no other name — was that I felt how voluntarily, how transcendently,° I *might*. It was like fighting with a demon for a human soul, and when I had fairly so appraised it I saw how the human soul — held out, in the tremor of my hands, at arms' length — had a perfect dew of sweat on a lovely childish forehead. The face that was close to mine was as white as the face against the glass, and out of it presently came a sound, not low nor weak, but as if from much further away, that I drank like a waft of fragrance.

"Yes — I took it."

At this, with a moan of joy, I enfolded, I drew him close; and while I held him to my breast, where I could feel in the sudden fever of his little body the tremendous pulse of his little heart, I kept my eyes on the thing at the window and saw it move and shift its posture. I have likened it to a sentinel, but its slow wheel, for a moment, was rather the prowl of a baffled beast. My present quickened courage, however, was such that, not too much to let it through, I had to shade, as it were, my flame. Meanwhile the glare of the face was again at the window, the scoundrel fixed as if to watch and wait. It was the very confidence that I might now defy him, as well as the positive certitude, by this time, of the child's unconsciousness,° that made me go on. "What did you take it for?"

"To see what you said about me."

"You opened the letter?"

"I opened it."

My eyes were now, as I held him off a little again, on Miles's own face, in which the collapse of mockery showed me how complete was the ravage of uneasiness. What was prodigious was that at last, by my success, his sense was sealed and his communication stopped: he knew that he was in presence, but knew not of what, and knew still less that I also was and that I did know. And what did this strain of trouble matter when my eyes went back to the window only to see that the air was clear again and — by my personal triumph — the influence quenched? There was nothing there. I felt that the cause was mine and that I should surely get *all*. "And you found nothing!" — I let my elation out.

He gave the most mournful, thoughtful little headshake. "Nothing."

"Nothing, nothing!" I almost shouted in my joy.

"Nothing, nothing," he sadly repeated.

---

transcendently: Intuitively; utterly.   *unconsciousness:* Miles is of course not "unconscious" in the modern sense, since he is awake and speaking. Rather, he is unaware, that is not conscious, of the presence of Peter Quint at the window.

I kissed his forehead; it was drenched. "So what have you done with it?"

"I've burnt it."

"Burnt it?" It was now or never. "Is that what you did at school?"

Oh what this brought up! "At school?"

"Did you take letters? — or other things?"

"Other things?" He appeared now to be thinking of something far off and that reached him only through the pressure of his anxiety. Yet it did reach him. "Did I *steal*?"

I felt myself redden to the roots of my hair as well as wonder if it were more strange to put to a gentleman such a question or to see him take it with allowances that gave the very distance of his fall in the world. "Was it for that you might n't go back?"

The only thing he felt was rather a dreary little surprise. "Did you know I might n't go back?"

"I know everything."

He gave me at this the longest and strangest look. "Everything?"

"Everything. Therefore *did* you — ?" But I could n't say it again. Miles could, very simply. "No. I did n't steal."

My face must have shown him I believed him utterly; yet my hands — but it was for pure tenderness — shook him as if to ask him why, if it was all for nothing, he had condemned me to months of torment. "What then did you do?"

He looked in vague pain all round the top of the room and drew his breath, two or three times over, as if with difficulty. He might have been standing at the bottom of the sea and raising his eyes to some faint green twilight. "Well — I said things."

"Only that?"

"They thought it was enough!"

"To turn you out for?"

Never, truly, had a person "turned out" shown so little to explain it as this little person! He appeared to weigh my question, but in a manner quite detached and almost helpless. "Well, I suppose I ought n't."

"But to whom did you say them?"

He evidently tried to remember, but it dropped — he had lost it. "I don't know!"

He almost smiled at me in the desolation of his surrender, which was indeed practically, by this time, so complete that I ought to have left it there. But I was infatuated — I was blind with victory, though even then the very effect that was to have brought him so much nearer was already that of added separation. "Was it to every one?" I asked.

"No; it was only to — " But he gave a sick little headshake. "I don't remember their names."

"Were they then so many?"

"No — only a few. Those I liked."

Those he liked? I seemed to float not into clearness, but into a darker obscure, and within a minute there had come to me out of my very pity the appalling alarm of his being perhaps innocent. It was for the instant confounding and bottomless, for if he *were* innocent what then on earth was I? Paralysed, while it lasted, by the mere brush of the question, I let him go a little, so that, with a deep-drawn sigh, he turned away from me again; which, as he faced toward the clear window, I suffered, feeling that I had nothing now there to keep him from. "And did they repeat what you said?" I went on after a moment.

He was soon at some distance from me, still breathing hard and again with the air, though now without anger for it, of being confined against his will. Once more, as he had done before, he looked up at the dim day as if, of what had hitherto sustained him, nothing was left but an unspeakable anxiety. "Oh yes," he nevertheless replied — "they must have repeated them. To those *they* liked," he added.

There was somehow less of it than I had expected; but I turned it over. "And these things came round — ?"

"To the masters? Oh yes!" he answered very simply. "But I did n't know they'd tell."

"The masters? They did n't — they've never told. That's why I ask you."

He turned to me again his little beautiful fevered face. "Yes, it was too bad."

"Too bad?"

"What I suppose I sometimes said. To write home."°

I can't name the exquisite pathos of the contradiction given to such a speech by such a speaker; I only know that the next instant I heard myself throw off with homely force: "Stuff and nonsense!" But the next after that I must have sounded stern enough. "What *were* these things?"

My sternness was all for his judge, his executioner; yet it made him avert himself again, and that movement made *me*, with a single bound and an irrepressible cry, spring straight upon him. For there again, against the glass, as if to blight his confession and stay his answer, was the hideous author of our woe — the white face of damnation. I felt a sick swim at

---

To write home: The things he said were so awful that the headmaster could not mention them in the letter "home" to Miles's uncle.

the drop of my victory and all the return of my battle, so that the wildness of my veritable leap only served as a great betrayal. I saw him, from the midst of my act, meet it with a divination, and on the perception that even now he only guessed, and that the window was still to his own eyes free, I let the impulse flame up to convert the climax of his dismay into the very proof of his liberation. "No more, no more, no more!" I shrieked to my visitant as I tried to press him against me.

"Is she *here*?" Miles panted as he caught with his sealed eyes° the direction of my words. Then as his strange "she" staggered me and, with a gasp, I echoed it, "Miss Jessel, Miss Jessel!" he with sudden fury gave me back.

I seized, stupefied, his supposition — some sequel to what we had done to Flora, but this made me only want to show him that it was better still than that. "It's not Miss Jessel! But it's at the window — straight before us. It's *there* — the coward horror, there for the last time!"

At this, after a second in which his head made the movement of a baffled dog's on a scent and then gave a frantic little shake for air and light, he was at me in a white rage, bewildered, glaring vainly over the place and missing wholly, though it now, to my sense, filled the room like the taste of poison, the wide overwhelming presence. "It's *he*?"

I was so determined to have all my proof that I flashed into ice to challenge him. "Whom do you mean by 'he'?"

"Peter Quint — you devil!"° His face gave again, round the room, its convulsed supplication. "*Where*?"

They are in my ears still, his supreme surrender of the name and his tribute to my devotion. "What does he matter now, my own? — what will he *ever* matter? *I* have you," I launched at the beast, "but he has lost you for ever!" Then for the demonstration of my work, "There, *there*!" I said to Miles.

But he had already jerked straight round, stared, glared again, and seen but the quiet day. With the stroke of the loss I was so proud of he uttered the cry of a creature hurled over an abyss, and the grasp with which I recovered him might have been that of catching him in his fall. I caught him, yes, I held him — it may be imagined with what a passion; but at the end of a minute I began to feel what it truly was that I held. We were alone with the quiet day, and his little heart, dispossessed, had stopped.

---

sealed eyes: Eyes that, like Mrs. Grose's, cannot see apparitions.   **you devil:** One of the critical questions in *The Turn of the Screw* is whether Miles refers here to the governess or to Peter Quint as a "devil."

Cultural Documents
and Illustrations

This collection of cultural documents and illustrations is designed to help readers at the beginning of the twenty-first century understand how *The Turn of the Screw* may have been understood at the end of the nineteenth. The documents presented here will help modern readers answer six key questions: (1) How might Miles and Flora have been damaged by their having been left in the care of servants for so long? (2) What were governesses of the Victorian era like, and how might a late-nineteenth-century audience have imagined them? (3) How did educated men and women react to narratives about ghosts and other "supernatural" phenomena, such as demonic possession? (4) How did readers react to *The Turn of the Screw* when it first came out? (5) How did Henry James himself respond to questions about his story? And (6) What did James say about the story in the Preface he wrote for it ten years after its initial publication?

Also in this section are a photograph of Henry James and his brother William, a painting of a young governess, the four illustrations that Eric Pape made for the original *Collier's Weekly* serialized publication, an 1891 painting of a haunted house, and a cover of *Borderland*, an 1890s journal devoted to the occult.

The title that I have given each of the written documents is a quotation taken directly from the book, essay, poem, or letter that follows. The title is selected to guide readers to a central point that the author of the subsequent piece is making.

Henry James and his brother William James, from a snapshot taken in
the summer of 1900 near the village of Rye, in East Sussex, England.
James lived at Rye in Lamb House when he wrote *The Turn of the Screw.*
The snapshot was taken several years after James wrote the story. For
much of his life the Harvard psychologist William (bearded, right) was
involved in research on apparitions and other paranormal phenomena.
By permission of the Houghton Library, Harvard University.

CHILDREN AND SERVANTS

MARIA EDGEWORTH

"It is the worst thing in the world to leave children with servants." (1798)

Originally published at the end of the eighteenth century in two volumes, Practical Education *was reprinted many times in the nineteenth century and was known to virtually everyone who pretended to care about the education of the young. Maria Edgeworth (1767–1849) was a well-known novelist. Her coauthor Richard Lovell Edgeworth (1744–1817) was her father, a noted author and educator. The sections reproduced below focus particularly on Maria Edgeworth's concern about the grave dangers of leaving young children under the supervision of servants. The parts quoted are all from chapters identified in the preface as hers. They are apparently based in large part on her experiences in raising her own children and in observing the effects of too-close contact with servants in other families in her acquaintance. Governesses were generally not considered to be "servants," though in some families they were treated like servants. Maria Edgeworth shows a particular interest in the negative effects of the language that servants teach young children. Miles and Flora are both accused of using inappropriate language that they apparently learned from others. The young governess's insistence on trying to keep the two children always in her physical presence can be seen as her response to the then-standard notion that responsible parents and governesses would do precisely that. Although Maria Edgeworth does not speak directly about the possibility of children's learning sexual vices from their servants, that possibility lurks just beneath the surface talk of "sugar," "other tastes," "temptations," "vulgarity," "evil," "contagion," and "vice." Edgeworth says in a note that the opening dialogue of a boy and a nursemaid is taken "verbatim from what has been really said to a boy."*

Chapter 4, Servants

"Now, Master," said a fond nurse to her favourite boy, after having given him sugared bread and butter for supper, "now, master, kiss me;

From Maria Edgeworth and Richard Lovell Edgeworth, *Practical Education* (London: J. Johnson, 1798), reprinted in facsimile by Garland in 1974, with a brief introduction by Gina Luria. I identify the chapters from which the excerpts are taken.

wipe your mouth, dear, and go up to the drawing room to mamma; and when mistress asks you what you have had for supper, you'll say, bread and butter, for you *have had* bread and butter, you know, master." "And sugar," said the boy; "I must say bread and butter and sugar, you know."

How few children would have had the courage to have added, "and sugar!" How dangerous it is to expose them to such temptations! The boy must have immediately perceived the object of his nurse's casuistry. He must guess that she would be blamed for the addition of the sugar, else why should she wish to suppress the word? His gratitude is engaged to his nurse for running this risk to indulge him; his mother, by the force of contrast, appears a severe person, who, for no reason that he can comprehend, would deprive him of the innocent pleasure of eating sugar. As to its making him sick, he has eaten it, and he is not sick; as to its spoiling his teeth, he does not care about his teeth, and he sees no immediate change in them: therefore he concludes that his mother's orders are capricious, and his nurse loves him better than his mother does, because she gives him the most pleasure. His honour and affection towards his nurse are immediately set in opposition to his duty to his mother. What a hopeful beginning in education! What a number of dangerous ideas may be given by a single word!

The taste for sugared bread and butter is soon over, but servants have it in their power to excite other tastes with premature and factitious enthusiasm. The waiting-maid, a taste for dress; the footman, a taste for gaming; the coachman and groom, for horses and equipage; and the butler, for wine. The simplicity of children is not a defence to them; and though they are totally ignorant of vice, they are exposed to adopt the principles of those with whom they live, even before they can apply them to their own conduct. . . .

The language and manners, the awkward and vulgar tricks which children learn in the society of servants, are immediately perceived, and disgust and shock well-bred parents. This is an evil which is striking and disgraceful; it is more likely to be remedied than those which are more secret and slow in their operation: the habits of cunning, falsehood, envy, which lurk in the temper, are not instantly visible to strangers, they do not appear the moment children are reviewed by parents; they may remain for years without notice or without cure.

All these things have been said a hundred times: and, what is more, they are universally acknowledged to be true. It has passed into a common maxim with all who reflect, and even with all who speak upon the subject of education, that "it is the worst thing in the world to leave children with servants." But, notwithstanding this, each person imagines that they have found some lucky exception to the general rule. There is some favourite maid or phoenix of a footman in each family, who is supposed to be unlike all other servants, and therefore qualified for the education of children. But, if their qualifications were scrupulously examined, it is to be feared they would not be found competent to the trust that is reposed in them. . . .

If children pass one hour in a day with servants, it will be in vain to attempt their education. Madame Roland, in one of her letters to De Bosc, says, that her little daughter Eudora had learned to swear; "and yet," continues she, "I leave her but one half hour a day with servants." . . .

Attention to the arrangement of a house is of material consequence. Children's rooms should not be passage rooms for servants; they should, on the contrary, be so situated, that servants cannot easily have access to them, and cannot on any pretense of business get in the habit of frequenting them. Some fixed employment should be provided for children, which will keep them in a different part of the house at those hours when servants must necessarily be in their bedchambers. There will be a great advantage in teaching children to arrange their own rooms, because this will prevent the necessity of servants being for any length of time in their apartments; their things will not be mislaid; their playthings will not be swept away or broken; no little temptations will arise to ask questions from servants; all necessity, and all opportunity of intercourse, will thus be cut off. . . .

Servants have so much the habit of talking to children, and think it such a proof of good-nature to be interested about them, that it will be difficult to make them submit to this total silence and separation. . . . It may be feared that some *secret* intercourse should be carried on between children and servants; but this will be lessened by the arrangements in the house which we have mentioned; by care in a mother or governess to know exactly where children are, and what they are doing every hour of the day.

Chapter 12, Books

Few books can safely be given to children without the previous use of the pen, the pencil, and the scissars. . . .

It may be laid down as a first principle, that we should preserve children from the knowledge of any vice, or any folly, of which the idea has never yet entered their minds. . . . The language of children, who have heard no language but what is good, must be correct. On the contrary, children who hear a mixture of low and high vulgarity before their own habits are fixed, must, whenever they speak, continually blunder; they have no rule to guide their judgment in selection from the variety of dialects which they hear; probably they may often be reproved for their mistakes, but these reproofs will be of no avail, whilst the pupils continue to be puzzled between the example of the nursery, and of the drawing room. It will cost much time and pains to correct these defects, which might have been with little difficulty prevented. It is the same with other bad habits. Falsehood, caprice, dishonesty, obstinacy, revenge, all the train of vices which are the consequences of mistaken or neglected education, which are learned by bad example, and which are not inspired by nature, need scarcely be known to children whose minds have from their infancy been happily regulated. Such children should be sedulously kept from contagion; their minds untainted; they are safe in that species of ignorance which alone can deserve the name of bliss.

Chapter 20, On Female Accomplishments, Masters, and Governesses

It is surely [in] the interest of parents to treat the person who educates their children with that perfect equality and kindness, which will conciliate her affection, and which will at the same time preserve her influence and authority over her pupils. And it is with pleasure we observe, that the style of behavior to governesses, in well-bred families, is much changed within these few years. A governess is no longer treated as an upper servant, or as an intermediate being between a servant and a gentlewoman: she is now treated as the friend and companion of the family, and she must, consequently, have warm and permanent interest in its prosperity: she becomes attached to her pupils from gratitude to their parents, from sympathy, from generosity, as well as from the strict sense of duty.

In fashionable life there is, however, some danger, that parents should go into extremes in their behavior towards their governesses. Those who disdain the idea of assuming superiority of rank and fortune, and who desire to treat the person who educates their children as their equal, act with perfect propriety; but if they make her their companion in all their amusements they go a step too far, and they defeat their own purposes. If a governess attends the card table, and the assembly room; if she is to visit, and be visited, what is to become of her pupils in her absence? They must be left to the care of servants.

Chapter 25, Summary

More failures in private education have been occasioned by the interference of servants and acquaintance than from any other cause. . . . [W]here parents have not sufficient firmness to prevent the interference of acquaintance, and sufficient prudence to keep children *from all private communication with servants*, we earnestly advise that the children be sent to some public seminary of education. We have taken some pains to detail the methods by which all hurtful communication between children and servants in a well regulated family may be avoided, and we have asserted, from the experience of above twenty years, that these methods have been found not only practicable, but easy.

THE VICTORIAN GOVERNESS

"The Introduction" by George Goodwin Kilburne (1839–1924). The painting shows a new governess in the schoolroom being introduced by a young gentleman to his sister.
Reproduced by courtesy of Sotheby's Picture Library, London.

ANNA JAMESON

"The occupation of governess is sought merely through necessity." (1846)

In an essay published in the 1840s at about the same time that the primary events in The Turn of the Screw *take place, Anna Jameson discusses the role of the governess. She emphasizes that, while women of what she calls the "servile classes" might with relative ease get jobs, for women of a higher class who did not marry and who had to leave their families there was only*

From Mrs. [Anna] Jameson, *Memoirs and Essays Illustrative of Art, Literature, and Social Morals* (London: Richard Bentley, 1846), 249–98.

one occupation possible, that of a governess to a wealthier or higher-class family. After the introductory section, Jameson couches many of her remarks in the form of direct address, first to mothers and then to the governesses themselves. Part of Jameson's purpose is to encourage mothers to understand the situation of their governesses and to support them whenever possible. The fact that the biological mother in The Turn of the Screw *is dead and that the absent uncle does not care about either the governess he has hired or the children he is guardian to makes the governess all the more isolated. The picture Jameson gives of the situation of the governess helps us to understand why the parson's daughter takes the strange job at Bly and accepts the uncle's main condition, that she leave him alone. The young governess has virtually no choice in the matter. Jameson says nothing whatever about how a governess should deal with the haunting spirits of former caretakers of her pupils. If the isolated young governess at Bly does become what Jameson calls "nervous" and "anxious," is it any wonder? Jameson couches her remarks in three parts, all of which are quoted from below: an introduction in which she lays out the history of problems between mothers and their governesses, an address to mothers, and an address to governesses.*

Of the relations which exist between one human being and another, some are necessary as arising out of our individual nature, our wants, our instincts, our affections, — and some are necessary as arising out of our common nature and the laws which bind us together in communities; — and all these relations, in some form or other, however modified by custom, are common to all periods and countries, and all degrees of civilization.

Other relations there are, not natural, not necessary, arising out of a very luxurious and complicate[d] state of society, most important in their bearing on our happiness, hard to define, harder to deal with, because society does not recognise in them any right or privilege — the law does not protect them — opinion does not reach them.

Of these merely conventional relations, one of the most artificial, the most anomalous, is the existence of a class of women whom we style private governesses; women employed to give such home training and instruction as are necessary to our children, and fulfil the highest of those duties which, in a simpler state of society, devolve on the parents. . . .

With every advance in civilization the position of instructor advances in importance and in dignity; how is it that precisely the reverse is the case where women are concerned? With them the task of education has ceased to have the sanctity and dignity of a religious calling; it has taken no rank as a profession; and it leads to nothing that I know of but a broken constitution, and a lonely unblessed old age. . . .

The inferior position of the woman, and the inferior value of her services, as compared with the same classes in the other sex, is in no instance so obvious, so bitterly felt, so unspeakably unjust, as in this.

One reason may be that the profession of a tutor infers the education of a scholar and a gentleman; that it is only one of the many paths in which a man going forth into the world, to fulfil the man's duty and destiny, may earn an honorable livelihood, by means which do not prevent him from mingling with society and with the world, nor shut him out from advancement and improvement; while with the woman, "whose proper sphere is home," — the woman who either has no home, or is exiled from that which she has, — the occupation of governess is sought merely through necessity, as the *only* means by which a woman not born in the servile classes *can* earn the means of subsistence.

It may be asked, "And why should this be such a very great hardship? if the training of the young be the woman's natural vocation — peculiarly fitted to the feminine organization — in harmony with her whole being — one would imagine that, under ordinary circumstances, it would be her choice, her aim, her happiness, to fulfil it. How is it then that the position should generally be one of such suffering, that a woman who knows anything of the world would, if the choice were left to her, be anything *in* the world rather than be a governess?"

It used to be only the titled and the rich who required governesses for their daughters; there were few women either inclined to the task, or by education qualified for it, and it was generally fulfilled by the poorer relatives of the family. It is within the last fifty years, since marriage has become more and more difficult, — forced celibacy, with all its melancholy and demoralizing consequences, more and more general, — that we find that governesses have become a class, and a class so numerous, that the supply has, in numbers at least, exceeded the demand. . . .

Granted that out of a thousand women who offer themselves as governesses, there is scarcely one qualified for the task — we must grant also that out of a thousand employers, there is scarcely one who has a proper idea of how a governess ought to be treated. Nevertheless, be it observed, the requisitions and the stipulations are all on one side, all on the part of the employer; the governess generally offers herself, and the best that is in her, for anything she can get. It is a contract without equality; a bargain in which, on one side at least, there is no choice. . . .

The misfortune is, that this mutual contract not only begins with an inequality, which leaves on one side no choice — it involves a *contradiction*. No social arrangements can violate certain natural and necessary premises with impunity, nor indeed without admixture of much evil. The relation which exists between the governess and her employer either places a woman of education and of superior faculties in an ambiguous and inferior position, with none of the privileges of a recognized profession, or places a vulgar, half-educated woman in a situation of high responsibility, requiring superior endowments. In either of these cases, and one or other is almost inevitable, the result cannot be good; *must* in fact bring with it more or less of evil consequences, to be dealt with as best we may. . . .

It is very possible, that the necessity of having private governesses, except in particular cases, may at some future time be done away with by a systematic and generally accessible education for women of all classes; and that some other means of earning a subsistence may be opened to the earnest woman, willing and able to work; mean time, the present evil lies a stumbling-block and a rock of offence before us; and in the midst of our hopes of what may, or might, or ought to be, let us look at what is. Private governesses exist, must live, must be employed by those who cannot do without them: and as the case is beyond the reach of public law or opinion, is it not worth while to try how far an exposition of this true relation between the mother and the governess might influence private opinion and individual feeling? . . .

And first, I address myself to the MOTHER. . . .

"I recollect an instance of a young girl of twenty, with the best will and intentions, and some qualities admirably suited to her task, who, within two years, became languid, nervous, hysterical, and at length utterly broken down. She was obliged to give up her situation. . . .

"If you engage a young governess, as less likely to have certain fixed habits [than an older one], and more likely to bring to her task a cheerful temper (though this by no means follows of course), you must remember that some patience will be necessary; you cannot expect to find her all at once efficient. She will be presumptuous, perhaps, or perhaps she will be nervous and over-anxious. In either case she will require your forbearance, or even help. There is much in making a good beginning. Give her all the benefit of your better knowledge of your children's characters; let no maternal vanity interfere with your truth in this respect; encourage her to refer to you. . . .

"It is presumed that you visit your children's study daily; not injudiciously to meddle, and dictate, and interrupt; but to encourage and to observe. . . ."

I turn now to the GOVERNESS: . . .

"You are in search of a situation as Governess, and deem yourself sufficiently prepared by study, and possessed of a fair share of the thousand qualifications usually required. If you are young, you probably set forth full of hope, of courage, and with such a lofty idea of the importance of the task you undertake, that you feel yourself uplifted. . . .

"I have never in my life heard of a governess who was such by choice: and when you look about for a family in which to enter, not only you will not have the power to choose, but in all probability your circumstances are such, that you will not have the power to refuse. . . .

"I have known those who began this sort of life, not only with spirit yet fresh and unbroken, but with the feeling that this so-called *dependence* might be, in fact, independence — the means of honourable self-support; with trust in others, with strong faith in herself, and not without some enthusiastic notions of training the young minds entrusted to her to all good — even such a one have I known to bend, to break down completely, under the crushing influences which met her at the very outset, and for which she was in nowise prepared. After all, the best preparation is to look upon the occupation to which you are devoted (I was going to say *doomed*) as what it really is, — a state of endurance, dependence, daily thankless toil; to accept it as such courageously and meekly, because you must, — cheerfully, if you can; — and so make the best of it. . . .

"Now everyone has a just horror of a nervous governess; complaints of the ill-health of governesses, as a class, are so common, one meets with them at every turn; and let the physician speak of what he knows! — he could make fearful revelations, if he dared, of the constitutions of young women ruined through fatigue, confinement, anxiety, in a sphere of life somewhat above those who make shirts, and fit on finery. You love your pupils, are anxious for their progress, are interested in their amusement; you have patience with them, and tenderness for them; and yet the dizzying effect produced by the constant presence of animated, active, high-spirited children, — the dulling effect of the drudgery of elementary teaching, cannot be told, nor conceived, but by those who have endured it."

MARY MAURICE

"Many were the daughters of clergymen."
(1847)

As one of several children of a poor country parson, the new governess at Bly would have had few options. Without a dowry her chances of marrying were slender, so the only profession open to her was that of governess. We are not told that she had to contribute to the support of her family, but we know that she receives letters from home reporting that things are not going well. We know little of Mary Maurice except that she wrote books giving advice to the governesses of her time. Here she outlines a family-of-origin scenario for a typical Victorian governess.

Many [governesses] were the children of affluent parents, who brought them up with every indulgence and refinement, that wealth could bestow: they moved in the best circles, and expected that their prosperity would last for ever; but a sudden loss of fortune, a failure in business, or death, has reversed the picture, and no alternative remains, but that they must support themselves, and no other way but this is open to them. Many were the daughters of clergymen, who were courted and followed; their houses were the resort of the wealthy members of their congregations; but their incomes were limited, and they had only a life-interest in them, and these were wholly swallowed up, in necessary expenses and in educating their children. The latter naturally acquired the tastes and feelings of the society with which they associated, and they were not unfrequently flattered too, till they fancied themselves the objects of admiration, instead of perceiving, that they were only sought after, as the ready means of access, to the popular preacher. But the father sickens, and dies, the orphaned family are at once reduced to want; the girls must find homes for themselves; perhaps the majority being only half educated, must be kept at school, by the scanty earnings of their elder sisters, till they too can find means of support.

Again, let us picture to ourselves the family of a country clergyman, which has been carefully brought up under the eye of a tender mother. The children are growing up and happy members of a peaceful home,

From [Mary Maurice], *Mothers and Governesses* (London: John W. Parker, 1847), 18–19; portions reprinted in *The Governess Anthology*, ed. Trev Broughton and Ruth Symes (Sutton: Phoenix Mill, Gloucestershire, 1997), 16–17.

where all the charities of life are in full exercise, where each heart is bound to each, by the holiest bonds, and the parents live for them, for each other, and for God. They are trained by the constant exercise of self-denial, to do good to the parish in which they dwell, and they shed a living light, the reflection of the truths their father teaches. Their house is one of the beautiful country parsonages, which so sweetly adorn our land, and give at once the idea of peace and repose; but the circle rapidly increasing, the utmost economy will not suffice to meet the growing expenditure; sickness enters the dwelling, and at length it becomes painfully evident, that the elder daughters must enter upon the life of governesses, and that they may save the rest from ruin, they quit the spot so much endeared to them — sisters who have never been separated before, must go out into the cold world.

MARY MAURICE

"There is a strong prejudice against governesses." (1849)

Youth and beauty were often seen as threatening qualities in a governess. Mrs. Grose reports that the former governess at Bly, Miss Jessel, was as young and pretty as the new governess, and while Mrs. Grose does not give details, it is obvious enough that as a result of a sexual affair with Peter Quint, Miss Jessel became pregnant. The youth and good looks of the new governess would have been held against her as she applied for many jobs because usually it was the mothers who did the hiring of governesses, and mothers would have been reluctant to have their husbands and sons tempted by near proximity to a pretty woman. In this case, since the children's uncle was doing the hiring, there was no mother to be concerned about the attractiveness of the new governess. Mary Maurice describes some of the problems that governesses, particularly pretty ones, had and some of the negative attitudes that their employers had about them.

It cannot be denied that there is a strong prejudice against governesses, particularly in the minds of men, and the reasons for this dislike we must not shrink from pointing out.

Frightful instances have been discovered in which she, to whom the

From [Mary Maurice], *Governess Life: Its Trials, Duties and Encouragements* (London: John W. Parker, 1849), 14–15; portions reprinted in Broughton and Symes, 181–82; see previous note.

care of the young has been entrusted, instead of guarding their minds in innocence and purity, has become their corrupter — she has been the first to lead and to initiate into sin, to suggest and carry on intrigues, and finally to be the instrument of destroying the peace of families. Very many instances, alas! are known in which habits of intemperance have been habitual, and others in which pilfering and theft have been practised to great extent — and we must rank under the same description those who indulge in reckless habits of expenditure, with the certainty of being unable to repay what they purchase. Does this deserve a milder name than swindling?

There are grosser forms of sin which have been generally concealed from public notice for the reasons before assigned — but none of the cases are imaginary ones, and they are but too well known in the circles amongst which they occurred. In some instances again, the love of admiration has led the governess to try and make herself necessary to the comfort of the father of the family in which she resided, and by delicate and unnoticed flattery gradually to gain her point, to the disparagement of the mother, and the destruction of mutual happiness. When the latter was homely, or occupied with domestic cares, opportunity was found to bring forward attractive accomplishments, or by sedulous attentions to supply her lack of them; or the sons were in some instances objects of notice and flirtation, or when occasion offered, visitors at the house.

This kind of conduct has led to the inquiry, which is frequently made before engaging an instructress, "Is she handsome or attractive?" If so, it is conclusive against her.

ELIZABETH MISSING SEWELL

"She is perfectly incompetent for her task." (1866)

Because many young governesses in Victorian times were not well educated themselves, they were but ill-suited to the teaching that was their central task as governesses. Boys and young men were sent to schools where they were taught many subjects, but girls stayed at home, where they were taught whatever their parents had the time, the knowledge, and the inclination to

From Elizabeth Missing Sewell, *Principles of Education, Drawn from Nature and Revelation, and Applied to Female Education in the Upper Classes* (New York: Appleton, 1866), 425–27.

teach them. Particularly in the less wealthy families, very little was actually taught to these girls, yet when the time came for them to seek employment, the only opportunity open to them was to be a governess, that is, a teacher. Most governesses were unprepared for their duties, as this excerpt from a chapter on "The Training of Governesses" in Elizabeth Missing Sewell's Principles of Education *shows.*

These pleasant-mannered, interesting young girls are destitute. They have to maintain themselves, and only one profession is open to them. They must be governesses. What can they teach? What do they know? They themselves will answer — in all humility and truthfulness — "Nothing." They have had a good education, they can play a little, and sing a little, and speak a little French, and read a little German; and of course they know something of geography and history. And then they are so thoroughly refined and well-bred, there can be no difficulty in procuring for them good situations. The young ladies are told that they must profess to teach all which they are supposed to know, and they obey. . . .

Only, unfortunately — it is very disappointing — she knows nothing. The bubble of information which in the clear air and the sunshine of prosperity shone so gaily, and floated so lightly, has burst. She is perfectly incompetent for her task. She has but a vague recollection of what she once knew. She feels no certainty about anything she attempts. She has not the slightest idea how to teach so as to interest children. She can but go through a dull routine which makes the daily lessons irksome to herself and her pupils. . . .

But the ranks of English governesses are continually recruited from these penniless, ignorant, yet well-born and well-bred young girls. What is to be done with them? . . .

Are we to give up education into their hands without an effort? Must our children necessarily be taught by superficial or under-bred governesses? Alas for English society if it is to be so!

MARIA ABDY

"Our governess left us, dear brother." (1838)

Governesses were sometimes the subject of lightly satirical poetry. In this poem, a minor poet named Maria Abdy sets up an imaginative conversation between a mother who has just lost her governess and her older brother, still a bachelor. The woman wants a governess who has had the benefit of a broad education, who can demonstrate many social and artistic accomplishments, and who can teach her children all sorts of subjects, yet not be a burden. Her brother, on the other hand, wants a wife with the same exaggerated and unrealistic qualifications. The poem is to be read as a dialogue, with the first five stanzas spoken by the mother to her brother, and the last two spoken as a reply by the brother. Both the sister and the brother are unreasonably idealistic in their demands and expectations.

A GOVERNESS WANTED

"Our governess left us, dear brother,
Last night, in a strange fit of pique,
Will you kindly seek out for another?
We want her at latest next week:
But I'll give you a few plain credentials,
The bargain with speed to complete;
Take a pen — just set down the essentials,
And begin at the top of the sheet!

"With easy and modest decision,
She ever must move, act, and speak;
She must understand French with precision,
Italian, and Latin, and Greek:
She must play the piano divinely,
Excel on the harp and the lute,
Do all sorts of needle-work finely,
And make feather-flowers, and wax-fruit.

"She must answer all queries directly,
And all sciences well understand,
Paint in oils, sketch from nature correctly,

From Maria Abdy, "A Governess Wanted" in *Poetry* (London: J. and W. Robins [for private circulation], 1838), 21–23; also reprinted in Broughton and Symes, 19–21.

And write German text, and short-hand:
She must sing with power, science, and sweetness,
Yet for concerts must sigh not at all,
She must dance with etherial fleetness;
Yet never must go to a ball.

"She must not have needy relations,
Her dress must be tasteful yet plain,
Her discourse must abound in quotations,
Her memory all dates must retain;
She must point out each author's chief beauties,
She must manage dull natures with skill,
Her pleasures must lie in her duties,
She must never be nervous or ill!

"If she write essays, odes, themes, and sonnets,
Yet be not pedantic or pert;
If she wear none but deep cottage bonnets,
If she deem it high treason to flirt,
If to mildness she add sense and spirit,
Engage her at once without fear;
I love to reward modest merit,
And I give — forty guineas a year."

"I accept, my good sister, your mission,
To-morrow, my search I'll begin —
In all circles, in every condition,
I'll strive such a treasure to win;
And, if after years of probation,
My eyes on the wonder should rest,
I'll engage her without hesitation,
But not on the terms you suggest.

"Of a bride I have ne'er made selection,
For my bachelor thoughts would still dwell
On an object so near to perfection,
That I blushed half my fancies to tell;
Now this list that you kindly have granted,
I'll quote and refer to through life,
But just blot out — 'A Governess Wanted,'
And head it with — 'Wanted a wife!'"

APPARITIONS AND DEMONIC POSSESSION

This illustration by John La Farge appeared at the start of each of the twelve installments of *The Turn of the Screw* as it was first published in *Collier's Weekly* in 1898. It apparently depicted the governess and Miles, probably in the final scene just before Miles died.
Courtesy of the New York State Historical Association Library.

On the following four pages appear the illustrations by Eric Pape that were distributed through the *Collier's Weekly* serialized version of the story that ran from January 27 to April 16, 1898. I give the actual date for each drawing in the caption beneath it. The quotations that appear underneath each illustration were given in the initial *Collier's* publication, though I give the page numbers for the quotations from this Bedford edition. Pape apparently read the story very much as a ghost story. The first of his four illustrations shows the horror registered on the faces of the guests who listen to Douglas's reading of the governess's narrative, while the other three all show the governess in proximity to the ghosts of Quint or Jessel. None of Pape's illustrations shows Miles or Flora.

"[T]he next night, by the corner of the hearth, in the best chair, he opened the faded red cover of a thin old-fashioned gilt-edged album. . . . But Douglas, without heeding me, had begun to read with a fine clearness that was like a rendering to the ear of the beauty of his author's hand" (p. 29). Eric Pape's illustration appeared in the first, or January 27, 1898, installment of the story in *Collier's Weekly*. The older man facing Douglas is apparently the narrator of the frame.

Courtesy of the New York State Historical Association Library.

"He did stand there! — but high up, beyond the lawn and at the very top of the tower" (p. 39). From the February 12, 1898, number of *Collier's*. Pape's drawing shows the governess's first encounter with the apparition of Peter Quint, though at first she thinks, from a distance, that it is the children's uncle making an unannounced visit from London. Courtesy of the New York State Historical Association Library.

"[H]olding my candle high, till I came within sight of the tall window"
(p. 67). From the March 5, 1898, number of *Collier's*. When the governess's candle goes out, she is able to see by the early dawn light the
ghost of Quint on the stairs. The outlines of his figure are just visible in
the darkness of the lower right corner of Pape's drawing.
Courtesy of the New York State Historical Association Library.

"I must have thrown myself, on my face, to the ground" (p. 104). From the April 2, 1898, number of *Collier's*. Pape's fourth and last drawing for *The Turn of the Screw* shows the governess and the apparition of Miss Jessel framed between two tree trunks with a pond or lake separating them. Mrs. Grose and Flora would just before have gone back to the house.

Courtesy of the New York State Historical Association Library.

REV. B. F. WESTCOTT

"A sufficient number of clear and well-attested cases." (1851)

A group of researchers at Trinity College, Cambridge, established what came to be known as the "Cambridge Ghost Club" in 1851. The purpose of the group was to solicit brief written statements from people who claimed to have seen a ghost or to have had some other experience with the "supernatural" — a term placed in quotation marks because many people believed that such experiences were perfectly natural. One of the members, Rev. B. F. Westcott, sent out a circular announcing the investigation of "phenomena popularly called supernatural." That circular is of interest to readers of The Turn of the Screw *for several reasons, but especially because Douglas, the frame-tale character who has the handwritten document that makes up most of James's story, was a student at Trinity College, Cambridge, when he first met the young woman who had been the governess at Bly and who was by then his own sister's governess. To judge by the somewhat vague dates given, he might have been a student at Cambridge at around the time the circular was sent out. In any case, to readers aware of the interest in phenomena variously called "supernatural," "psychical," or, more recently, "paranormal," Douglas's association with Trinity might well have indicated his professional or at least his academic interest in ghostly phenomena. The circular calls for personal statements and specifically states that names need not be given. James rarely used first-person narration in his fiction and almost always gives the names of his central characters. In* The Turn of the Screw, *however, James has a first-person narrator but does not have her reveal her name, possibly because she did not want to identify herself. Are we to understand that Douglas is a ghost-narrative investigator for one of his professors at Trinity, that he specifically asks the governess to write her story down, and that he gives, in the opening frame, a positive statement of her character? Modern readers who think that the new young governess at Bly is subject to "delusions of the mind or senses" will note that Rev. Westcott is aware that some of those who report ghostly phenomena might be that sort of person, and that he specifically asks that those who gather reports of these cases should give "particulars as to the observer's natural temperament." Douglas informally does that in his introduction to the narrative before the governess's manuscript*

From the appendix of Robert Dale Owen's *Footfalls on the Boundary of Another World* (Philadelphia: Lippincott, 1860), 513–16.

reaches him from London. Whether or not Douglas is to be seen as a reporter or gatherer of ghostly narratives from Trinity College, it is interesting that the governess's written narrative has certain similarities to several of the ghost narratives that I include below, after Westcott's circular and the statements by Gurney and Stead.

Circular of a Society, Instituted by Members of the University of Cambridge, England, for the Purpose of Investigating Phenomena Popularly Called Supernatural

The interest and importance of a serious and earnest inquiry into the nature of the phenomena which are vaguely called "supernatural" will scarcely be questioned. Many persons believe that all such apparently mysterious occurrences are due either to purely natural causes, or to delusions of the mind or senses, or to willful deception. But there are many others who believe it possible that the beings of the unseen world may manifest themselves to us in extraordinary ways. . . . The main impediment to investigations of this kind is the difficulty of obtaining a sufficient number of clear and well-attested cases. Many of the stories current in tradition, or scattered up and down in books, may be exactly true; others must be purely fictitious; others, again, — probably the greater number, — consist of a mixture of truth and falsehood. But it is idle to examine the significance of an alleged fact of this nature until the trustworthiness, and also the extent, of the evidence for it are ascertained. Impressed with this conviction, some members of the University of Cambridge are anxious, if possible, to form an extensive collection of authenticated cases of supposed "supernatural" agency. . . . From all those, then, who may be inclined to aid them, they request written communications, with full details of persons, times, and places; but it will not be required that names should be inserted without special permission, unless they have already become public property: it is, however, indispensable that the person making any communication should be acquainted with the names, and should pledge himself for the truth of the narrative from his own knowledge or conviction. . . . Every narrative of "supernatural" agency which may be communicated will be rendered far more instructive if accompanied by any particulars as to the observer's natural temperament, (*e.g.* sanguine, nervous, &c.,) constitution, (*e.g.* subject to fever, somnambulism, &c.,) and state at the time, (*e.g.* excited in mind or body, &c.).

Communications may be addressed to
Rev. B. F. Westcott, *Harrow, Middlesex.*

EDMUND GURNEY

"Common-sense persists in recognizing . . . a single natural group." (1886)

The Cambridge Ghost Club never organized itself sufficiently to conduct much actual research or to publish its findings, but several of its most prominent early members organized the Society for Psychical Research in 1882. This major research group, with meetings, funding, and officers, still exists today. Edmund Gurney, with a little help from two other members, published in 1886 the monumental two-volume Phantasms of the Living, *a collection and discussion of hundreds of carefully researched reports of ghostly or other unusual phenomena. The book was essentially Gurney's work, but he had some research and editorial assistance from his coauthors. Both the Society for Psychical Research and* Phantasms of the Living *have important connections for Henry James. For one thing, James's brother William James was active in the Society and was its president during the 1890s. Because William could not attend one of the meetings in London at which he was to present the findings of one of his research projects, his brother Henry attended on his behalf and read the paper. Furthermore, we know that Henry James knew personally the authors of* Phantasms of the Living *and purchased his own copy of their book not long after it came out. The phrase "phantasms of the living" referred to apparitions that appeared, as most of them did, within twelve months after death. The apparitions of people who had died a year or more before their spirits appeared, a far fewer number, were called "phantasms of the dead." I quote below Gurney's scientific statement about the conclusions to be drawn from the sheer number of ghostly phenomena reported in his book and about the difficulty of the alternative explanations offered for those phenomena by people who did not accept their reality. In the part of his discussion that I quote here, Gurney is answering the objections of those who question the evidence that he has presented through more than 800 specific narratives, each of which was personally investigated either by himself or by another trained investigator, and almost all of which involved a personal interview with the person who claimed to witness the phenomenon. To be sure, Gurney says, there are various ways witnesses could misinterpret the evidence, could have made errors, or could even try to deceive the researchers with lies or deceptions. Such errors and deceptions are possible*

From *Phantasms of the Living*, by Edmund Gurney, Frederic W. H. Myers, and Frank Podmore, vol. 1 (London: Trubner, 1886), 163–64.

in the individual case, Gurney says, but to assume them in all cases is downright unscientific, particularly when the researchers have carefully interviewed the witnesses.

One advantage, however, which we ourselves have had, cannot be communicated to our readers — namely, the increased power of judgment which a personal interview with the narrator gives. The effect of these interviews on our own minds has been on the whole distinctly favourable. They have greatly added to our confidence that what we are here presenting is the testimony of trustworthy and intelligent witnesses. And if the collection be taken as a whole, this seems to be a sufficient guarantee. . . . But we have naturally preferred to be on the safe side. We have therefore, excluded all narratives where, on personal acquaintance with the witnesses, we felt that we should be uneasy in confronting them with a critical cross-examiner; and we have frequently thought it right to exclude cases, otherwise satisfactory, that depended on the reports of uneducated persons. . . .

But the point on which we desire to lay stress is the *number* of improbable hypotheses that will have to be propounded if the [evidence for apparitions] is rejected. . . . Not only have we to assume such an extent of forgetfulness and inaccuracy, about simple and striking facts of the immediate past, as is totally unexampled in any other range of experience. Not only have we to assume that distressing or exciting news about another person produces a havoc in the memory which has never been noted in connection with distress or excitement in any other form. We must leave this merely general ground, and make suppositions as detailed as the evidence itself. We must suppose that some people have a way of dating their letters in indifference to the calendar, or making entries in their diaries on the wrong page and never discovering the error; and that whole families have been struck by the collective hallucination that one of their members had made a particular remark, the substance of which had never even entered that member's head; and that it is a recognized custom to write mournful letters about bereavements which have never occurred; and that when A describes to a friend how he has distinctly heard the voice of B, it is not infrequently by a slip of the tongue for C; and that when D says he is not subject to hallucinations of vision, it is through momentary forgetfulness of the fact that he has a spectral illusion once a week; and that when a wife interrupts her husband's slumbers with words of distress or alarm, it is only her fun, or a sudden morbid craving for undeserved sympathy; and that when people assert that they were in sound health, in good spirits, and wide awake, at a particular time which they had occasion to note, it is a safe conclusion that they were having a nightmare, or were the prostrate victims of nervous hypochondria. Every one of these improbabilities is, perhaps, in itself a possibility; but as the narratives drive us from one desperate expedient to another, when time after time we are compelled to own that deliberate falsification is less unlikely than the assumptions we are making, and then again when we submit the theory of deliberate falsification to the cumulative test, and see what is involved in the supposition that hundreds of persons of established character, known to us for the most part and unknown to one another, have simultaneously formed a plot to deceive us — there comes a point where the reason rebels. Common-sense persists in recognizing that when phenomena, which are united by a fundamental characteristic and have every appearance of forming a single natural group, are presented to be explained, an explanation which multiplies causes is improbable, and an explanation which multiplies improbable causes becomes, at a certain point, incredible.

"The Haunted House" by T. Griffiths appeared in the Christmas 1891 number of the weekly illustrated London review called *Black and White* (II, 39). We know little about illustrator Tom Griffiths except that he did most of his work between 1880 and 1904. We can be reasonably certain that Henry James saw this drawing because James's own story, "Sir Edmund Orme," appeared for the first time in the same issue. "The Haunted House" did not illustrate a story in the *Black and White*, but was included as filler. It shows two young people, apparently a man and a woman, looking across a body of water to a ghostly mansion. Whether or not it influenced James's conception of the setting for Bly in *The Turn of the Screw*, written seven years later, "The Haunted House" does suggest the interest that audiences in the 1890s had in such scenes. For more information, see the article by Wolff referenced on p. 222. The Henry James story that appeared in this issue of *Black and White* bears interesting comparison to *The Turn of the Screw*. "Sir Edmund Orme" is about an apparition that appears to a woman named Mrs. Marden. The story, said to have been found in a locked drawer by the person who publishes it, is the first-person account of a man who falls in love with Mrs. Marden's daughter. He comes to see a man whom he takes to be alive, but is finally told by Mrs. Marden that it is the ghost of Sir Edmund Orme. Cast aside by his fiancee, who fell in love and finally married Mr. Marden, Sir Edmund had poisoned himself and now from time to time returns to punish the woman who threw him over. Only a few people can see Orme's ghost.

WILLIAM T. STEAD

"The absurd delusion that there is no such thing as ghosts." (1897)

William T. Stead was a journalist and publisher who collected, edited, and sold several volumes of what he called "real ghost stories." In 1890 he became founding editor of a journal called Review of Reviews. *In the Christmas issue of 1891 and the January issue of 1892, Stead published a large number of "real" stories about ghosts. In 1893 Stead established a new quarterly called* Borderland, *devoted entirely to reporting evidence about "supernatural" phenomena. These were stories about ghosts that seemed to him to constitute evidence that ghosts really did exist. In 1897, the year Henry James wrote* The Turn of the Screw, *Stead combined and republished the two earlier collections under the title* Real Ghost Stories. *He gave the book version a new introduction. The excerpt below is from that introduction. It may be overstated, but there is no question that Stead was serious. That it appeared the year James wrote* The Turn of the Screw *suggests that James may well have been assuming an audience at least some of whom would have agreed with Stead that ghosts absolutely did exist. An interesting side note is that Stead booked a cabin on the* Titanic *in 1912 and was last seen helping others get into lifeboats.*

Of all the vulgar superstitions of the half educated, none dies harder than the absurd delusion that there is no such thing as ghosts. All the experts, whether spiritual, poetical, or scientific, and all the others, non-experts, who have bestowed any serious attention upon the subject, know that they do exist. . . . There is endless variety of opinion as to what a ghost may be. But as to the fact of its existence, whatever it may be, there is no longer any serious dispute among honest investigators. If any one questions this, let him investigate for himself. In six months, possibly in six weeks, or even in six days, he will find it impossible to deny the reality of the existence of the phenomena popularly entitled ghostly. He may have a hundred ingenious explanations of the origin and nature of the ghost, but as to the existence of that entity itself there will no longer be any doubt. . . .

The time has surely come when the fair claim of ghosts to the impartial attention and careful observation of mankind should no

From the author's "Introduction" and "A Prefatory Word" to William T. Stead's *Real Ghost Stories* (Philadelphia: Lippincott, 1897), v–viii.

longer be ignored. . . . [I]t is necessary to begin from the beginning and to convince a skeptical world that apparitions really appear. In order to do this it is necessary that your ghost should no longer be ignored as a phenomenon of Nature. He has a right to be examined and observed, studied and defined, which is equal to that of any other natural phenomenon. It is true that he is a rather difficult phenomenon; his comings and goings are rather intermittent and fitful, his substance is too shadowy to be handled, and he has avoided hitherto equally the obtrusive inquisitiveness of the microscope and telescope. A phenomenon which you can neither handle nor weigh, analyze nor dissect, is naturally regarded as intractable and troublesome; nevertheless, however intractable and troublesome he may be to reduce to any of the existing scientific categories, we have no right to allow his idiosyncrasies to deprive him of his innate right to be regarded as a phenomenon. . . .

Eclipses in old days used to drive whole nations half mad with fright. To this day the black disc of the moon no sooner begins to eat into the shining surface of the sun than millions of savage men feel "creepy," and begin to tremble at the thought of the approaching end of the world. But in civilised lands even the most ignorant regard an eclipse with imperturbable composure. Eclipses are scientific phenomena observed and understood. It is our object to reduce ghosts to the same level, or rather to establish the claim of ghosts to be regarded as belonging as much to the order of Nature as the eclipse.

MRS. VATAS-SIMPSON

"There must be some foundation for the rumours." (1885)

This narrative is taken from the diary of a Mrs. Vatas-Simpson. The case was carefully investigated by researchers in the Society for Psychical Research, who found that Mrs. Vatas-Simpson was a reliable witness, not given to lying or hysteria. The case involves a woman's first-person account of two ghosts, one of either sex, that appeared in an old house to her two children. Other parallels with The Turn of the Screw *are the presence of servants, the presence of a second woman named "L." (apparently the children's governess), the strange noises and the mysterious cry of an infant, the staying awake late into the night, the reading of a book, the appearance of*

From the *Proceedings of the Society for Psychical Research* 3 (1885): 127–30.

a ghost on the stairs, and the verbal parallels of "Now, then, how did that man get in? — or rather, how did he get out?" with the exchange in James's story between the governess and Mrs. Grose: "Then how did he get in?" "And how did he get out?" (p. 47). Below is the first half of Mrs. Vatas-Simpson's narrative, without the subsequent account of her skeptical husband's becoming a believer after he also unaccountably sees the ghost of an old lady in his study. The narrative is reproduced as it was published in the proceedings of the Society for Psychical Research, then in its third year of existence. The ellipses indicate passages left out of Mrs. Vatas-Simpson's diary by the original editors who published the narrative in 1885.

This is very strange. What can it mean? The servants say that they see queer things moving about, and that they hear peculiar noises. One servant has left us in consequence. To-day I was told by a neighbour that the people who lived here before we came could not remain, because there were always noises and sounds about the house at night, and that even their little children were disturbed by them. At last they became so very unbearable he was obliged to go elsewhere. One hardly knows whether to believe such reports or to laugh at them. At present we have had no nocturnal visitors, and I shall not tell my dear ones, to cause apprehension of ghosts and hobgoblins. . . .

There must be some foundation for the rumours regarding the sounds, noises, and appearances in this old house. It has stood here since the Fire of London. The lower part of the house is very extensive; and then, underground, dark, big, cavernous cellarage (which, it is said, has not been thoroughly explored or examined for years) where secret passages are believed to exist, and from whence issue sounds of moaning and sighing, clearly and quite unmistakably, after dark, when the hum of the busy world is hushed. Any one then, by placing themselves over the window grating may hear distinctly the peculiar noises within. I try to turn a deaf ear to all this, and to combat the fears such revelations inspire in the household, but am unsuccessful with the servants, as they leave me in consequence. My husband says the sounds are produced by the contrary winds careering through the gratings, and perhaps they are.

A severe illness has kept my pen idle for several weeks. Not so, however, events. To-day, L. told me that when the children are playing upstairs an old woman will persist in standing in the doorway, looking in very disconsolately. She believes in the reality of the occurrence; says that it is an annoyance; would I give orders to the servants to keep our gate on the staircase locked? — the iron gate that shuts in the private portion of the house from that which is below, making it thus quite impossible to pass up the stairs from the offices below. . . .

So late, so tired and weary. Every night now L. and I have to sit up long, dreary hours to wait my husband coming home, for we are afraid to go to bed till he returns. There is no feeling of security with only women in this big, grim, and hollow-sounding house, and though we are both free from all superstitious fears, and far from timid, we cannot but be sensible of our unprotected helplessness, left alone, as we are, till the night wanes into morning.

To-night, and for several nights now, we have had our courage put to the test, and most decidedly it has not been found wanting. . . . The first evening, about 11 o'clock, sitting with the drawing-room door open, a man's face was clearly seen above the balustrade, while the old-fashioned size and the carvings of the supports hid his form from our view. Instantly we both jumped up, and as instantly started forward. Both thought that he had come up by mistake, or purposely, perhaps, to see someone in the house. Ere we could speak he was gone.

The servants, not having gone to bed, were summoned, told to go and fasten the iron gate, and reprimanded for their negligence in forgetting to do so. The gas was alight, illuminating the house from the ground-floor to the very roof of the house. We stood upon the landing. The servants went down, protesting that they had locked and fastened securely the gate: and so they had — it was securely fast.

Then I went for the key, and downstairs, and satisfied myself of the fact, and also went below to satisfy myself that all doors and every place below were firmly secured for the night.

Now, then, how did that man get in? — or rather, how did he get *out?* It is possible he might have been concealed during the evening, and so have been on the stairs — but where could he go, instantaneously as he had been followed, and by both of us, neither of us suspecting anything more than that he had obtained entrance through the forgetfulness of the servants, and nothing doubting but that he would wait to be spoken to? Where could he go? — for in an instant, in the twinkling of an eye, the spot where he had appeared was vacant.

Well, when my husband came home I told him. He treated it as a good joke, laughed at our bewilderment, and said we must all have been asleep and dreaming. He has such a supreme contempt for any supposition of the supernatural. Has no belief in spiritual visions, in "ghosts," or visions of the night. He is far too practical, and only derides my credulity. At present I have been able to keep all suspicion of these things from the household. . . .

Twice late, sitting up during the night hours, my L. and I have been disturbed by that same appearance on the stairs, and each time have done our best to discover the mystery. The face is pale to sickliness, and the eye steady and mournful. The figure is shrouded in a sort of dark, shadowy indistinctness, and his departure is sudden and noiseless. The first time he came we slowly advanced to him, side by side, quite silently, and with firm decision of manner, intending to show him our determination to enforce an interview, and ask explanation for his intrusion. Ah! he is gone.

The second time I was reading an interesting book. L. looked up from her employment and, seeing him, touched me gently (we were close together), when both of us made a sudden dart forward, only to find the spot vacant which had, one instant previously, been occupied by his face and figure. It is impossible that we can be mistaken or deceived. No, No, we are not. There is no misapprehension, because no fear quells our courage; no cowardice prevents the full action of our powers of perception; no alarm frustrates our intention of grappling with him if we can, or of pursuing him, or of holding him if we can come up with him. We are on our guard against surprise, and our nerves steady, prepared to make a decided unequivocal effort to find out who and what this nocturnal intruder may be.

But nothing avails; he is not here; he is not anywhere near. Looking keenly at him one moment, the next he has fled, quick as a flash of lightning. But he *was* standing there; we both saw him, positively and undoubtedly. . . .

It is useless to contend against facts. Nervous terrors and timorous imaginations have nothing whatever to do in suggesting the various appearances and the indescribable sounds which pervade the rooms, the corners, and the recesses of this great house. Superstition might indeed supply one person with food for miracles or for belief in deception and witchcraft; but when there are several witnesses of all ages there must be a foundation of truth, and, at all events, each and every one could not be deceived. If all that is going on here is a strange delusion, then all would not be affected at the same moment. If it is but a mere sensation or impression, then it would only be conceived by *one* mind, not by all. If it were capable of detection, then so many persons gathered together would surely find out that it was imposture and deception.

Besides, there is nothing done to annoy any of us; no attempt is made to frighten or even to surprise us. There seems no system or organization in all these mysteries. In addition to the little old woman who goes about the upper floor, and the man who comes occasionally upon the stairs, there are other sights and sounds, and other nocturnal disturbances. Very often a babe is heard wailing and crying in the kitchen, generally in the evening. We heard these piteous wailings when we first came here to live, and then imagined that a babe was really within hearing; but when, after the lapse of many months, the sounds were still those of a new-born babe, no stronger in tone or different in expression, then we began to wonder, and to strive to penetrate the mystery, and are constrained to believe that no living infant causes those sounds.

Then, again, close to my bedroom door, in a recess, there are notes of the most mournful singing the ear can hear — real notes — soft and sad, but clear and thrilling. Then, in an instant, the notes are prolonged, and change into short, sharp screams of agony. Then total silence.

All this takes place in the very interior of the house — in parts where there is no outside wall, but where the wall, thick and massive, divides one room from another.

MISS C.

"I plainly saw the figure of a female dressed in black." (1885)

Miss C. was an Irish governess who, like many of the men and women who reported experiences with ghosts, did not give her full name because she wanted to protect her privacy. Miss C.'s narrative has several parallels with James's story: the young woman is governess to two children, one of whom sleeps in her bedroom, and she sees a woman dressed in black. When Miss C. was asked how she could be sure of the dates, she replied that she kept a diary and that she had consulted it before writing her narrative. It may or may not be relevant that investigation by a member of the Society for Psychical Research revealed vague reports by neighbors that a woman had died in a fire in the house in 1752.

On the 18th of April (Thursday), 1867, about 7:40 p.m., I was going to my room, which I at that time shared with one of my pupils, when just as I had reached the top of the stairs I plainly saw the figure of a female dressed in black, with a large white collar or kerchief, very dark

From the *Proceedings of the Society for Psychical Research* 3 (1885): 119–22.

hair, and pale face. I only saw the side face. She moved slowly and went into my room, the door of which was open. I thought it was Marie, the French maid, going to see about A.'s clothes, but the next moment I saw that the figure was too tall and walked better. I then fancied it was some visitor who had arrived unexpectedly (Mrs. S. had done so a few days previously), and had gone into the wrong bedroom, and as I had only been at F. H. a short time, I felt rather shy at speaking to strangers, so waited where I was a minute or two expecting to see the lady come out, but I *never* lost sight of the door. At last I went in, and there was no one in the room. I looked everywhere, and even felt the back of the hanging side of the wardrobe to see whether there was any concealed door leading into the next room. This idea would not have occurred to me had I been able in any way to account for the lady's disappearance. She could not have gone by the window, as the room was on the second storey. Going downstairs, I met the cook and another maid, and asked them if any stranger had arrived, and was answered in the negative. I had never heard of any strange appearances in the house, and could not account for what I had seen that evening.

Some years after, in December, 1874, as I was going to bed, about 10 o'clock (the house had been slightly altered), I saw most distinctly a lady in black leaning over the fire in the room occupied by the eldest daughter. She was shading her eyes with her hand, and seemed looking for something by the fender; her other hand was on the chimney-piece. I walked slowly toward the room, and said, "Take care, C., you will burn your face, it is *so* near the flame." As there was no answer I spoke again, I suppose louder, for at that moment C., whom I supposed the lady to be, came out of her *sister's room* and asked what I was talking about and why I was in such a fright about her burning her face. There was no one in her room and no one could have passed me unobserved, as I was standing close to the door.

Another time, late one evening in September, I was sitting in the schoolroom with the door open, when I saw the figure again, standing on the far side of the stove in the lower hall. I at once got up to see who it was, but it had vanished. I think it seemed to go up one step of the stairs, but am not sure, as this was the only time I felt rather nervous when seeing it, and that, perhaps, from thinking it was someone who had no business in the house, or that someone was playing me a trick. Each time I have seen "the black lady" she has been dressed in what appeared to be black serge or cashmere — something soft and in heavy folds — with the same large white collar or kerchief on her neck. Whatever it was, I feel as certain of having seen it as that I am now writing this account of it, and it may be as well to mention that I am by no means a nervous person — quite the contrary.

MRS. G.

"What has happened to the children?" (1889)

Mrs. G.'s narrative concerns a woman with two small children in a house that appears to be haunted. It has several parallels with James's story: strange noises, a female and a male ghost, the white face and the hint of suicide of one of them, the man at the window who disappears, the wicked servant of a former occupant, the ability of only certain individuals to see a ghost that is not visible to others, the child sent away because of a sickness caused in part by the presence of a ghost, and so on. Frank Podmore, a member of the Society for Psychical Research, investigated Mrs. G.'s report. He found a newspaper article dated April 5, 1870, reporting that a 42-year-old woman had earlier hanged herself in the house. The ellipses in the narrative indicate my omission of paragraphs that are of no relevance to readers of The Turn of the Screw.

We had not been more than a fortnight in our new home (it was in December) when I was aroused by a deep sob and moan. "Oh," I thought, "what has happened to the children?" I rushed in, their room being at the back of mine; found them sleeping soundly. So back to bed I went, when again another sob, and such a thump of somebody or something very heavy. "What can be the matter?" I sat up in bed, looked all round the room, then to my horror a voice (and a very sweet one) said, "Oh, do forgive me!" three times. I could stand it no more; I always kept the gas burning, turned it up, and went to the maid's room. She was fast asleep, so I shook her well, and asked her to come into my room. Then in five minutes the sobs and moans recommenced, and the heavy tramping of feet, and such thumps, like heavy boxes of plate being thrown about. She suggested I should ring the big bell I always keep in my room, but I did not like to alarm the neighbourhood. "Oh, do, ma'am, I am sure there are burglars next door, and they will come to us next." Anything but pleasant, on a bitter cold night, standing bell in hand, a heavy one, too, awaiting a burglar. Well, I told her to go to bed, and hearing nothing for half-an-hour, I got into mine, nearly frozen with cold and fright. But no sooner had I got warm than the sobs, moans, and noises commenced again. I heard the policeman's steady step, and I thought of the words, "What of the night, Watchman? what of the night?" If he only could have known what we, a few paces off, were going through. Three times I called Anne in, and then in the morning it all died away in a low moan. Directly it was daylight, I looked in the glass to see if my hair had turned white from the awful night I spent. Very relieved was I to find it still brown.

Of course nothing was said to the children, and I was hoping I should never experience such a thing again. I liked the house, and the children were so bonny. I had too much furniture for that small house, so stowed it away in the room next to the kitchen, and we used the small room at the top of the kitchen stairs as a dining-room, and then I had a pretty double drawing-room, where I always stayed. Still the children had no play-room, and no place for their doves. I therefore had most of the furniture and boxes taken out and put in the back kitchen. It seems from that day our troubles commenced, for the children were often alarmed by noises and a crash of something, and did not like sleeping alone. I felt a little uncomfortable, and thought it was all rather strange, but had so much business affairs to settle, having no one else to help me, that I had not much time to think.

I was in the drawing-room deeply thinking about business matters, when I was startled by Edith giving such a scream. I ran to the door, and found her running up, followed by Florence and the servant, the child so scared and deadly white, and could hardly breathe. "Oh, Birdie dear, I have seen such a dreadful white face peeping round the door! I only saw the head. I was playing with Floss (dog), and looking up, I saw this dreadful thing. Florence and Anne rushed in at once, but saw nothing." I pacified them by saying someone was playing a trick by a magic lantern, but after that for months they would not go upstairs or down alone.

It was very tiresome, and thinking seriously over the matter, I resolved to return my neighbour's call, which she honored me with the day after the first terrible night. I was ushered into the presence of two portly dames, and I should think they had arrived at that age not given to pranks. I looked at them, and mentally thought, "That sweet voice does not belong to either of you." They informed me that they had lived in that house 18 years, so I thought I might venture to ask whether anything had ever taken place of a disagreeable nature in my house, as we were so constantly alarmed by heavy noises, and that my eldest daughter, aged 10, had seen a dreadful white face looking round the door at her, and of course I should be glad to know; that as far as I was concerned, I feared nothing and no one, but if my children were frightened I should leave, but I liked the house very much, and thought perhaps I might buy it. They said, "Don't do that, but there is nothing to hurt you," and I saw sundry nods and winks which meant more, so in desperation I said, "Won't you tell me what has occurred?" "Well, a few years ago, the bells commenced to ring, and there was quite a commotion, but then the former tenant, a Miss M., had a wicked servant." The other dame replied, "I may say, a very wicked servant." Well, I could not get much more, but of course I imagined this very wicked servant had done something, and felt very uneasy.

On my return, Edith said, "Oh, dear, I have seen such a little woman pass, and I often hear pitter patter; what is it? Of course magic lanterns couldn't do that." So I said nothing, and said I was too tired to talk. That night I felt a very creeping feeling of shivering, and thought I would have Florence to sleep with me, so when I went to bed around 10, I carried her in wrapped up in a shawl, leaving Edith asleep with the maid. It was about 11; I had tucked my little pet in and was about to prepare to go to sleep, when it seemed as if something electric was in the room, and that the ceiling and roof were coming on the top of us. The bed was shaken, and such a thump of something very heavy. I resolved not to risk my child's life again, for whatever it was came down on me, she would be safe in the next room with the others, but I dreaded going to bed, as I never knew what might happen before the morning. . . .

I found that house very expensive, and I had to keep the gas burning downstairs and up all night I asked a young friend from Richmond to stay, a clergyman's daughter. She laughed at such a thing as a ghost. We both went up the trap-door and explored the space over the bedroom, and next to the roof; it was very dark, but I took a candle, and then discovered three holes as large as a plate between my house and the old ladies'. The next morning I walked down to the landlord who owns both houses, and told him again what we were continually going through and that I and my children were getting ill, and that it was quite impossible to live in the house. He came up on the following day, and told me that a woman had hanged herself, he thought, in the room the children slept in. The holes were filled up, and I thought now nothing can come in to alarm us. What puzzled my friend was that the two old dames being invalids should go out in the snow and wet between 9 and 10 most nights in their garden; it certainly was odd, but, of course, they had a right to do what they liked in their own house, only they banged the back door; when Anne locked up she scarcely made a sound.

Florence was often saying to her eldest sister, "You see it was your imagination, for I never see anything." "Wait till you do, you won't forget it!" The next morning, as Florence was passing the room on the stairs, she saw a man standing by the window staring fixedly; blue eyes, dark brown hair, and freckles. She rushed up to me, looking very white and frightened; the house was searched at once, and nothing seen.

I had forgotten to mention that the night after the knocks came to my bedroom I resolved that the dog, who is very sharp, should sleep outside, but oh, that was worse than all, for at a quarter past 12 I looked at my clock. He commenced to cry, it was not exactly howling, and tore at the carpet in a frantic manner. I threw my fur cloak on, threw the door wide open, and demanded what was the matter. The poor little animal was so delighted to see me; I saw he had biscuits and water, and the children were then awake, and asked me why Floss was making that noise. I went to bed, and in ten minutes he recommenced. I went out three times, and then made up my mind not to move again, for I felt so cold and angry.

Another night something seemed to walk to the children's door, and turn the handle, walk up to the washstand, shake the bed, and walk out. It really was enough to shake anyone's nerves. My sister and brother-in-law, Mr. B., came for a couple of nights, but that was when I first went in. They heard nothing. I then had my husband's first wife's sister, who is very fond of me, to stay over Easter. She, fortunately, did not hear anything. . . .

I then had an interview with Miss M., the former tenant, who told me she had gone through precisely what I had, but had said very little about it, for fear of being laughed at. I was far too angry to take notice whether anyone laughed or not. Miss M. said one afternoon between four and five she was in very good spirits, and was playing the piano, and as she crossed the room a figure enveloped in black, with a very white face, and such a forlorn look, stood before her, and then it faded away. She was so terrified, but did not tell anyone about it. For some time after she was ill from fright on two occasions, but her aunt being old did not care to move, and she was too much attached to her to leave. It was satisfactory to find someone else who had gone through what we were daily experiencing. March 20th. I was resting in the drawing-room, when as I thought, I heard Edith's voice saying three times, "Darling!" I ran downstairs, much to their astonishment, and said, "Well, what is it now?" They replied, "We were coming directly, why did you come down?" "Well, that is cool; why did you call me?" "But we didn't; you called to us to put on our hats at once as you were going to the town." Anne said she distinctly heard me say it when I had not even spoken. I believe it was that same night as they were going upstairs to bed, they saw a white figure standing by the little room. How I hated that room! . . .

Having had very heavy expenses all the year, I thought I would if possible stay till September, as the evenings would be light, and we should be out all day, but even that I was not allowed to do, for coming home from paying visits, I found Florence looking deathly white, and in a very nervous state, and in breathless haste she said she had seen the same face, but the figure was crawling in the little room as if it would spring on her. I at once called on my doctor who advised me to take the children away as soon as possible, and let them be amused, so I left my servant and her father in charge, locked my bedroom door, and took the key, went to London, where Edith was so ill that I had to call in Dr. F. . . .

And so ended my sojourn of five months in that very extraordinary house. All is quite true that I have stated, whether mortal or immortal I know not. I am glad to say my children are recovering, though Edith is still very weak, and I am suffering dreadfully from neuralgia, the result of the anxiety and worry I have gone through.

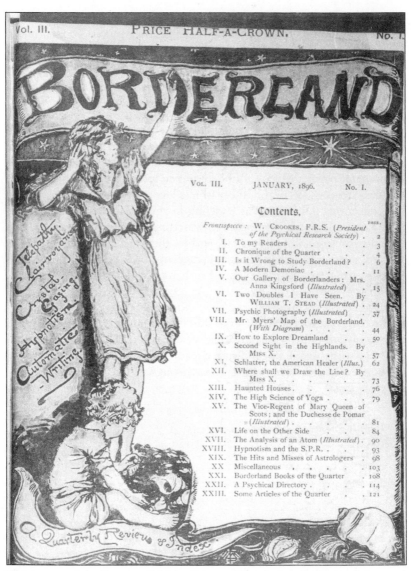

The cover of the January 1896 edition of *Borderland,* a journal devoted to reporting research on the occult. *Borderland* was published, and much of it written, by William T. Stead. Of particular interest here is the fourth item announced on the cover of this issue, Stead's narrative of "A Modern Demoniac," republished here.

WILLIAM T. STEAD

"I no longer felt I belonged to myself."
(1896)

In addition to the "real ghost stories" that he published in the 1890s, William T. Stead started in 1893 his own journal, called Borderland. *In that journal he gathered and published reports of matters having to do with spiritualism — such matters as telepathy, clairvoyance, hypnotism, automatic handwriting, and demonic possession. In the third volume of* Borderland, *for January of 1896, Stead published "A Modern Demoniac," an account of a young man who came to his office and described his experience with possession by the spirit of the enraged grandfather of a young woman he had seduced. It appeared a little more than a year before James wrote* The Turn of the Screw. *Readers may see certain parallels between the behavior of Miles and Flora near the end of James's story and this moving story of demonic possession. The grandfather's epithets "d——" and "b——" stand for "damned" or "damn" and "bloody," terms deemed too harsh to print in polite Victorian circles. All ellipses are in the original and indicate pauses or interruptions in speech.*

One Thursday afternoon in January, when coming in after lunch, I met at the foot of the stairs a young man, who somewhat nervously asked the lift-boy whether Mr. Stead came down to the office nowadays.

"What do you want?" said I. "I am Mr. Stead."

"O!" said he, "might I speak to you?"

"Certainly," said I, and so he followed me into my office without going through the usual preliminary of sending in his name, therefore I do not know to this day who my visitor was, or where he came from. I only know that he said he was an officer in the British army, and that he is now, and has been for some time, on sick leave.

He said that he wished to speak to me because he had been interested in spiritualism and thought he could tell me something that was interesting, and at the same time he hoped I might be able to give him some advice.

Some time ago he had taken to experimenting, and had found that he had great facility in automatic writing. His hand had moved within

From "A Modern Demoniac," a journalistic account that William T. Stead wrote and published in his journal, *Borderland* 3 (1896): 11–14.

five minutes of the time he had first taken the pen in his hand, and left it free to move as it pleased. Fascinated by the unusual phenomena he had gone on and, neglecting his duties and abandoning himself for hours — eight, nine, and ten at a stretch — to receiving the communications which were written by his hand. It became a passion with him. After a time he found that there was no necessity for him to use a pen as his hand would automatically trace the characters in the air, and he could read them wherever he might be. This after a time was succeeded by a further form of development, when he became partially entranced, and would talk under control when he was either wholly unconscious or only partially conscious. Thus by gradually sapping the mind, the invisible Intelligence which had established itself as his control, gradually gained such complete possession of his faculties that, as he said, "I no longer felt I belonged to myself. It dominates me by its will, and I do not know what the end will be."

He spoke quietly, with simple earnestness, as of a man caught in the grip of a mighty, invisible force which was bearing him irresistibly down into the abyss against which it was in vain even to struggle. I said to him at once that he had been frightfully reckless, that the one condition of safety in all such experiments was never to abandon the control of your own personality to that of any agency whatever, and that he must break it once and for all.

He smiled sadly. "It is all very well to talk about my giving him up, but he won't give me up," said he.

"But," said I, "did the agency itself never warn you as to consequences of this frightful over-indulgence?"

"Ah!" said he, " it is not a good spirit. It is a very bad one that sticks to me, not for my good but for my harm, and I cannot shake it off."

"Nonsense!" said I. "It is all a matter of will."

"Yes," said he, "that may be, but he dominates my will. I cannot stand up against him, and he tells me that now he has got me he will never let me go until he has killed me."

"This is madness," said I; "he may tell you that a thousand times, but it is only because you give in to it."

"But," said he,"how can I help it? He seizes me when he pleases. He jerks my head from one side to the other, or forces me to go here and there at his own caprice; nay, he will suddenly drive me as it were out of himself, extinguishing my own consciousness and taking possession of my body, using it as his own."

"Do you mean to say you cannot stay him?" said I.

"No!" said he; "he has such power over me, he uses me just as if my body were his and not mine."

"But you must stop that, and at once. Otherwise you are lost."

"Yes," he said, mournfully. "I am afraid I am; at least he says so. He says that he will do me all the evil he can while I live, and that after, I am to be damned. But," said he, "will you speak to him?"

"Certainly," said I. "Will he take possession of you now?"

"At any time," he replied.

I paused for a moment; but I thought that as the Evil Spirit was in the habit of seizing him without his will at all times and to his own detriment, it would be permissible to allow him to enter in by an act of his own volition when he was with one who might possibly be the means of helping in his deliverance; so I said, "Yes, if he will talk he may come."

My visitor walked across the room and sat down without saying a word in a large easy chair. In a moment he became convulsed, his eyes closed, he fell backwards with his head on the couch, his chest heaved, rising and falling, while his body writhed as if convulsed. Not a word was said. I stood watching him silently, nor did he speak or make a sound beyond a low moan when the convulsions became more violent. After waiting for two or three minutes standing over him, I at last said, "Well!"

Then there was another writhing movement of the prostrate form before me, and a very curious voice, quite different from that of my visitor, said to me,

"Well! A b—— queer fellow it is, is it not?"

"Who are you?" I said.

"I will tell you," said he, as the body was more violently contorted. "I will tell you. I am the grandfather of a girl, that d—— carcass . . ." Then he writhed again and the voice ceased.

"Come," I said sharply; "why can't you talk decently and tell me who you are and what you want? Will you talk to me?" I said.

"Yes," said he, and then with another shuddering convulsion he raised himself upon the chair and said,

"Yes, I will tell you. I am the grandfather of a girl who was a d—— pretty girl, with whom this b—— carcass, ugh . . ."

Once more the convulsions recommenced, and he flung himself back with his head on the couch writhing and moaning.

"Come, come," I said; "why do you play the fool like that? Sit up straight and talk to me like a gentleman."

He continued, however, lying as he was.

"Talk to you respectably?" said he. "Talk to you like a gentleman, and this d—— carcass . . ."

His head jerked backwards violently over the side of the chair. Then he was silent for a moment, apparently collecting himself.

He said, "I like to do that, it hurts him; it hurts this old carcass, doesn't it, ugh." Then he struck himself a violent blow to the chest. The face twinged with pain, "Does it not hurt him? I like to do it. I am going to kill him, kill him; yes, kill him. D—— him, d—— him!"

"Nonsense," I said. "You will not kill him, or do anything of the kind."

"Won't I, though! You will see. He knows. He dare not shave himself for fear he will cut his throat. Ho! I have got him. I have got him."

I replied, "What is the meaning of all this? Who are you? Why have you got him? And what is it all to you? Can't you speak straight and tell me without all this?"

"Are you a father?" he said? "You can understand then what I feel towards this brute. Ugh! How I loathe having to touch him. I only do it to torment him. Well, you know my granddaughter."

"What about your granddaughter?"

"Pretty girl, very pretty girl. Well this brute . . ."

He writhed again.

"What about her? What happened?"

"He made love to her for four months. For four months he did, d—— him, and for four months I have had him. I have tortured him night and day, and for four months more I will make his life horrible. Oh, yes, I will cut his throat. I will, and he will be damned for ever, and serve him right."

"Now," I said, "how dare you talk like this? You are only making your own torment worse."

"What do I care? I would willingly be tormented for eternity to have the joy of punishing him."

"But," I said, "what right have you?"

"Right!" said he. "Listen. My granddaughter, a lady, girl of good family, one of the best families. Oh, yes! And this d—— carcass came along, made love to her he did. Such a nice young man! D—— fool, don't you know — always says 'Don't you know' — came along and made love to her."

"Did he marry her?"

"Wanted to," said he. "Would now if he could get the chance, but he never will. He will never see her again. Don't know what would happen. D—— swine, he is as ugly as sin; ugly, yes. Yet, she is such a fool that if she saw him again I don't know what would happen. They will never meet again. Never! Never! I take care of that."

"But," I said, "what is the matter? He wanted to marry her, made love to her. There is no wrong in that. I can't understand. Did he ruin . . ."

"Ruined her. Seduced her. Lived with her for four months. Nobody knew. Nobody. Then she turned round and sent him away. She said, 'You have made me a beast. I will have nothing more to do with you.' And he goes, the wretch, the carcass."

Again there was a convulsion. The breast heaved, and again he struck himself a heavy blow on the chest, writhing with passion, and continued,

"I can do anything with him now. Anything. He is mine, altogether. I make him go where I like, talk to him when I like; night and day torment him. Keep it up. O! yes, keep it up. And in four months cut his throat." And as he said so, he drew his hand across his neck, making a hideous gurgling sound in his throat.

"Nothing can save him," he said. "Nothing."

"You are quite wrong," I said. "You have no business to torment him in this way whatever wrong he has done. And he will turn you out."

"Turn me out! Ho! Ho!" he cried out. "The other day he called on God to have mercy on him. Did I not laugh? He did not talk much to God before I took him in hand. No! he is mine and I keep him."

"But," I said, "where is the girl now? Would he marry her now?"

"Of course he would. But she won't have him, and he will never get the chance. Never! never!"

"How long have you been on the other side?"

"Fifty years!" he said. "Fifty years."

"In fifty years," said I, "you ought to have made better progress than to be giving way to all this hideous passion. What have you been doing all the time?"

"I have been in Hell," said he. "In Hell, tormented, going about everywhere, doing this kind of thing."

"But," I said, "are you all alone?"

"Yes, all alone."

"Well," I said, "how did you come to get hold of him?"

"Listen," said he. "I was an officer in the army in my time, and I think I ruined more women than any man I know. Then I came over here, and for fifty years what have I had to do but to go about seeing girls, pretty girls, falling in love with them, not being able to speak to them. What could they do to me? What could I do to them? I could not touch them, but the desire was there all the time, and I go about seeing it all. Tormented with desire that could never be satisfied, and then to go and see my relations doing as I did. My granddaughter, to see her ruined! D—— him! d——— ! and he will be d——— . Oh curse it!" he said, striking his head against the edge of the couch, "to think of it, this carcass, oh this carcass. But I will pay him out. Four months more, night and day, night and day, and then to be d—— with him for ever. That is good." And he laughed a hideous, hollow laugh.

"But," I said, "is there no one to care for you at all?"

"None!" he said, "no."

"But," I said, "you must have loved many women."

"Seduced them, you mean," he said. "They are in Hell, all in Hell. Do you think they love me? No, they curse me."

"No," I said, "I don't believe they are in Hell, and if they were — women are very good, and some of them must have loved you."

"No; none!"

"But," I persisted, "you are quite wrong. No one knows how deep, how great is a woman's love. But did you never do an unselfish thing in your life?"

"Never! never! I pleased myself."

"Poor wretch," I said. "I am awfully sorry for you."

A violent convulsion shook the frame of my unfortunate visitor.

"Don't," he said, in a ghastly grating voice. "Don't pity me! Don't pity me. I can't bear it."

"But I do pity you," I said. "I am awfully sorry for you. It must be ghastly to go on like this."

"I don't want pity, I want vengeance, and I am taking it now. Don't I take it out of him, and won't I take it out of him?"

"No," I said, "you have taken enough out of him. You will have to go."

"Who will make me go?"

"He will."

"He has no will."

"May I ask you a question?"

"Yes," he said, "ask what you like."

"Did you approve of him coming here?"

"No," said he, "that I did not."

"Then," I said, "why did he come?"

"Because," he said, speaking as if with reluctance, "because in what that d—— fellow calls his mind — *his* mind . . . it is mine, not his — there is one little bit that sometimes makes him do what he pleases."

"Then," I said, "that means he came here in spite of you."

"That is it," he said. "He did," writhing and making horrible faces. His lips would be protruded until they almost became like a pig's snout, not round, but with a circular protrusion very hideous to see.

"Well," I said, "the same will that brought him here against you will drive you out."

"Ha! ha!" said he. "Never! never! He is mine. I can do with him what I like. I say to Carcass, turn your head to the right, he turns it. Lay it on the right shoulder, he lays it. I turn his head right round. I say, Carcass, turn to the right! he does; to the left, he does. I can use his body as I please, this d—— carcass, it is mine."

"How did you gain possession of it?"

"I will tell you," he said. "Listen. There is some b—— nonsense called spiritualism. He tried with the Ouija Board, got answers from somebody, then thinks he will try handwriting. Takes a pen. I see him, I see him. I am passing, I see what he is doing. Remember about my granddaughter. Pretty girl, pretty girl, and this d—— ugly carcass."

"Never mind about that. Go on."

"I wait, I think I can get at him. So one day he thinks he will try automatic handwriting. Takes a pen in his b—— old fist, ugh!" and he writhed. "I took his hand and wrote. Called myself 'Lucy,' I did. Lucy, nice girl, always said her prayers, beautiful spirit; come to lead him into the paths of virtue. Ho! did I not fool him! I wrote, 'Your perseverance is rewarded.' Then I tell him. What do I tell him? Oh! I write with his hand and tell him everything that he thinks is only known to himself about his girl and himself. He writes and writes for hours together. I torture him by everything that I can think of to give him pain, even when I am 'Lucy,' then he goes on and on. B—— fool that he is; always say b—— fool, 'don't you know.' Nice young man; nice young officer. But at last I get hold of him, and he can't shake me off."

"Oh! yes he could," I said. "He could banish you by his will."

"He hasn't got one. I have it. It is mine. You see how I use his old carcass. I use it, I hate it, curse it! — I hate it! I have tortured him for four months; I will torture him for another four, then I will cut his throat! — yes, I will."

"No," I said, "you won't. You will do nothing of the kind. What is more, now, you will have to clear out; you have been here quite long enough."

He did not speak again. A few convulsive moments followed, a long sigh, and then my visitor slowly rose to his feet, rubbing his eyes.

"Well," he said. "You see he can use me as he likes."

I said, "He has told me a great deal about you."

"What has he told you?" said he.

"He told me first about himself. He says he is the grandfather of a lady whom you ruined. Of course, I know nothing at all about it; I only tell you what he said."

He was silent.

"Well?" I said, "is there any truth in what he said?"

"Well, yes," he said, "I am afraid there is."

"Then," I said, "my friend, I think you are in a position of great difficulty, for which it will be absolutely necessary for you to escape at once."

"But how can I?" said he.

"By simply declining to obey him," said I. "You can banish him if you will it."

"I can't. He comes and talks to me whether I like it or not; he uses my hand to write what he wishes to say in the air."

"But," I said, "the moment he begins to use your hand put it in your pocket."

"But he will talk to me."

"Then," I said, "don't answer him back; don't listen to him. You can't pull on with this any longer; you have to fight it tooth and nail, as if you were fighting for your immortal soul."

"Yes," he said. "I am fighting for my life. I know that perfectly well. I dare not shave now."

"Yes," said I. "He told me that. I told him it was all bosh. But the question is this. He has overrun your territory, but the citadel is still intact. You came here in spite of his will. Regard this as the turning point of your destiny. Never do anything he wants you to do; and every time you baffle him and assert your own will you weaken his forces and strengthen yourself."

"But," I said, "what about the lady?"

He said, "I don't wish to speak about her. She is not in this country. It is all off between us."

"But," I said, "would you marry her if you had the chance?"

"Would I not?" said he. "But she will not hear of it."

"How was it broken off?"

"O!" he said. "She had a great spasm of repentance, bitterly upbraided me, and would not see me any more."

"Does no one know about it?"

"No one but she and me."

"Well," I said; "if she really repented, as I have no doubt she has, she must help you to escape from this domination. You must tell her."

He seemed for a moment as if he were going to be controlled; then he said, with a shudder: "Do you know what he says to me now? — 'I will kill you to-night if you do. Kill you to-night.'"

I will break off the narrative at this point. I saw my unknown visitor once again. His control was more blasphemous and more defiant than before. The convulsions were worse and the contortions more violent. It was a ghastly sight to see him writhing on the floor, tossed about until he was stiff and sore.

It may have been incipient insanity. It certainly was not fooling. When the control passed the victim was calm and sane. If it be madness, it was madness resulting from excessive experimentalizing with spiritualism. But I wish any materialistic doctor would take the man in hand. He would, I am sure, be less scornful in his comments upon that "exploded superstition Demoniacal Possession."

Reactions, 1898

It is useful to balance our own twenty-first-century reactions to The Turn of the Screw *with a sampling of the reactions of others in James's own times. The following five reactions all were written in 1898, just after the story appeared as one of two stories in a book called* The Two Magics, *published shortly after its serialization in* Collier's. *These documents, along with James's responses to a series of letters about the story in the following section, constitute a grouping of readings in the year of the initial publication of* The Turn of the Screw.

"A horribly successful study of the magic of evil."

[*The Turn of the Screw* is] a deliberate, powerful, and horribly successful study of the magic of evil, of the subtle influence over human hearts and minds of the sin with which this world is accursed. . . . We have called it "horribly successful," and the phrase seems to still stand, on second thought, to express the awful, almost overpowering sense of the evil that human nature is subject to derive from it by the sensitive reader. . . . The strongest and most affecting argument against sin we have lately encountered in literature (without forcing any didactic purpose upon the reader) it is nevertheless free from the slightest hint of grossness. Of any precise form of evil Mr. James says very little, and on this head he is never explicit. Yet, while the substance of his story is free from all impurity and the manner is always graceful and scrupulously polite, the very breath of hell seems to pervade some of its chapters, and in the outcome goodness, though depicted as alert and militant, is scarcely triumphant. . . . [Miles and Flora] are accursed, or all but damned, and are shown to have daily, almost hourly, communication with lost souls, the souls that formerly inhabited the bodies of a vicious governess and her paramour, who, in the flesh, began the degradation of their victims. The awful "imagination of evil" this fair boy and girl must possess, the oldness of the heart and soul in each young body, the terrible precocity which enables them to deceive their "pastors and masters" as to their knowledge of the presence of their ghostly mentors, these set forth with perfect clearness and the sobriety of a matter-of-fact narrative are what serve to produce the thrilling effect.

From *The New York Times Saturday Review of Books and Art* 3 (October 15, 1898): 681–82.

"The deep mistake of writing the story."

The plottings of the good governess and the faithful Mrs. Grose to combat the evil, very gradually discovered, are marvellously real. You cannot help but assist at their interviews, and throb with their anxiety. You are amply convinced of the extraordinary charm of the children, of the fascination they exercise over all with whom they come in contact. The symbolism is clumsy; but only there in the story has Mr. James actually failed. It is not so much from a misunderstanding of child nature that he has plunged into the deep mistake of writing the story at all. Here, as elsewhere in his work, there are unmistakable signs of a close watchfulness and a loving admiration of children of the more distinguished order. A theory has run away with him. It is flimsily built on a few dark facts, so scattered and uncertain that they cannot support a theory at all. He has used his amiable knowledge of child life in its brighter phases to give a brilliant setting to this theory. His marvellous subtlety lends his examination of the situation an air of scientific precision. But the clever result is very cruel and untrue.

"The most monstrous and incredible ghost-story."

The subject-matter of *The Turn of the Screw* is also made up of feminine intuitions, but the heroine — this time a governess — has nothing in the least substantial upon which to base her deep and startling cognitions. She perceives what is beyond all perception, and the reader who begins by questioning whether she is supposed to be sane ends by accepting her conclusions and thrilling over the horrors they involve.

The story, in brief, concerns itself with the hideous fate of two beautiful and charming children who have been subjected to the baneful and corrupting influence of two evil-intentioned servants. These, dying, are unable to give up their hold upon so much beauty and charm, but while suffering the torments of damnation, come back to haunt the children as influences of horror and evil, with "a fury of intentions" to complete the ruin they have begun. The story is told by the governess, who recounts her slow recognition of the situation and

From *The Bookman* 15 (November, 1898): 54.
From *The Critic*, old series 33 (December 1898): 523–24.

her efforts to shield and save her charges. It is the most monstrous and incredible ghost-story that ever was written. At the same time it grasps the imagination in a vise. The reader is bound to the end by the spell, and if, when the lids of the book are closed, he is not convinced as to the possibility of such horrors, he is at least sure that Mr. James has produced an imaginative masterpiece.

"A tale of the Poe sort."

Henry James has frequently given his readers shivers by the coldness with which he treats intense emotions. But it is a new thing for him to create a semblance of terror by a genuine story of "uncanny ugliness and horror and pain." In his latest volume, *The Two Magics* (Macmillan), he has shown what he can do with a tale of the Poe sort — and he does it extremely well. He calls the story *The Turn of the Screw*, and he does not hesitate to give it the extra twist that makes the reader writhe under it. And when you sift the terror to its essential facts, there does not seem to be anything in it to make a fuss about. That two supremely beautiful children should be under the evil spell of the ghosts of a dead governess and a wicked valet is not, on the face of it, a very awe-inspiring situation. Indeed, the ludicrousness of it, in these enlightened days, is always in danger of breaking through the hedge which the author had ingeniously constructed around it.

But right there is the place for the literary artist to show what he can do — and Henry James does it in a way to raise goose-flesh! He creates the atmosphere of the tale with those slow, deliberate phrases which seem fitted only to differentiate the odors of rare flowers. Seldom does he make a direct assertion, but qualifies and negatives and double negatives, and then throws in a handful of adverbs, until the image floats away upon a verbal smoke. But while the image lasts, it is, artistically, a thing of beauty. When he seems to be vague he is by elimination creating an effect of terror, of unimaginable horrors.

While his art is present in every sentence, the artist is absolutely obliterated. His personality counts for nothing in the effect. He is like a perfect lens which focuses light, but is itself absolutely colorless.

From *Life* 32 (November 10, 1898): 368. The author of this piece identifies himself as "Droch," the pen name of Robert Bridges. I am grateful to Martha Banta for first directing me, a decade ago, to this review.

"Lesbian love" and "pederastic passion."

Henry James has written a forceful story of country-home life, — *The Turn of the Screw*, in a book called *The Two Magics*. The hero and heroine are two sweet and lovely children, — a boy of 9 and a girl of 6. The little girl feels lesbian love for the partially-materialized ghost of a harlot-governess; and the little boy (who is expelled from school for obscenity) feels pederastic passion for the partially-materialized ghost of a corrupt manservant. The story is told by a governess (a good and virtuous one) with much force and dignity. The manservant seduces the first governess, who kills herself in pregnancy; he is himself killed by some apparently male victim of his lust. On this simple groundwork some striking and even tragic scenes are inwrought; — the main *motif* being the natural desire of the ghosts to carry off the children to hell.

From a letter that one psychical researcher, Frederic W. H. Myers, wrote to another, Oliver Lodge, on October 28, 1898. The letter (number 1520) is in the Lodge Collection in the Society for Psychical Research in London. Myers gets Miles's age wrong (he is really ten), and Flora's age he erroneously gives as six (she is really eight, though in the original *Collier's* version she had been six). Myers would have had a particular interest in *The Turn of the Screw*. He was a friend of Henry James and spent a good part of his professional life investigating reported cases of ghostly visitations. He was coauthor, with Edmund Gurney and Frank Podmore, of *Phantasms of the Living* (1886), a book that Henry James himself purchased not long after it came out.

HENRY JAMES RESPONDS, 1898

A number of people wrote to Henry James after The Turn of the Screw *appeared. Virtually all of those letters have been lost — that is, James destroyed them after he read and answered them. But some of his responses to these letters are still extant because the recipients held onto them. Sometimes we can guess from James's response what questions, opinions, or issues the original letter writer raised, but for the most part we are left in the dark about the specific contents of their letters. Nevertheless, James's response letters give some clues — sometimes ambiguous ones — about the way James read his own story. The letters should be read in conjunction with James's note about the anecdote told by Edward White Benson, the Archbishop of Canterbury (p. 15) and his own 1908 Preface to the story in the New York Edition of his works (see pp. 179–86).*

To Arthur C. Benson: "The ghostly and ghastly."

My dear Arthur, . . .

But à propos, precisely, of the ghostly and ghastly, I have a little confession to make to you that has been on my conscience these three months and that I hope will excite in your generous breast nothing but tender memories and friendly sympathies.

On one of those two memorable — never to be obliterated — winter nights that I spent at the sweet Addington, your father, in the drawing-room by the fire, where we were talking a little, in the spirit of recreation, of such things, repeated to me the few meagre elements of a small and gruesome spectral story that had been told *him* years before and that he could only give the dimmest account of — partly because he had forgotten details and partly — and much more — because there had *been* no details and no coherency in the tale as he received it, from a person who also but half knew it. The vaguest essence only was there — some dead servants and some children. This essence *struck* me and I made a note of it (of a most scrappy kind) on going home. There the note remained till this autumn, when, struck with it afresh, I wrought it into a fantastic fiction which, first intended to be of the briefest, finally became a thing of some length and is now being "serialised" in an American periodical.

From a March 11, 1898, letter to A. C. Benson (1862–1925), son of the recently deceased Edward W. Benson, Archbishop of Canterbury. Quoted from *The Letters of Henry James*, ed. Percy Lubbock, vol. 1 (New York: Octagon, 1970), 279.

To Louis Waldstein, M.D.: "My bogey-tale dealt with things so hideous."

Dear Sir, . . .

That the *Turn of the Screw* has been suggestive and significant to you — in any degree — it gives me great pleasure to hear; and I can only thank you very kindly for the impulse of sympathy that made you write. I am only afraid, perhaps, that my conscious intention strikes you as having been larger than I deserve it should be thought. It is the intention so primarily, with me, always, of the artist, the *painter*, that *that* is what I most, myself, feel in it — and the lesson, the idea — ever — conveyed is only the one that deeply lurks in any vision prompted by life. And as regards a presentation of things so fantastic as in that wanton little Tale, I can only rather blush to see real substance read into them — I mean for the generosity of the reader. *But*, of course, where there *is* life, there's truth, and the truth was at the back of my head. The poet is always justified when he is not a humbug; always grateful to the justifying commentator. My bogey-tale dealt with things so hideous that I felt that to save it at all it needed some infusion of beauty or prettiness, and the beauty of the pathetic was the only attainable — was indeed inevitable. But ah, the exposure indeed, the helpless plasticity of childhood that isn't dear or sacred to *some*body! That *was* my little tragedy.

To H. G. Wells: "I had to rule out subjective complications."

My dear H. G. Wells, . . .

Bless your heart, I think I could easily say worse of the T. of the S., the young woman, the spooks, the style, the everything, than the worst any one else could manage. One knows the *most* damning things about one's self. Of course I had, about my young woman, to take a very

---

From an October 21, 1898, letter to Louis Waldstein (1853–1915). In 1897 Waldstein published *The Subconscious Self and Its Relation to Education and Health*. Quoted from *The Letters of Henry James*, ed. Leon Edel, vol. 4 (Cambridge, MA: Harvard UP, 1974, 1984), 84.

From a December 9, 1898, letter to H. G. Wells (1866–1946). Quoted from *The Letters of Henry James*, ed. Leon Edel, vol. 4 (Cambridge, MA: Harvard UP, 1974, 1984), 86. A "pot-boiler" is a piece of writing designed to put food in the pot, that is to make enough money to keep one from starving. In literary parlance it usually means something written *just* for the money. A "*jeu d'esprit*" is a "play of the spirit" — in this context a light-hearted game rather than something of depth or great seriousness.

sharp line. The grotesque business I had to make her picture and the childish psychology I had to make her trace and present, were, for me at least, a very difficult job, in which absolute lucidity and logic, a single-ness of effect, were imperative. Therefore I had to rule out subjective complications of her own — play of tone etc.; and keep her impersonal save for the most obvious and indispensable little note of neatness, firmness and courage — without which she wouldn't have had her data. But the thing is essentially a pot-boiler and a *jeu d'esprit*.

To Frederic W. H. Myers: "The most infernal imaginable evil and danger."

My dear Myers, . . .

The *T. of the S.* is a very mechanical matter, I honestly think — an inferior, a merely *pictorial*, subject and rather a shameless pot-boiler. The thing that, as I recall it, I most wanted not to fail of doing, under penalty of extreme platitude, was to give the impression of the commu-nication to the children of the most infernal imaginable evil and danger — the condition, on their part, of being as *exposed* as we can humanly conceive children to be. This was my artistic knot to untie, to put any sense of logic into the thing, and if I had known any way of pro-ducing *more* the image of their contact and condition I should assuredly have been proportionally eager to resort to it. I evoked the worst I could.

From a December 19, 1898, letter to Frederic W. H. Myers (1843–1901). Quoted from *The Letters of Henry James*, ed. Leon Edel, vol. 4 (Cambridge, MA: Harvard UP, 1974, 1984), 88. Myers was a friend of Henry James and an active member of the Society for Psychical Research.

From the Preface to Henry James's 1908 Edition
of *The Turn of the Screw*

In his 1908 Preface to the New York Edition of The Turn of the Screw, *written a decade after the story was initially published in 1898, Henry James gave a detailed explanation of the way he read his own story. That reading need not, of course, necessarily influence the way we read the story a century later. Although at times his language is somewhat confusing and elliptical, James made five major points in the Preface: (1) He saw* The Turn of the Screw *as a fanciful romance based on an anecdote he had heard about how the spirits of two dead servants tried to get hold of two small children; the resulting story was a fairy tale so simple in its effect that it would not attract earnest criticism. (2) He was not interested in offering a full characterization of the young governess; rather, he worked hard to have her keep clear her record of the events she was engaged in, though her explanation of those events was not always correct. (3) He saw the spirits of Peter Quint and Miss Jessel not as the kinds of ghosts reported by psychical researchers (and exemplified by the narratives of Mrs. Vatas-Simpson, Miss C., and Mrs. G. reproduced earlier in this section), but rather as evil demons or witches, predatory villains wooing Miles and Flora to their destruction. (4) He did not want to specify the precise nature of the evil done by Quint and Jessel, with each other or with the children, because to do so would make their actions seem less evil; rather, he wanted to give only vague hints, leaving it to his readers to imagine for themselves whatever worst-case evil they could visualize. (5) He saw* The Turn of the Screw *as a thing of beauty, a work of art designed to terrify and move his readers.*

This perfectly independent and irresponsible little fiction rejoices, beyond any rival on a like ground, in a conscious provision of prompt retort to the sharpest question that may be addressed to it. For it has the small strength — if I should n't say rather the unattackable ease — of a perfect homogeneity, of being, to the very last grain of its virtue, all of a kind; the very kind, as happens, least apt to be baited by earnest criticism, the only sort of criticism of which account need be taken. To have handled again this so full-blown flower of high fancy is to be led back by it to easy and happy recognitions. Let the first of these be that of the starting-point itself — the sense, all charming again, of the circle, one winter afternoon, round the hall-fire of a grave old country-house where (for all the world as if to resolve itself promptly and obligingly into convertible, into "literary" stuff) the talk turned, on I forget what homely pretext, to apparitions and night-fears, to the marked and sad drop in the general supply, and still more in the general quality, of such commodities. The good, the really effective and heart-shaking ghost-stories (roughly so to term them) appeared all to have been told, and neither new crop nor new type in any quarter awaited us. The new type indeed, the mere modern "psychical" case,° washed clean of all queer-ness as by exposure to a flowing laboratory tap, and equipped with cre-dentials vouching for this — the new type clearly promised little, for the more it was respectably certified the less it seemed of a nature to rouse the dear old sacred terror. Thus it was, I remember, that amid our lament for a beautiful lost form, our distinguished host expressed the wish that he might but have recovered for us one of the scantest of frag-ments of this form at its best. He had never forgotten the impression made on him as a young man by the withheld glimpse, as it were, of a dreadful matter that had been reported years before, and with as few particulars, to a lady with whom he had youthfully talked. The story would have been thrilling could she but have found herself in better possession of it, dealing as it did with a couple of small children in an out-of-the way place, to whom the spirits of certain "bad" servants, dead in the employ of the house, were believed to have appeared with the design of "getting hold" of them. This was all, but there had been more, which my friend's old converser had lost the thread of: she could only assure him of the wonder of the allegations as she had anciently heard them made. He himself could give us but this shadow of a shadow — my own appreciation of which, I need scarcely say, was exactly wrapped up in that thinness. On the surface there was n't much, but another grain, none the less, would have spoiled the precious pinch addressed to its end as neatly as some modicum extracted from an old silver snuff-box and held between finger and thumb. I was to remember the haunted children and the prowling servile spirits as a "value," of the disquieting sort, in all conscience sufficient; so that when, after an inter-val, I was asked for something seasonable by the promoters of a period-ical° dealing in the time-honoured Christmas-tide toy, I bethought myself at once of the vividest little note for sinister romance that I had ever jotted down.

"psychical" case: Case reported by or commented on by a member of the Society for Psy-chical Research. Men and women who claimed to have seen ghosts were investigated and reported on by trained scientists in James's time.   *periodical: Collier's Weekly.* In 1897 Robert Collier had invited James to submit a tale for its Christmas number.

Such was the private source of "The Turn of the Screw"; and I wondered, I confess, why so fine a germ, gleaming there in the wayside dust of life, had never been deftly picked up. The thing had for me the immense merit of allowing the imagination absolute freedom of hand, of inviting it to act on a perfectly clear field, with no "outside" control involved, no pattern of the usual or the true or the terrible "pleasant" (save always of course the high pleasantry of one's very form) to consort with. This makes in fact the charm of my second reference, that I find here a perfect example of an exercise of the imagination unassisted, unassociated — playing the game, making the score, in the phrase of our sporting day, off its own bat. To what degree the game was worth playing I need n't attempt to say: the exercise I have noted strikes me now, I confess, as the interesting thing, the imaginative faculty acting with the *whole* of the case on its hands. The exhibition involved is in other words a fairy-tale pure and simple — save indeed as to its springing not from an artless and measureless, but from a conscious and cultivated credulity. Yet the fairy-tale belongs mainly to either of two classes, the short and sharp and single, charged more or less with the compactness of anecdote (as to which let the familiars of our childhood, Cinderella and Blue-Beard and Hop o' my Thumb and Little Red Riding Hood and many of the gems of the Brothers Grimm directly testify), or else the long and loose, the copious, the various, the endless, where, dramatically speaking, roundness is quite sacrificed — sacrificed to fulness, sacrificed to exuberance, if one will: witness at hazard almost any one of the Arabian Nights. The charm of all these things for the distracted modern mind is in the clear field of experience, as I call it, over which we are thus led to roam; an annexed but independent world in which nothing is right save as we rightly imagine it. We have to do *that*, and we do it happily for the short spurt and in the smaller piece, achieving so perhaps beauty and lucidity; we flounder, we lose breath, on the other hand — that is we fail, not of continuity, but of an agreeable unity, of the "roundness" in which beauty and lucidity largely reside — when we go in, as they say, for great lengths and breadths. And this, oddly enough, not because "keeping it up" is n't abundantly within the compass of the imagination appealed to in certain conditions, but because the finer interest depends just on *how* it is kept up.

Nothing is so easy as improvisation, the running on and on of invention; it is sadly compromised, however, from the moment its stream breaks bounds and gets into flood. Then the waters may spread indeed, gathering houses and herds and crops and cities into their arms

and wrenching off, for our amusement, the whole face of the land —
only violating by the same stroke our sense of the course and the chan-
nel, which is our sense of the uses of a stream and the virtue of a story.
Improvisation, as in the Arabian Nights, may keep on terms with
encountered objects by sweeping them in and floating them on its
breast; but the great effect it so loses — that of keeping on terms with
itself. This is ever, I intimate, the hard thing for the fairy-tale; but by
just so much as it struck me as hard did it in "The Turn of the Screw"
affect me as irresistibly prescribed. To improvise with extreme freedom
and yet at the same time without the possibility of ravage, without the
hint of a flood; to keep the stream, in a word, on something like ideal
terms with itself: that was here my definite business. The thing was to
aim at absolute singleness, clearness, and roundness, and yet to depend
on an imagination working freely, working (call it) with extravagance;
by which law it would n't be thinkable except as free and would n't be
amusing except as controlled. The merit of the tale, as it stands, is
accordingly, I judge, that it has struggled successfully with its dangers.
It is an excursion into chaos while remaining, like Blue-Beard and Cinderella, but an anecdote — though an anecdote amplified and highly
emphasised and returning upon itself; as, for that matter, Cinderella
and Blue-Beard return. I need scarcely add after this that it is a piece of
ingenuity pure and simple, of cold artistic calculation, an *amusette*° to
catch those not easily caught (the "fun" of the capture of the merely
witless being ever but small), the jaded, the disillusioned, the fastidious.
Otherwise expressed, the study is of a conceived "tone," the tone of
suspected and felt trouble, of an inordinate and incalculable sort — the
tone of tragic, yet of exquisite, mystification. To knead the subject of
my young friend's, the supposititious° narrator's, mystification thick,
and yet strain the expression of it so clear and fine that beauty would
result: no side of the matter so revives for me as that endeavour. Indeed
if the artistic value of such an experiment be measured by the intellectual echoes it may again, long after, set in motion, the case would make
in favour of this little firm fantasy — which I seem to see draw behind it
to-day a train of associations. I ought doubtless to blush for thus confessing them so numerous that I can but pick among them for reference. I recall for instance a reproach made me by a reader° capable
evidently, for the time, of some attention, but not quite capable of

---

amusette: Idle pleasure, trivial pastime, something for fun only.   *supposititious:*
Imaginary, fictional.   *reader:* This reader was probably H. G. Wells. We do not have
the letter, but we do have James's December 9, 1898, response to it (see pp. 177–78).

enough, who complained that I had n't sufficiently "characterized" my young woman engaged in her labyrinth; had n't endowed her with signs and marks, features and humours, had n't in a word invited her to deal with her own mystery as well as with that of Peter Quint, Miss Jessel, and the hapless children. I remember well, whatever the absurdity of its now coming back to me, my reply to that criticism — under which one's artistic, one's ironic heart shook for the instant almost to breaking. "You indulge in that stricture at your ease, and I don't mind confiding to you that — strange as it may appear! — one has to choose ever so delicately among one's difficulties, attaching one's self to the greatest, bearing hard on those and intelligently neglecting the others. If one attempts to tackle them all one is certain to deal completely with none; whereas the effectual dealing with a few casts a blest golden haze under cover of which, like wanton mocking goddesses in clouds, the others find prudent to retire. It was 'déjà très-joli,'° in 'The Turn of the Screw,' please believe, the general proposition of our young woman's keeping crystalline her record of so many intense anomalies and obscurities — by which I don't of course mean her explanation of them, a different matter; and I saw no way, I feebly grant (fighting, at the best too, periodically, for every grudged inch of my space) to exhibit her in relations other than those; one of which, precisely, would have been her relation to her own nature. We have surely as much of her own nature as we can swallow in watching it reflect her anxieties and inductions. It constitutes no little of a character indeed, in such conditions, for a young person, as she says, 'privately bred,' that she is able to make her particular credible statement of such strange matters. She has 'authority,' which is a good deal to have given her, and I could n't have arrived at so much had I clumsily tried for more."

For which truth I claim part of the charm latent on occasion in the extracted reasons of beautiful things — putting for the beautiful always, in a work of art, the close, the curious, the deep. Let me place above all, however, under the protection of that presence the side by which this fiction appeals most to consideration: its choice of its way of meeting its gravest difficulty. There were difficulties not so grave: I had for instance simply to renounce all attempt to keep the kind and degree of impression I wished to produce on terms with the to-day so copious psychical record° of cases of apparitions. Different signs and circumstances, in the

---

déjà très-joli: French for "already quite pretty enough." **psychical record:** Published narratives and analyses of them by members of the Society for Psychical Research. Thousands of such reports about appearances of apparitions (ghosts) had been published in the quarter-century before James wrote *The Turn of the Screw.*

reports, mark these cases; different things are done — though on the whole very little appears to be — by the persons appearing; the point is, however, that some things are never done at all: this negative quantity is large — certain reserves and proprieties and immobilities consistently impose themselves. Recorded and attested "ghosts" are in other words as little expressive, as little dramatic, above all as little continuous and conscious and responsive, as is consistent with their taking the trouble — and an immense trouble they find it, we gather — to appear at all. Wonderful and interesting therefore at a given moment, they are inconceivable figures in an *action* — and "The Turn of the Screw" was an action, desperately, or it was nothing. I had to decide in fine between having my apparitions correct and having my story "good" — that is producing my impression of the dreadful, my designed horror. Good ghosts, speaking by book, make poor subjects, and it was clear that from the first my hovering prowling blighting presences, my pair of abnormal agents, would have to depart altogether from the rules. They would be agents in fact;° there would be laid on them the dire duty of causing the situation to reek with the air of Evil. Their desire and their ability to do so, visibly measuring meanwhile their effect, together with their observed and described success — this was exactly my central idea; so that, briefly, I cast my lot with pure romance, the appearances conforming to the true type being so little romantic.

This is to say, I recognise again, that Peter Quint and Miss Jessel are not "ghosts" at all, as we now know the ghost, but goblins, elves, imps, demons as loosely constructed as those of the old trials for witchcraft; if not, more pleasingly, fairies of the legendary order, wooing their victims forth to see them dance under the moon. Not indeed that I suggest their reducibility to any form of the pleasing pure and simple; they please at the best but through having helped me to express my subject all directly and intensely. Here it was — in the use made of them — that I felt a high degree of art really required; and here it is that, on reading the tale over, I find my precautions justified. The essence of the matter was the villainy of motive in the evoked predatory creatures; so that the result would be ignoble — by which I mean would be trivial — were this element of evil but feebly or inanely suggested. Thus arose on behalf of my idea the lively interest of a possible suggestion and process of adumbration;° the question of how best to convey that sense of the

---

agents in fact: Spirits, evil "agents" from "the other side."   *adumbration:* Indication, signification, specification.

depths of the sinister without which my fable would so woefully limp. Portentous evil — how was I to save that, as an intention on the part of my demon-spirits, from the drop, the comparative vulgarity, inevitably attending, throughout the whole range of possible brief illustration, the offered example, the imputed vice, the cited act, the limited deplorable presentable instance? To bring the bad dead back to life for a second round of badness is to warrant them as indeed prodigious, and to become hence as shy of specifications as of a waiting anti-climax. One had seen, in fiction, some grand form of wrong-doing, or better still of wrong-being, imputed, seen it promised and announced as by the hot breath of the Pit — and then, all lamentably, shrink to the compass of some particular brutality, some particular immorality, some particular infamy portrayed: with the result, alas, of the demonstration's falling sadly short. If *my* bad things, for "The Turn of the Screw," I felt, should succumb to this danger, if they should n't seem sufficiently bad, there would be nothing for me but to hang my artistic head lower than I had ever known occasion to do.

The view of that discomfort and the fear of that dishonour, it accordingly must have been, that struck the proper light for my right, though by no means easy, short cut. What, in the last analysis, had I to give the sense of? Of their being, the haunting pair, capable, as the phrase is, of everything — that is of exerting, in respect to the children, the very worst action small victims so conditioned might be conceived as subject to. What would *be* then, on reflexion, this utmost conceivability? — a question to which the answer all admirably came. There is for such a case no eligible *absolute* of the wrong; it remains relative to fifty other elements, a matter of appreciation, speculation, imagination — these things moreover quite exactly in the light of the spectator's, the critic's, the reader's experience. Only make the reader's general vision of evil intense enough, I said to myself — and that already is a charming job — and his own experience, his own imagination, his own sympathy (with the children) and horror (of their false friends) will supply him quite sufficiently with all the particulars. Make him *think* the evil, make him think it for himself, and you are released from weak specifications. This ingenuity I took pains — as indeed great pains were required — to apply; and with a success apparently beyond my liveliest hope. Droll enough at the same time, I must add, some of the evidence — even when most convincing — of this success. How can I feel my calculation to have failed, my wrought suggestion not to have worked, that is, on my being assailed, as has befallen me, with the charge of a monstrous emphasis, the charge of all indecently expatiat-ing?° There is not only from beginning to end of the matter not an inch of expatiation, but my values are positively all blanks save so far as an excited horror, a promoted pity, a created expertness — on which punctual effects of strong causes no writer can ever fail to plume him-self — proceed to read into them more or less fantastic figures. Of high interest to the author meanwhile — and by the same stroke a theme for the moralist — the artless resentful reaction of the entertained person who has abounded in the sense of the situation. He visits his abun-dance, morally, on the artist — who has but clung to an ideal of fault-lessness. Such indeed, for this latter, are some of the observations by which the prolonged strain of that clinging may be enlivened!

expatiating: Wandering on, writing or explaining at greater length than necessary.

PART TWO

The Turn of the Screw: A Case Study in Contemporary Criticism

A Critical History
of *The Turn of the Screw*

The fundamental question dealt with in the scholarship on *The Turn of the Screw* is how real the ghosts are. Are Peter Quint and Miss Jessel real in the sense that they are spirits of the dead come back to haunt the living? Or are they real only in the sense that the governess has hallucinations that make them *seem* real to her? Do they haunt the children or do they haunt only the governess's troubled imagination? Virtually every book and article on *The Turn of the Screw* — and there have been hundreds — deals at least indirectly with that question. It is almost impossible to read the story without taking sides and almost impossible to approach the story critically without knowing where one stands on it. Indeed, that question — and the fun that scholars and their students have had debating it — has elevated to star status what might otherwise have been seen as a rather ordinary James story. The two basic readings are so radically different and so apparently mutually exclusive that it is amazing that both sides have agreed on one essential fact: that *The Turn of the Screw* is a wonderfully successful story. It is an amazingly fine creepy, scary, soul-shuddering ghost story or, alternatively, it is an amazingly fine psychological case study of a neurotic young woman. The fact that the two readings seem mutually exclusive — how, after all, can a woman be both sane and insane, how can ghosts be both real and imaginary? — has not prevented a third position from emerging in recent years: that *The Turn of the Screw* is at once *both* a ghost story *and* a psychological study. Those who argue for this third or dualistic view also agree that it is an amazingly fine story — fine precisely because James has told it with such skillful ambiguity that readers can hold *both* views simultaneously.

Because of this rich disagreement about how to read it and because of the paradoxical agreement that whichever way we read it the story is brilliant, *The Turn of the Screw* is Henry James's most frequently read, taught, and discussed piece of fiction. The story compels us partly because we all want to discuss our own ways of answering its commanding question: Is this or is this not a story about ghosts? Related questions are sure to evoke spirited class discussions and interesting papers. Can we trust the governess's perceptions? Is she sane? What is the purpose of the "prologue"? Are the children innocent or corrupt? How does Mrs. Grose know from the governess's description that the ghost is that of Peter Quint? How does Miles die? Is this a story about sexual coercion or homosexuality? Is there a "best" way to read this story, or are all ways acceptable?

So fascinated have scholars been with *The Turn of the Screw*, and so insistent have they been about convincing other scholars that *their* view is right, that the published scholarship on this story has taken on a life of its own. This essay reviews that scholarship, but so much has been written on *The Turn of the Screw* that I cannot begin to report on all of it. This critical history paints the critical controversy with broad brushstrokes but with enough detail to suggest both the richness and the heat of that controversy. The full citations to the books and articles of the scholars I name appear in the list of Works Cited at the end of this essay.

ORIGINS OF THE STORY

In his notebooks for January 12, 1895, Henry James described in some detail an account he had heard two days earlier during a visit to Edward W. Benson, the Archbishop of Canterbury (quoted in full in my introduction, p. 15 in this volume). No one seriously doubts that the Archbishop's story *was* the central source for *The Turn of the Screw*. From the beginning, however, scholars have shown an eagerness to discover other literary and scientific influences that helped to shape *The Turn of the Screw*. Among the candidates for direct textual influence are these (in parentheses are the names of the critics who suggested them): a drawing entitled "The Haunted House" by T. Griffiths, showing two young people looking across a lake at a mysterious house (Robert Lee

Wolff; see p. 149 in the Cultural Documents and Illustrations section); Mrs. Gaskell's "The Old Nurse's Story" (Miriam Alcott); Goethe's "Erlkönig" (Ignace Feuerlicht); Dickens's *Oliver Twist* (Jean Frantz Blackall); an anonymous serialized novel *Temptation* (Leon Edel and Adeline R. Tintner); Charlotte Brontë's *Jane Eyre* (Alice Hall Petry); a nineteenth-century medical book describing governesses (William J. Scheick); another medical text describing "temporal lobe epilepsy" (J. Purdon Martin); plays by Ibsen (E. A. Sheppard); Fielding's *Amelia* (May L. Ryburn); German literature (Ernst Braches); various fairy tales (Lisa G. Chinitz, Mary Y. Hallab).

Other scholars have suggested influences other than literary or scientific ones. They have suggested, for example, that some of the characters in *The Turn of the Screw* may be "drawn from life": the governess from "Miss Lucy R.," a patient of Sigmund Freud's, and from Henry James's sister, Alice, who had a history of mental illness (Oscar Cargill); Miles from an orphan James had known as a child (Vincent P. Pecora's 1989 article); Quint from the playwright George Bernard Shaw, and Douglas from Edward W. Benson (E. A. Sheppard). And a number of critics have tried to show that *The Turn of the Screw* grows more generally out of social attitudes prevalent at the end of the nineteenth century. Elliot Schrero reports, for example, that a study of late Victorian attitudes toward parents, servants, governesses, and children indicates that James was very much a part of his time in demonstrating that young children who are allowed to associate too freely with servants can be corrupted and that governesses can be successful in providing the loving care and protection that a child's own mother does not provide. And Daniel R. Schwarz urges that we consider the broad cultural relationships among *The Turn of the Screw*, the paintings of Edouard Manet, and Thomas Mann's *Death in Venice*.

Although scholars have tried to connect *The Turn of the Screw* with other fictional "ghost stories" in the gothic tradition, a more persistent approach has been to connect it with "ghost cases" reported to and by practitioners of "psychical research." Henry James's brother William, the distinguished Harvard psychology professor, took active leadership in the Society for Psychical Research (established in 1882). Henry James never became a member of the society, but just seven years before he wrote *The Turn of the Screw* he attended one of its meetings, where he read one of his brother's professional papers about a spirit medium named Mrs. Piper.

Francis X. Roellinger was one of the first to write about the possible influence on *The Turn of the Screw* of the published reports and articles about people who had seen ghosts. He points out three or four of the cases that presented characters and situations similar to those in James's story, and he shows that James's Preface to the 1908 Edition of the story proves that he knew about psychical research. Ernest Tuveson sees the governess as a medium, a person who enables the spirits of the dead to manifest themselves. Martha Banta suggests that we not allow late-twentieth-century disbelief in ghosts to influence our reading of a story written when there was more widespread belief in them. E. A. Sheppard gives us a hundred-page chapter on the connection between James's story and psychical research, demonstrating parallels between the characters and events in *The Turn of the Screw* and those in the reports in the various publications of the Society for Psychical Research. David S. Miall connects *The Turn of the Screw* with one particular ghostly case history. A good discussion of the ghosts appears in an Italian book by Giovanna Mochi. For more on these matters, see also my own 1989 book, in which I review the evidence for James's knowledge of ghost cases and consider the evidence that James had knowledge of demonic possession and was influenced by that knowledge to hint that Miles and Flora are at times "possessed" by the spirits of Quint and Jessel.

All critics recognize that, despite the many influences that might have contributed to the story, *The Turn of the Screw* is very much its own thing: an amazingly original piece of fiction. And there is no question that for many critics a key feature of that originality is the character of the young woman whose first-person retrospective is *The Turn of the Screw.*

PSYCHOLOGICAL CASE STUDY

The possibility that the governess may be insane has never been far from the consciousness of readers of *The Turn of the Screw.* Although virtually all of James's contemporaries read it as a spine-chilling ghost story, as early as 1919 Henry A. Beers wrote, "I have sometimes thought . . . that the woman who saw the phantoms was mad" (44). At about that time Harold C. Goddard, a professor of English at Swarthmore, wrote an essay he never published. At his death his daughter found among his papers a manuscript, written apparently around 1920, arguing that by a close reading of the governess's language and of her notations about the reactions of others to her, sensitive readers can see that she is insane. By the time the essay was published in 1957, the view that the ghosts exist only in the mind of a deranged governess had already been popularized by others. Edna Kenton got the "mad gov erness" theory moving in 1924, when she published an article suggesting that the story is only on the surface about ghosts and children; more fundamentally it is about the "little personal mystery" of the governess, for whom the ghosts and children are merely "figures for the ebb and flow of troubled thought within her mind" (255).

The landmark study of the governess's psychological makeup came in 1934 with Edmund Wilson's influential essay "The Ambiguity of Henry James." That essay, strongly influenced by Freud's ideas, has been so important that I must quote at some length from Wilson's 1948 revised and enlarged revision of it. Wilson's theory is that "the governess who is made to tell the story is a neurotic case of sex repression, and that the ghosts are not real ghosts but hallucinations of the governess" (88). Her infatuation with the uncle in Harley Street, combined with the sexual repression that would have been natural to the sheltered daughter of a country parson, makes her transfer her feelings for the uncle onto a self-generated vision of his former valet atop the tower at Bly. Later, by the lake, as she observes Flora trying to force a play mast into a play boat, the governess imagines that she sees the ghost of the dishonored Miss Jessel. "Observe," Wilson says, "from the Freudian point of view, the significance of the governess' interest in the little girl's pieces of wood and of the fact that the male apparition first takes shape on a tower and the female apparition on a lake" (90). These objects and settings become, then, literary representations of "Freudian symbols": the tower and mast as phallus, the boat hull and the lake as vagina. The governess's repression of her natural sexual drives, in Wilson's view, forces her into a neurotic pattern of visions and interpretations that are revealed to us through the story she tells. Indeed, according to Wilson, the story of the children and the ghosts at Bly is important not for its own sake, but as a kind of soliloquy "primarily intended as a characterization of the governess" (95). Quint and Jessel exist not to endanger or tempt the children but to prove to readers that the governess is insane.

Wilson's thesis has shaped subsequent criticism on *The Turn of the Screw*. That criticism culminated in a 1965 book-length study of *The Turn of the Screw* by Thomas M. Cranfill and Robert L. Clark, Jr. Building on the work of Wilson and Goddard, Cranfill and Clark show the governess growing more and more neurotic and dangerously insane as the story progresses. Their book is a relentless analysis, word by word, scene by scene, of the narrator's madness. But many others besides these two have built on the Freudian foundations laid by Wilson. John Lydenberg sees the governess as a "hysterical, compulsive, sado-masochistic" (57) woman who deprives Miles and Flora of the love that might have let them develop into adults. Mark Spilka finds that even the Freudian critics have overlooked the evidence for precocious sexuality and infant repression in the story. The possibility of a psychoanalytic reading of the story is reinforced by Leon Edel, the most influential single interpreter of James's life and works, when he says in his biography of Henry James that the governess's "courage is a mask for a deep hysteria" and that Bly is filled "not so much with the evil of the ghosts, as the terror of the governess, her wild suppositions and soothing self-consoling explanations" (194). In Edel's reading it is not the ghosts but "the governess herself who haunts the children" (195). In an interesting variation on this reading, Elizabeth Schultz finds that the ghosts are kindly and "human" but that in misreading their characters and intentions as evil, the governess harms rather than helps the children.

A different kind of psychoanalytic reading examines *The Turn of the Screw* for what it may reveal about Henry James's own childhood. M. Katan, a practicing psychiatrist, finds in the story evidence that James had probably, at a very young age, seen his parents in a "primal scene" — that is, making love. Connected to efforts to understand James's own psychological self by reading *The Turn of the Screw* are several readings that emphasize the author's purported homosexuality. Ronald Knowles, for example, posits a homoerotic connection between Henry and his older brother William and sees that connection working itself out in the story: "he partly re-enters his effeminate early self by cross-dressing as the virginal governess" (172). C. Knight Aldrich, another practicing clinician, suggests that Mrs. Grose may be based, if only unconsciously, on James's mother, "a destructive woman" (173).

Arno Bohlmeijer thinks that a Jungian analysis of the story is more promising than a Freudian one, while Karen Halttunen encourages us to seek in the works of Henry James's brother William for clues to the possible multiple personalities and spirit mediumship of the governess.

REACTIONS AGAINST THE
PSYCHOANALYTIC READING

Almost immediately scholars began to argue against the Wilson theory. Nathan Bryllion Fagin, for example, finding it strange that Wilson focused on the influence of Freud, whom James could scarcely have read, takes *The Turn of the Screw* to be a Hawthornesque "allegory which dramatizes the conflict between Good and Evil" (200). Robert Heilman, by a different route, reads the story as a reflection of "the struggle of evil to possess the human soul" (278). For Heilman the children are symbolic representations of Adam and Eve, Bly is the Garden of Eden, Quint the devil. Similarly, Joseph J. Firebaugh finds the governess to be not sexually repressed but nonetheless dangerous to the two children, to whom she denies the knowledge that would allow them to grow and mature. Maxwell Geismar finds that denying the reality of the ghosts removes the emphasis from where it ought to be — on the servile sexual experiences of the two children. Eli Siegel rejects both Wilson and Heilman and finds Miles and Flora not to be caught in a struggle between good and evil but to be just plain evil.

Several other scholars (Glenn A. Reed, Oliver Evans, Charles G. Hoffman, Alexander E. Jones, Dorothea Krook, John J. Allen, and Charles K. Wolfe) note problems with the psychoanalytic interpretation. Why, for example, if the governess is so neurotically unreliable and insane, does she go on to become the respected and much-loved governess of other small children? Why, if we are to see her as a danger to Miles and Flora, does Douglas give such a positive report of her character in the prologue? Why, since James wrote some half dozen other stories about ghosts, must we read *this* one alone as a hallucination story? Why does the good Mrs. Grose, initially skeptical and unable to see the ghosts herself, admit by the end of the story that she believes that the spirits of Quint and Jessel have been visiting and corrupting the children? Why, if James wanted to write a psychological case study of a deranged governess, does he say in his 1908 Preface that *The Turn of the Screw* is a "fairy-tale pure and simple" (p. 181) in which he means Peter Quint and Miss Jessel to be "fairies of the legendary order, wooing their victims" (p. 184) into the moonlight? Why, if he wanted the story to focus on the governess, does James in that same Preface speak of "intelligently neglecting" the teller's "relation to her own nature," so that he could spend time on other subjects, such as making his "demon-spirits" seem "sufficiently bad" (pp. 183–85)? Why, if the ghosts are imaginary, does James in his letters to others who asked him about the story insist that he was much more interested in the ghosts and the children than in the governess who tells their story? And why, if the governess is really a pathological liar, should we believe *any*thing she says — that there is an uncle in Harley Street, that there is a place called Bly, that there are two children, that she is their governess?

One of the most telling pieces of evidence against Wilson's theory is the scene in which the governess describes Peter Quint in such detail that Mrs. Grose can positively identify him as the former valet. J. A. Waldock puts the case against Wilson this way: "How did the governess succeed in projecting on vacancy, out of her own subconscious mind, a perfectly precise, point-by-point image of a man, then dead, whom she had never seen in her life and never heard of? What psychology, normal or abnormal, will explain that? And what is the right word for such a vision but 'ghost'?" (333–34). So telling is this argument that Wilson retracted his thesis — for a time.

DEFENDING WILSON

Other scholars, distressed with Wilson's retraction, have come to Wilson's defense on this issue of the identification of Peter Quint by suggesting various "realistic" explanations for the governess's description of Quint and Mrs. Grose's identification of him. John Silver suggests that the governess had gone to town to make inquiries and had learned there about the details of Quint's appearance. John A. Clair thinks that Mrs. Grose is a liar who tries to deceive the governess about the real nature of the man she sees; the "ghost" of Peter Quint is no more than a living "prowler" whom Mrs. Grose falsely identifies as the spirit of a dead man. In a similar reading, C. Knight Aldrich believes that Mrs. Grose, quite possibly the mother of the two children by a former liaison with the "uncle" in Harley Street, is jealous of the younger, prettier governess and wants both to discredit the governess and drive her mad. She therefore identifies the man — and would have identified *any* man the governess described — as the dead former valet. (It is interesting that in this argument Aldrich was to some extent anticipated by a tongue-in-cheek article by Eric Solomon.) John Harmon McElroy questions the governess's details by asserting that the governess could scarcely have seen Quint clearly because of the hour of the day and the fact that the window would have been "blurred" by the recent rain. James B. Scott thinks that the governess's ghosts are hoaxes played on her by Miles: Miles dresses up in Quint's clothes and appears on the tower and at the window "to throw a little mystery" into the governess's life (115). Other scholars — C. B. Ives, A. W. Thompson, Sidney E. Lind, Fred L. Milne, Robert W. Hill, and Dennis Chase, for example — have risen to defend the Wilson-Goddard theory on other grounds. And Stanley Renner, in a psychoanalytic reading (pp. 271–88), tells us that the governess's fear of sexuality causes her to project onto the "man" on the tower certain sexual stereotypes embedded in the collective mind of her culture.

HAVING IT BOTH WAYS

Are the ghosts real? Is the governess mad? These two choices had long been considered mutually exclusive: if the ghosts are real, then the governess is sane; if she is mad, then the ghosts are mere figments of her imagination. One of the identifying features of contemporary criticism of *The Turn of the Screw* is that it has tended to move away from the "either-or" choices offered by earlier criticism. Instead of "X *or* Y," contemporary scholars tend to say "X *and* Y." Several earlier scholars — John J. Enck, Paul N. Siegel, and Juliet McMaster, for example — had suggested that the story permits both readings simultaneously, and in the early 1970s Dorothea Krook tried to encompass both readings by drawing a distinction between what James wrote *consciously* (a story of children haunted by evil spirits) and what he wrote *unconsciously* (a story about a young woman essentially good but whose moral nature is "compounded by the . . . sexual complications of her maiden state" [370]). The newer view, however, was not raised to prominence until the late 1970s, when several scholars brought to bear the influence of the structuralist Tzvetan Todorov and the psychoanalyst Jacques Lacan. Todorov argues that the literature of the "fantastic" requires unresolved possibilities and says specifically of *The Turn of the Screw* that it "does not permit us to determine finally whether ghosts haunt the old estate, or whether we are confronted by the hallucinations of a hysterical governess victimized by the disturbing atmosphere which surrounds her" (43).

Three studies form the foundation for the postmodern "we-can-have-it-both-ways" view. In a three-part essay entitled "The Squirm of the True," Christine Brooke-Rose dismisses most previous scholarship on the tale as limiting or just plain wrong and tries to "preserve the total ambiguity" of the story: "I shall not argue for the ghosts or for the hallucinations, but take it as accepted there is no word or incident in the story that cannot be interpreted both ways" (II, 513). In an essay published at about the same time, Shlomith Rimmon writes about the "impossibility of choice between mutually exclusive interpretations" (116) of *The Turn of the Screw* and speaks of the "double-directedness" of many of the linguistic and psychological "clues" James gives his readers. The third study proclaiming the inconclusiveness of *The Turn of the*

Screw is Shoshana Felman's long article "Turning the Screw of Interpretation." Influenced by Lacan and Jacques Derrida, Felman "decon-
structs" the story. Felman asserts that much of the governess's
unconscious is inaccessible to readers — who are inevitably frustrated
in their attempts to understand fully either the governess or her story.
Certainly they are frustrated in their efforts to find the *one* right way to
read the story. Felman says, for example, that the question is not "simply to decide whether in effect the 'Freudian' reading is true or false,
correct or incorrect. It can be both at the same time" (117). She would
have readers not try to solve the mysteries of *The Turn of the Screw* but
"to follow, rather, the significant path of its flight" (119).

In the 1980s and 1990s critics felt increasingly uncomfortable asking "either-or" questions about this story. The only "correct" answer is
likely to be "both" or "we cannot decide." Ned Lukacher suggests that
readers can never "be on the right track" when reading the story, and
John Carlos Rowe backs away from some provocative suggestions he
makes about Miles's uncle and concludes that the issue is "undecidable": "we cannot know . . . we are forever 'dupes' of the language that
employs us" (144). In a study of James's revisions to two paragraphs in
chapter IX of *The Turn of the Screw,* Norman Macleod supports the
general indeterminacy of the author's intentions: "The evidence of
punctuation and revisions reveals, not an author elucidating the particular meaning he strives for in his text, but an author intent on establishing a text that cannot be interpreted in a definite way" (134). And
Richard Dilworth Rust speaks of many of the characters and events and
settings in the story as "liminal": that is, as on the "threshold" between
one condition and another and therefore inevitably ambiguous. Vivien
Jones thinks it reductive even to try to decide whether *The Turn of the
Screw* is a ghost story or a psychological case study, since "a sophisticated reading . . . keeps both stories in play at once, without the felt
need to decide between them" (21). Willie van Peer and Ewout van der
Knaap find the Freudian reading quite compatible with the notion that
the ghosts are real because the two readings "relate to different aspects
of the work and its meaning, aspects that complement rather than
exclude each other" (707).

In a book-length study Terry Heller resolves the "are-the-ghosts-
real?" question by answering "yes, then no." Heller tells us that *The
Turn of the Screw* demands two readings. On a first reading virtually all
view it as a ghost story told by a sympathetic and reliable governess.
The mysterious death of Miles at the end, however, pulls these readers
back into a rereading of the story. The second time it is quite a different

experience. The governess is now suspect, and readers focus more and more on her questionable motives, on possible inconsistencies in her narrative, and on her own psychology. They see her in this second reading as a love-starved woman for whom the various "characters" in the novel, such as Jessel and Quint, shadow forth repressed aspects of her own clouded personality. In a somewhat similar reading, but argued from a semantic base, José A. Á. Amorós posits three "stages" in the reading of *The Turn of the Screw:* in the first stage readers trust the governess, in the second stage readers accept the possibility that the governess is unreliable, and in the third stage readers accept the "radical ambiguity" (64) of the work.

Others besides Amorós have applied the technical methods and terminology of semantic, linguistic, and syntactic theory to *The Turn of the Screw.* Helen A. Dry and Susan Kucinkas, for example, locate "the textual ambiguity of the ghosts" in James's "extensive use of presuppositional constructions" (71). T. J. Lustig has counted more than six hundred dashes (—) in the story; for him "the long dash bears a metonymic relation to the text as a whole; it certainly operates as an effective index of the extent to which the narrative becomes pitted and vesicular at times of crisis" (124). And in a book-length study of the story, Sigrid Renaux decodes the narrative by means of "the spiral of the turn of the screw" and concludes that the sign of that spiral "thus becomes an icon of the dialectic overcoming the proposition of a constantly changing interpretant" (274).

Most of those who accept the bipolarity of the novel do so in less technical language. David A. Cook and Timothy J. Corrigan, for example, find the very point of *The Turn of the Screw* to be the "tension" between the two opposing but equally legitimate readings of the story: "The subject of *The Turn of the Screw* is the nature of narrative. . . . By constantly undermining and restoring his narrator's credibility, James transforms a narrative which is potentially either a ghost story or a mystery tale about a demented governess into a very subtle fiction about the process of fiction itself" (63, 65). William R. Goetz finds in the puzzlement of the governess and her being cut off from any recourse to truth or authority a reflection of the situation of all readers of the story: "If *The Turn of the Screw* is an exemplary fiction for hermeneutic problems, this is not because it will support radically divergent, even mutually exclusive, readings, but because it obliges the reader to choose one reading and at the same time to see the inadequacy of his choice" (74). Marcia M. Eaton applies "speech-act theory" to a reading of the story and finds that James "is doing at least two things at once: he provides us with utterances (in many-tiered narrative mouths) that at the same time tell *two* tales, one about ghosts, the other about a deranged governess" (336–37). Millicent Bell believes that the governess's problem — and by implication the problem of most scholars — is that she cannot accept ambiguity: she must have the children either all good or all bad; she must have Quint and Jessel either ghosts or nonghosts. According to Bell, the truth — for the governess and for critics — must remain uncertain and indeterminate: "The prolonged debate about the reality or irreality of the ghosts in the story, the principal pivot of controversy, seems finally to have come to a halt in the acceptance of the idleness of such a question" (228).

One variation on the "we-can-have-it-both-ways" reading is that whether the ghosts are real or the governess is delusional is not important and not what *The Turn of the Screw* is about in any case. John H. Pearson, who is interested in the way the governess subverts the patriarchal authority at Bly, gives succinct expression to this view: "Whether Quint and Jessel are ghosts or delusions is ultimately irrelevant in this reading. What they signify, and that they do signify, both to the governess and in her text, are important here" (83). Pearson's interest in the governess as a woman who gradually asserts her power at Bly leads us to the next section, which takes us directly into the political and gendered overtones of the story.

MARXIST AND GENDER-BASED READINGS

As the debate about the reality of the ghosts has subsided in recent years, a different kind of debate has replaced it — a debate about Marxist and gender-based interpretations of *The Turn of the Screw*. In a stimulating review of the scholarship on *The Turn of the Screw*, Brenda Murphy (1979) writes that "practically the only critical frameworks I don't remember having seen are the Marxist framework of class struggle . . . and the feminist approach" (198). The lack was not to last long. Edwin Fussell, in an early Marxist reading, reminds us that *The Turn of the Screw* is a story not by the educated and sophisticated Henry James but by the lower-class governess. Of particular interest in Fussell's reading is his suggestion that James has this oppressed governess rise above her station by proving that she can write a novel:

> The governess fits a pattern of economic and social exploitation all too well. She is a worker; she is poor; her security of employment

is dubious; upward mobility is almost always denied her. . . .
James's governess turns the screw on her own situation and on the
people who grow sleek by her labor. . . . If a woman writes a novel
as good as a man — the same novel as a man — why indeed
should she be a governess? (128)

More squarely in the Marxist tradition is Heath Moon's assertion that
in *The Turn of the Screw* James was showing the moral decline of the
upper classes — "the fashionable leisured London 'society' preoccupied with self-gratification" (19). The uncle comes under particular
attack in Moon's reading: "The master has abandoned his property,
abdicated his responsibility over the most precious but inconvenient
embodiment of his inheritance, the burdensome guardianship over his
niece and nephew" (22). The governess does what she can to save
them, but the outcome of the story suggests to Moon that James
thought there was little hope for the upper classes.

Graham McMaster's Marxist reading makes much of the fact that
Miles and Flora are "Indian orphans" — thus placing the events in the
story squarely within what readers would have recognized as a particular social and political context. In this reading questions of imperialism,
race, class, nationalism, and mobility come to the surface. McMaster
believes, for example, that *The Turn of the Screw* "deals with a threat to
the hegemony of the landed plutocracy" (32) and that "the ghosts at
Bly represent an avenging, repressed class, taking advantage of moments of political crisis" (36). Bruce Robbins argues that the governess
is both horrified at and fascinated by the prospect of "love between the
classes" — a notion he develops further in an essay from a Marxist perspective on *The Turn of the Screw* (pp. 333–46).

One of the most interesting features of the criticism on *The Turn of
the Screw* is the way it transforms the governess into whatever it wants.
It makes her into anything from an innocent but responsible young
woman resisting the forces of evil to a sexually obsessed neurotic who
murders one of her pupils. One way of looking at the Wilson-Goddard
critics is that they make the governess the victim of a subtle antifemi-
nism that refuses to trust women to be what they say they are. One kind
of feminist approach to the story would ask whether a *male* narrator of
the story would have been so easily molded to fit into so many different
critical interpretations, and whether he would have been considered
"hysterical" in so many of them. A study having a distinctly feminist
cast is Paula Marantz Cohen's 1986 comparison of James's treatment
of the governess with Freud's treatment (written three years later) of a

neurotic young woman named Dora. Cohen finds that James, by allowing the governess to speak for herself, was much more sympathetic to
the situation and oppression of women than was Freud. Indeed, Cohen
classifies the two basic critical camps as "patriarchal" and "matriarchal":

> Those who, with Edmund Wilson, "diagnose" the governess
> simply as mad as a result of sexual repression would fall into the
> *patriarchal* camp. They read the governess as Freud reads Dora —
> as a collection of symptoms — and hence exclude her point of
> view. The *matriarchal* reading, in contrast, would posit the gov-
> erness' point of view as a salutary reversal of patriarchal interpreta-
> tion — as the rightful if violent return of the repressed in the
> assertion of the female perspective. (84)

Although Cohen is properly postmodern in her refusal to take sides ("It
no longer," she says, "seems a matter of deciding whether she has *either*
gone mad *or* has really encountered ghosts, but of accepting the possibility that *both* situations may be true" [79]), she clearly appreciates
James's appearing to have taken a more matriarchal view of the governess. The focus of Patricia N. Klingenberg's essay is not directly on
The Turn of the Screw, but she does call attention to the fact that James's
story "expels the female," if only because the governess's story is
"framed and reframed in the introduction by two different male narrators, Douglas and the story's first 'I'" (493). For an extended discussion of James's "disruption" of the feminine in this story and in several
of his longer works of fiction, see Priscilla Walton's book on the subject.

    In recent years there has been a growing interest in homoerotic
readings of *The Turn of the Screw.* The story has, from the very beginning, prompted some readers to wonder about the possibility of
pederastic sexuality between Quint and Miles (see the Myers letter on
p. 175). M. Katan, a practicing psychiatrist, sees Henry James's own
homosexuality reflected in the story. Richard Ellmann finds it notable
that "James has Miles go off for hours with Peter Quint" (7). Anthony
J. Mazzella tells us that the homoeroticism between Quint and Miles is
"attributable to the relationship between Douglas and the narrator"
(333). Michael J. H. Taylor seeks to avoid the suggestion that there
may be a "homosexual union of some kind between Douglas and the
narrator" (719) by arguing that the narrator of the frame may well be a
woman. Taylor's suggestion has been picked up and extended by others, including Beth Newman. Mary Cappello thinks that the gay painter
Charles Demuth has uncovered in his five illustrations for the story "the

possibility of homoeroticism that critics have read as everywhere subli-
mated and secret" (155). In an essay devoted mostly to a discussion of
Whitman, Michael Moon talks about the homosexual implications of
The Turn of the Screw: "Much in the tale turns on the mystery (or non-
mystery) of little Miles's having been sent down from school for shocking misconduct toward some of his schoolmates — conduct into which
he may have earlier been initiated by the literally haunting figure of
Peter Quint" (256). In an interesting twist on gendered readings of the
story, Helen Killoran thinks that the real secret of the story is that most of
the characters — the governess, the uncle, Mrs. Grose, the children —
are bisexual.

The move to queer readings of the story gained impetus from the
work of Eve Sedgwick in 1990. Although she did not discuss *The Turn
of the Screw,* others have done so. Neill Matheson, for example, suggests
that reading *The Turn of the Screw* within the context of the Oscar
Wilde trial helps us to understand the veiled hints in the story about the
children's sexuality, desires, and practices. Matheson sees certain telling
parallels between the governess's questioning of Miles about what he
did at school and the trials of Oscar Wilde. For a discussion of several
possible applications of queer theory to *The Turn of the Screw,* see Priscilla
Walton's gender perspective written for this volume (pp. 305–16).

NOSTALGIA

As we have seen, it is fashionable in these postmodern times for
scholars to reject all efforts to find "the" answer to the questions raised
by the story. The ghosts are both real and imaginary, the governess is
both sane and mad, the text both feminist and antifeminist, Quint both
gay and straight. I begin to sense, however, a nostalgia for readings
tending toward a more definite outcome, a growing annoyance with
readings that refuse to decide. Readers may be starting to question the
slippery conclusions of critics like Tobin Siebers, Darrel Mansell, Don
Anderson, and Myler Wilkinson. Reading the story through the lenses
provided by literary theorists like Tzvetan Todorov, Michel Foucault,
and Claude Lévi-Strauss, Siebers reaches this conclusion: "The reader
may choose to hesitate once more over the visitants, governess, or children; or he may choose to hesitate over hesitation" (571). In an analysis
of the way words mean, Mansell finds in *The Turn of the Screw* only "a
text describing merely itself. . . . The story begins as a mailable or send-
able letter, and ends as an unsendable one" (60). Anderson tells us that

reading James's story "is no longer possible" because "reading" suggests finding a meaning, attempting to answer the questions of the text, and such readings are sure to be "reductive, 'totalitarian,' 'terroristic'" (148). And Myler Wilkinson tells us that all is contradiction and indiscrimination: "good exists within evil, true becomes false, trust becomes fear, love doubles with hate, purity within corruption, the known within the unknowable — and James works very hard to eliminate all the markers that would help us discriminate between them" (164).

I begin to sense, as I say, a growing dissatisfaction with such readings. Dieter Freundlieb, for example, thinks that the multiplicity of interpretations of *The Turn of the Screw*, many of them advanced with little more justification than that "no one thought of this one before" and with even less in the way of proof is "an intellectual scandal" (79); he suggests that literary "interpretation should never have been turned into an academic discipline" (94). And Vincent P. Pecora tells us that "the 'question' of the narrative has now become almost completely metacritical: one can hardly see the text except through the nearly opaque screen of more than half a century of professional critical argument" (*Reflection* 176). Do readers long to read *The Turn of the Screw* as a story once again, quite ignoring the critical baggage it has acquired? Are they growing impatient with being told that *The Turn of the Screw* is ambiguous or indeterminate or undecidable or unreadable? Or do they merely yearn for the days when critics proposed definite readings and defended their readings with old-fashioned arguments and evidence drawn from a lovingly close reading of *The Turn of the Screw*?

To put the matter more specifically, are scholars beginning to insist that not all possible readings of Miles's death are equally valid, and that one of our jobs as readers is to *decide*, to argue on clear grounds and in clear language which is best? A prolific British novelist named Anthony Trollope died in 1882, just as Henry James was finding his own literary voice. Among his literary remains was his autobiography. A year later, in accordance with his father's wishes, his son published it. At the very start of the fourteenth chapter, entitled "On Criticism," Trollope wrote a nostalgic reflection: "Literary criticism has in the present day become a profession, — but it has ceased to be an art. Its object is no longer that of proving that certain literary work is good and other literary work is bad, in accordance with rules which the critic is able to define" (261). One cannot help wondering what Henry James would have thought of the professionalization of literary criticism a century and more later. He would be pleased, no doubt, to learn that virtually all critics agree that *The Turn of the Screw* is "good," but would he understand the diverse "rules" by which they have deemed it so?

THE DEATH OF MILES

In what remains of this essay I present a series of critical comments about Miles's death. I present them without comment of my own, thinking that perhaps students will want to test their own readings of the closing pages of the story against those of other readers. It is impossible, in any case, for readers *not* to pay some attention to Miles's death. Whether we see the ghosts as real or imaginary, whether we see the governess as insane or sane, whether we see the children as corrupt or innocent, whether we think the story resolves any questions, Miles's heart stops for us all — well almost all — in the last line of the story, and that stopping cries out to be explained. Explaining Miles's death has always been frustrating. Robert W. Hill puts it this way: "The narrative record ing Miles's death is designed to be as uncooperative to a clear understanding as anything in literature can be" (69). In the following paragraphs I give a chronological medley of comments about Miles's death. To be fully understood, they should be read in the context of the books and articles from which they are taken. See the Works Cited for bibliographic details for each citation.

Wilson, 1934: "She has literally frightened him to death." (94)

Fagin, 1941: "Little Miles is dead . . . exhausted by the ordeal . . . too corrupted to live without evil." (201)

Liddell, 1947: "Miles's soul is purged by confession. . . . He dies, worn out by the struggle between good and evil, in the moment of triumph." (141)

Heilman, 1948: "His face gives a 'convulsive supplication' — that is, actually a prayer, for and to Quint, the demon who has become his total deity. But the god isn't there, and Miles despairs and dies." (285)

Hoffman, 1953: "Miles's death is caused by the governess's insistence on his confession; the confession is wrested from him, but he dies from the shock. . . . Miles is saved, Peter Quint has lost. But the experience — the fright, the horror, the recognition of evil — is too much for Miles." (104–05)

Firebaugh, 1957: "Small wonder that Miles dies; he has been forced to see the only source of knowledge he has known in his brief life, Quint, as an embodiment of evil, and himself as a victim of Original Sin." (62)

Lydenberg, 1957: "Recall again the last long scene of Miles' death — or murder. She will make him confess, by whatever third-degree methods prove necessary; she will find a way to demonstrate that all actions, all explanations prove his guilt. He will not escape like Flora. She will hold him tight and keep him all for herself, even though she can possess him as she wishes only in death." (55)

Feuerlicht, 1959: "The death of a healthy child from mere mental shock seems . . . almost as unbelievable as the existence of evil ghosts. Miles's 'little heart,' as the governess says, — this, by the way, is the moving style of a loving and lovable person, not of a lunatic or a sadist — has stopped because it has been 'dispossessed' . . . exorcised." (74)

Katan, 1962: "The boy had a homosexual dependency upon Peter Quint. This power of Peter Quint's extends even after the valet's death. Yet this relation with Peter Quint protects him against the dangerous attachment to a mother figure. When the governess destroys Peter Quint's influence, she turns the clock back. The warded-off exciting oedipal relationship comes again to the fore. Out of necessity the boy has to die, for James had no other solution left. It was this dramatic ending through which James hoped to prevent the reader from having any discharge of the castration anxiety that James intended to arouse." (489)

Rubin, 1964: "What I am suggesting, of course, is . . . that Douglas *is* Miles, and that the story Douglas reads, supposedly about another little boy and the governess, is in fact about him. If this were so, then the scarcely-disguised erotic implications of the narrative are of direct importance. They would mean that . . . Miles [did] not die at all at the close." (318)

West, 1964: "The governess indulges in an exuberant debauch of violence that contributes to the sudden death of the little Miles — or she dreams that she did." (288)

Clair, 1965: "In a burst of fear and terror . . . he dies of shock." (54)

Cranfill and Clark, 1965: "The children suffer prolonged, helpless, lethally dangerous exposure to the mad governess. . . . Their exposure ends only when Flora lies delirious and Miles lies dead in the governess' arms, both victims of her endless harassment and of mortal terror." (169)

Aldrich, 1967: *"The Turn of the Screw* is . . . a tragedy about an evil older woman [Mrs. Grose] who drove an unstable younger woman completely out of her mind, and whose jealousy was the indirect cause of a little boy's death." (176–77)

Eli Siegel, 1968: "The reason Miles dies is because he can't decide. 'Extinction through indecision' would be the aesthetic coroner's statement about him. . . . Because of this indecision, Miles gets what can be called a quiet tantrum. It is a little bit like what happens when babies turn blue with indecision: frantic indecision." (135, 148)

Sheppard, 1974: "She kills Miles on the spot, with mingled excitement, fright, rage, and despair." (210)

Felman, 1977: "*The Turn of the Screw* could thus be read not only as a remarkable *ghost* story but also as a no less remarkable *detective* story: the story of the discovery of a corpse and of a singularly redoubtable crime: *the murder of a child.* . . . Ironically enough, however, not knowing what the crime really consists of, the governess-detective finally ends up *committing it herself.*" (175)

O'Gorman, 1980: "The ultimate 'Turn of the Screw' is not the death of little Miles, but rather, a few lines earlier, the governess's revealing use of the pronoun 'we.' With reference to her harrowing experience by the lake on the previous day, she speaks of 'what we had done to Flora.' And the reader shudders to learn that the Devil, still in full possession after so many years, is slyly dictating the words she writes." (256)

Hill, 1981: "It is he, Miles, whom she has been intent upon destroying all along. . . . Certainly 'his little heart, dispossessed, had stopped' — dispossessed not of Quint's influence as the governess had always supposed, but of a murderous plot against others which had recoiled upon its maker." (70)

Milne, 1981: "The governess sees Quint again at the window and desperately attempts to force Miles to enter her hallucination. When the moment is over, Quint has vanished and Miles lies dead in the governess' smothering grasp. Ironically, her attempt to escape her 'small smothered life' has smothered the life out of Miles." (298–99)

Schrero, 1981: "To deprive a person of sexuality is to deprive him of life; for, on an unconscious level, it may well seem that the loss of erotic freedom is what kills little Miles at the end of the tale." (274)

Crowe, 1982: "She is the evil force, or at least its vehicle. Miles . . . is dead, dispossessed, not of ghosts he never sees, but of the governess. For she, a bit like Hawthorne's Dr. Chillingworth, has presumed to invade the human heart; she has wanted to possess the very soul of another." (42)

Matheson, 1982: "There are many indications throughout the concluding scenes which point to Miles having been smothered by the frantic, raving governess, that his death is the result of asphyxiation rather than strain, fright, or 'dispossession.'" (173)

Scott, 1983: "Miles collapses into the governess's arms, dead of a terror-induced heart-stoppage. . . . He has finally seen what he had caused the governess to see seven times . . . and since he is exhausted from a summer's sleeplessness, the shock of that single appearance proves fatal." (128)

Krieg, 1988: "The governess's perception of evil at Bly has at last been communicated to the child, but the enormity of that perception is so great that, as the governess says, his 'little heart, dispossessed, had stopped.' The moral question, which cannot be avoided, is whether it is truly Miles's heart which is 'dispossessed,' or his mind, dispossessed of its intellectual freedom." (152)

McMaster, 1988: "Miles, the male heir to the estate, dies, either of the overprotection of the governess's regime (she stifles him against her own spinsterly breast) or of the uncle's prior neglect (which has allowed his immortal soul to be filched from him). Either way, an end to empire is foretold." (34)

Haggerty, 1989: "She seems to know that in liberating Miles from Quint she has lost him as well. She catches him and holds him for a minute before she realizes that Miles has succumbed to his own liberation. And his death leaves us ever to wander in the darkness of our own confusion." (157)

Heller, 1989: "Miles becomes angry in the end because he believes he has failed to expel Jessel; the governess possesses or is possessed by her, and he is helpless. His fear of the consequences, added to the other stresses of the situation, prove too much for his sensitive frame." (112)

Kaplan, 1992: "The insidious sexual element in the story — which combines Henry senior's fear of corruption and his role as a corrupting force, Miles's homoerotic sexual adventures, for which he

has been expelled from school, and death by shock . . . — res-
onates as an artistic rendering of homosexual panic." (414)

Pearson, 1992: "[Miles] is the last living presence with any pretensions to authority over the governess. His survival to adulthood
would defeat the governess's subversion of patriarchy. She could
not allow him to repeat the degenerate presence of Quint, nor
the irresponsible absence of his uncle. He dies into silence and
absence. . . . Like Quint, he is 'hurled over an abyss,' and like
Quint, he falls out of the text." (285)

Renaux, 1993: "The screw of torture, in eradicating evil from
Miles's soul, has also made his heart stop. . . . Thus, by means of
the governess's inquisition, . . . the boy's ill-health increases, as if
at each turn, piercing more and more inside his body and his soul
through coercion and torture, Miles would become more sick
and anxious, until his ordeal ends in death. His death suggests
that the complementarity of the concepts of good and evil cannot
be ignored; one cannot extirpate evil without concomitantly root-
ing out good, for both coexist, and duality is at the core of
things." (171)

Chinitz, 1994: "But Miles dies from overexposure. Unlike Hansel,
he survives neither the penetrating chill of the forest nor the sear
ing flames of the witch's passion. He dies because the governess
cannot quench the consequences of her own urgent desire to possess the ghosts of Bly." (279)

Mitchell, 1994: "Although the governess refers several times to
the children as angels, the concluding paragraph describes the
death of Miles in a way which seems to echo Biblical descriptions
of Lucifer's more spectacular plummet from grace, while his
expulsion from school repeats the original expulsion from the
Garden of Eden." (113)

Houston, 1996: "Only one possibility for the sudden death of
Miles can be elucidated from the governess's revelation, assuming
of course, that the governess is not hallucinating about the death
of her ward. . . . [S]he has constrained him through her unsup-
pressed violence and produced what is medically known as a
'Valsalva effect,' here, perhaps, the sudden sharp and continuous
increase of pressure on the thoracic cavity to cause the dead-stop
of Miles's heart. The governess more than 'contributes' to Miles'
death — she is the absolute cause of death, and knowingly or
unknowingly, willingly or unwillingly, she is the murderess of
Miles." (75)

Mahbobah, 1996: "The abuse and eventual murder of Miles is the inevitable outcome. . . . This embrace, however, is fatal, and Miles is dead. The ghost of the Master finally disappears as well, since the governess's indictment of and revenge against the Master, finally takes shape. As he seduced and stifled her at the beginning, so does she seduce and smother his two representatives in a fatal love embrace at the ending. The reversal is perfect in its symmetry." (158, 160)

Smith, 1998: "Miles is actually killed by the stress of articulating the name of 'Peter Quint.' . . . To name Quint, in the context of the governess's intervention . . . is to strip away the child's defenses (his 'innocence') in naming as disgusting or evil the activities he has been shaped by. This is what kills him. . . . That it should be Miles who dies . . . suggests that the focus here is mostly on homosexual attraction." (151-53)

Wagenknecht, 1998: "*The Turn of the Screw* . . . allegorizes a homophobic collapse and . . . sees its outcome as death." (445)

Kane, 1999: "The ominous ghost of Peter Quint is so essential a part of Miles's life that when the child's heart is 'dispossessed,' that heart must stop. The governess cannot preserve the children's angelic innocence because such innocence can never exist in this imperfect world; such innocence can only be imaginary. The ghosts, unfortunately, are all too real." (46)

Lundén, 2000: "All the governess wants is an honest answer as to whether [Douglas's] feelings are reciprocated. She realizes, however, from his cowardly behavior that he will never dare affirm and express his feelings for her. And so, she must kill their love to be able to go on. And therefore, as a writer, she symbolically takes Douglas/Miles' life at the end of the story she wrote about Bly, the love letter she later sends to Douglas." (43)

Haralson, 2002: "The governess — or rather, the regulatory apparatus that lays to rest the ghost of homosexuality — only finishes the job, eliminating in the process a prospective bearer of civilization. 'If he *were* innocent,' the governess ponders, just moments before the circumstances of Miles's death appear to prove otherwise, 'what then on earth was *I*?' [p. 119] This is a timely and potentially productive doubt, for what if Miles's nominal crime — incipient same-sex desire — were grasped as purely a cultural fabrication, rather than a theological 'evil' or a pathological 'deviance'? How on earth would one then judge 'his executioner'?" (146–47)

How are we to account for such enormous variety in the ways of reading Miles's death? Is it that James failed to tell his story well, leaving readers all at sea about the ending? Is it that, for James, Miles's death was not nearly as important as other aspects of the story? Is it that readers have refused to take James at his word when he said that his tale was "pure romance" (p. 184), and have been trying ever since to read it as if it were pure realism? Is it that scholars fancy themselves as participants in the creative process and see it as their job to fill in the narrative blanks that James left in the story? That there is some little truth to this last possibility is suggested in the next section, where we look at several modern efforts to write the deaths not only of Miles, but of Quint and Jessel, as well.

DEATH BY FICTION

Henry James wrote the first fictional account of the death of Miles, an event that, as we saw in the previous section, has challenged readers ever since to ask whether he died, how he died, why he died, who was responsible for the fact that he died, and what his death means. In answering these questions scholars have often crossed that fine line between criticism and fiction by reconstructing the story line to make what seems to them better sense of it. In doing so they try to explain what Henry James left unexplained. It should be no surprise that fiction writers in the late twentieth century have tried to rework the materials that James left vague, to make explicit the deaths that he left inexplicit. How did Miss Jessel and Peter Quint and Miles die? James gives hints but no answers. Some answers have come through scholars, but they also come from makers of music and drama and film and fiction.

In 1954 the first of many productions of Benjamin Britten's operetta *The Turn of the Screw* was staged. Based very much on James's story, it nevertheless makes some changes. In it, for example, Peter Quint speaks — that is, sings. In the last scene, Miles runs into the governess's arms, and the disappointed Quint says, "Ah, Miles, we have failed." The governess retorts, "Ah Miles, you are saved, now all will be well. Together we have destroyed him." When she realizes that Miles is dead, her final question is the enigmatic, "What have we done between us?" (taken from Myfanwy Piper's libretto, as excerpted on page 62 of Patricia Howard's book-length analysis of the operetta).

A movie named *The Nightcomers* appeared in 1972. As an imaginative prequel to *The Turn of the Screw*, it ends where James's story begins, with the uncle hiring a new governess to go to Bly to take care of a boy named Miles and a girl named Flora. Mrs. Grose is there to greet the new governess and introduce them to her two pupils. The story line itself, almost entirely made up, is the story of the tragic love affair between Miss Jessel, the former governess, and Peter Quint, the gardener, played by Marlon Brando. In *The Nightcomers* we do not find out how Miles dies — he is, of course, still alive at the end of the movie — but we do find out how Jessel and Quint die: Flora drowns Miss Jessel in the lake and Miles shoots an arrow into Peter Quint's head. Other film versions have appeared, and I have no doubt that still others will be coming. The most recent that I am aware of is *The Others* (2001), starring Nicole Kidman, in which the young woman and the two children, it turns out, are themselves ghosts. *The Others,* of course, is based only very loosely on James's *The Turn of the Screw.* It takes place on an island off the coast of England at the end of World War II, and Kidman plays the mother of two small children, not their governess. Still, its indebtedness to James's story is obvious enough and at the same time suggests the creativity with which postmodern readers — and writers — reconstruct the events at Bly.

In the 1990s two fiction writers working with the story line that James provided reconstructed it in creative ways. The only part I will focus on here is what they did with the death of Miles. In 1994 Joyce Carol Oates published a thirty-page short story she called "Accursed Inhabitants of the House of Bly." It was a retelling of some of the events in James's century-old *The Turn of the Screw,* mostly from the point of view of the dead Miss Jessel and the dead Peter Quint. Oates radically alters the ending in such a way that Miles does not die after all, but escapes. In this scene the governess points an accusing figure out the window to direct Miles's gaze:

> "There! — as you've known all along, you wicked, wicked boy!"
> Yet, it seems, Miles, though staring straight at Quint, cannot see him. "What?" he cries. " 'Peter Quint' — where?"
> "There, I say — *there!*" In a fury, the governess taps against the glass, as if to break it. Quint shrinks away.
> Miles gives an anguished cry. His face has gone dead-white, he appears on the verge of a collapse, yet, when [the governess] tries to secure him in her arms, he shoves her away. "Don't touch me, leave me alone!" he shouts. "*I hate you.*" . . .
> Into the balmy-humid night the child Miles runs, runs for his life, damp hair sticking to his forehead, and his heart, that slithery

fish, thumping against his ribs. Though guessing it is futile, for the madwoman was pointing at nothing, Miles cries, in a hopeful, dreading voice, "Quint? — *Quint?*" (282)

The events at Bly take quite a different shape in Hilary Bailey's 1997 *Miles and Flora,* a 281-page novel. (For brief discussion of this novel, see pages 380–82 in the book by Adeline R. Tintner; see also the article by Beth A. Boehm.) The novel has an unlikely plot that focuses on Flora, still alive in 1913, who is about to get married. Her former governess is still alive but has tuberculosis. Near death, she reconnects with Mrs. Grose. Miles's death is reported by the uncle who, in a moment of remorse, tells his friend Henry (who is apparently modeled in some ways on Henry James) what little he knows about it. Bailey plays fast and loose with the facts of *The Turn of the Screw*. She re-spells "Jessel" as "Jessell" and makes the unnamed bachelor uncle in her novel a recent widower named Geoffrey Bennett. Geoffrey gives this vague account of the strange events at Bly:

> "It begins fourteen years ago, when my brother and his wife died suddenly in India. At that time I was suffering bitterly from the loss of my first wife. Then came this second blow. I found myself in a black cloud, from which I could not escape. I was left in charge of my nephew and niece, a boy of nine, Miles, and a girl of seven, Flora, without any mental resources to deal with them. None. I decided, therefore, to put them with the reliable house-keeper at Bly and appoint a governess. The boy, in any case, was coming up to the age when he would go away to school. I appointed a young woman, with excellent references, to act as governess. All, I supposed, was well. Then the governess, Miss Jessell, left with little warning. The reasons for her going were obscure, the housekeeper could tell me nothing. And by now I was about to be married to Beth. Without any further thought, I appointed another governess, at the point when the boy was going off to school. I do not know what happened. At one moment all seemed well, then Miles was dismissed from school. Then," he said, "Then — alas — he killed himself. A boy of ten — to kill himself . . . "(72–73)

And we readers never know much more than that about Miles's suicide. Did he drown himself? Shoot himself? Cut his wrists? Fling himself off the tower? We never do find out, nor do we find out why he killed himself.

Fiction, criticism, and now fiction once again continue to struggle with what *really* happened — or ought to have happened, or might have happened — at Bly.

What is the governess *really* like? Are the ghosts *really* real? Is Flora *really* corrupt? How does Miles *really* die? It is evident that there are almost as many readings of *The Turn of the Screw* as there are readers. In 1979 Wayne Booth referred to "the appalling chaos of critical opinions" on the story. In 1985 Vincent Pecora found so many published opinions about the story that he spoke of "the disappearance of the sense that anything about *The Turn of the Screw* matters at all. . . . [I]t has become a 'game'" (28). In her "combined approaches" essay written for this second edition (pp. 349–62), Sheila Teahan begins by remarking on "the sheer volume of scholarly commentary" on James's story. How are we to react to the fact that scholars have written thousands of pages interpreting this one little story of less than one hundred pages? Do we praise critics for their marvelous ingenuity? Do we blame readers for not reading more carefully? Do we praise James for the wonderful and all-encompassing ambiguity of his story? Do we blame James for this chaos, wishing that he had made his meaning clearer? Or do we dispense with all praise and blame and take on the stance of one kind of reader-response scholar and say that virtually any reading is legitimized by the very fact that some reader, somewhere, has offered it?

In the essays that follow we have five different ways of reading *The Turn of the Screw* — and its ending. In view of the multiplicity of readings possible, it makes most sense to begin with an account of what reader-response criticism is all about and with a reader-response interpretation written by Wayne Booth for this volume.

WORKS CITED

Alcott, Miriam. "Mrs. Gaskell's 'The Old Nurse's Story': A Link between *Wuthering Heights* and *The Turn of the Screw*." *Notes and Queries* 8 (1961): 101–02.

Aldrich, C. Knight, M.D. "Another Twist to *The Turn of the Screw*." *Modern Fiction Studies* 13 (1967): 167–78.

Allen, John J. "The Governess and the Ghosts in *The Turn of the Screw*." *Henry James Review* 1 (1979): 73–80.

Amorós, José Antonio Álvarez. "Possible-World Semantics, Frame Text, Insert Text, and Unreliable Narration: The Case of *The Turn of the Screw*." *Style* 25 (1991): 42–70.

Anderson, Don. " 'A Fury of Intention': The Scandal of Henry
    James's *The Turn of the Screw.*" *Sydney Studies in English* 15
    (1989–90): 140–52.

Bailey, Hilary. *Miles and Flora: A Sequel to Henry James's "The Turn of
    the Screw."* London: Touchstone Books, 1997.

Banta, Martha. "The Berkelian Ghosts at Bly." *Henry James and the
    Occult.* Bloomington: Indiana UP, 1972. 114–29.

Beers, Henry A. *Four Americans.* New Haven: Yale UP, 1919.

Beidler, Peter G. *Ghosts, Demons, and Henry James: "The Turn of the
    Screw" at the Turn of the Century.* Columbia: U of Missouri P,
    1989.

Bell, Millicent. *"The Turn of the Screw."* In *Meaning in Henry James.*
    Cambridge: Harvard UP, 1991. 223–44.

Blackall, Jean Frantz. "Cruikshank's *Oliver* and *The Turn of the
    Screw.*" *American Literature* 51 (1979): 161–78.

Boehm, Beth A. "A Postmodern Turn of *The Turn of the Screw.*"
    Henry James Review 19 (1998): 245–54

Bohlmeijer, Arno. "Henry James and *The Turn of the Screw.*"
    Encounter 69 (1987): 41–50.

Booth, Wayne C. *Critical Understanding: The Powers and Limits of
    Pluralism.* Chicago: U of Chicago P, 1979. 284–301.

Braches, Ernst. *Engel en afrond over "The Turn of the Screw" van
    Henry James.* Amsterdam: Meulenhoff, 1983.

Britten, Benjamin, *The Turn of the Screw* (operetta). Libretto by
    Myfanwy Piper. 1954. Film version, dir. Petr Weigl. Perf. Helen
    Donath as the governess. Unitel, 1982.

Brooke-Rose, Christine. "The Squirm of the True: I, An Essay in
    Non-Methodology; II, A Structural Analysis of Henry James's *The
    Turn of the Screw;* III, Surface Structure in Narrative." *PTL: A
    Journal for Descriptive Poetics and Theory of Literature* 1 (1976):
    265–94 [Part I]; 1 (1976): 513–46 [Part II]; 2 (1977): 517–62
    [Part III].

Cappello, Mary. "Governing the Master('s) Plot: Frames of Desire in
    Demuth and James." *Word and Image* 8 (1992): 154–70.

Cargill, Oscar. "*The Turn of the Screw* and Alice James." *PMLA* 78
    (1963): 238–49.

Chase, Dennis. "The Ambiguity of Innocence: *The Turn of the Screw.*"
    Extrapolation 27 (1986): 197–202.

Chinitz, Lisa G. "Fairy Tale Turned Ghost Story: James's *The Turn of
    the Screw.*" *Henry James Review* 15 (1994): 264–85.

Clair, John A. *"The Turn of the Screw."* In *The Ironic Dimension in the Fiction of Henry James*. Pittsburgh: Duquesne UP, 1965. 37–58.

Cohen, Paula Marantz. "Freud's *Dora* and James's *Turn of the Screw:* Two Treatments of the Female 'Case.'" *Criticism* 28 (1986): 73–87.

Cook, David A., and Timothy J. Corrigan. "Narrative Structure in *The Turn of the Screw:* A New Approach to Meaning." *Studies in Short Fiction* 17 (1980): 55–65.

Cranfill, Thomas Mabry, and Robert Lanier Clark, Jr. *An Anatomy of "The Turn of the Screw."* Austin: U of Texas P, 1965.

Crowe, M. Karen. "The Tapestry of Henry James's *The Turn of the Screw.*" *Nassau Review* 4 (1982): 37–48.

Dry, Helen Aristar, and Susan Kucinkas. "Ghostly Ambiguity: Presuppositional Constructions in *The Turn of the Screw.*" *Style* 25 (1991): 71–88.

Eaton, Marcia M. "James's Turn of the Speech-Act." *British Journal of Aesthetics* 23 (1983): 333–45.

Edel, Leon. "The Little Boys." In *Henry James: The Treacherous Years, 1895–1901*. London: Hart-Davis, 1969. 191–203.

———, and Adeline R. Tintner. "The Private Life of Peter Quin[t]; Origins of *The Turn of the Screw.*" *Henry James Review* 7 (1985): 2–5.

Ellmann, Richard. "A Late Victorian Love Affair." *New York Review of Books,* August 4, 1977: 6–7.

Enck, John J. "*The Turn of the Screw* and the Turn of the Century." In the Norton Critical Edition of Henry James's *The Turn of the Screw,* ed. Robert Kimbrough. New York: Norton, 1966. 259–69.

Evans, Oliver. "James's Air of Evil: *The Turn of the Screw.*" *Partisan Review* 16 (1949): 175–87.

Fagin, Nathan Bryllion. "Another Reading of *The Turn of the Screw.*" *Modern Language Notes* 56 (1941): 196–202.

Felman, Shoshana. "Turning the Screw of Interpretation." *Yale French Studies* 55/56 (1977): 94–207. Rpt. in *Writing and Madness: Literature/Philosophy/Psychoanalysis*. Ithaca: Cornell UP, 1985. 141–247.

Feuerlicht, Ignace. "'Erlkönig' and *The Turn of the Screw.*" *Journal of English and German Philology* 58 (1959): 68–74.

Firebaugh, Joseph J. "Inadequacy in Eden: Knowledge and *The Turn of the Screw.*" *Modern Fiction Studies* 3 (1957): 57–63.

Freundlieb, Dieter. "Explaining Interpretation: The Case of

Henry James's *The Turn of the Screw.*" *Poetics Today* 5 (1984): 79–95.

Fussell, Edwin. "The Ontology of *The Turn of the Screw.*" *Journal of Modern Literature* 8 (1980): 118–28.

Geismar, Maxwell. *Henry James and the Jacobites.* Boston: Houghton Mifflin, 1963.

Goddard, Harold C. "A Pre-Freudian Reading of *The Turn of the Screw.*" Prefatory note by Leon Edel. *Nineteenth-Century Fiction* 12 (1957): 1–36.

Goetz, William R. "The 'Frame' of *The Turn of the Screw:* Framing the Reader In." *Studies in Short Fiction* 18 (1981): 71–74.

Haggerty, George E. *Gothic Fiction/Gothic Form.* University Park: Pennsylvania State UP, 1989.

Hallab, Mary Y. "The Governess and the Demon Lover: The Return of a Fairy Tale." *Henry James Review* 8 (1987): 104–15.

Halttunen, Karen. "'Through the Cracked and Fragmented Self': William James and *The Turn of the Screw.*" *American Quarterly* 40 (1988): 472–90.

Haralson, Eric. "'His little heart, dispossessed': Ritual Sexorcism in *The Turn of the Screw.*" In *Questioning the Master: Gender and Sexuality in Henry James's Writings,* ed. Peggy McCormack. Newark, DE: U of Delaware P, 2002.

Heilman, Robert. "*The Turn of the Screw* as Poem." *U of Kansas City Review* 14 (1948): 277–89.

Heller, Terry. "*The Turn of the Screw*": *Bewildered Vision.* Boston: Twayne, 1989.

Hill, Robert W., Jr. "A Counterclockwise Turn in James's *The Turn of the Screw.*" *Twentieth-Century Literature* 27 (1981): 53–71.

Hoffman, Charles G. "Innocence and Evil in James's *The Turn of the Screw.*" *U of Kansas City Review* 20 (1953): 97–105.

Houston, Neal B. "A Footnote to the Death of Miles in James's *The Turn of the Screw.*" *RE:AL: The Journal of Liberal Arts* 21 (1996): 74–76.

Howard, Patricia, ed. *Benjamin Britten: "The Turn of the Screw."* Cambridge: Cambridge UP, 1985.

Ives, C. B. "James's Ghosts in *The Turn of the Screw.*" *Nineteenth-Century Fiction* 18 (1963): 183–89.

Jones, Alexander E. "Point of View in *The Turn of the Screw.*" *PMLA* 74 (1959): 112–22.

Jones, Vivien. "Henry James's *The Turn of the Screw.*" In *Benjamin*

Britten: "The Turn of the Screw," ed. Patricia Howard. Cambridge: Cambridge UP, 1985. 1–22.

Kane, Carolyn. "The Strange Case of *The Turn of the Screw.*" *Publications of the Missouri Philological Association* 24 (1999): 40–47.

Kaplan, Fred. *Henry James: The Imagination of Genius.* New York: Morrow, 1992.

Katan, M., M.D. "A Causerie on Henry James's *The Turn of the Screw.*" *The Psychoanalytic Study of the Child* 17 (1962): 473–93.

Kenton, Edna. "Henry James to the Ruminant Reader: *The Turn of the Screw.*" *The Arts* 4 (1924): 245–55.

Killoran, Helen. "The Governess, Mrs. Grose, and 'the Poison of an Influence' in *The Turn of the Screw.*" *Modern Language Studies* 23 (1993): 13–24.

Kimbrough, Robert, ed. *"The Turn of the Screw": An Authoritative Text, Backgrounds, and Sources.* New York: Norton, 1966.

Klingenberg, Patricia N. "The Feminine 'I': Silvina Ocampo's Fantasies of the Subject." *Romance Language Annual* 6 (1989): 488–94.

Knowles, Ronald. " 'The hideous obscure': *The Turn of the Screw* and Oscar Wilde." In *"The Turn of the Screw" and "What Maisie Knew,"* ed. Neil Cornwell and Maggie Malone. New York: St. Martin's, 1998. 164–78.

Krieg, Joann P. "A Question of Values: Culture and Cognition in *The Turn of the Screw.*" *Language and Communication* 8 (1988): 147–54.

Krook, Dorothea. "Intentions and Intentions: The Problem of Intention and Henry James's *The Turn of the Screw*" in *The Theory of the Novel: New Essays,* ed. John Halperin. New York: Oxford UP, 1974. 353–72.

Liddell, Robert. "The 'Hallucination' Theory of *The Turn of the Screw.*" In *A Treatise on the Novel.* London: Jonathan Cape, 1947. 138–45.

Lind, Sidney E. *"The Turn of the Screw:* The Torment of Critics." *Centennial Review* 14 (1970): 225–40.

Lukacher, Ned. " 'Hanging Fire': The Primal Scene of *The Turn of the Screw.*" In *Primal Scenes: Literature, Philosophy, Psychoanalysis.* Ithaca: Cornell UP, 1986. 115–32.

Lundén, Rolf. " 'Not in any literal, vulgar way': The Encoded Love Story of Henry James's *The Turn of the Screw.*" *American Studies in Scandinavia* 31 (2000): 30–44.

Lustig, T. J. *Henry James and the Ghostly.* Cambridge: Cambridge UP, 1994.

Lydenberg, John. "The Governess Turns the Screws." *Nineteenth-Century Fiction* 12 (1957): 37–58.

Macleod, Norman. "Stylistics and the Ghost Story: Punctuation, Revisions, and Meaning in *The Turn of the Screw*." In *Edinburgh Studies in the English Language*, ed. John M. Anderson and Norman Macleod. Edinburgh: John Donald, 1988. 133–55.

Mahbobah, Albaraq. "Hysteria, Rhetoric, and the Politics of Reversal in Henry James's *The Turn of the Screw*." *Henry James Review* 17 (1996): 149–61.

Mansell, Darrell. "The Ghost of Language in *The Turn of the Screw*." *Modern Language Quarterly* 46 (1985): 48–63.

Martin, J. Purdon. "Neurology in Fiction: *The Turn of the Screw*." *British Medical Journal* 4 (1973): 717–21.

Matheson, Neill. "Talking Horrors: James, Euphemism, and the Specter of Wilde." *American Literature* 71 (1999): 709–50.

Matheson, Terence J. "Did the Governess Smother Miles?: A Note on James's *The Turn of the Screw*." *Studies in Short Fiction* 19 (1982): 172–75.

Mazzella, Anthony J. "An Answer to the Mystery of *The Turn of the Screw*." *Studies in Short Fiction* 17 (1980): 327–33.

McElroy, John Harmon. "The Mysteries at Bly." *Arizona Quarterly* 37 (1981): 214–36.

McMaster, Graham. "Henry James and India: A Historical Reading of *The Turn of the Screw*." *Clio* 18 (1988): 23–40.

McMaster, Juliet. "'The Full Image of a Repetition' in *The Turn of the Screw*." *Studies in Short Fiction* 6 (1969): 377–82.

Miall, David S. "Designed Horror: James's Vision of Evil in *The Turn of the Screw*." *Nineteenth-Century Fiction* 39 (1984): 305–27.

Milne, Fred L. "Atmosphere as Triggering Device in *The Turn of the Screw*." *Studies in Short Fiction* 18 (1981): 293–99.

Mitchell, Domhnall. "Narrative Failure and the Fall in Henry James's *The Turn of the Screw*." *American Studies in Scandinavia* 26 (1994): 113–25.

Mochi, Giovanna. *Le "cose cattive" di Henry James*. Parma: Pratiche Editrice Cooperativa, 1982.

Moon, Heath. "More Royalist Than the King: The Governess, the Telegraphist, and Mrs. Gracedew." *Criticism* 24 (1982): 16–35.

Moon, Michael. "Disseminating Whitman." *South Atlantic Quarterly* 88 (1989): 247–65.

Murphy, Brenda. "The Problem of Validity in the Critical Controversy over *The Turn of the Screw*." *Research Studies* 47 (1979): 191–201.

Newman, Beth. "Getting Fixed: Feminine Identity and the Scopic Crisis in *The Turn of the Screw*." *Novel* 26 (1992): 43–63.

The Nightcomers. Dir. Michael Winner. Perf. Marlon Brando as Peter Quint. Avco Embassy, 1972.

Oates, Joyce Carol. "Accursed Inhabitants of the House of Bly." In *Haunted: Tales of the Grotesque.* New York: Dutton, 1994. 254–83.

O'Gorman, Donal. "Henry James's Reading of *The Turn of the Screw*: Parts II and III." *Henry James Review* 1 (1980): 228–56.

The Others. Dir. Alejandro Amenábar. Perf. Nicole Kidman. Dimension Films, 2001.

Pearson, John H. "Repetition and Subversion in Henry James's *The Turn of the Screw*." *Henry James Review* 13 (1992): 276–91.

Pecora, Vincent P. "Of Games and Governesses." *Perspectives on Contemporary Literature* 11 (1985): 28–36.

———. "Reflection Rendered: James's *The Turn of the Screw*." In *Self and Form in Modern Narrative.* Baltimore: Johns Hopkins UP, 1989. 176–213.

Petry, Alice Hall. "Jamesian Parody, *Jane Eyre,* and *The Turn of the Screw*." *Modern Language Studies* 4 (1983): 61–78.

Reed, Glenn A. "Another Turn on James's *The Turn of the Screw*." *American Literature* 20 (1949): 413–23.

Renaux, Sigrid. *"The Turn of the Screw": A Semiotic Reading.* New York: Peter Lang, 1993.

Rimmon, Shlomith. *"The Turn of the Screw*." In *The Concept of Ambiguity — the Example of James.* Chicago: U of Chicago P, 1977. 116–66.

Robbins, Bruce. "Shooting Off James's Blanks: Theory, Politics, and *The Turn of the Screw*." *Henry James Review* 5 (1984): 192–99.

Roellinger, Francis X. "Psychical Research and *The Turn of the Screw*." *American Literature* 20 (1949): 401–12.

Rowe, John Carlos. "Psychoanalytical Significances: The Use and Abuse of Uncertainty in *The Turn of the Screw*." In *The Theoretical Dimensions of Henry James.* Madison: U of Wisconsin P. 1984. 120–46.

Rubin, Louis D., Jr. "One More Turn of the Screw." *Modern Fiction Studies* 9 (1964): 314–28.

Rust, Richard Dilworth. "Liminality in *The Turn of the Screw*." *Studies in Short Fiction* 25 (1988): 441–46.

Ryburn, May L. "*The Turn of the Screw* and *Amelia*: A Source for Quint?" *Studies in Short Fiction* 16 (1979): 235–37.

Scheick, William J. "A Medical Source for *The Turn of the Screw*." *Studies in American Fiction* 19 (1991): 217–20.

Schrero, Elliot M. "Exposure in *The Turn of the Screw*." *Modern Philosophy* 78 (1981): 261–74.

Schultz, Elizabeth. "'The Pity and the Sanctity and the Terror': The Humanity of the Ghosts in *The Turn of the Screw*." *Markham Review* 9 (1980): 67–71.

Schwarz, Daniel R. "Manet, James's *The Turn of the Screw*, and the Voyeuristic Imagination." *Henry James Review* 18 (1997): 1–21.

Scott, James B. "How the Screw Is Turned: James's *Amusette*." *U of Mississippi Studies in English* 4 (1983): 112–31.

Sedgwick, Eve Kosofsky. *Epistemology of the Closet*. Berkeley: U of California P, 1990.

Sheppard, E[lizabeth]. A. *Henry James and "The Turn of the Screw*." Auckland: Auckland UP, 1974.

Siebers, Tobin. "Hesitation, History, and Reading: Henry James's *The Turn of the Screw*." *Texas Studies in Literature and Language* 25 (1983): 558–72.

Siegel, Eli. *James and the Children: A Consideration of Henry James's "The Turn of the Screw*." New York: Definition P, 1968.

Siegel, Paul N. "'Miss Jessel': Mirror Image of the Governess." *Literature and Psychology* 18 (1968): 30–38.

Silver, John. "A Note on the Freudian Reading of *The Turn of the Screw*." *American Literature* 29 (1957): 207–11.

Smith, Allan Lloyd. "A Word Kept Back in *The Turn of the Screw*." *Victorian Literature and Culture* 24 (1998): 139–58.

Solomon, Eric. "The Return of the Screw." In the *Norton Critical Edition of "The Turn of the Screw*," ed. Robert Kimbrough. New York: Norton, 1966. 237–45.

Spilka, Mark. "Turning the Freudian Screw: How Not to Do It." *Literature and Psychology* 13 (1963): 105–11.

Taylor, Michael J. H. "A Note on the First Narrator of *The Turn of the Screw*." *American Literature* 4 (1982): 717–22.

Thompson, A. W. "*The Turn of the Screw*: Some Points on the Hallucination Theory." *Review of English Literature* 6 (1965): 26–36.

Tintner, Adeline R. *Henry James's Legacy: The Afterlife of His Figure and Fiction*. Baton Rouge: Louisiana State UP, 1998.

Todorov, Tzvetan. *Introduction à la littérature fantastique*. Paris: Éditions du Seuil, 1970. Trans. Richard Howard as *The Fantastic: A Structural Approach to a Literary Genre*. Ithaca: Cornell UP, 1977.

Trollope, Anthony. *An Autobiography.* 1883. Ed. Michael Sadleir and Frederick Page. Oxford: Oxford UP, 1980.

Tuveson, Ernest. "*The Turn of the Screw:* A Palimpsest." *Studies in English Literature* 12 (1972): 783–800.

van Peer, Willie, and Ewout van der Knaap. "(In)compatible Interpretations?: Contested Readings of *The Turn of the Screw.*" *Modern Language Notes* 110 (1995): 692–710.

Wagenknecht, David. "Here's Looking at You, Peter Quint: *The Turn of the Screw,* Freud's *Dora,* and the Aesthetics of Hysteria." *American Imago* 55 (1998): 423–58.

Waldock, J. A. "Mr. Edmund Wilson and *The Turn of the Screw.*" *Modern Language Notes* 62 (1947): 331–34.

Walton, Priscilla L. *The Disruption of the Feminine in Henry James.* Toronto: U of Toronto P, 1992.

West, Muriel. "The Death of Miles in *The Turn of the Screw.*" *PMLA* 89 (1964): 283–88.

Wilkinson, Myler. "Henry James and the Ethical Moment." *Henry James Review* 11 (1990): 153–75.

Willen, Gerald, ed. *A Casebook on Henry James's "The Turn of the Screw."* 2nd ed. New York: Crowell, 1969.

Wilson, Edmund. "The Ambiguity of Henry James." *Hound and Horn* 7 (1934): 385–406. All quotations from *The Triple Thinkers,* rev. and enl. ed. New York: Oxford UP, 1948. 88–132.

Wolfe, Charles K. "Victorian Ghost Story Technique: The Case of Henry James." *Romantist* 3 (1979): 67–72.

Wolff, Robert Lee. "The Genesis of *The Turn of the Screw.*" *American Literature* 13 (1941): 1–8.

Reader-Response Criticism
and *The Turn of the Screw*

WHAT IS READER-RESPONSE CRITICISM?

Students are routinely asked in English courses for their reactions to texts they are reading. Sometimes there are so many different reactions that we may wonder whether everyone has read the same text. And some students respond so idiosyncratically to what they read that we say their responses are "totally off the wall." This variety of response interests reader-response critics, who raise theoretical questions about whether our responses to a work are the same as its meanings, whether a work can have as many meanings as we have responses to it, and whether some responses are more valid than others. They ask what determines what is and what isn't "off the wall." What, in other words, is the wall, and what standards help us to define it?

In addition to posing provocative questions, reader-response criticism provides us with models that aid our understanding of texts and the reading process. Adena Rosmarin has suggested that a literary text may be likened to an incomplete work of sculpture: to see it fully, we must complete it imaginatively, taking care to do so in a way that responsibly takes into account what exists. Other reader-response critics have suggested other models, for reader-response criticism is not a monolithic school of thought but, rather, an umbrella term covering a variety of approaches to literature.

Nonetheless, as Steven Mailloux has shown, reader-response critics *do* share not only questions but also goals and strategies. Two of the basic goals are to show that a work gives readers something to do and to describe what the reader does by way of response. To achieve those goals, the critic may make any of a number of what Mailloux calls "moves." For instance, a reader-response critic might typically (1) cite direct references to reading in the text being analyzed, in order to justify the focus on reading and show that the world of the text is continuous with the one in which the reader reads; (2) show how other nonreading situations in the text nonetheless mirror the situation the reader is in ("Fish shows how in *Paradise Lost* Michael's teaching of Adam in Book XI resembles Milton's teaching of the reader throughout the poem"); and (3) show, therefore, that the reader's response is, or is analogous to, the story's action or conflict. For instance, Stephen Booth calls *Hamlet* the tragic story of "an audience that cannot make up its mind" (Mailloux, "Learning" 103).

Although reader-response criticism is often said to have emerged in the United States in the 1970s, it is in one respect as old as the foundations of Western culture. The ancient Greeks and Romans tended to view literature as rhetoric, a means of making an audience react in a certain way. Although their focus was more on rhetorical strategies and devices than on the reader's (or listener's) response to those methods, the ancients by no means left the audience out of the literary equation. Aristotle thought, for instance, that the greatness of tragedy lay in its "cathartic" power to cleanse or purify the emotions of audience members. Plato, by contrast, worried about the effects of artistic productions, so much so that he advocated evicting poets from the Republic on the grounds that their words "feed and water" the passions!

In our own century, long before 1970, there were critics whose concerns and attitudes anticipated those of reader-response critics. One of these, I. A. Richards, is usually associated with formalism, a supposedly objective, text-centered approach to literature that reader-response critics of the 1970s roundly attacked. And yet in 1929 Richards managed to sound surprisingly *like* a 1970s-vintage reader-response critic, writing in *Practical Criticism* that "the personal situation of the reader inevitably (and within limits rightly) affects his reading, and many more are drawn to poetry in quest of some reflection of their latest emotional crisis than would admit it" (575). Rather than deploring this fact, as many of his formalist contemporaries would have done, Richards argued that the reader's feelings and experiences provide a kind of reality check, a way of testing the authenticity of emotions and events represented in literary works.

Approximately a decade after Richards wrote *Practical Criticism,* an American named Louise M. Rosenblatt published *Literature as Exploration* (1938). In that seminal book, now in its fourth edition (1983), Rosenblatt began developing a theory of reading that blurs the boundary between reader and text, subject and object. In a 1969 article entitled "Towards a Transaction Theory of Reading," she sums up her position by writing that "a poem is what the reader lives through under the guidance of the text and experiences as relevant to the text" (127). Rosenblatt knew her definition would be difficult for many to accept: "The idea that a *poem* presupposes a *reader* actively involved with a text," she wrote, "is particularly shocking to those seeking to emphasize the objectivity of their interpretations" ("Transactional" 127).

Rosenblatt implicitly and generally refers to formalists (also called the "New Critics") when she speaks of supposedly objective interpreters shocked by the notion that a "poem" is something cooperatively produced by a "reader" and a "text." Formalists spoke of "the poem itself," the "concrete work of art," the "real poem." They had no interest in what a work of literature makes a reader "live through." In fact, in *The Verbal Icon* (1954), William K. Wimsatt and Monroe C. Beardsley defined as fallacious the very notion that a reader's response is relevant to the meaning of a literary work:

> The Affective Fallacy is a confusion between the poem and its
> *results* (what it *is* and what it *does*). . . . It begins by trying to
> derive the standards of criticism from the psychological effects of a
> poem and ends in impressionism and relativism. The outcome . . .
> is that the poem itself, as an object of specifically critical judgment,
> tends to disappear. (21)

Reader-response critics have taken issue with their formalist predecessors. Particularly influential has been Stanley Fish, whose early work is seen by some as marking the true beginning of contemporary reader-response criticism. In "Literature in the Reader: Affective Stylistics" (1970), Fish took on the formalist hegemony, the New Critical establishment, by arguing that any school of criticism that would see a work of literature as an object, claiming to describe what it *is* and never what it *does,* is guilty of misconstruing the very essence of literature and reading. Literature exists when it is read, Fish suggests, and its force is an affective force. Furthermore, reading is a temporal process. Formalists assume it is a spatial one as they step back and survey the literary work as if it were an object spread out before them. They may find elegant patterns in the texts they examine and reexamine, but they fail to take into account that the work is quite different to a reader who is turning the pages and being moved, or affected, by lines that appear and disappear as the reader reads.

In discussing the effect that a sentence penned by the seventeenth-century physician Thomas Browne has on a reader reading, Fish pauses to say this about his analysis and also, by extension, about his critical strategy: "Whatever is persuasive and illuminating about [it] is the result of my substituting for one question — what does this sentence mean? — another, more operational question — what does this sentence do?" He then quotes a line from John Milton's *Paradise Lost,* a line that refers to Satan and the other fallen angels: "Nor did they not perceive their evil plight." Whereas more traditional critics might say that the "meaning" of the line is "They did perceive their evil plight," Fish relates the uncertain movement of the reader's mind *to* that half-satisfying interpretation. Furthermore, he declares that "the reader's inability to tell whether or not 'they' do perceive and his involuntary question . . . are part of the line's *meaning,* even though they take place in the mind, not on the page" (*Text* 26).

This stress on what pages *do* to minds (and what minds do in response) pervades the writings of most, if not all, reader-response critics. Stephen Booth, whose book *An Essay on Shakespeare's Sonnets* (1969) greatly influenced Fish, sets out to describe the "reading experience that results" from a "multiplicity of organizations" in a sonnet by Shakespeare (*Essay* ix). Sometimes these organizations don't make complete sense, Booth points out, and sometimes they even seem curiously contradictory. But that is precisely what interests reader-response critics, who, unlike formalists, are at least as interested in fragmentary, inconclusive, and even unfinished texts as in polished, unified works. For it is the reader's struggle to *make sense* of a challenging work that reader-response critics seek to describe.

The German critic Wolfgang Iser has described that sense-making struggle in his books *The Implied Reader* (1974) and *The Act of Reading: A Theory of Aesthetic Response* (1978). Iser argues that texts are full of "gaps" (or "blanks," as he sometimes calls them). These gaps powerfully affect the reader, who is forced to explain them, to connect what they separate, to create in his or her mind aspects of a poem or novel or play that aren't *in* the text but that the text incites. As Iser puts it in *The Implied Reader,* the "unwritten aspects" of a story "draw the reader into the action" and "lead him to shade in the many outlines suggested by the given situations, so that these take on a reality of their own." These "outlines" that "the reader's imagination animates" in turn "influence" the way in which "the written part of the text" is subsequently read (276).

In *Self-Consuming Artifacts: The Experience of Seventeenth-Century Literature* (1972), Fish reveals his preference for literature that makes readers work at making meaning. He contrasts two kinds of literary presentation. By the phrase "rhetorical presentation," he describes literature that reflects and reinforces opinions that readers already hold; by "dialectical presentation," he refers to works that prod and provoke. A dialectical text, rather than presenting an opinion as if it were truth, challenges readers to discover truths on their own. Such a text may not even have the kind of symmetry that formalist critics seek. Instead of offering a "single, sustained argument," a dialectical text, or self-consuming artifact, may be "so arranged that to enter into the spirit and assumptions of any one of [its] . . . units is implicitly to reject the spirit and assumptions of the unit immediately preceding" (*Artifacts* 9). Whereas a critic of another school might try to force an explanation as to why the units are fundamentally coherent, the reader-response critic proceeds by describing how the reader deals with the sudden twists and turns that characterize the dialectical text, returning to earlier passages and seeing them in an entirely new light.

"The value of such a procedure," Fish has written, "is predicated on the idea of meaning as *an event*," not as something "located (presumed to be embedded) *in* the utterance" or "verbal object as a thing in itself" (*Text* 28). By redefining meaning as an event rather than as something inherent in the text, the reader-response critic once again locates meaning in time: the reader's time. A text exists and signifies while it is being read, and what it signifies or means will depend, to no small extent, on *when* it is read. (*Paradise Lost* had some meanings for a seventeenth-century Puritan that it would not have for a twentieth-century atheist.)

With the redefinition of literature as something that only exists meaningfully in the mind of the reader, with the redefinition of the literary work as a catalyst of mental events, comes a concurrent redefinition of the reader. No longer is the reader the passive recipient of those ideas that an author has planted in a text. "The reader is *active*," Rosenblatt insists ("Transactional" 123). Fish begins "Literature in the Reader" with a similar observation: "If at this moment someone were to ask, 'what are you doing,' you might reply, 'I am reading,' and thereby acknowledge that reading is . . . something *you do*" (*Text* 22).

Iser, in focusing critical interest on the gaps in texts, on what is not expressed, similarly redefines the reader as an active maker.

Amid all this talk of "the reader," it is tempting and natural to ask, "Just who *is* the reader?" (Or, to place the emphasis differently, "Just who is *the* reader?") Are reader-response critics simply sharing their own idiosyncratic responses when they describe what a line from *Paradise Lost* does in and to the reader's mind? "What about my responses?" you may want to ask. "What if they're different? Would reader-response critics be willing to say that my responses are equally valid?"

Fish defines "the reader" in this way: "*the* reader is the *informed* reader." The informed reader (whom Fish sometimes calls "the *intended* reader") is someone who is "sufficiently experienced as a reader to have internalized the properties of literary discourses, including everything from the most local of devices (figures of speech, etc.) to whole genres." And, of course, the informed reader is in full possession of the "semantic knowledge" (knowledge of idioms, for instance) assumed by the text (*Artifacts* 406).

Other reader-response critics define "*the* reader" differently. Wayne C. Booth, in *A Rhetoric of Irony* (1974), uses the phrase "the implied reader" to mean the reader "made by the work itself" [228]. (Only "by agreeing to play the role of this created audience," Susan Suleiman explains, "can an actual reader correctly understand and appreciate the work" [8].) Gerard Genette and Gerald Prince prefer to speak of "the narratee, . . . the necessary counterpart of a given narrator, that is, the person or figure who receives a narrative" (Suleiman 13). Like Booth, Iser employs the term "the implied reader," but he also uses "the educated reader" when he refers to what Fish calls the "informed" reader.

Jonathan Culler, who in 1981 criticized Fish for his sketchy definition of the informed reader, set out in *Structuralist Poetics* (1975) to describe the educated or "competent" reader's education by elaborating those reading conventions that make possible the understanding of poems and novels. In retrospect, however, Culler's definitions seem sketchy as well. By "competent reader," Culler meant competent reader of "literature." By "literature," he meant what schools and colleges mean when they speak of literature as being part of the curriculum. Culler, like his contemporaries, was not concerned with the fact that curricular content is politically and economically motivated. And "he did not," in Mailloux's words, "emphasize how the literary competence he described was embedded within larger formations and traversed by political ideologies extending beyond the academy" ("Turns" 49). It remained for a later generation of reader-oriented critics to do those things.

The fact that Fish, following Rosenblatt's lead, defined reader-response criticism in terms of its difference from and opposition to the New Criticism or formalism should not obscure the fact that the formalism of the 1950s and early 1960s had a great deal in common with the reader-response criticism of the late 1960s and early 1970s. This has become increasingly obvious with the rise of subsequent critical approaches whose practitioners have proved less interested in the close reading of texts than in the way literature represents, reproduces, and/or resists prevailing ideologies concerning gender, class, and race. In a retrospective essay entitled "The Turns of Reader-Response Criticism" (1990), Mailloux has suggested that, from the perspective of hindsight, the "close reading" of formalists and "Fish's early 'affective stylistics'" seem surprisingly similar. Indeed, Mailloux argues, the early "reader talk of . . . Iser and Fish enabled the continuation of the formalist practice of close reading. Through a vocabulary focused on a text's manipulation of readers, Fish was especially effective in extending and diversifying the formalist practices that continued business as usual within literary criticism" (48).

Since the mid-1970s, however, reader-response criticism (once commonly referred to as the "School of Fish") has diversified and taken on a variety of new forms, some of which truly *are* incommensurate with formalism, with its considerable respect for the integrity and power of the text. For instance, "subjectivists" like David Bleich, Norman Holland, and Robert Crosman have assumed what Mailloux calls the "absolute priority of individual selves as creators of texts" (*Conventions* 31). In other words, these critics do not see the reader's response as one "guided" by the text but rather as one motivated by deep-seated, personal, psychological needs. What they find in texts is, in Holland's phrase, their own "identity theme." Holland has argued that as readers we use "the literal work to symbolize and finally to replicate ourselves. We work out through the text our own characteristic patterns of desire" ("UNITY" 816). Subjective critics, as you may already have guessed, often find themselves confronted with the following question: If all interpretation is a function of private, psychological identity, then why have so many readers interpreted, say, Shakespeare's *Hamlet* in the same way? Different subjective critics have answered the question differently. Holland simply has said that common identity themes exist, such as that involving an oedipal fantasy.

Meanwhile, Fish, who in the late 1970s moved away from reader-response criticism as he had initially helped define it, came up with a different answer to the question of why different readers tend to read the same works the same way. His answer, rather than involving common individual identity themes, involved common *cultural* identity. In "Interpreting the *Variorum*" (1976), he argues that the "stability of interpretation among readers" is a function of shared "interpretive strategies." These strategies, which "exist prior to the act of reading and therefore determine the shape of what is read," are held in common by "interpretive communities" such as the one constituted by American college students reading a novel as a class assignment (*Text* 167, 171). In developing the model of interpretive communities, Fish truly has made the break with formalist or New Critical predecessors, becoming in the process something of a social, structuralist, reader-response critic. Recently, he has been engaged in studying reading communities and their interpretive conventions in order to understand the conditions that give rise to a work's intelligibility.

Fish's shift in focus is in many ways typical of changes that have taken place within the field of reader-response criticism — a field that, because of those changes, is increasingly being referred to as "reader-*oriented*" criticism. Less and less common are critical analyses examining the transactional interface between the text and its individual reader. Increasingly, reader-oriented critics are investigating reading communities, as the reader-oriented cultural critic Janice A. Radway has done in her study of female readers of romance paperbacks (*Reading the Romance*, 1984). They are also studying the changing reception of literary works across time; see, for example, Mailloux in his "pragmatic readings" of American literature in *Interpretive Conventions* (1982) and *Rhetorical Power* (1989).

An important catalyst of this gradual change was the work of Hans Robert Jauss, a colleague of Iser's whose historically oriented reception theory (unlike Iser's theory of the implied reader) was not available in English book form until the early 1980s. Rather than focusing on the implied, informed, or intended reader, Jauss examined actual past readers. In *Toward an Aesthetics of Reception* (1982), he argued that the reception of a work or author tends to depend upon the reading public's "horizons of expectations." He noted that, in the morally conservative climate of mid-nineteenth-century France, *Madame Bovary* was literally put on trial, its author Flaubert accused of glorifying adultery in passages representing the protagonist's fevered delirium via free indirect discourse, a mode of narration in which a third-person narrator tells us in an unfiltered way what a character is thinking and feeling.

As readers have become more sophisticated and tolerant, the popularity and reputation of *Madame Bovary* have soared. Sometimes, of course, changes in a reading public's horizons of expectations cause a work to be *less* well received over time. As American reception theorists influenced by Jauss have shown, Mark Twain's *Adventures of Huckleberry Finn* has elicited an increasingly ambivalent reaction from a reading public increasingly sensitive to demeaning racial stereotypes and racist language. The rise of feminism has prompted a downward revaluation of everything from Andrew Marvell's "To His Coy Mistress" to D. H. Lawrence's *Women in Love.*

Some reader-oriented feminists, such as Judith Fetterley, Patrocinio Schweickart, and Monique Wittig, have challenged the reader to become what Fetterley calls "the resisting reader." Arguing that literature written by men tends, in Schweickart's terms, to "immasculate" women, they have advocated strategies of reading that involve substituting masculine for feminine pronouns and male for female characters in order to expose the sexism inscribed in patriarchal texts. Other feminists, such as Nancy K. Miller in *Subject to Change* (1988), have suggested that there may be essential differences between the way women and men read and write.

That suggestion, however, has prompted considerable disagreement. A number of gender critics whose work is oriented toward readers and reading have admitted that there is such a thing as "reading like a woman" (or man), but they have also tended to agree with Peggy Kamuf that such forms of reading, like gender itself, are cultural rather than natural constructs. Gay and lesbian critics, arguing that sexualities have been similarly constructed within and by social discourse, have argued that there is a homosexual way of reading; Wayne Koestenbaum has defined "the (male twentieth-century first world) gay reader" as one who "reads resistantly for inscriptions of his condition, for texts that will confirm a social and private identity founded on a desire for other men. . . . Reading becomes a hunt for histories that deliberately foreknow or unwittingly trace a desire felt not by author but by reader, who is most acute when searching for signs of himself " (in Boone and Cadden 176–77).

Given this kind of renewed interest in the reader and reading, some students of contemporary critical practice have been tempted to conclude that reader-oriented theory has been taken over by feminist, gender, gay, and lesbian theory. Others, like Elizabeth Freund, have suggested that it is deconstruction with which the reader-oriented approach has mixed and merged. Certainly, all of these approaches have informed and been informed by reader-response or reader-oriented theory. The case can be made, however, that there is in fact still a distinct reader-oriented approach to literature, one whose points of tangency are neither with deconstruction nor with feminist, gender, and so-called queer theory but, rather, with the new historicism and cultural criticism.

This relatively distinct form of reader theory is practiced by a number of critics, but is perhaps best exemplified by the work of scholars like Mailloux and Peter J. Rabinowitz. In *Before Reading: Narrative Conventions and the Politics of Interpretation* (1987), Rabinowitz sets forth four conventions or rules of reading, which he calls the rules of "notice," "signification," "configuration," and "coherence" — rules telling us which parts of a narrative are important, which details have a reliable secondary or special meaning, which fit into which familiar patterns, and how stories fit together as a whole. He then proceeds to analyze the misreadings and misjudgments of critics and to show that politics governs the way in which those rules are applied and broken ("The strategies employed by critics when they read [Raymond Chandler's] *The Big Sleep*" Rabinowitz writes, "can teach us something about the structure of misogyny, not the misogyny of the novel itself, but the misogyny of the world outside it" [195]). In subsequent critical essays, Rabinowitz proceeds similarly, showing how a society's ideological assumptions about gender, race, and class determine the way in which artistic works are perceived and evaluated.

Mailloux, who calls his approach "rhetorical reception theory" or "rhetorical hermeneutics," takes a similar tack, insofar as he describes the political contexts of (mis)interpretation. In a recent essay on "Misreading as a Historical Act" (1993) he shows that a mid-nineteenth-century review of Frederick Douglass's *Narrative* by proto-feminist Margaret Fuller seems to be a misreading until we situate it "within the cultural conversation of the 'Bible politics' of 1845" (Machor 9). Woven through Mailloux's essay on Douglass and Fuller are philosophical pauses in which we are reminded, in various subtle ways, that all reading (including Mailloux's and our own) is culturally situated and likely to seem like *mis*reading someday. One such reflective pause, however, accomplishes more; in it, Mailloux reads the map of where reader-oriented criticism is today, affords a rationale for its being there, and plots its likely future direction. "However we have arrived at our present juncture," Mailloux writes,

the current talk about historical acts of reading provides a welcome opportunity for more explicit consideration of how reading
is historically contingent, politically situated, institutionally
embedded, and materially conditioned; of how reading any text,
literary or nonliterary, relates to a larger cultural politics that goes
well beyond some hypothetical private interaction between an
autonomous reader and an independent text; and of how our particular views of reading relate to the liberatory potential of literacy
and the transformative power of education. (5)

In the pages that follow this introduction, one of the great literary
critics of the twentieth century, Wayne C. Booth, poses a series of
related questions. Why have so many interpretations of *The Turn of the
Screw* been published? Why are they all so different, even contradictory?
(Critics don't even agree on whether the ghosts are real or invented;
how Miles dies; and whether James's tale is a classic "horror story" or a
subtle example of modern psychological fiction.) In addition to asking
why *The Turn of the Screw* has proved so controversial, Booth asks even
more basic and important questions, such as: "What is the value of writing and reading controversial essays about such a work?" (p. 241).
Indeed, what is to be gained by debating the meaning of *any* text?

To reveal the answers that Booth eventually arrives at would be to
spoil the fun of his essay's unfolding argument. Suffice it to say here
that in the process of coming to his carefully worked-out conclusions
he roughly divides all known interpretations of *The Turn of the Screw*
into three broad groups: those readings he calls "straight" (a straight
reading views the ghosts as being real, the story as a horror story);
those readings he calls "ironic" (according to an ironic reading, the
ghosts are the imaginings of a mad governess and the tale is a disguised
psychological study); and those readings he calls "mazed" (these are
"readings that see the story as itself rejecting any one interpretation"
[p. 244]). Booth then proceeds by weighing the positive and negative
effects of these three kinds of readings on the *reader*, asking in each case
how a friend might be affected or changed — psychologically and/or
morally — by being a "straight," "ironic," or "mazed" reader of *The
Turn of the Screw*.

Booth states early on that he is writing "ethical criticism," which he
classifies as "a version of what is now generally called reader-response
criticism." As old as Plato's aesthetic philosophy, ethical criticism is
interested not only in how readers respond to the same text in a variety
of ways but also in the ethical implications of those various responses.
As a practitioner of ethical criticism, Booth consistently — in his own

words — invites us "to probe . . . the possible rewards for responding to this story in one way rather than another" (p. 241).

However much he may believe that we, as readers, may and should choose between compelling readings, Booth should not be confused with the kind of subjectivist critic who believes that a text means whatever we make it out to mean. Booth views the author as one who guides the reader's responses — and views readers as agents who are only free within certain limits to make interpretive choices. "Though no one reading can ever triumph over all others," Booth writes, "there *are* better and worse readings. In short, 'my' readings, like yours, are inherently corrigible, improvable" (p. 252).

As the quotation above amply demonstrates, Booth proves himself to be a reader-oriented critic not only by focusing on a variety of interpretive responses and their affective dimensions but also via his writing style. Throughout his essay, he addresses us directly, dares us to invent readings more preposterous than any that are extant, implores us to see that some readings are more dispensable than others, characterizes himself not as a writer of criticism but as a reader of James, and places his own readings in the contexts of other readings, including the four other readings (and the editor's critical history of the text) published in this volume!

Because of its provocative, reader-involving style, the essay you are about to read is one you will probably find highly unusual: unusual in that it is personal; unusual in that it is sometimes emotionally moving; and unusual, too, insofar as it suggests that what you are doing at this very moment has a value far greater than you may have supposed.

Ross C Murfin

READER-RESPONSE CRITICISM:
A SELECTED BIBLIOGRAPHY

Some Introductions to
Reader-Response Criticism

Beach, Richard. *A Teacher's Introduction to Reader-Response Theories.* Urbana: NCTE, 1993.

Fish, Stanley E. "Literature in the Reader: Affective Stylistics." *New Literary History* 2 (1970): 123–61. Rpt. in Fish *Text* 21–67, and in Primeau 154–79.

Freund, Elizabeth. *The Return of the Reader: Reader-Response Criticism.* London: Methuen, 1987.

Holub, Robert C. *Reception Theory: A Critical Introduction.* New York: Methuen, 1984.

Leitch, Vincent B. *American Literary Criticism from the Thirties to the Eighties.* New York: Columbia UP, 1988.

Mailloux, Steven. "Learning to Read: Interpretation and Reader-Response Criticism." *Studies in the Literary Imagination* 12 (1979): 93–108.

———. "Reader-Response Criticism?" *Genre* 10 (1977): 413–31.

———. "The Turns of Reader-Response Criticism." *Conversations: Contemporary Critical Theory and the Teaching of Literature.* Ed. Charles Moran and Elizabeth F. Penfield. Urbana: NCTE, 1990. 38–54.

Rabinowitz, Peter J. "Whirl Without End: Audience-Oriented Criticism." *Contemporary Literary Theory.* Ed. G. Douglas Atkins and Laura Morrow. Amherst: U of Massachusetts P, 1989. 81–100.

Rosenblatt, Louise M. "Towards a Transactional Theory of Reading." *Journal of Reading Behavior* 1 (1969): 31–47. Rpt. in Primeau 121–46.

Suleiman, Susan R. "Introduction: Varieties of Audience-Oriented Criticism." Suleiman and Crosman 3–45.

Tompkins, Jane P. "An Introduction to Reader-Response Criticism." Tompkins ix–xxiv.

Reader-Response Criticism
in Anthologies and Collections

Flynn, Elizabeth A., and Patrocinio P. Schweickart, eds. *Gender and Reading: Essays on Readers, Texts, and Contexts.* Baltimore: Johns Hopkins UP, 1986.

Garvin, Harry R., ed. *Theories of Reading, Looking, and Listening.* Lewisburg: Bucknell UP, 1981. Essays by Cain and Rosenblatt.

Machor, James L., ed. *Readers in History: Nineteenth-Century American Literature and the Contexts of Response.* Baltimore: Johns Hopkins UP, 1993. Contains Mailloux essay "Misreading as a Historical Act: Cultural Rhetoric, Bible Politics, and Fuller's 1845 Review of Douglass's *Narrative.*"

Primeau, Ronald, ed. *Influx: Essays on Literary Influence.* Port Washington: Kennikat, 1977. Essays by Fish, Holland, and Rosenblatt.

Suleiman, Susan R., and Inge Crosman, eds. *The Reader in the Text: Essays on Audience and Interpretation*. Princeton: Princeton UP, 1980. See especially the essays by Culler, Iser, and Todorov.

Tompkins, Jane P., ed. *Reader-Response Criticism: From Formalism to Post-Structuralism*. Baltimore: Johns Hopkins UP, 1980. See especially the essays by Bleich, Fish, Holland, Prince, and Tompkins.

Reader-Response Criticism: Some Major Works

Bleich, David. *Subjective Criticism*. Baltimore: Johns Hopkins UP, 1978.

Booth, Stephen. *An Essay on Shakespeare's Sonnets*. New Haven: Yale UP, 1969.

Booth, Wayne C. *A Rhetoric of Irony*. Chicago: U of Chicago P, 1974.

Eco, Umberto. *The Role of the Reader: Explorations in the Semiotics of Texts*. Bloomington: Indiana UP, 1979.

Fish, Stanley Eugene. *Doing What Comes Naturally: Change, Rhetoric, and the Practice of Theory in Literary and Legal Studies*. Durham: Duke UP, 1989.

———. *Is There a Text in This Class? The Authority of Interpretive Communities*. Cambridge: Harvard UP, 1980. This volume contains most of Fish's most influential essays, including "Literature in the Reader: Affective Stylistics," "What It's Like to Read *L'Allegro* and *Il Penseroso*," "Interpreting the *Variorum*," "How to Recognize a Poem When You See One," "Is There a Text in This Class?" and "What Makes an Interpretation Acceptable?"

———. *Self-Consuming Artifacts: The Experience of Seventeenth-Century Literature*. Berkeley: U of California P, 1972.

———. *Surprised by Sin: The Reader in Paradise Lost*. 2nd ed. Berkeley: U of California P, 1971.

Holland, Norman N. *5 Readers Reading*. New Haven: Yale UP, 1975.

———. "UNITY IDENTITY TEXT SELF." *PMLA* 90 (1975): 813–22.

Iser, Wolfgang. *The Act of Reading: A Theory of Aesthetic Response*. Baltimore: Johns Hopkins UP, 1978.

———. *The Implied Reader: Patterns of Communication in Prose Fiction from Bunyan to Beckett*. Baltimore: Johns Hopkins UP, 1974.

Jauss, Hans Robert. *Toward an Aesthetics of Reception*. Trans. Timothy Bahti. Intro. Paul de Man. Brighton, Eng.: Harvester, 1982.

Mailloux, Steven. *Interpretive Conventions: The Reader in the Study of American Fiction.* Ithaca: Cornell UP, 1982.

———. *Rhetorical Power.* Ithaca: Cornell UP, 1989.

Messent, Peter. *New Readings of the American Novel: Narrative Theory and Its Application.* New York: Macmillan, 1991.

Prince, Gerald. *Narratology.* New York: Mouton, 1982.

Rabinowitz, Peter. *Before Reading: Narrative Conventions and the Politics of Interpretation.* Ithaca: Cornell, UP, 1987.

Radway, Janice A. *Reading the Romance: Women, Patriarchy, and Popular Literature.* Chapel Hill: U of North Carolina P, 1984.

Rosenblatt, Louise M. *Literature as Exploration.* 4th ed. New York: MLA, 1983.

———. *The Reader the Text, the Poem: The Transactional Theory of the Literary Work.* Carbondale: Southern Illinois UP, 1978.

Slatoff, Walter J. *With Respect to Readers: Dimensions of Literary Response.* Ithaca: Cornell UP, 1970.

Steig, Michael. *Stories of Reading: Subjectivity and Literary Understanding.* Baltimore: Johns Hopkins UP, 1989.

Exemplary Short Readings of Major Texts

Anderson, Howard. "*Tristram Shandy* and the Reader's Imagination." *PMLA* 86 (1971): 966–73.

Berger, Carole. "The Rake and the Reader in Jane Austen's Novels." *Studies in English Literature, 1500–1900* 15 (1975): 531–44.

Booth, Stephen. "On the Value of Hamlet." *Reinterpretations of English Drama: Selected Papers from the English Institute.* Ed. Norman Rabkin. New York: Columbia UP, 1969. 137–76.

Easson, Robert R. "William Blake and His Reader in *Jerusalem.*" *Blake's Sublime Allegory.* Ed. Stuart Curran and Joseph A. Wittreich. Madison: U of Wisconsin P, 1973. 309–28.

Kirk, Carey H. "*Moby-Dick:* The Challenge of Response." *Papers on Language and Literature* 13 (1977): 383–90.

Leverenz, David. "Mrs. Hawthorne's Headache: Reading *The Scarlet Letter.*" *Nathaniel Hawthorne, "The Scarlet Letter."* Ed. Ross C Murfin. Case Studies in Contemporary Criticism Series. Boston: Bedford, 1991. 263–74.

Lowe-Evans, Mary. "Reading with a 'Nicer-Eye': Responding to *Frankenstein.*" *Mary Shelley, "Frankenstein."* Ed. Johanna M. Smith. Case Studies in Contemporary Criticism Series. Boston: Bedford, 1992. 215–29.

Rabinowitz, Peter J. " 'A Symbol of Something: Interpretive Vertigo in 'The Dead.' " *James Joyce, "The Dead."* Ed. Daniel R. Schwarz. Case Studies in Contemporary Criticism. Boston: Bedford, 1994. 137–49.

Other Works Referred to in "What Is Reader-Response Criticism?"

Culler, Jonathan. *Structuralist Poetics: Structuralism, Linguistics, and the Study of Literature.* Ithaca: Cornell UP, 1975.

Koestenbaum, Wayne. "Wilde's Hard Labor and the Birth of Gay Reading." *Engendering Men: The Question of Male Feminist Criticism.* Ed. Joseph A. Boone and Michael Cadden. New York: Routledge, 1990.

Miller, Nancy K. *Subject to Change: Reading Feminist Writing.* New York: Columbia UP, 1988.

Richards, I. A. *Practical Criticism.* New York: Harcourt, 1929. Rpt. in *Criticism: The Major Texts.* Ed. Walter Jackson Bate. Rev. ed. New York: Harcourt, 1970. 575.

Wimsatt, William K., and Monroe C. Beardsley. *The Verbal Icon.* Lexington: U of Kentucky P, 1954. See especially the discussion of "The Affective Fallacy," with which reader-response critics have so sharply disagreed.

Reader-Response Approaches to *The Turn of the Screw*

Boehm, Beth. "A Postmodern Turn of *The Turn of the Screw.*" *Henry James Review* 19 (1998): 245–54.

Booth, Wayne C. *Critical Understanding: The Powers and Limits of Pluralism.* Chicago: U of Chicago P, 1979.

Heller, Terry. *"The Turn of the Screw": Bewildered Vision.* Boston: Twayne, 1989.

A READER-RESPONSE PERSPECTIVE

WAYNE C. BOOTH

"He began to read to our hushed little circle": Are We Blessed or Cursed by Our Life with *The Turn of the Screw*?

No one who reads Peter Beidler's "Critical History" of *The Turn of the Screw* (pp. 189–214 in this volume) is likely to call the readers of *The Turn of the Screw* a "hushed little circle." The circle is not little, and there has been no hush. Indeed, *The Turn of the Screw* has probably been discussed more than any other modern story.[1] Some older, longer classics have no doubt had more pages devoted to them: Homer's great epics, the *Iliad* and the *Odyssey;* Dante's *Divine Comedy;* Shakespeare's *Hamlet*. And some longer modern novels may well outdo this story in the number of printed discussions. But among short works of fiction this one is surely king. In English alone I have counted, before I got too bored to go on, more than five hundred titles of books and articles about it, and since it has been translated and discussed in dozens of other languages the total must yield more than a lifetime's possible reading. To this one might add all the unpublished doctoral dissertations and students' essays. And here we are, in this volume, adding to the total!

If this sheer quantity seems puzzling, what can we say of the intense contradictions among the readings the critical history reveals? About many great works most readers agree on the basic facts of plot and character and about the responses called for; in discussion, public and private, readers discover that they have felt similar emotions and been led to similar thoughts — in other words, they discover agreement at least about the kind of work they have read. Nobody has ever seriously suggested, for example, that the tragedy *Hamlet* should be responded to as a comedy, or that Hamlet doesn't really die at the end but is just pretending, or that the ghost of Hamlet's father is only Hamlet's crazy invention, or that Hamlet killed his own father.[2] Nobody has ever seriously

---

[1]Stories like this one that are too long to be called short stories but shorter than most of what we call novels are often called novellas, especially when, as in this case, they cover an elaborate sequence of events of the kind one finds in novels.

[2]Of course there are many playful parodies and transformations of the classics, like Tom Stoppard's turning of *Hamlet* into the story of two minor characters in *Rosencrantz and Guildenstern Are Dead*. But the clever readings that such games offer are quite

suggested that the hero of Dickens's *A Tale of Two Cities,* Sidney Carton, should be viewed as really a villain at heart, responsible for all the woes in that book, including the French Revolution itself, or that the events of the novel were all made up by one of the minor characters. Nobody has ever seriously suggested that Jane Austen's *Pride and Prejudice* is a tragedy, or that Elizabeth Bennet, the heroine, really made the whole thing up, as an old maid regretting her spinsterhood. But readers of *The Turn of the Screw* have found themselves unable to agree about the kind of story it is, about the emotional or intellectual responses it calls for, about who does what to whom, or even about who tells which parts of the story. I can think of no other work of art that has stimulated as many contradictory readings.

I want to pursue here the tricky question of what we readers are to make out of all this controversy. It might almost lead us to think that reading such stories and talking about our responses is a pointless, even crazy business — until we remember the variety of "readings" we meet of events in so-called real life. How many interpretations do you think we could find, if we searched hard, for what really happened in the American revolution or the Vietnam War or the 2003 war with Iraq, or for your true motives in some important choice you have made, such as choosing a college or a major?

Still, such disagreement about a story, among readers who all seem to think it is worth reading and discussing, raises many difficult questions. Why do readers, like the five of us you find here, feel compelled to go on reading and re-reading a story the very nature of which we cannot even agree on? Why bother? What is the appeal to us, both of the re-reading and of the debates we engage in? As readers responding to the responses of us "literary critics," how should *you* respond? Should you just give it up as a bad job and go do something more obviously worthwhile? Or should you dig in and read the story again — and again?

Before you decide, you might think a bit about just how much re-reading most critics conduct when they are tempted to write about any literary work. While many of the interpretations Beidler reports seem to me to have been invented without enough attention to the words on the page, most of the authors had read the story many times before

---

different from the conflicting readings we consider here. Not only do they not question the "facts" of the originals, they depend on those facts, because readers and spectators cannot fully enjoy the jokes without full knowledge and acceptance of the originals.

feeling comfortable about offering an interpretation. My own experience may be a bit extreme, since this is my third printed discussion, but
I think it resembles that of most critics we pay any attention to. Over
the years I've read the story many times; I haven't counted but I would
guess at least twenty-five. And that's not counting the many times I've
re-read puzzling sentences, paragraphs, and whole sections. Last week I
read it again, and just today I looked once more at the death of
Miles — for the hundred and forty-seventh time! This seemingly irrelevant digression is offered, of course, to convince you that I am the only
critic whose incredible care should lead you to accept his views as
clinchers!

Of all the challenging questions that such buzzing attention over
one small flower raises, it is surprising that so few have asked, "Just
what is the value of all this activity for those who engage in it?" What
good is it? Does responding to this story, whether we read as we think
Henry James would want us to or read looking for interpretations he
would never have dreamed of, enhance our lives? This is the main question I am addressing here, but it will lead me to a second, closely related
one: What is the value of writing and reading controversial essays about
such a work? To read *The Turn of the Screw* is one thing; to write criticism about it, and to read, as you are now doing in this volume, a variety of seemingly conflicting views of what the story is about — that is
quite a different thing. And again I ask, What good is it?

In short, I invite you now to probe with me the possible rewards for
responding to this story in one way rather than another.

I

As we attempt such thinking, we shall be practicing a kind of literary criticism that for thousands of years was the most popular kind: a
version of what is now generally called reader-response criticism. I call
my version *ethical criticism:* the discussion of what stories do to the
ethos of those who respond to them with full attention (*ethos* is the
Greek word for "character"; its meanings include but go beyond what
we call personality). Almost all readers took it for granted until quite
recently that the most important questions to ask about any story were:
How does it ask me to respond, and will that kind of response be good
or bad for me? What will this story do to anyone who allows himself
(for thousands of years hardly anyone worried about whether female
readers might respond differently from males) to get caught up in the

events — caught up in the sense of hoping for happiness for some characters and hoping to see other characters punished? Readers who chose
to write down their opinions for other readers — "critics" like the five
of us in this book — saw their job as in part that of helping others to
think about what good or harm a given story or kind of story might
yield.

When Plato, writing in *The Republic* almost twenty-five hundred
years ago, raised doubts about the possible mis-education resulting
from a sympathetic reading of Homer's epics, or when Samuel Johnson, the greatest English critic of the eighteenth century, raised tough
questions about the wonderfully comic novel *Tom Jones,* it was as if they
thought of their readers as friends whose fate they cared about, asking
themselves, Would I want the experience I have had with this story, or
the experience that readers are likely to have, to serve other people as a
guide to life? or, Do I think of this story as a valuable gift from the
author to me and my friends, or do I think of it as some kind of disguised poison? Such readers shared the assumption — one that to me is
self-evident but that some modern critics have questioned — that readers are in fact influenced by the stories they read. They also assumed
that talking together and writing and reading criticism about our experiences would heighten the good effects of worthwhile stories and
weaken the bad effects of potentially harmful ones.[3]

Sometimes such critics seemed to embrace a fairly simple notion of
how stories affect us — as if we were likely to imitate any behavior that
any story presents, especially if the story asks us to admire that behavior.
It is this belief that leads some people to try to ban the publication of
certain books or prevent their being on the reading lists in schools and
colleges. Like the ancient critics, they rightly assume that readers, and
especially young readers, will probably imitate whatever they admire in
a story's characters, and the would-be censors conclude — wrongly, in
my view — that it would be better for everyone to see or hear only
admirable forms of behavior and the purest of language, whether in
movies and television or in mental pictures built from books. Such
narrowly moral or moralistic criticism could easily ban from our experience large portions of the Bible, many of Chaucer's poems, most of

---

[3]If this question seems a bit remote from your interests, you might want to think
about recent debates over whether a constant diet of violent scenes on television or in the
movies is harmful to the young. And if that leads you to want to do further reading and
thinking, you might start with an article by Ken Auletta on how moviemakers themselves
talk about the potential harm of the violence their "products" exploit ("What Won't
They Do," *The New Yorker,* May 17, 1993: 45–53).

Shakespeare's plays, modern novels like Mark Twain's *The Adventures of Huckleberry Finn* and J. D. Salinger's *The Catcher in the Rye,* and — though perhaps not quite so obviously — *The Turn of the Screw.*[4]

The ethical criticism that is worth practicing avoids that kind of censorship. It does not look for this or that violation of some simple moral code: four-letter words, acts of violence, sexist or racist comments. For the careful ethical critic, everything will depend on the quality of the whole experience that a story offers; every detail, even if it is in itself highly offensive, will be judged in the context of what is seen as that total experience. That many of the heroes of the Torah (Old Testament) commit outrageous sins — Jacob cheating his brother Esau out of his inheritance, the various shenanigans of the young David and other leaders — does not mean that the Bible is a wicked book; to decide whether it is, one must look at the experiences it provides those readers who really pay attention to the context of the various vicious acts. For responsible ethical critics, it is what an author does with a character's actions, and what the reader then does, in turn, that determines the ethical effect.

It will always remain true that some careless readers will tear details out of their context and may thus harm themselves with works that, like the Bible, are written by authors intending nothing but good. The censors are thus right in insisting that stories do change us and can change us harmfully as well as beneficially. Perhaps you can remember a time when, after seeing an exciting movie, you found yourself trying to walk or talk like your favorite character — or thinking that it would be really cool to have an apartment or car or costume or sexy vocabulary of the kind your hero or heroine displayed. And you may by now have decided that a particular temptation to imitate was a mistake. I have known many self-reproaching smokers who claimed that what they considered a vicious addiction had resulted not from cigarette ads but from observing heroes and heroines in movies lighting up with a sexy flourish or actually sharing — what a thrill! — the same cigarette.

But how can we write or talk about such influencing? How could you warn someone else against a work that had "worked" ill on you,

---

[4]Every year hundreds of works are attacked by purification committees or individuals — "Unfit for young readers!" — and some of the attacks work. You may have experienced in your own schooling the effects of such purges, when your teachers or the school board in your town surrendered to the attackers. I'm not aware that anyone has ever proposed cutting *The Turn of the Screw* from reading lists, but we can be sure that if James had dared make explicit the words that little Miles and Flora were taught by the two villains, it would have been banned by many today, and by all when it first came out.

without sounding merely preachy and dogmatic? The task is so difficult that many critics in this century have decided not to attempt it at all. It too often leads to writing that sounds like a simple sermon touting the critic's private morality — as my statement above reveals my strong bias against smoking.

That is only one of the reasons that have led critics to avoid ethical criticism. If the ethical task is to appraise the value of a reading experience (or of listening to musical "stories" or viewing paintings or statues), how do we deal with the troublesome fact — dramatized in extreme form by *The Turn of the Screw* — that different readers experience different responses to the "same" story and argue for seemingly contradictory readings? How can we appraise the experience offered by a story as "good for us" or "bad for us" if there is no single experience — if your response is radically different from mine?

II

Surely the experience of *The Turn of the Screw* by a reader who believes that ghosts are real and who feels personally threatened by characters like Peter Quint and Miss Jessel requires an entirely different appraisal from what we would offer when discussing the response of someone who does not believe in ghosts — one who knows that ghosts do not exist and who feels neither fear nor horror but only curiosity about why James wrote the story in just this way. What is even more troublesome is disagreement among critics about just what standards are to be applied. Two "straight" readers, seeing the ghosts as real and the story as an attempt to "turn the screws" of horror as thrillingly as possible, might flatly disagree with each other about whether the literary experience of thrilling horror is good or bad for "us," or for a given immature reader, or for a former governess now incarcerated in a mental institution.

Because of all this variety, we have to ask our questions as if we were dealing not with one *The Turn of the Screw* but many different ones. Without simplifying too much, we can consider them under the three categories that Beidler's "Critical History" has led us to: straight, ironic, and what I'll call "mazed" — the readings that see the story as itself rejecting any one interpretation.

What is the quality of the experience of the "straight" reader, who assumes that whether or not ghosts actually exist in real life, they can be real at least in ghost stories? Such readers take seriously what is said in the opening section — the part that is sometimes called the frame or prologue; they accept the governess at her own word, and they take literally, as I confess that I do, Douglas's praise of the governess in the opening frame story: "a most charming person . . . the most agreeable woman I've ever known in her position" as governess. She was his sister's governess long ago — she's been herself dead for twenty years — and he's thus had every chance to discover whether she was trustworthy as a governess. His judgment is that "she'd have been worthy of any [position] whatever" (p. 24) — presumably not just as a governess.[5]

Such readers of course find themselves responding to a horrifying story of how two utterly corrupt people return from the dead in the hope of possessing the souls of two helpless little children; of how their innocent and courageous governess, learning of their plans, fights them off, hoping to save the children. For some readers responding in this way, she fails, fails utterly. The ghosts succeed: they do corrupt the children, and despite the governess's best efforts, one of them "possesses" little Miles to the horrifying point of killing him. For some other straight readers, though the governess loses the battle for little Miles's body, she saves his soul from the ultimate human disaster: being possessed by evil.

Readers who see victory for the ghosts naturally see the story as aiming to horrify. What could be more horrifying than the corruption — not just the destruction but the utter possession by evil forces — of two little children who are potentially ideal types of innocence? What could be more horrifying — and many a current movie and television show dramatizes this point — than the portrait of real moral monsters come back from the dead to poison the lives of little "angels"?

While sharing much of this horror, those who see Miles as saved see the story as clearly intending some degree of exultation or sense of triumph: evil is defeated, even though at the cost of Miles's life. At least his soul is saved.

If we ask ethical questions about the offering and acceptance of such a straight gift, whether ending in total disaster or salvation, we face the same comparatively simple problems that would face us if we asked

---

[5]I offered a brief tracing of my then devotedly straight reading in *The Rhetoric of Fiction* (311–16, 369–71). My later reading in *Critical Understanding* (284–301) was still essentially on the governess's side, but it tried to account more fully for the evidence of her increasing approach to psychological breakdown as the battle tensions mount; that reading thus moved somewhat toward the uneasy version of a "mazed" reading that I hint at below.

that question about the latest horror movie. The experience itself is conventional, demanding little of us except intense emotional response. We may believe that to be roused to intense emotional response is itself a good thing — especially if it is done by reading words rather than simply surrendering to filmed images and if it happens to people who are otherwise emotional deadheads: Wake up, sluggard, and live for a while with this exciting stuff. Or we may want to say that for some readers — relatively immature or on the brink of emotional breakdown — such stuff is dangerous and ought to be avoided. Or we might want to stress the moral effects of identifying with the governess: the straight reader is invited to be courageous in the face of intense danger and to be a tough, honest defender of decency and justice. Even if her efforts are seen as failing, we will surely want to practice her kind of spunk if we ever find ourselves facing similar wickedness. And if her efforts have in fact saved Miles from possession, we have had a confirmation of just how important it is to face evil head on.

We see, then, that we get no single answer when we ask the question: Was this straight experience of terror and horror worth offering as a gift to our best friend? Or — what is the same thing, really — should your teacher have required you to read it? Since the world of literature is crowded with ghost stories, to have one more is neither especially good nor especially bad. James himself talked of *The Turn of the Screw* as a kind of potboiler, an effort to earn some needed cash by horrifying as many readers as possible. Neither the writing of such a story nor the reading of it matters very much to us one way or another, except as we may be thankful for skillful stories that cure our boredom. No doubt it would be harmful to spend most of our time reading such stuff, but an occasional few hours spent being scared out of our wits can't harm us very much — as those titillated ladies who appear in James's frame make clear: they love the thrill of it (though one suspects that James's way of portraying them reveals his own contempt for simple unalloyed horrifying).

Turning to ironic readings, what is the likely experience of the reader who for one reason or another mistrusts the governess's or Douglas's or the first narrator's account? This reader may or may not believe that Henry James intended us to mistrust one or another of the three, but all or part of what they say happened did not happen as they report it. Such a reader is likely to be absolutely sure that ghosts are not real, and that no ghost ever returned to corrupt an innocent child; that Henry James is himself too sophisticated to believe in ghosts and must have hoped for similarly sophisticated readers; and that James decided to create a story that would no doubt fool some careless readers into overlooking his portrait of a neurotic governess who goes mad and in one way or another destroys an innocent child.

Ironic readers will thus look for every clue that betrays untrustworthiness in the governess's account (or for some, in Douglas's, and for a very small number, the account of the opening narrator, the "I" who says "I remember" on the first page). Such readers usually report considerable pleasure in the ways in which James deliberately misleads the innocent into taking things straight. They also have the fun of becoming shrewd detectives, deciphering increasingly subtle clues that only the cleverest readers can catch. For example, they cite as a deliberate lie the account the governess gives Mrs. Grose of her encounter with Miss Jessel (early in chapter XVI), since it is different from and more detailed than the account she has given earlier. Or they quote her own words about being guilty of "endless obsession" (p. 91), and her admission that she "ached for the proof" (p. 96) that Miles actually did something to get expelled, and that she feels a "thrill of joy at having brought on a proof" (p. 101).

In this reading, the governess's courage will seem entirely deceptive, an obsessive cover-up for her increasingly mad pursuit of imaginary horrors; she herself says, again and again, that the alternative to seeing the ghosts as real is to see herself as "cruel" or "mad" (p. 101).

Like the straight story, this one is also likely to produce horrified responses in readers who engage fully with it; what the governess is seen as doing is awful. The children are victimized, whether we think of the governess as herself totally unsympathetic — a mad tyrant — or, as she is seen in some new interpretations, as herself a sympathetic victim of her own sincere delusions.[6] Straight readers may feel that they have reason to fear that the same kind of disaster might strike them or their own children. In the ironic response, by contrast, readers can feel that simple precautions will protect anyone from allowing such a madwoman to succeed: just conduct more careful interviews before you hire your governesses! The master in London is the one who is to blame for not recognizing a madwoman when he sees one. He has consigned his helpless wards to their doom.

---

[6]Critics who deal with horror stories too seldom distinguish the radically differing ethical quality of stories that, while horrifying, disgust us, stories that scare us, stories that make us laugh, and — to cut the list short — stories that, like the horror in Shakespeare's *King Lear* and *Macbeth*, both teach us about the nature of evil and also lead us to want to combat it.

The fun of such a reading is likely to be somewhat less innocent than that of the first. Part of the pleasure in it seems to lie in feeling superior to straight readers: You uneducated, superstitious, lazy folks "down there" ought to feel sort of silly not to have caught the subtle clues that we smarties up here have worked out. Critics are like other people: they compete with one another for the badge of Most Perceptive, and the desire to win can tempt them into looking for the most unlikely readings.

On the other hand, if we become convinced that James intended an ironic reading, we can hardly claim that to read the story straight is ethically superior: it would be just plain wrong. Still, I must ask myself, Would I recommend to my best friends that they spend hours and hours working out the "correct" ironic reading of such a story — seeing the governess, say, as a psychopathic killer? I think not. It would not only reinforce my friends' natural temptation to feel superior to other people; it would also confirm any temptation those friends have to feel that women tend to be hysterical and destructive of those they love: "Watch out for women who pretend to be deeply concerned about the moral welfare of their loved ones; and when you read stories told by them, be sure to look behind any masks of virtue they have put on."

According to one view of human nature, however, we could turn that charge around: we should surely praise the ironic story for alerting us to the inherent inclination of every human creature to sin: as some religions suggest, we are "originally sinful." Behind every virtuous-seeming exterior there does indeed lie a heart that was created flawed, "in the beginning," and it is the highest purpose of literature to pull down the facades and expose the viciousness within. A reader who believes that and who possesses sufficient humility might well be led to conclude, reading the ironic story, "I am too much like that destructive governess: I go about the world judging other people's wickedness and ignoring my own. Lord protect me from my own pride. I must change my life, or I will find myself behaving like the governess." This defense does not, however, answer the charge reported by Beidler, a charge that I share, that some of the ironic readings are prompted by sexism (see "Critical History" p. 201).

But what can we say happens to the "mazed readers" who see the story (as Beidler shows that more and more critics are urging us to do) as a maze with many intentionally deceptive false turns and dead ends? Regardless of what James said he intended, they see the story as ensuring the constant frustration of every interpreter; it leads readers on a merry chase through one failed reading after another. If, as a careful reader, you pursue the straight story, with the governess generally trust-worthy, you will soon find many signs of her unreliability — the kind I have already cited — and you will see increasing signs of her pathologi-cal over-reaction to ambiguous clues. On the other hand, if you pursue the ironic story you will soon be balked by signs that James intends us to see the governess as reliable, the ghosts as absolutely real, and Miles as already in the process of being corrupted — not just the testimony of Douglas to her reliability but a long list of corroborating facts: Miles's expulsion from school before he meets the governess; Miles's strange blowing out of the candle; tiny Flora's ability to row a large boat across the pond; Mrs. Grose's ability to identify Peter Quint from the gov-erness's detailed description of what she has seen; the initially skeptical housekeeper's final assertion that she believes the governess.

For some, the result of such endless revisions of reading responses should be not bitter frustration but a kind of thrill as bafflement yields illumination about the true nature of literature and life: no interpreta-tion of any story, or indeed of any event in real life, can ever be fixed, determinate, counted on to be *the* interpretation; all views are under-minable, "deconstructible" — in short, not only should every conclu-sion be held as temporary, but all controversies must be seen as unresolvable, undecidable, or as some critics put it, "unreadable." The story-as-maze confirms this "sophisticated" — and for some quite exciting — view of life. Miles is both persecuted by ghosts and not per-secuted by ghosts; the governess is both mad and not mad; Douglas is both involved in the story as a (disguised) character, and not involved. And so on.

Would I recommend such a "mazed" experience to my best friends? Again the answer must depend on "where my friends are coming from," or "where they are at." If they are already members of that elite club who know that there is only one truth, which is that there is no truth, then I think the story might very well be harmful to them: along with whatever bliss they may initially experience at the sense of libera-tion from other people's truth is likely to come a complacent sense of cynical superiority. They will feel a bit too comfortable with the "proof," offered by James himself, that they have been right all along: like every other story, *The Turn of the Screw*, if it is read carefully, con-firms an anti-truth-truth that only a select band of right-thinking folks have discovered.

On the other hand, I may have friends who are too firmly fixed in certain conventional views of the world — readers who read a story once and know then precisely what to think about it; readers who look at a character, in or out of a story, and quickly decide, whether reading straight or ironically, that he or she belongs to this or that conventional category of good or bad. Such friends could do with some shaking up; things are not what they seem. First readings are almost always inadequate. Every truth proclaimed by any human being is sure to be at best fragmentary, correctable by further truth to be discovered on down the road. *The Turn of the Screw* as maze could well wake up such friends and lead them on to further discovery.

III

Imagine now any teacher — you if you are actually one, your teacher if you are now "here" because of an assignment — trying to decide, on the basis of what I have said so far, whether to require students to read and discuss and write about this story. No teacher can know much in advance about just what kind of response students will have — whether they will most need waking up or settling down, whether they are too much or too little inclined to doubt what anyone says. What is the teacher to do?

Now I could easily offer that teacher a summary of my own reading — one that by now is somewhat different from the ones I printed in 1961 and 1979. It is of course the one reading that is really correct, the one that all readers ought to hold and that would lead to a decisive proclamation about whether your teacher should have recommended *The Turn of the Screw* to you and you should recommend it to your friends.[7] But if I am right in believing that a personal response to the story, and then an honest discussion with others about it, are much more important than being right about any one reading, it will be much more valuable to leave you to work out your own response, encouraged as I hope by my turning here to my second large question: What is the value of debating about *The Turn of the Screw*? What can we say about those hundreds of thousands of hours people have spent arguing in print, in classrooms, and in private conversation, not only about the printed version but about the movies and opera based on it?

[7]I hope, but cannot believe, that my own irony here will never be quoted against me. And I should perhaps add that though I still see James as consciously intending (at least most of the time) a straight story, I am forced to agree now with those who see James-the-imaginer as having been to some degree deflected from his conscious intentions by the intensities of his own encounters with disturbed and superstitious minds. Thus, having changed my mind about it several times over the years, I can hardly agree with those who expect to find the one right final reading.

The question clearly applies sharply to us critics you are meeting in this volume. We are not in any obvious agreement about what the story is or how to discuss it. Even if we got together for prolonged discussion, we would not come out in full agreement about every detail. We know that, and yet we continue to debate — knowing full well that such inherently interminable debate is not actually required of us. Even those among us who must publish or perish could easily write about other matters. Why *The Turn of the Screw*? As I've said, few stories have been subjected to anything like this much debate. About most stories that we tell one another, we feel little temptation to spend much time in discussion: they are simply gripping or boring and we leave it at that. How can we judge the value of the time and energy and specific kind of attention that are spent on this story and others like it?

Here we must face the same complication that troubled us in appraising the three contrasting stories themselves: straight, ironic, and mazed. Much will depend on the presuppositions of the reader who engages in debate about James's complex gift. If that reader is already convinced, before reading, that no debate can ever lead to genuine improvement of views, that no views about anything are inherently superior to any other views, then debate about the story is not in itself an activity to value. Why bother? Critical debate in this view can have value only to the degree that it results in persuading us to believe that all ideas are equally questionable.[8] If there will always be counter-evidence for anyone clever enough to locate it, then to persuade readers to have the maze experience in its extremer versions may feel worthwhile, but the time spent on the debate itself will simply be a means to the end of coming to the truth-of-non-truth. On the other hand the reader may have been, in past reading and discussion, unduly eager to land in certainty, or unwilling to change a reading in the face of hard evidence — Miles's death is obviously sad or horrifying or triumphant, or deliberately puzzling, and so on. For such a reader the experience of having to debate a particular story, the engagement with evidence and counter-evidence, the irresistible temptation to go back and read the story again, can all be in themselves educational: the very process is valuable, regardless of where, at a given stage in the argument, we come out. But that value depends on one strong assumption too often

[8]One well-known critic, who shall be nameless, has sometimes argued that no interpretations are inherently better than others, and that debating about them has only one unquestionable value: it gains jobs and promotions for professors. But I can't believe that he takes himself seriously in such claims, because he often shows a passionate concern to get things right.

repudiated by the "mazers": though no one reading can ever triumph over all others, there *are* better and worse readings. In short, "my" readings, like yours, are inherently corrigible, improvable.

As someone who began his mental life expecting to get "the whole thing taped," convinced that sooner or later he could, "in principle," know the truth about just about everything, I would claim that to have been led, by teachers and other critics, to debate just how this or that story ought to be read, just what experience of it ought to be achieved, has been one of life's most precious gifts. Again and again I have found myself, after expressing a firm conclusion in talk or print, simply and embarrassingly proved wrong. I have then had to draw back, re-think, re-read, and try again. Often I have been shocked, or angry, or disoriented. I have then sometimes developed fancy hypotheses in the effort to prove my opponents wrong — only to discover that the hypotheses had nothing to say for themselves except that they were mine. I was wrong again — and again.

Perhaps you will not be surprised to find me concluding, then, that to live in that kind of constantly revising state is not a bad way to live. When are we more fully alive than when grappling with Henry James and then being forced by other readers to go back for another look at his beautiful intricate prose, and then debating further about whether one has re-read those often puzzling words in the best possible — or at least a defensible — way? It's not a bad way to go, not a bad way to go at all. On the contrary I would say that the hours I have spent on this story in the past, and the hours I am spending now, trying to rise to the level of James's kind of mind and of the best of the other minds who have found him worth reading, including yours, my anonymous friends who read me here — these hours have been among the best of my days, or weeks, or years.

Just compare the time we have spent together so far here, you and I, with the time we spent last night watching the latest re-run of the most popular mystery or horror film or the hottest talk show or rock video, or whatever political convention happens to have been on, or the latest sport championship; or the time we spent this morning reading the sports page or the comic strips. While I don't feel any deep regret about the time I spend on activities like that — and I spend time on all of them — I haven't the least doubt about valuing more highly the time I've spent on Henry James and his critics, whether I have agreed with their readings or not. Though some critics have seemed to be merely playing trivial self-promotional games, most have been engaged in the activity Henry James himself most honored: constructing, or in our case re-constructing with his help, a complex, challenging story that becomes, almost miraculously, theirs.

Most of my other valued experiences in life select out from many possible values one or another and play it to the hilt. Sports, sex, food, travel seem to offer shallow pleasures compared with the hours we're spending "here" — here in this curious mental space/nonspace where you as my reader and I as a fellow-reader of Henry James somehow meet. Our experience here is rivaled only by other deep activities: loving, making friends, trying to help others or obtaining help from them — you can no doubt add to this short list. And one wonderful bonus of experiencing stories is the way they can deepen those other deepest experiences. A great part of the fun of seeing a good movie, for example, is arguing about its meanings afterward, with someone whose challenges we respect.

Many of my other valued experiences produce strong emotional responses — "We won the championship!" — but little or no thought. Some other experiences make me think — "Why did Karpov choose just this move at this point in the championship chess match?" — but do not engage my deeper emotions. Some experiences engage me emotionally and also make me think — "How can I outsmart X in this championship match?" — but do not sharpen my sensitivity to and concern for other people's feelings. Responding to Henry James's story, however, and then discussing it with other readers, can "deepen" me in all three dimensions at once. Whether I find myself feeling with the governess or against her, I am, in most though perhaps not all conceivable readings, engaged with the imaginative richness of extraordinary minds and hearts — not just Henry James's but other readers'.

To wrestle with minds and hearts like that, to make my own sense out of one rich piece of the world, that piece itself consisting of characters who themselves think and feel and talk and act in concern for what is good or bad about one another — is not such wrestling the best possible life-instructor as we construct the day-by-day story of our own lives? We all meet many characters daily, some who wish us well and some who will gladly turn the screw another notch in our troubles and pains. Who better than Henry James and his critics can teach us the complex skills we need in "reading" these would-be friends?

Psychoanalytic Criticism
and *The Turn of the Screw*

WHAT IS PSYCHOANALYTIC CRITICISM?

It seems natural to think about novels in terms of dreams. Like dreams, literary works are fictions, inventions of the mind that, although based on reality, are by definition not literally true. Like a literary work, a dream may have some truth to tell, but, like a literary work, it may need to be interpreted before that truth can be grasped. We can live vicariously through romantic fictions, much as we can through daydreams. Terrifying novels and nightmares affect us in much the same way, plunging us into an atmosphere that continues to cling, even after the last chapter has been read — or the alarm clock has sounded.

The notion that dreams allow such psychic explorations, of course, like the analogy between literary works and dreams, owes a great deal to the thinking of Sigmund Freud, the famous Austrian psychoanalyst who in 1900 published a seminal essay, *The Interpretation of Dreams*. But is the reader who feels that Emily Brontë's *Wuthering Heights* is dreamlike — who feels that Mary Shelley's *Frankenstein* is nightmarish — necessarily a Freudian literary critic? To some extent the answer has to be yes. We are all Freudians, really, whether or not we have read a single work by Freud. At one time or another, most of us have referred to ego, libido, complexes, unconscious desires, and sexual repression. The premises of Freud's thought have changed the way the

Western world thinks about itself. Psychoanalytic criticism has influenced the teachers our teachers studied with, the works of scholarship and criticism they read, and the critical and creative writers *we* read as well.

What Freud did was develop a language that described, a model that explained, a theory that encompassed human psychology. Many of the elements of psychology he sought to describe and explain are present in the literary works of various ages and cultures, from Sophocles' *Oedipus Rex* to Shakespeare's *Hamlet* to works being written in our own day. When the great novel of the twenty-first century is written, many of these same elements of psychology will probably inform its discourse as well. If, by understanding human psychology according to Freud, we can appreciate literature on a new level, then we should acquaint ourselves with his insights.

Freud's theories are either directly or indirectly concerned with the nature of the unconscious mind. Freud didn't invent the notion of the unconscious; others before him had suggested that even the supposedly "sane" human mind was conscious and rational only at times, and even then at possibly only one level. But Freud went further, suggesting that the powers motivating men and women are *mainly* and *normally* unconscious.

Freud, then, powerfully developed an old idea: that the human mind is essentially dual in nature. He called the predominantly passional, irrational, unknown, and unconscious part of the psyche the *id,* or "it." The *ego,* or "I," was his term for the predominantly rational, logical, orderly, conscious part. Another aspect of the psyche, which he called the *superego,* is really a projection of the ego. The superego almost seems to be outside of the self, making moral judgments, telling us to make sacrifices for good causes even though self-sacrifice may not be quite logical or rational. And, in a sense, the superego *is* "outside," since much of what it tells us to do or think we have learned from our parents, our schools, or our religious institutions.

What the ego and superego tell us *not* to do or think is repressed, forced into the unconscious mind. One of Freud's most important contributions to the study of the psyche, the theory of repression, goes something like this: much of what lies in the unconscious mind has been put there by consciousness, which acts as a censor, driving underground unconscious or conscious thoughts or instincts that it deems unacceptable. Censored materials often involve infantile sexual desires, Freud postulated. Repressed to an unconscious state, they emerge only in disguised forms: in dreams, in language (so-called Freudian slips), in

creative activity that may produce art (including literature), and in neurotic behavior.

According to Freud, all of us have repressed wishes and fears; we all
have dreams in which repressed feelings and memories emerge disguised, and thus we are all potential candidates for dream analysis. One
of the unconscious desires most commonly repressed is the childhood
wish to displace the parent of our own sex and take his or her place in
the affections of the parent of the opposite sex. This desire really
involves a number of different but related wishes and fears. (A boy —
and it should be remarked in passing that Freud here concerns himself
mainly with the male — may fear that his father will castrate him, and
he may wish that his mother would return to nursing him.) Freud
referred to the whole complex of feelings by the word *oedipal,* naming
the complex after the Greek tragic hero Oedipus, who unwittingly
killed his father and married his mother.

Why are oedipal wishes and fears repressed by the conscious side of
the mind? And what happens to them after they have been censored? As
Roy P. Basler puts it in *Sex, Symbolism, and Psychology in Literature*
(1975), "from the beginning of recorded history such wishes have been
restrained by the most powerful religious and social taboos, and as a
result have come to be regarded as 'unnatural,'" even though "Freud
found that such wishes are more or less characteristic of normal human
development":

> In dreams, particularly, Freud found ample evidence that such
> wishes persisted. . . . Hence he conceived that natural urges, when
> identified as "wrong," may be repressed but not obliterated. . . .
> In the unconscious, these urges take on symbolic garb, regarded
> as nonsense by the waking mind that does not recognize their sig-
> nificance. (14)

Freud's belief in the significance of dreams, of course, was no more
original than his belief that there is an unconscious side to the psyche.
Again, it was the extent to which he developed a theory of how dreams
work — and the extent to which that theory helped him, by analogy,
to understand far more than just dreams — that made him unusual,
important, and influential beyond the perimeters of medical schools
and psychiatrists' offices.

The psychoanalytic approach to literature not only rests on the theories of Freud; it may even be said to have *begun* with Freud, who was

interested in writers, especially those who relied heavily on symbols. Such writers regularly cloak or mystify ideas in figures that make sense only when interpreted, much as the unconscious mind of a neurotic disguises secret thoughts in dream stories or bizarre actions that need to be interpreted by an analyst. Freud's interest in literary artists led him to make some unfortunate generalizations about creativity; for example, in the twenty-third lecture in *Introductory Lectures on Psycho-Analysis* (1922), he defined the artist as "one urged on by instinctive needs that are too clamorous" (314). But it also led him to write creative literary criticism of his own, including an influential essay on "The Relation of a Poet to Daydreaming" (1908) and "The Uncanny" (1919), a provocative psychoanalytic reading of E. T. A. Hoffman's supernatural tale "The Sandman."

Freud's application of psychoanalytic theory to literature quickly caught on. In 1909, only a year after Freud had published "The Relation of a Poet to Daydreaming," the psychoanalyst Otto Rank published *The Myth of the Birth of the Hero*. In that work, Rank subscribes to the notion that the artist turns a powerful, secret wish into a literary fantasy, and he uses Freud's notion about the "oedipal" complex to explain why the popular stories of so many heroes in literature are so similar. A year after Rank had published his psychoanalytic account of heroic texts, Ernest Jones, Freud's student and eventual biographer, turned his attention to a tragic text: Shakespeare's *Hamlet*. In an essay first published in the *American Journal of Psychology*, Jones, like Rank, makes use of the oedipal concept: he suggests that Hamlet is a victim of strong feelings toward his mother, the queen.

Between 1909 and 1949, numerous other critics decided that psychological and psychoanalytic theory could assist in the understanding of literature. I. A. Richards, Kenneth Burke, and Edmund Wilson were among the most influential to become interested in the new approach. Not all of the early critics were committed to the approach; neither were all of them Freudians. Some followed Alfred Adler, who believed that writers wrote out of inferiority complexes, and others applied the ideas of Carl Gustav Jung, who had broken with Freud over Freud's emphasis on sex and who had developed a theory of the *collective* unconscious. According to Jungian theory, a great work of literature is not a disguised expression of its author's personal, repressed wishes; rather, it is a manifestation of desires once held by the whole human race but now repressed because of the advent of civilization.

It is important to point out that among those who relied on Freud's models were a number of critics who were poets and novelists as well.

Conrad Aiken wrote a Freudian study of American literature, and poets such as Robert Graves and W. H. Auden applied Freudian insights when writing critical prose. William Faulkner, Henry James, James Joyce, D. H. Lawrence, Marcel Proust, and Toni Morrison are only a few of the novelists who have either written criticism influenced by Freud or who have written novels that conceive of character, conflict, and creative writing itself in Freudian terms. The poet H. D. (Hilda Doolittle) was actually a patient of Freud's and provided an account of her analysis in her book *Tribute to Freud*. By giving Freudian theory credibility among students of literature that only they could bestow, such writers helped to endow earlier psychoanalytic criticism with a largely Freudian orientation that has begun to be challenged only in the last two decades.

The willingness, even eagerness, of writers to use Freudian models in producing literature and criticism of their own consummated a relationship that, to Freud and other pioneering psychoanalytic theorists, had seemed fated from the beginning; after all, therapy involves the close analysis of language. René Wellek and Austin Warren included "psychological" criticism as one of the five "extrinsic" approaches to literature described in their influential book *Theory of Literature* (1942). Psychological criticism, they suggest, typically attempts to do at least one of the following: provide a psychological study of an individual writer; explore the nature of the creative process; generalize about "types and laws present within works of literature"; or theorize about the psychological "effects of literature upon its readers" (81). Entire books on psychoanalytic criticism began to appear, such as Frederick J. Hoffman's *Freudianism and the Literary Mind* (1945).

Probably because of Freud's characterization of the creative mind as "clamorous" if not ill, psychoanalytic criticism written before 1950 tended to psychoanalyze the individual author. Poems were read as fantasies that allowed authors to indulge repressed wishes, to protect themselves from deep-seated anxieties, or both. A perfect example of author analysis would be Marie Bonaparte's 1933 study of Edgar Allan Poe. Bonaparte found Poe to be so fixated on his mother that his repressed longing emerges in his stories in images such as the white spot on a black cat's breast, said to represent mother's milk.

A later generation of psychoanalytic critics often paused to analyze the characters in novels and plays before proceeding to their authors. But not for long, since characters, both evil and good, tended to be seen by these critics as the author's potential selves, or projections of various repressed aspects of his or her psyche. For instance, in *A Psycho-*

analytic Study of the Double in Literature (1970), Robert Rogers begins with the view that human beings are double or multiple in nature. Using this assumption, along with the psychoanalytic concept of "dissociation" (best known by its result, the dual or multiple personality), Rogers concludes that writers reveal instinctual or repressed selves in their books, often without realizing that they have done so.

In the view of critics attempting to arrive at more psychological insights into an author than biographical materials can provide, a work of literature is a fantasy or a dream — or at least so analogous to daydream or dream that Freudian analysis can help explain the nature of the mind that produced it. The author's purpose in writing is to gratify secretly some forbidden wish, in particular an infantile wish or desire that has been repressed into the unconscious mind. To discover what the wish is, the psychoanalytic critic employs many of the terms and procedures developed by Freud to analyze dreams.

The literal surface of a work is sometimes spoken of as its "manifest content" and treated as a "manifest dream" or "dream story" would be treated by a Freudian analyst. Just as the analyst tries to figure out the "dream thought" behind the dream story — that is, the latent or hidden content of the manifest dream — so the psychoanalytic literary critic tries to expose the latent, underlying content of a work. Freud used the words *condensation* and *displacement* to explain two of the mental processes whereby the mind disguises its wishes and fears in dream stories. In condensation, several thoughts or persons may be condensed into a single manifestation or image in a dream story; in displacement, an anxiety, a wish, or a person may be displaced onto the image of another, with which or whom it is loosely connected through a string of associations that only an analyst can untangle. Psychoanalytic critics treat metaphors as if they were dream condensations; they treat metonyms — figures of speech based on extremely loose, arbitrary associations — as if they were dream displacements. Thus figurative literary language in general is treated as something that evolves as the writer's conscious mind resists what the unconscious tells it to picture or describe. A symbol is, in Daniel Weiss's words, "a meaningful concealment of truth as the truth promises to emerge as some frightening or forbidden idea" (20).

In a 1970 article entitled "The 'Unconscious' of Literature," Norman Holland, a literary critic trained in psychoanalysis, succinctly sums up the attitudes held by critics who would psychoanalyze authors, but without quite saying that it is the *author* that is being analyzed by the psychoanalytic critic. "When one looks at a poem psychoanalytically," he writes, "one considers it as though it were a dream or as though some ideal patient [were speaking] from the couch in iambic pentameter." One "looks for the general level or levels of fantasy associated with the language. By level I mean the familiar stages of childhood development — oral [when desires for nourishment and infantile sexual desires overlap], anal [when infants receive their primary pleasure from defecation], urethral [when urinary functions are the locus of sexual pleasure], phallic [when the penis or, in girls, some penis substitute is of primary interest], oedipal." Holland continues by analyzing not Robert Frost but Frost's poem "Mending Wall" as a specifically oral fantasy that is not unique to its author. "Mending Wall" is "about breaking down the wall which marks the separated or individuated self so as to return to a state of closeness to some Other"— including and perhaps essentially the nursing mother ("'Unconscious'" 136, 139).

While not denying the idea that the unconscious plays a role in creativity, psychoanalytic critics such as Holland began to focus more on the ways in which authors create works that appeal to *our* repressed wishes and fantasies. Consequently, they shifted their focus away from the psyche of the author and toward the psychology of the reader and the text. Holland's theories, which have concerned themselves more with the reader than with the text, have helped to establish another school of critical theory: reader-response criticism. Elizabeth Wright explains Holland's brand of modern psychoanalytic criticism in this way: "What draws us as readers to a text is the secret expression of what we desire to hear, much as we protest we do not. The disguise must be good enough to fool the censor into thinking that the text is respectable, but bad enough to allow the unconscious to glimpse the unrespectable" (117).

Holland is one of dozens of critics who have revised Freud significantly in the process of revitalizing psychoanalytic criticism. Another such critic is R. D. Laing, whose controversial and often poetical writings about personality, repression, masks, and the double or "schizoid" self have (re)blurred the boundary between creative writing and psychoanalytic discourse. Yet another is D. W. Winnicott, an "object relations" theorist who has had a significant impact on literary criticism. Critics influenced by Winnicott and his school have questioned the tendency to see reader/text as an either/or construct; instead, they have seen reader and text (or audience and play) in terms of a *relationship* taking place in what Winnicott calls a "transitional" or "potential" space — space in which binary terms such as *real* and *illusory, objective* and *subjective,* have little or no meaning.

Psychoanalytic theorists influenced by Winnicott see the transitional or potential reader/text (or audience/play) space as being *like* the space entered into by psychoanalyst and patient. More important, they also see it as being similar to the space between mother and infant: a space characterized by trust in which categorizing terms such as *knowing* and *feeling* mix and merge and have little meaning apart from one another.

Whereas Freud saw the mother-son relationship in terms of the son and his repressed oedipal complex (and saw the analyst-patient relationship in terms of the patient and the repressed "truth" that the analyst could scientifically extract), object-relations analysts see both relationships as *dyadic* — that is, as being dynamic in both directions. Consequently, they don't depersonalize analysis or their analyses. It is hardly surprising, therefore, that contemporary literary critics who apply object-relations theory to the texts they discuss don't depersonalize critics or categorize their interpretations as "truthful," at least not in any objective or scientific sense. In the view of such critics, interpretations are made of language — itself a transitional object — and are themselves the mediating terms or transitional objects of a relationship.

Like critics of the Winnicottian school, the French structuralist theorist Jacques Lacan focused on language and language-related issues. He treated the unconscious *as* a language and, consequently, viewed the dream not as Freud did (that is, as a form and symptom of repression) but rather as a form of discourse. Thus we may study dreams psychoanalytically to learn about literature, even as we may study literature to learn more about the unconscious. In Lacan's seminar on Poe's "The Purloined Letter," a pattern of repetition like that used by psychoanalysts in their analyses is used to arrive at a reading of the story. According to Wright, "the new psychoanalytic structural approach to literature" employs "analogies from psychoanalysis . . . to explain the workings of the text as distinct from the workings of a particular author's, character's, or even reader's mind" (125).

Lacan, however, did far more than extend Freud's theory of dreams, literature, and the interpretation of both. More significantly, he took Freud's whole theory of psyche and gender and added to it a crucial third term — that of language. In the process, he both used and significantly developed Freud's ideas about the oedipal stage and complex.

Lacan pointed out that the pre-oedipal stage, in which the child at first does not even recognize its independence from its mother, is also a pre*verbal* stage, one in which the child communicates without the medium of language, or — if we insist on calling the child's communications a language — in a language that can only be called *literal*. ("Coos," certainly, cannot be said to be figurative or symbolic.) Then, while still in the pre-oedipal stage, the child enters the *mirror* stage.

During the mirror period, the child comes to view itself and its mother, later other people as well, *as* independent selves. This is the stage in which the child is first able to fear the aggressions of another, to desire what is recognizably beyond the self (initially the mother), and, finally, to want to compete with another for the same desired object. This is also the stage at which the child first becomes able to feel sympathy with another being who is being hurt by a third, to cry when another cries. All of these developments, of course, involve projecting beyond the self and, by extension, constructing one's own self (or "ego" or "I") as others view one — that is, as *another*. Such constructions, according to Lacan, are just that: constructs, products, artifacts — fictions of coherence that in fact hide what Lacan called the "absence" or "lack" of being.

The mirror stage, which Lacan also referred to as the *imaginary* stage, is fairly quickly succeeded by the oedipal stage. As in Freud, this stage begins when the child, having come to view itself as self and the father and mother as separate selves, perceives gender and gender differences between its parents and between itself and one of its parents. For boys, gender awareness involves another, more powerful recognition, for the recognition of the father's phallus as the mark of his difference from the mother involves, at the same time, the recognition that his older and more powerful father is also his rival. That, in turn, leads to the understanding that what once seemed wholly his and even indistinguishable from himself is in fact someone else's: something properly desired only at a distance and in the form of socially acceptable *substitutes*.

The fact that the oedipal stage roughly coincides with the entry of the child into language is extremely important for Lacan. For the linguistic order is essentially a figurative or "Symbolic" order; words are not the things they stand for but are, rather stand-ins or substitutes for those things. Hence boys, who in the most critical period of their development have had to submit to what Lacan called the "Law of the Father"— a law that prohibits direct desire for and communicative intimacy with what has been the boy's whole world — enter more easily into the realm of language and the Symbolic order than do girls, who have never really had to renounce that which once seemed continuous with the self: the mother. The gap that has been opened up for boys, which includes the gap between signs and what they substitute — the gap marked by the phallus and encoded with the boy's sense of his maleness — has not opened up for girls, or has not opened up in the same way, to the same degree.

For Lacan, the father need not be present to trigger the oedipal stage; nor does his phallus have to be seen to catalyze the boy's (easier) transition into the Symbolic order. Rather, Lacan argued, a child's recognition of its gender is intricately tied up with a growing recognition of the system of names and naming, part of the larger system of substitutions we call language. A child has little doubt about who its mother is, but who is its father, and how would one know? The father's claim rests on the mother's *word* that he is in fact the father; the father's relationship to the child is thus established through language and a system of marriage and kinship — names — that in turn is basic to rules of everything from property to law. The name of the father (*nom du père*, which in French sounds like *non du père*) involves, in a sense, nothing of the father — nothing, that is, except his word or name.

Lacan's development of Freud has had several important results. First, his sexist-seeming association of maleness with the Symbolic order, together with his claim that women cannot therefore enter easily into the order, has prompted feminists not to reject his theory out of hand but, rather, to look more closely at the relation between language and gender, language and women's inequality. Some feminists have gone so far as to suggest that the social and political relationships between male and female will not be fundamentally altered until language itself has been radically changed. (That change might begin dialectically, with the development of some kind of "feminine language" grounded in the presymbolic, literal-to-imaginary communication between mother and child.)

Second, Lacan's theory has proved of interest to deconstructors and other poststructuralists, in part because it holds that the ego (which in Freud's view is as necessary as it is natural) is a product or construct. The ego-artifact, produced during the mirror stage, *seems* at once unified, consistent, and organized around a determinate center. But the unified self, or ego, is a fiction, according to Lacan. The yoking together of fragments and destructively dissimilar elements takes its psychic toll, and it is the job of the Lacanian psychoanalyst to "deconstruct," as it were, the ego, to show its continuities to be contradictions as well.

The author of the psychoanalytic essay that follows, Stanley Renner, is one in a long line of critics who have assumed that the "true" and "richer" reading of *The Turn of the Screw* is one that views the text not as a ghost story but, rather, as a "dramatization of a woman's psychosexual problem and the damage it does to the children in her charge." One thing that makes Renner's approach new and different is the fact that it seeks to answer a question previous psychoanalytic critics have by and large avoided: If we are to take the "ghosts" of the story as the projections of a mentally skewed governess, then why does James see to it that the governess's description of the male ghost is identified by an astonished Mrs. Grose as Peter Quint, a deceased former valet?

Having posed the question, Renner sets it aside for awhile, taking a close look at the character of the governess and showing that her "background, inexperience, vulnerability, anxiety and fear, and susceptibility to romantic emotions" all make her a candidate for what James's contemporaries would have called "sexual hysteria" in general and, more specifically, a "hysterical fit." The governess, in Renner's view, experiences just such a fit when the erotically charged, attractive male figure she at first thinks she sees suddenly becomes a very different sort of figure, a frightening male with a pale, long face, small but penetrating eyes, thin lips, and curly red hair. This transformation of an erotically attractive image of man into a decidedly repulsive one is, according to Renner, driven by a "fear of male sexuality" that would have gone hand in hand with the erotic longings of a nineteenth-century parson's daughter.

James, Renner shows, would have been familiar with the term "sexual hysteria"; indeed, it seems likely that he knew Breuer and Freud's *Studien über Hysterie*. Furthermore, as Oscar Cargill has shown, James's own sister, Alice, had been said to be a sexual hysteric. But James was drawing and commenting upon more than his sister, more than Freudian theory, and more than sexual hysteria in *The Turn of the Screw*. He was also, Renner believes, exploring "the physiognomies of fictional characterization" — that is, the *stereotypical* nature of the way in which Victorian minds would have hallucinated about the sexual male, and the stereotypical way in which Victorian writers (whose works at once influenced and reflected the influences of contemporary thinking) represented "evil, which in Victorian times tended to mean sexual evil." (The pale, red-haired, sharp-eyed physiognomy of Quint as envisioned by the governess, Renner argues, resembles any number of "bad men" in late eighteenth- and nineteenth-century Victorian and continental novels.)

Renner's approach to *The Turn of the Screw* is typical of Freudian psychoanalytic criticism insofar as it grounds literary images and even plots in psychic fantasies and their inhibition or repression — in this case the governess's sexual longings and simultaneous attempts to bury those longings at great psychic cost to herself and her charges. But Renner, unlike Freud and early psychoanalytic critics influenced by Freud, does not attempt to psychoanalyze the author by reading the text as if it were James's unintentionally revealing dream. Rather, he views James as a highly deliberative framer of words who understood human nature along lines suggested by Freud and who, therefore, fashioned the characters in his fiction accordingly.

If that were all Renner did, his psychoanalytic approach would be of interest, although less than contemporary. But Renner goes further by adding a *cultural* dimension to our understanding of psychology and of the psychological dimensions of texts. The hallucination that a person experiences when undergoing an attack of something like hysteria, Renner argues, is not just some private imagining; rather, it is historically determined — that is, a representation of a cultural stereotype. (If such a hallucination takes place in an influential work of fiction, it is a reinforcement, as well as a representation, of a cultural stereotype.) To put this another way: cultures, as well as individuals, have fantasies and fears — fantasies and fears that they "write" through novelists such as Dickens and Thackeray and, of course, Henry James.

Ross C Murfin

PSYCHOANALYTIC CRITICISM: A SELECTED BIBLIOGRAPHY

Some Short Introductions to Psychological and Psychoanalytic Theory

Holland, Norman. "The 'Unconscious' of Literature: The Psychoanalytic Approach." *Contemporary Criticism.* Ed. Malcolm Bradbury and David Palmer. Stratford-Upon-Avon Studies 12. New York: St. Martin's, 1971. 131–53.

Natoli, Joseph, and Frederik L. Rusch, comps. *Psychocriticism: An Annotated Bibliography*. Westport: Greenwood, 1984.

Scott, Wilbur. *Five Approaches to Literary Criticism*. London: Collier-Macmillan, 1962. See the essays by Burke and Gorer as well as Scott's introduction to the section "The Psychological Approach: Literature in the Light of Psychological Theory."

Wellek, René, and Austin Warren. *Theory of Literature*. New York: Harcourt, 1942. See the chapter "Literature and Psychology" in pt. 3, "The Extrinsic Approach to the Study of Literature."

Wright, Elizabeth. "Modern Psychoanalytic Criticism." *Modern Literary Theory: A Comparative Introduction*. Ed. Ann Jefferson and David Robey. Totowa: Barnes, 1982. 113–33.

Freud, Lacan, and Their Influence

Althusser, Louis. *Writings on Psychoanalysis: Freud and Lacan*. Ed. Olivier Corpet and Francois Matheron. Trans. Jeffrey Mehlman. New York: Columbia UP, 1996.

Basler, Roy P. *Sex, Symbolism, and Psychology in Literature*. New York: Octagon, 1975. See especially 13–19.

Clement, Catherine. *The Lives and Legends of Jacques Lacan*. Trans. Arthur Goldhammer. New York: Columbia UP, 1983.

Copjec, Joan. *Read My Desire: Lacan Against the Historicists*. Cambridge: MIT P, 1994.

Feldstein, Richard, Bruce Fink, and Maire Jaanus, eds. *Reading Seminar XI: Lacan's Four Fundamental Concepts of Psychoanalysis*. Albany: State U of New York P, 1995.

Fink, Bruce. *The Lacanian Subject: Between Language and Jouissance*. Princeton: Princeton UP, 1995.

Freud, Sigmund. *The Interpretation of Dreams*. Trans. James Strachey. New York: Avon, 1965.

———. *Introductory Lectures on Psycho-Analysis*. Trans. Joan Riviere. London: Allen, 1922.

Hill, Philip. *Lacan for Beginners*. New York: Writers and Readers, 1997.

Lacan, Jacques. *Ecrits: A Selection*. Trans. Alan Sheridan. New York: Norton, 1977.

———. *The Ego in Freud's Theory and in the Technique of Psychoanalysis 1954–1955*. Ed. Jacques-Alain Miller. Trans. Sylvana Tomaselli. The Seminar of Jacques Lacan Book II. New York: Norton, 1988.

————. *The Ethics of Psychoanalysis: 1959–1960.* Ed. Jacques-Alain Miller. Trans. Dennis Porter. The Seminar of Jacques Lacan Book VII. New York: Norton, 1992.

————. *Feminine Sexuality: Lacan and the ecole freudienne.* Ed. Juliet Mitchell and Jacqueline Rose. Trans. Rose. New York: Norton, 1982.

————. *The Four Fundamental Concepts of Psychoanalysis.* Trans. Alan Sheridan. London: Penguin, 1980.

————. *Freud's Papers on Technique 1953–1954.* Ed. Jacques-Alain Miller. Trans. John Forrester. The Seminar of Jacques Lacan Book I. New York: Norton, 1988.

————. *On Feminine Sexuality: The Limits of Love and Knowledge.* Ed. Jacques-Alain Miller. Trans. Bruce Fink. The Seminar of Jacques Lacan Book XX: Encore 1972–1973. New York: Norton, 1998.

Lee, Jonathan Scott. *Jacques Lacan.* Boston: Twayne, 1990.

Ragland-Sullivan, Ellie. *Essays on the Pleasures of Death: From Freud to Lacan.* New York: Routledge, 1995.

Roudinesco, Elisabeth. *Jacques Lacan.* Trans. Barbara Bray. New York: Columbia UP, 1997.

Schneiderman, Stuart. *Jacques Lacan: The Death of an Intellectual Hero.* Cambridge: Harvard UP, 1983.

Zizek, Slavoj. *Enjoy Your Symptom: Jacques Lacan in Hollywood and Out.* New York: Routledge, 1992.

————. *The Metastases of Enjoyment: Six Essays on Woman and Causality.* New York: Verso, 1994.

————. *The Sublime Object of Ideology.* New York: Verso, 1989.

Psychoanalysis, Feminism, and Literature

Barr, Marleen S., and Richard Feldstein. *Discontented Discourses: Feminism/Textual Intervention/Psychoanalysis.* Urbana: U of Illinois P, 1989.

Benjamin, Jessica. *The Bonds of Love: Psychoanalysis, Feminism and the Problem of Domination.* New York: Pantheon, 1988.

Bernheimer, Charles, and Claire Kahane, eds. *In Dora's Case: Freud-Hysteria-Feminism.* New York: Columbia UP, 1985.

de Lauretis, Teresa. *The Practice of Love: Lesbian Sexuality and Perverse Desire.* Bloomington: Indiana UP, 1994.

Elliott, Patricia. *From Mastery to Analysis: Theories of Gender in Psychoanalytic Criticism.* Ithaca: Cornell UP, 1991.

Felman, Shoshana. *What Does a Woman Want? Reading and Sexual Difference.* Baltimore: Johns Hopkins UP, 1993.

Gallop, Jane. *The Daughter's Seduction: Feminism and Psychoanalysis.* Ithaca: Cornell UP, 1982.

———. *Thinking Through the Body.* New York: Columbia UP, 1988.

Garner, Shirley Nelson, Claire Kahane, and Madelon Sprengnether. *The (M)other Tongue: Essays in Feminist Psychoanalytic Interpretation.* Ithaca: Cornell UP, 1985.

Grosz, Elizabeth. *Jacques Lacan: A Feminist Introduction.* New York: Routledge, 1990.

Irigaray, Luce. *This Sex Which Is Not One.* Trans. Catherine Porter. Ithaca: Cornell UP, 1985.

———. *Speculum of the Other Woman.* Trans. Gillian C. Gill. Ithaca: Cornell UP, 1985.

Jacobus, Mary. "Is There a Woman in This Text?" *New Literary History* 14 (1982): 117–41.

Kristeva, Julia. *The Kristeva Reader.* Ed. Toril Moi. New York: Columbia UP, 1986. See especially the selection from *Revolution in Poetic Language* 89–136.

MacCannell, Juliet Flower. *The Regime of the Brother: After the Patriarchy.* New York: Routledge, 1991.

Mitchell, Juliet. *Psychoanalysis and Feminism.* New York: Random, 1974.

Mitchell, Juliet, and Jacqueline Rose, Introduction I and Introduction II. Lacan, *Feminine Sexuality: Jacques Lacan and the ecole freudienne* 1–26, 27–57.

Rose, Jacqueline. *Sexuality in the Field of Vision.* New York: Verso, 1986.

Sprengnether, Madelon. *The Spectral Mother: Freud, Feminism, and Psychoanalysis.* Ithaca: Cornell UP, 1990.

Psychological and Psychoanalytic Studies of Literature, Culture, and the Arts

Apollon, Willy, and Richard Feldstein, eds. *Lacan. Politics, Aesthetics.* Albany: State U of New York P, 1996.

Bersani, Leo. *Baudelaire and Freud.* Berkeley: U of California P, 1977.

———. *The Freudian Body: Psychoanalysis and Art.* New York: Columbia UP, 1986.

Bettelheim, Bruno. *The Uses of Enchantment: The Meaning and Importance of Fairy Tales.* New York: Knopf, 1976.

Bracher, Mark. *Lacan, Discourse, and Social Change: A Psychoanalytic Cultural Criticism.* Ithaca: Cornell UP, 1993.

Grosz, Elizabeth. *Space, Time, and Perversion: Essays on the Politics of Bodies.* New York: Routledge, 1995.

Hartman, Geoffrey, ed. *Psychoanalysis and the Question of the Text.* Baltimore: Johns Hopkins UP, 1978.

Hertz, Neil. *The End of the Line: Essays on Psychoanalysis and the Sublime.* New York: Columbia UP, 1985.

Jacobus, Mary. *First Things: The Maternal Imaginary in Literature, Art, and Psychoanalysis.* New York: Routledge, 1995.

Krauss, Rosalind. *The Optical Unconscious.* Cambridge: MIT P, 1994.

Poizat, Michel. *The Angel's Cry: Beyond the Pleasure Principle in Opera.* Trans. Arthur Denner. Ithaca: Cornell UP, 1992.

Salecl, Renata, and Slavoj Zizek, eds. *Gaze and Voice as Love Objects.* Durham: Duke UP, 1996.

Silverman, Kaja. *The Threshold of the Visible World.* New York: Routledge, 1996.

Lacanian Psychoanalytic Studies of Literature

Booker, M. Keith. "Notes Toward a Lacanian Reading of Wallace Stevens." *Journal of Modern Literature* 16 (1990): 493–509.

Davis, Robert Con, ed. *The Fictional Father: Lacanian Readings of the Text.* Amherst: U of Massachusetts P, 1981.

——. *Lacan and Narration: The Psychoanalytic Difference in Narrative Theory.* Baltimore: Johns Hopkins UP, 1984.

Devlin, Kim. "Castration and Its Discontents: A Lacanian Approach to *Ulysses.*" *James Joyce Quarterly* 29 (1991): 117–44.

Felman, Shoshana, ed. *Literature and Psychoanalysis: The Question of Reading: Otherwise.* Baltimore: Johns Hopkins UP, 1982. Includes Lacan's seminar on Shakespeare's *Hamlet.*

Homans, Margaret. *Bearing the Word: Language and Female Experience in Nineteenth-Century Women's Writing.* Chicago: U of Chicago P, 1986.

Lacan, Jacques. "The Essence of Tragedy: A Commentary on Sophocles's *Antigone.*" Lacan, *The Ethics of Psychoanalysis* 243–87.

Mellard, James M. *Using Lacan, Reading Fiction.* Urbana: U of Illinois P, 1991.

Miller, David Lee. "Writing the Specular Son: Jonson, Freud, Lacan, and the (K)not of Masculinity." *Desire in the Renaissance:*

Psychoanalysis and Literature. Ed. Valeria Finucci and Regina
Schwartz. Princeton: Princeton UP, 1994. 233–60.

Muller, John P., and William J. Richardson, eds. *The Purloined Poe:
Lacan, Derrida. and Psychoanalytic Reading.* Baltimore: Johns
Hopkins UP, 1988. Includes Lacan's seminar on Poe's "The
Purloined Letter."

Netto, Jeffrey A. "Dickens with Kant and Sade." *Style* 29 (1995):
441–58.

Rapaport, Herman. *Between the Sign & the Gaze.* Ithaca: Cornell UP,
1994.

Schad, John. " 'No One Dreams': Hopkins, Lacan, and the
Unconscious." *Victorian Poetry* 32 (1994): 141–56.

Psychoanalytic Approaches to James
and *The Turn of the Screw*

Cranfill, Thomas Mabry, and Robert Lanier Clark, Jr. *An Anatomy of
"The Turn of the Screw."* Austin: U of Texas P. 1965.

Edel, Leon. "The Little Boys." In *Henry James: The Treacherous Years,
1895–1901.* London: Hart-Davis, 1969. 191–203.

Goddard, Harold C. "A Pre-Freudian Reading of *The Turn of the
Screw.*" *Nineteenth-Century Fiction* 12 (1957): 1–36.

Halttunen, Karen. " 'Through the Cracked and Fragmented Self':
William James and *The Turn of the Screw.*" *American Quarterly* 40
(1988): 472–90.

Katan, M., M.D. "A Causerie on Henry James's *The Turn of the
Screw.*" *The Psychoanalytic Study of the Child* 17 (1962): 473–93.

Levander, Caroline. " 'Informed Eyes': The 1890s Child Study
Movement and Henry James's *The Turn of the Screw.*" *Critical
Matrix* 12 (2001): 8–25.

Lydenberg, John. "The Governess Turns the Screws." *Nineteenth-
Century Fiction* 12 (1957): 37–58.

Mahbobah, Albaraq. "Hysteria, Rhetoric, and the Politics of Reversal
in Henry James's *The Turn of the Screw.*" *Henry James Review* 17
(1996): 149–61.

Spilka, Mark. "Turning the Freudian Screw: How Not to Do It."
Literature and Psychology 13 (1963): 105–11.

Wagenknecht, David. "Here's Looking at You, Peter Quint. *The Turn
of the Screw,* Freud's *Dora,* and the Aesthetics of Hysteria."
American Imago 55 (1998): 423–58.

Wilson, Edmund. "The Ambiguity of Henry James." *Hound and Horn* 7 (1934): 385–406. Rpt. in *The Triple Thinkers,* rev. and enl. ed. New York: Oxford UP, 1948. 88–132.

A PSYCHOANALYTIC PERSPECTIVE

STANLEY RENNER

"Red hair, very red, close-curling": Sexual Hysteria, Physiognomical Bogeymen, and the "Ghosts" in *The Turn of the Screw*

For readers and critics for whom the true — and clearly the richer — story of James's *The Turn of the Screw* is its dramatization of a woman's psychosexual problem and the damage it does to the children in her charge, the immovable stumbling block has always been the governess's detailed description of Peter Quint, a man dead and buried whom she has never seen. If James does not mean for readers to take Quint (and subsequently Miss Jessel) as a bona fide ghost, so the argument runs, why does he arrange things so that the only way to account for her description of him is that she has seen a supernatural manifestation? As Peter Beidler has shown in his "Critical History" of the story earlier in this volume (pp. 189–214), efforts thus far to circumvent this obstacle have not settled the issue. In this essay I want to show that the story provides its own eminently logical, quite unsupernatural, indeed, deeply naturalistic, accounting for the manifestations the governess describes. The logic of this line of development has escaped observation, I believe, because it derives from idea structures that have since faded from general awareness: the symptomatology of female sexual hysteria and the supposed behavioral significance of human physiognomy. What the governess sees on her first encounter with the famous "ghosts" of Bly, the experience that sets in motion the story's central line of development, is thus not the ghost of a dead man she has never seen but the projection of her own sexual hysteria in the form of stereotypes deeply embedded in the mind of the culture. The story's spectral figures, colored by the governess's sexual fear and disgust, symbolize the adult sexuality just beginning to "possess" Miles and Flora as they hover on the brink of puberty. Frantically trying to block the emergence of their sexuality, the governess does damage to their natural development that, in the case of the male child, proves fatal.

The first appearance of an apparition in the story and the governess's state of mind on that occasion are, of course, crucial to understanding the ghosts and their place in James's design. As the story itself asserts, "the fact to be in possession of" is that the governess is a parson's daughter leaving the shelter of home for the first time, coming up to London in "trepidation," and encountering a young gentleman presented in the story as a girl's romantic dream, from whom she accepts employment (p. 26 in this volume). As the Jamesian narrator of the prologue deduces, and Douglas, who knew the governess and tells her story, does not deny, she "succumbed" to the "seduction exercised by the splendid young man" (p. 28). Thus James pointedly calls attention to a group of characterizing details about the governess — her sheltered religious background, inexperience, vulnerability, anxiety and fear, and susceptibility to romantic emotions — that establish her as a virtual Victorian cliché of sexual ambivalence. With her almost classic conflict between idealistic innocence and naive romantic impulses she is the virginal ingénue encountering sexual danger in the form of a "handsome," "bold" young gentleman bachelor with "charming ways with women," enjoying a life of pleasurable self-indulgence (pp. 26–27). This emphasis on the governess's susceptibility to romantic emotions is an important feature of the buildup to the first apparition.

With this preparation the reader comes to the governess's first encounter with the apparitions that harrow her throughout the story: she sees a frightening male ghost that she later describes so particularly that Mrs. Grose, in astonishment and consternation, identifies it as Peter Quint, deceased former valet of the children's uncle and guardian, who, with the last governess, also deceased, had previously shared the charge of the children. When, however, the episode is read closely in the light of the turn-of-the-century understanding of sexual hysteria, it unfolds as a remarkably astute dramatization of an actual hysterical attack.

Although she suppresses the erotic component of her impulses, it is clear that the governess is indulging in romantic fantasies of her dashing young gentleman employer as she enjoys an evening stroll, the children "tucked away" in bed: how "charming" it would be, she fancies, if "[s]ome one would appear there at the turn of a path and would stand before me and smile and approve" (p. 39). And then she does see him. Whatever the psychic validity of the phenomenon James presents in this scene, it is clear that the governess is able to conjure up in her fantasy such a powerful impression that she feels she is actually seeing someone not present. And what she sees, at least at first, is her gentleman employer's "handsome face" reflecting the "kind light" of approval with which she has hoped he will notice her. With "the sense that [her] imagination had . . . turned real," she declares unequivocally, "[h]e did stand there!" (p. 39).

But then as she views this figure from her own imagination she experiences an indescribable "bewilderment of vision": the figure now before her, she explains, "was not the person I had precipitately supposed" (p. 39). Readers have customarily accepted the governess's own explanation for what happens to her vision: that her first impression was mistaken and that the figure that ultimately stands before her has been there all along. But the fact is that she was not mistaken; her identification of the handsome gentleman is too positive, too emphatic to have been a mistake. What has actually happened is that the attractive male figure she first imagines is transformed in her own mind into the frightening male figure she subsequently projects. That the transformation is brought about by fear — specifically fear of male sexuality — is the clear implication of the terms in which the governess explains the "shock" to her sensibility caused by the figure that ultimately met her eyes: "[a]n unknown man in a lonely place is a permitted object of fear to a young woman privately bred" (pp. 39–40).

James's technical knowledge of sexual hysteria has been well established, both his almost certain familiarity with Breuer and Freud's *Studien über Hysterie* and his "personal acquaintance" with an actual case of hysteria in "the illness of his sister [Alice] and with the delusions and fantasies of that illness" (Cargill 247). Thus it should not be surprising that in *The Turn of the Screw* he could portray an accurate, virtually textbook case of sexual hysteria. The most convenient source for the understanding of sexual hysteria at the time of *The Turn of the Screw* is Havelock Ellis, who provides, in "Auto-Erotism," an exhaustive survey of contemporary opinion on the subject. James could not have known Ellis's discussion, which was not published until 1901, but he would have gotten his information from the same sources. I make no claims, by the way, for the validity of turn-of-the-century assumptions about sexual hysteria, which are presently being challenged. My point is only how faithfully James reproduces these assumptions in his characterization of the governess.

Briefly summarized, sexual hysteria, as it was understood in the milieu of *The Turn of the Screw*, is a psychosexual disorder mainly afflicting women, particularly women with "fine qualities of mind and character." It is caused by a profound conflict between their natural sexual impulses and the repression of sexuality required by society and exaggerated by Victorian idealism — a conflict in the hysterical, Havelock Ellis explains, "between their ideas of right and the bent of their inclinations" (220). The classic symptom of hysteria is thus "'a paradoxical sexual instinct' . . . by which, for instance, sexual frigidity is combined with intense sexual preoccupations"(213). The resulting conflict can be of such intensity as to precipitate some kind of "nervous explosion" (231). "Pitres and others," Ellis notes, "refer to the frequently painful nature of sexual hallucinations in the hysterical" (217). In some cases "nausea and vomiting" or an "actual hysterical fit" may occur (223, 225).

Today the term "sexual hysteria" is familiar, but less so is its substance, the actual syndrome designated by the name. Thus, even though the term has been applied to the governess (Huntley 229), no one has shown how exactly she fits the profile of a typical sexual hysteric. It would be hard to imagine a more classic manifestation of its symptomatology than James's governess. Her "superiority of character" (Ellis 220) revealed in her sense of responsibility for the children is unquestionable. She exhibits, in classic form, the conflict between sexual impulse and inhibition found by clinicians of the time at the root of the disorder, suffering from "sexual needs . . . and in large measure, indeed, . . . precisely through the struggle with them, through the effort to thrust sexuality aside" (Ellis 224). A "fluttered anxious girl out of a Hampshire vicarage," the governess is clearly in a state of extreme tension of the kind most likely to trigger an attack of hysteria. And she fits the profile of the typical female hysteric in several ways: she is a "single woman . . . whose sexual needs are unsatisfied"; she appears to be "attractive to men"; she leads the kind of "small, smothered life" conducive to hysteria; and she is extremely suggestible (218, 229). Indeed, in typifying the hysterical situation Ellis mentions the case of a governess much like that of James's protagonist: "in one case," he writes, "a governess, whose training has been severely upright, is, in spite of herself and without any encouragement, led to experience for the father of the children under her care an affection which she refuses to acknowledge even to herself" (221).[1] James's governess, according to all the evidence in *The Turn of the Screw, is* the product of a training "severely upright," and she feels, "without any encouragement," an

---

[1] Ellis is most likely alluding to "The Case of Miss Lucy R.," included in *Studien über Hysterie,* the case that Oscar Cargill convincingly links to *The Turn of the Screw* (156).

attraction to the paternal figure (if not the father) of the household in which she is employed, which she regards as only the desire to please an employer and merit his approval.

Not only does James's governess fit the classic profile of the female sexual hysteric, she also experiences the "hysterical fit" observed by turn-of-the-century clinicians. That her first hallucination precipitates a "nervous explosion" of some intensity is clear from her own account. Like that of the classic hysteric, her "mental activity . . . is split up, and only a part of it is conscious" (Ellis 220). Her initial fantasy of her handsome employer is conscious, but his transformation into a figure embodying her fear of sexuality is generated by deep-rooted unconscious inhibitions. The effect — "the shock I had suffered," as she describes it — is a manifestation of the kind of "shock to the sexual emotions" that, according to Freud, could "scarcely fail sometimes to produce such a result" (231). "Something is introduced into psychic life which refuses to merge in the general flow of consciousness" (222), and that something is the governess's unacknowledged sexual attraction to the charming gentleman: it does not fit with her idealized romantic and spiritualized notions about love. The resulting "collision," as she herself terms the experience, between her conscious ideals and her unconscious impulses triggers in her emotions a profound disturbance. "Driven" by her "[a]gitation," as she confesses, and only half conscious, she "must, in circling about the place, have walked three miles" (p. 41). As the hysterical shock involves shame and disgust and often "cannot even be talked about" (Ellis 222), so the governess, upon encountering Mrs. Grose, "somehow measured the importance of what I had seen by my thus finding myself hesitate to mention it" (p. 41).

If the figure the governess "sees" is an example of the "frequently painful nature of sexual hallucinations in the hysterical" (Ellis 217), a manifestation of her deep fear of sexuality engendered when her unacknowledged sexual impulses intrude themselves into her idealized romantic fantasy of her employer — when, to put it another way, the relationship she fantasizes begins to take its natural course toward a sexual consummation — the logical question to be addressed is "What form would such a hallucination take?" Obviously, it would be a male figure, and it would be sexually threatening. The figure the governess sees is male, and the "fear" she feels is like that stirred in "a young woman privately bred" by "an unknown man in a lonely place." Assuming, then, this generalized embodiment of a threatening sexual male figure, if the governess were to imagine the apparition in human form, what particular features might it be expected to have? The answer is that there existed in the culture a widely recognized stereotype of the predatory sexual male, a set of typical features and characteristics that such a figure would be presupposed to manifest. Logically enough, it is this figure that the governess describes in *The Turn of the Screw*.

I

Europe in the nineteenth century was much intrigued by the theory that there exists in human nature a determinative relationship between physiognomical features and character. In a recent book Graeme Tytler documents "the universality of physiognomy in nineteenth-century Europe" and in particular the immense influence of the physiognomical speculations of Johann Caspar Lavater, an eighteenth-century Swiss clergyman, whose monumental *Essays on Physiognomy* was certainly, Tytler says, known about by "most nineteenth-century men of letters" (316). Widely popularized in newspapers and periodicals, physiognomical theory exercised a significant influence on the novel during the period from the early 1770s to about the 1880s as the pseudo-scientific spuriousness of its conclusions came to be increasingly recognized. There is no evidence that James knew Lavater's work firsthand. But there is evidence beyond the elaborate physiognomical portrait the governess describes in *The Turn of the Screw* that he knew something of the subject, as when in his description of Caspar Goodwood in *The Portrait of a Lady* he mentions "blue eyes of a remarkable fixedness . . . and a jaw of the somewhat angular mould which is supposed to bespeak resolution" (47). And it is certain that James would have been well versed secondhand in the physiognomies of fictional characterization: the roster of writers named by Tytler as most influenced by physiognomy — Fielding, Dickens, the Brontës, Thackeray, Balzac, Flaubert, George Sand — reads like a gallery of novelists most familiar to James.

To demonstrate the physiognomical stereotypicality of the fearful male figure the governess hallucinates, whose actual unreality James may be implying in her remark that " 'he's like nobody,' " it will be useful to reproduce her description at length:

> "He has no hat. . . . He has red hair, very red, close-curling, and a pale face, long in shape, with straight good features and little rather queer whiskers that are as red as his hair. His eyebrows are somehow darker; they look particularly arched and as if they

might move a good deal. His eyes are sharp, strange — awfully; but I only know clearly that they're rather small and very fixed. His mouth's wide, and his lips are thin, and except for his little whiskers he's quite clean-shaven. He gives me a sort of sense of looking like an actor. . . . He's tall, active, erect, . . . but never — no, never! — a gentleman. . . ."

[Mrs. Grose] visibly tried to hold herself. "But he *is* handsome?"

I saw the way to help her. "Remarkably!"

"And dressed — ?"

"In somebody's clothes. They're smart, but they're not his own."

She broke into a breathless affirmative groan. "They're the master's!" (p. 48)

Certain details of this description can be traced to more general assumptions than those of physiognomical theory. The figure is remarkably handsome, and "the handsome man," according to general prejudice, particularly in men, "is likely to be a cad." Quite ready "for his own immediate profit . . . to defy the conventions that other men subscribe to," the cad "may dress and adorn himself in what is commonly condemned as bad taste" as "a crude and external manifestation of his disregard of the conventions of masculine behaviour." Thus he has no scruples against "taking advantage of the susceptibility which women exhibit in the presence of good-looking men." Usually with "neat and symmetrical features" and "attractive to many women," the cad is hampered neither by "a bad reputation nor bad manners . . . : his aim is not love or even philandering, but amour" (Brophy 85–86). Presumably, the fearful male figure the governess hallucinates, with his "straight good features," his somehow not quite suitable clothes, his "secret disorders, vices more than suspected," and his success with women — "He did what he wished," Mrs. Grose says, "[w]ith them all" (pp. 48, 53, 58) — emanates from some such stereotype.

Beyond conveying this general aura of sexual danger, however, the governess's description of the threatening male specter she conjures up turns out to be a detailed physiognomical portrait, the most telling feature of which is its "red hair, very red, close-curling." "Most nineteenth-century novelists," Tytler observes, "are concerned, like their predecessors, almost entirely with the color of the hair" (213). While red hair, according to Lavater, is said to characterize "a person supremely good or supremely evil" (Tytler 215), the consensus has always favored the latter view, a prejudice that can be traced as far back as the Bible. Indeed, there is a close connection, not at all surprising in view of Lavater's clerical vocation, between physiognomical stereotypes and biblical personifications of evil. In the Old Testament the association of red hair with evil would have been reinforced by the story of Esau, who yielded to fleshly appetite, sold his God-given birthright for a mess of pottage, and spawned the lineage repudiated by Jehovah. More telling against red hair was the suspicion that Judas must have been a redhead (Cooper 75). Still more relevant to the governess's hallucinations in *The Turn of the Screw* is the knowledge that in ancient lore it was held that Satan materialized in the form of a red-haired male. It would not be surprising if a parson's daughter, hysterically projecting an image of her sexual fear and revulsion, were to envision a figure embodying features of this long-standing assumption about the human form assumed by the Tempter himself.

Indeed, the correspondence is striking. The threatening male figure she projects has "*very* red" hair (emphasis added). In *The Devil in Legend and Literature* Maximilian Rudwin observes that "the Devil's beard as well as his hair is usually of a flaming red color" (48). The figure she sees is associated with "vices more than suspected" (p. 53); among other things, to be sure, "Satan is famed as the greatest gambler ever known upon or under the earth" (Rudwin 143). And other details of her portrait whose place in the design of the story has remained obscure are at least traceable to lore about Satan. The odious figure gave the governess "a sort of sense of looking like an actor." "The Devil is likewise regarded as the inventor of the drama," Rudwin reports; "indeed, the actors were regarded by the Catholic Church in the Middle Ages, and even for many centuries afterwards, as servants of Satan" (259). Finally, the penchant of the governess's projected figure to wear the clothes of a gentleman in order to be taken for what he decidedly is not is very much a part of his Satanic aura:

> The Devil . . . has on clothes which any gentleman might
> wear. . . . It has been his greatest ambition to be a gentleman, in
> outer appearance at least; and to his credit it must be said that he
> has so well succeeded in his efforts to resemble a gentleman that it
> is now very difficult to tell the two apart. (Rudwin 50)

Thus, in projecting in human form the embodiment of her deep, puritanical fear of evil, which in Victorian times tended to mean sexual evil, the governess envisions an attractive male figure, one to whom she would instinctively respond — a figure projected in the form of the

Tempter himself, as that form was imprinted in the mind of the culture of which she is representative. But her projection draws also on stereotypes established in the physiognomical lore of the preceding centuries. The importance of Lavater in the considerable influence of physiognomical theories on the nineteenth century, and particularly on important novelists, has been mentioned. But there were many other practitioners in the field, and in their writings, as well as in those of novelists influenced by physiognomical lore, can be found most of the details of the apparition the governess projects. This is a precarious business at best: the spuriousness of the science assures that one can find almost as many different readings of the same features and expressions as there are physiognomists. But there is pretty solid agreement supporting Lavater's suspicion of red hair. The mind of Chaucer's Miller, for example, with a beard red "as any sowe or fox" (A552), runs to "synne and harlotries" (A561). Swift equips Gulliver with the prevailing prejudice against red hair. In describing the Yahoos — "cunning, malicious, treacherous and revengeful" as well as "cowardly . . . insolent, abject, and cruel" — Gulliver observes "that the *Red-Haired* of both Sexes are more libidinous and mischievous than the rest" and finds it curious that the female Yahoo with a lecherous eye for him did not have "Hair . . . of a Red Colour, (which might have been some Excuse for an Appetite a little irregular)" (232–33). Among physiognomists, Joseph Simms, after acknowledging that "many cases might be cited in which red-haired persons have been very amiable," finds nevertheless that this color, "if curliness is added [Quint's hair is "very red, close-curling"], indicates a . . . disposition to ardent love," and if it is very coarse "is a sign of propensities much too animal" (402). Paolo Mantegazza agrees that "red hair, although rare, is disliked by nearly all because it is an almost monstrous type" (62). Although, as Tytler points out, physiognomical (as well as phrenological) explanations for human behavior had lost credibility for perceptive people by the end of the nineteenth century, their assumptions remained in some minds so ingrained as to be almost taken for granted. Thus in *Ann Veronica* (1914), as Ann and her fellow suffragettes are arraigned after their raid on the House of Commons, H. G. Wells describes "a disagreeable young man, with red hair and a loose mouth, seated at the reporter's table . . . sketching her" (252).

If, by general agreement, red hair is a sign of lechery, other features of the male sex villain the governess projects can also be found with threatening significance in physiognomical lore. The figure's eyes, for example, — "sharp, strange — awfully; . . . rather small and very fixed" — which give the governess "such a bold hard stare" (pp. 48, 42), have a strong sexual significance. According to Simms, "there is a close connection between the eyes and the sexual organs" (229). To the authoritative Lavater, "small, and deep sunken eyes, [are] bold in opposition; not discouraged, intriguing, and active in wickedness" (3:179). The significance of the figure's eyebrows — "particularly arched and as if they might move a great deal" — is also explained by physiognomy: the arch by Mantegazza, who finds that the proud and impudent "have arched eyebrows which are often raised" (180), the movement by Lavater, who explains that "the motion of the eyebrows contains numerous expressions, especially of ignoble passions; pride, anger and contempt: the supercilious man . . . despises, and is despicable" (3:183). The wide mouth and thin lips of the governess's figure fit Mantegazza's observation that "no face recalls the expression of cruelty so much as a wanton one," and "the expression of cruelty is almost exclusively concentrated round the mouth; . . . The mouth is closed, the corners are drawn back as far as possible, . . . The eye is clear, widely opened, and fixed upon the victim" (178). Even the "habit of going about bareheaded" (the governess's figure "has no hat" [p. 48]) attracts physiognomical attention (Tytler 294). Indeed, the essence of the governess's projected figure, embodying her hysterical but unconscious sexual horror, is very like what Lavater says one would see if he or she were to imagine a wicked, lecherous man:

> Rude, savage, ruffianly, danger-contemning, strength. It is a crime to him to have committed small mischief; his stroke, like his aspect, is death. He does not oppress, he destroys. To him murder is enjoyment, and the pangs of others a pleasure. The form of his bones denotes his strength, his eye a thirst of blood, his eyebrow habitual cruelty, his mouth deriding contempt, his nose grim craft, his hair and beard choleric power. (3:249–50)

II

Not only is it reasonably certain that James knew about physiognomical theories and the use of such devices by novelists familiar to him, then, but he also creates in his governess a character who fits the profile of the typical sexual hysteric, who has a hysterical hallucination, and whose mind projects her sexual fear in a form that draws on the very religious and physiognomical stereotypes with which such a mind as hers would logically be furnished. It remains to show some striking prototypes of the governess's physiognomically stereotypical redheaded sex villain in popular novels of the era.

A link to one such prototype exists in *The Turn of the Screw* itself: the governess is reading Fielding's *Amelia* just before her third hallucination of the figure identified as Quint (p. 66). *Amelia* contains a similar figure, Robinson, who has Quint's long pale face, red hair (actually "a red Beard"), and clothes that call a kind of disreputable attention to themselves.[2] Although Robinson is not, to the reader's knowledge, sexually villainous, his life resembles Quint's, at least the latter's reputation for "strange passages and perils, secret disorders, vices more than suspected" (p. 53). Robinson is a gambler, cheat, thief, and criminal conspirator. The governess, not having finished the novel, would not know of his repentance in the end and thus could be expected to regard him with emotions that might contribute to her fearful hallucinations. Even more terrifying, however, in this novel with its undercurrent of sexual danger and ruin are its interpolated histories of young women betrayed by their naive indulgence in the pleasurable sensations excited by the attentions of attractive men: Miss Mathews, seduced by a soldier under false promises of marriage, and Mrs. Bennet, seduced by a nobleman after quaffing only "Half a Pint of Small Punch," which had been drugged. The latter's case would have been especially terrible to the governess, for Mrs. Bennet was the naive, sheltered daughter of a clergyman and got into trouble precisely by entertaining romantic fantasies of an attractive man: she intended only to "indulge [her] Vanity and Interest at once, without being guilty of the least Injury" (295). The warnings of both these wretched fallen women must surely have terrified the governess. Miss Mathews offers her fate as a warning to every woman "to deal with Mankind with Care and Caution . . . and never to confide too much in the Honesty of a Man, nor in her own Strength, where she has so much at Stake; let her remember she walks on a Precipice, and the bottomless Pit is to receive her, if she slips; nay, if she makes but one false Step" (53). Mrs. Bennet warns "that the Woman who gives up the least Outwork of her Virtue, doth, in that very Moment, betray the Citadel" (295). Indulging in romantic fantasies of her dashing gentleman employer, the governess, had she read thus far into *Amelia*, might indeed suddenly discover herself on the way to ruin,

---

[2]May L. Ryburn has called attention to the resemblance between Fielding's Robinson and the figure the governess describes. Ryburn observes quite logically that this parallel "would seem to lay the ghosts to rest forever, except as they existed in the governess's mind" (237).

the outworks of her virtue undermined by her own susceptibility to an attractive male. Small wonder, in such a case, that the gentleman of her fantasy should metamorphose into a villainous projection of sexual fear.

Although my primary focus here is on Quint, I might mention that, just as the governess does not need (and indeed does not have) any knowledge of Peter Quint to accomplish the transformation, so her complementary projection of the female counterpart of her sexual fear does not require knowledge of Miss Jessel and her shame: it is, in an important sense, the governess herself, the awful projection of herself ruined by the sexual evil toward which her own sexual impulses are urging her. Paul N. Siegel is another critic who views the female figure the governess sees, a genteel woman ruined by indulging her sexual impulses, as a fearful projection of the governess herself and also of the adult sexual female Flora will become. Siegel discusses James's subtle dramatization of the governess's psychosexual ambivalence: she is horrified at Miss Jessel's sexuality and its consequences and terrified of her own susceptibility to sexual feeling, of which she is subconsciously aware; but she is also fascinated and excited, because of her powerful attraction to her employer, by identifying herself with Miss Jessel and her indulgence of sexual desires. Although he does not pursue its consequences, Siegel also senses James's implication that Miss Jessel in some way prefigures in the governess's mind a Flora grown up and hardened by sexual experience (36). The story's most telling hint of this is in the episode of the girl's second excursion to the lake. With the awful vision of Miss Jessel burning in her mind, the governess sees that Flora's "incomparable childish beauty had suddenly failed, had quite vanished. . . . She was hideously hard; she had turned common and almost ugly." Flora's indignant response to her accusations seems to the governess like "that of a vulgarly pert little girl in the street" (p. 103).

Tytler's demonstration of the physiognomical awareness reflected in *Amelia* is corroborated by Fielding's mention of the term "physiognomist" in the novel (47) as well as by the physiognomical description of the villainous Robinson. But Robinson is not a sexual villain. The projection of the governess's fear is even more in the lineage of numerous red-haired male villains rendered, like her projected figure, in detailed physiognomical portraits in some of the best-known novels of the era. One such character, who appeared just before the governess's ordeal at Bly, is Fagin, the consummate villain of Dickens's *Oliver Twist*. Fagin insinuated his way into the consciousness of thousands of readers every month from February 1837 to April 1839. Beyond the "quantity of matted red hair" that obscured his "villainous-looking and repulsive face," there is scant description of Fagin with physiognomical import, although he is "lynx-eyed," has a "pale lip," and is seen on one occasion "raising his eyebrows" (294, 87, 325). But he is certainly "hideously" villainous, personifying an evil power capable of entrapping a tender, angelic child in a hideous morass of evil, and the typifying description of him as "like some loathsome reptile, engendered in the slime and darkness through which he moved: crawling forth by night, in search of some rich offal for a meal" (128, 135), might conceivably have contributed to the governess's vision of Quint. Today, a time deeply troubled by the specter of child sexual abuse, it might even be suspected that Fagin's lasciviousness extends beyond the jewels and coins he hoards to the children he manipulates so greedily and that his possession of the pure, innocent Oliver might involve designs such as those the governess fears Quint has on Miles. If the governess had indeed read *Oliver Twist,* Fagin's embodiment of all that would have been lawless and vile to someone with her proper upbringing, together with his particular penchant for seducing children into lives of evil, could hardly have failed to color her projection of her fears.

Later Dickens would elaborate with fuller physiognomical detail and more pointed sexual innuendo on this character type in the figure of Uriah Heep, with his slimy designs on the saintly Agnes in *David Copperfield*. Although Heep, like Fagin, is anything but handsome, "this red-bearded animal," "this detestable Rufus," has the hair color, pale face, wide mouth, and piercing eyes of the figure the governess projects in *The Turn of the Screw*. Heep's face is "pale" and "cadaverous," "his mouth [is] widened" like a gargoyle's, and his eyes, "sleepless . . . like two red suns," were a "shadowless red" and "looked as if they had scorched their lashes off" (362).

An older, aristocratic version of the same character type is Lord Steyne, the sharkish nobleman who undoes Becky Sharp in Thackeray's *Vanity Fair.* Steyne's description captures the grotesquerie, as well as several details, of the portrait of Heep. His "shining bald head . . . was fringed with red hair. He had thick bushy eyebrows, with little twinkling bloodshot eyes. . . . His jaw was underhung, and when he laughed, two white buck-teeth protruded themselves and glistened savagely in the midst of the grin" (366).

In *Daniel Deronda,* Henleigh Mallinger Grandcourt, like the governess's figure, is handsome, and, as Gwendolyn Harleth discovers, trails, like Quint, a past of secret disorders and vices, like gambling and keeping a mistress, more than suspected. Grandcourt is "decidedly handsome," has "a mere fringe of reddish-blond hair," a complexion of "a faded fairness resembling that of an actress," and "long narrow grey eyes" that "looked at Gwendolyn persistently with a slightly exploring gaze" (79, 80).

This list of prototypes for the figure the governess describes could be extended considerably — even, it has been argued, into the realm of real life. It is deliciously pertinent to note, at this point, that in view of his "reddish, untamed beard," descriptions of him as "an ugly fellow" with a "pasty" face, "red nose," "rusty red beard," and "little slatey-blue eyes," his reputation as a "dangerous seducer of women," and his own self-perception that "there clung about him a 'faint but unmistakable flavor of brimstone,'" the figure upon whom Peter Quint is based has been decisively identified by E. A. Sheppard: "He is George Bernard Shaw" (61–62).

To be sure, the governess, whose ordeal takes place in the 1840s, could not have known the red-haired sexual villains Heep, Steyne, and Grandcourt, although she might have known Fagin. My point is, rather, that James, writing in 1897, surely did know them and that in creating the figure she describes he drew the same *type* of character, one whose lineage in literary history, James is careful to imply, she would have been familiar with. The only book she is shown reading in *The Turn of the Screw* is *Amelia,* but through her remarks about her reading at Bly James implies that, free from the strict censorship of the vicarage, utterly on her own, and with a good deal of time on her hands, the governess fell with avidity on the "roomful of old books at Bly" — books of a kind that had come into her "sequestered home" only "to the extent of a distinctly deprecated reknown" — the very category of books that could not fail to whet "the unavowed curiosity of [her] youth." No catalog of the library at Bly has survived, but one category of its holdings was "last-century fiction" (p. 66) — fiction, that is, full of the ordeals of virginal ingenues pursued by sexual villains. At the time of her first manifestation of hysterical symptoms when she projects the red-haired sex fiend, she has already been some weeks at Bly. If she is, as is likely, immersed in eighteenth-century fiction full of Gothic terror — fiction, as Tytler demonstrates, steeped in physiognomical lore — the figure she describes is exactly what might be expected.

There can be no doubt that James *could* have done what I have proposed. His own upbringing as a boy in a proper household, "surrounded by admonishing governesses, a permissive father, an often stern ambiguous mother" (Edel 22), would have provided, in general outlines, a prototype for the situation as well as the atmosphere at Bly. (Indeed, there is good reason to suspect, in view of James's own well-known sexual problem [pp. 8–9][3] and Douglas's pointed hints to the Jamesian narrator of the opening frame that when "he looked at me, . . . he saw what he spoke of" [p. 23], that it is his own story James tells in *The Turn of the Screw*.) In his familiarity with the work of his brother William, coupled with his knowledge of sexual hysteria, its supposed causes, and its manifestations, James certainly possessed the requisite psychological acumen to dramatize the psychology of sexual fear in a maternal figure and its effect on the children in her charge. And, given his artistic seriousness and penchant for subtlety, as well as the persistent undercurrent of sexual preoccupation in his work, despite his prim distaste for the explicit airing of sexual matters, what I have suggested is, I believe, precisely what he *would* do with the story. Indeed, the demonstrable extent to which the governess represents a classic case of sexual hysteria and the fact that the figure she projects is a classic example of physiognomical cliché, deliberately elaborated for ironic effect, serve to indicate James's intentions in *The Turn of the Screw*. It is not a ghost story but a psychological drama about the disastrous effects of Victorian sexual attitudes on the development of children.[4]

In light of the foregoing, a belated, perhaps ironic sympathy is due poor Edmund Wilson for his ordeal (referred to by Beidler on pp. 193–96 of his "Critical History") over *The Turn of the Screw:* he was on the right track but could never get over the obstacle of the ghosts. Wilson was right: the problem *is* with the troubled sexuality of the governess, who, the story pointedly emphasizes, was greatly attracted to the gentleman who employed her but was also, in an exaggerated but quintessentially Victorian way, deeply fearful of and hostile toward sexuality. As she indulges her romantic feelings toward her attractive employer, she senses subconsciously that by thus relaxing her sexual defenses even so innocuously she has set foot on the path to ruin. At that point, the attractive male projection of her pleasurable sensations changes to the terrifying male projection of her fear. The figure she projects emerges from her own subconscious imprinting by religious and cultural stereotypes of the villainously libidinous male, with numerous precedents in the literature of the period, colored, conceivably, by some awareness of the views of Lavater himself, who had established a reputation throughout Europe as a preacher as well as a physiognomist

[3]See also Edel, especially in Preface (xi–xii) and the index under "James, Henry: Psychosexual problems."
[4]A conclusion also reached by Jane Nardin, who asserts that *The Turn of the Screw* "is neither about evil metaphysically conceived, nor about madness clinically conceived, but rather [about] a particular social milieu and the way it affects people living in it" (142).

(Tytler 24). Thus awakened, the governess's hysterical fear of sexuality is superadded to her sense of her duty as governess of two children approaching puberty. Not really mad, merely deeply Victorian in the grip of a powerful cultural ideal, she takes upon herself the role of angel in the house — guardian of idealized, spiritualized love and sexual purity. Along the same line she is, as James seems to have realized, a manifestation of the Great Governess of the era, representing maternal control over the sexual mores of the household and thus of the culture at large.

Through the figures the governess projects — one representing her fear and revulsion at male sexuality, the other her fear and disgust at female reciprocation of male lust (she realizes with a spasm of ambivalence that what went on between Quint and Jessel "must have been also what *she* [Miss Jessel] wished!" [p. 59]) — James contrives to objectify her sexual state of mind. But the main line of development in the story is the effect such a deep aversion to sexual phenomena has on the development of children. But how does one dramatize in fiction such psychological effects? James's solution to the problem is masterful. The "ghosts," which work well enough on the literal level (where many learned critics have enjoyed them), become, on the figurative level, a means of objectifying the psychology of both the governess and the children and also the psychological meaning and consequences of her behavior toward them: they represent both her fear and her revulsion at the children's natural sexual development. For, of course, the sexual male and female figures so fearfully on the governess's mind *are* possessing Miles and Flora: they are merely the adult sexual beings the children will become when the sexuality latent in childhood emerges through adolescence and establishes itself in adulthood. This possession, however, is not evil; it is merely natural. The many elaborate explications of the evil in *The Turn of the Screw* notwithstanding, the only evil the story presents is that Quint and Jessel were sexually active. The powerful aura of evil that pervades the story emanates from the psyche of the governess, who, after all, tells the story: it is her hysterical aversion to sexuality, heightened for satirical effect by James's subtle irony.

In her compulsion to keep the children from being possessed with this evil, then, the governess is actually blocking their normal sexual development. Naturally, when she looks so anxiously at Miles and Flora, children entering puberty, she sees signs of their sexual maturation — the adult male with an attraction to young and pretty women in Miles and the adult female with a reciprocal attraction to handsome young men in Flora. In trying to suppress all manifestations of their natural sexual development she inflicts grievous damage on their psyches. With apt oedipal implications, James allows Flora to escape to the protection of the father figure; but the male child, trapped in the psychosexual undertow of the mother-son relationship, is destroyed.

So James does not arrange things so that the only way to account for the governess's description of the apparition Mrs. Grose identifies as Peter Quint is that she has seen a supernatural manifestation: he contrives it so that she describes a hysterical projection of her own sexual aversion coupled with a powerful sense of duty to keep the children in her charge free of sexual taint. But a question yet remains. If the red-headed sexual male does, as I have demonstrated, well up hysterically in the governess's mind from physiognomical stereotypes, how does it happen that this figure so closely resembles the real person Peter Quint? The answer is not, certainly, that James believed in physiognomical science and meant to represent through Quint an actual living embodiment of the theory. For, as he was undoubtedly aware, the physiognomical stereotype, as well as the evil ascribed to Quint and Jessel, was a purely subjective phenomenon, an attitude of mind. In an atmosphere of increasing rationality, Tytler explains, there emerged, as the nineteenth century wore on, a "subtler treatment of physiognomy" which tended to treat it "as a problematic sign of the observer's own moral character" (319). Thus in *The Turn of the Screw* the governess's physiognomical imprinting, like her sense of sexual evil, is part of her characterization as an upright and idealistic person, but one with problematically unhealthy attitudes toward sexuality. I suspect rather that James made it appear that the governess describes a real person dead and buried because he felt it imperative that the story appear to be a ghost story. Such dissembling would help explain the notorious ambiguity of his various comments on the story. With the example fresh on his mind of the storm of opprobrium that had fallen upon Thomas Hardy when he ventured to criticize Victorian sexual sanctities — showing, for example, through Tess that a sexual lapse did not really commit a girl to hopeless depravity and through Jude that the spiritual-love ideal could turn marriage into a torment for people with normal sexual desires — James knew that he could not say openly what he wanted to say in *The Turn of the Screw.* What he wanted to say was that the angel in the house might really be an angel of psychic destruction, votary of an ideal moving through society from house to house doing mortal damage to human sexual development and especially, since male sexuality has always seemed more irrepressible than female, to the sexual development of boys like Miles, whose death, of course, is not

actual but symbolic of the permanent harm done to the very core —
the "heart" — of his sexual being. Thus James produced *The Turn
of the Screw*, a ghost story that would materialize interestingly on the
figurative level as one of the most remarkable psychological dramas in
literature.

For that, ultimately, is the story of *The Turn of the Screw* — a more
significant story, I maintain, than either a ghost story or a parable of
some amorphous good and evil. If that is still debatable, the assertion
that the psychological drama is more humanly relevant both to James's
time and to our own is surely not. At least a story about the damage
done to the sexual development of children by Victorian sexual fear and
disgust would satisfy James's own requirement that the art of fiction
must achieve an imitation of life.

WORKS CITED

Breuer, Josef, and Sigmund Freud. *Studien über Hysterie*. Leipzig:
F. Deuticke, 1895.

Brophy, John. *The Human Face*. London: Harrap, 1945.

Cargill, Oscar. "*The Turn of the Screw* and Alice James." *PMLA* 78
(1963): 238–49.

Chaucer, Geoffrey. *The Canterbury Tales* in *The Riverside Chaucer*, 3rd
ed. Ed. Larry D. Benson. Boston: Houghton, 1987.

Cooper, Wendy. *Hair, Sex, Society, Symbolism*. New York: Stein, 1971.

Dickens, Charles. *David Copperfield*. New York: Washington Square,
1958.

———. *Oliver Twist*. New York: Holt, 1962.

Edel, Leon. *Henry James: A Life*. New York: Harper, 1985.

Eliot, George. *Daniel Deronda*. New York: Harper, 1961.

Ellis, Havelock. "Auto-Erotism." *Studies in the Psychology of Sex*. 2
vols. New York: Random, 1936. 1, pt. 1: 163–283.

Fielding, Henry. *Amelia*. Middletown: Wesleyan UP, 1983.

Huntley, H. Robert. "James's *The Turn of the Screw:* Its 'Fine
Machinery.'" *American Imago* 34 (1977): 224–37.

James, Henry. *The Portrait of a Lady*. Norton Critical Edition. Ed.
Robert D. Bamberg. New York: Norton, 1975.

Lavater, J. C. *Essays on Physiognomy; for the Promotion of Knowledge
and the Love of Mankind*. Trans. Thomas Holcroft. 3 vols.
London: Robinson, 1789.

Mantegazza, Paolo. *Physiognomy and Expression*. New York: Scribner's, 1914.

Nardin, Jane. "*The Turn of the Screw:* The Victorian Background." *Mosaic* 12 (1978): 131–42.

Rudwin, Maximilian. *The Devil in Legend and Literature*. Chicago and London: Open Court, 1931.

Ryburn, May L. "*The Turn of the Screw* and *Amelia:* A Source for Quint?" *Studies in Short Fiction* 16 (1979): 235–37.

Sheppard, E[lizabeth]. A. *Henry James and "The Turn of the Screw."* Auckland: Auckland UP, 1974.

Siegel, Paul N. "'Miss Jessel': Mirror Image of the Governess." *Literature and Psychology* 18 (1968): 30–38.

Simms, Joseph. *Physiognomy Illustrated; or Nature's Revelation of Character*. New York: Murray, 1889.

Swift, Jonathan. *Gulliver's Travels*. Norton Critical Edition. Ed. Robert A. Greenberg. New York: Norton, 1961.

Thackeray, William Makepeace. *Vanity Fair*. Riverside Edition. Boston: Houghton, 1963.

Tytler, Graeme. *Physiognomy in the European Novel: Faces and Fortunes*. Princeton: Princeton UP, 1982.

Wells, H. G. *Ann Veronica*. New York: Harper, 1914.

Gender Criticism
and *The Turn of the Screw*

WHAT IS GENDER CRITICISM?

Feminist criticism was accorded academic legitimacy in American universities "around 1981," Jane Gallop claims in her book *Around 1981: Academic Feminist Literary Theory.* With Gallop's title and amusing approximation in mind, Naomi Schor has since estimated that, "around 1985, feminism began to give way to what has come to be called gender studies" (Schor 275).

In explaining her reason for saying that feminism began to give way to gender studies "around 1985," Schor says that she chose that date "in part because it marks the publication of *Between Men*," a book whose author, the influential gender critic Eve Kosofsky Sedgwick, "articulates the insights of feminist criticism onto those of gay-male studies, which had up to then pursued often parallel but separate courses (affirming the existence of a homosexual or female imagination, recovering lost traditions, decoding the cryptic discourse of works already in the canon by homosexual or feminist authors)" (Schor 276). Today, gay and lesbian criticism is so much a part of gender criticism that some people equate "sexualities criticism" with the gender approach.

Many would quarrel with the notion that feminist criticism and women's studies have been giving way to gender criticism and gender studies — and with the either/or distinction that such a claim implies.

Some would argue that feminist criticism is by definition gender criticism. (When Simone de Beauvoir declared in 1949 that "one is not born a woman, one becomes one" [301], she was talking about the way in which individuals of the female sex assume the feminine gender — that is, that elaborate set of restrictive, socially prescribed attitudes and behaviors that we associate with femininity.) Others would point out that one critic whose work *everyone* associates with feminism (Julia Kristeva) has problems with the feminist label, while another critic whose name, like Sedgwick's, is continually linked with the gender approach (Teresa de Lauretis) continues to refer to herself and her work as feminist.

Certainly, feminist and gender criticism are not polar opposites but, rather, exist along a continuum of attitudes toward sex and sexism, sexuality and gender, language and the literary canon. There are, however, a few distinctions to be made between those critics whose writings are inevitably identified as being toward one end of the continuum or the other.

One distinction is based on focus: as the word implies, "feminists" have concentrated their efforts on the study of women and women's issues. Gender criticism, by contrast, has not been woman centered. It has tended to view the male and female sexes — and the masculine and feminine genders — in terms of a complicated continuum, much as we are viewing feminist and gender criticism. Critics like Diane K. Lewis have raised the possibility that black women may be more like white men in terms of familial and economic roles, like black men in terms of their relationships with whites, and like white women in terms of their relationships with men. Lesbian gender critics have asked whether lesbian women are really more like straight women than they are like gay (or for that matter straight) men. That we refer to gay and lesbian studies as gender studies has led some to suggest that gender studies is a misnomer; after all, homosexuality is not a gender. This objection may easily be answered once we realize that one purpose of gender criticism is to criticize gender as we commonly conceive of it, to expose its insufficiency and inadequacy as a category.

Another distinction between feminist and gender criticism is based on the terms *gender* and *sex*. As de Lauretis suggests in *Technologies of Gender* (1987), feminists of the 1970s tended to equate gender with sex, gender difference with sexual difference. But that equation doesn't help us explain "the differences among women, . . . the differences *within women*." After positing that "we need a notion of gender that is not so bound up with sexual difference," de Lauretis provides just such a notion by arguing that "gender is not a property of bodies or something originally existent in human beings"; rather, it is "the product of various social technologies, such as cinema" (2). Gender is, in other words, a construct, an effect of language, culture, and its institutions. It is gender, not sex, that causes a weak old man to open a door for an athletic young woman. And it is gender, not sex, that may cause one young woman to expect old men to behave in this way, another to view this kind of behavior as chauvinistic and insulting, and still another to have mixed feelings (hence de Lauretis's phrase "differences *within women*") about "gentlemanly gallantry."

Still another, related distinction between feminist and gender criticism is based on the *essentialist* views of many feminist critics and the *constructionist* views of many gender critics (both those who would call themselves feminists and those who would not). Stated simply and perhaps too reductively, the term *essentialist* refers to the view that women are essentially different from men. *Constructionist,* by contrast, refers to the view that most of those differences are characteristics not of the male and female sex (nature) but, rather, of the masculine and feminine genders (nurture). Because of its essentialist tendencies, "radical feminism," according to Sedgwick, "tends to deny that the meaning of gender or sexuality has ever significantly changed; and more damagingly, it can make future change appear impossible" (*Between Men* 13).

Most obviously essentialist would be those feminists who emphasize the female body, its difference, and the manifold implications of that difference. The equation made by some avant-garde French feminists between the female body and the *maternal* body has proved especially troubling to some gender critics, who worry that it may paradoxically play into the hands of extreme conservatives and fundamentalists seeking to reestablish patriarchal family values. In her book *The Reproduction of Mothering* (1978), Nancy Chodorow, a sociologist of gender, admits that what we call "mothering" — not having or nursing babies but mothering more broadly conceived — is commonly associated not just with the feminine gender but also with the female sex, often considered nurturing by nature. But she critically interrogates the common assumption that it is in women's nature or biological destiny to "mother" in this broader sense, arguing that the separation of home and workplace brought about by the development of capitalism and the ensuing industrial revolution made mothering *appear* to be essentially a woman's job in modern Western society.

If sex turns out to be gender where mothering is concerned, what differences *are* grounded in sex — that is, nature? *Are* there *essential* differences between men and women — other than those that are purely anatomical and anatomically determined (for example, a man can exclusively take on the job of feeding an infant milk, but he may not do so from his own breast)? A growing number of gender critics would answer the question in the negative. Sometimes referred to as "extreme constructionists" and "postfeminists," these critics have adopted the viewpoint of philosopher Judith Butler, who in her book *Gender Trouble* (1990) predicts that "sex, by definition, will be shown to have been gender all along" (8). As Naomi Schor explains their position, "there is nothing outside or before culture, no nature that is not always and already enculturated" (278).

Whereas a number of feminists celebrate women's difference, post feminist gender critics would agree with Chodorow's statement that men have an "investment in difference that women do not have" (Eisenstein and Jardine 14). They see difference as a symptom of oppression, not a cause for celebration, and would abolish it by dismantling gender categories and, ultimately, destroying gender itself. Because gender categories and distinctions are embedded in and perpetuated through language, gender critics like Monique Wittig have called for the wholesale transformation of language into a nonsexist, and nonheterosexist, medium.

Language has proved the site of important debates between feminist and gender critics, essentialists and constructionists. Gender critics have taken issue with those French feminists who have spoken of a feminine language and writing and who have grounded differences in language and writing in the female body.[1] For much the same reason, they have disagreed with those French-influenced Anglo-American critics who, like Toril Moi and Nancy K. Miller, have posited an essential relationship between sexuality and textuality. (In an essentialist sense, such critics have suggested that when women write, they tend to break the rules of plausibility and verisimilitude that men have created to evaluate fiction.) Gender critics like Peggy Kamuf posit a relationship only between *gender* and textuality, between what most men and women *become* after they are born and the way in which they write. They are

---

[1]Because feminist/gender studies, not unlike sex/gender, should be thought of as existing along a continuum of attitudes and not in terms of simple opposition, attempts to highlight the difference between feminist and gender criticism are inevitably prone to reductive overgeneralization and occasional distortion. Here, for instance, French feminism is made out to be more monolithic than it actually is. Hélène Cixous has said that a few men (such as Jean Genet) have produced "feminine writing," although she suggests that these are exceptional men who have acknowledged their own bisexuality.

therefore less interested in the author's sexual "signature"— in whether the author was a woman writing — than in whether the author was (to borrow from Kamuf) "Writing like a Woman."

Feminists such as Miller have suggested that no man could write the "female anger, desire, and selfhood" that Emily Brontë, for instance, inscribed in her poetry and in *Wuthering Heights* (*Subject* 72). In the view of gender critics, it is and has been possible for a man to write like a woman, a woman to write like a man. Shari Benstock, a noted feminist critic whose investigations into psychoanalytic and poststructuralist theory have led her increasingly to adopt the gender approach, poses the following question to herself in *Textualizing the Feminine* (1991): "Isn't it precisely 'the feminine' in Joyce's writings and Derrida's that carries me along?" (45). In an essay entitled "Unsexing Language: Pronomial Protest in Emily Dickinson's 'Lay This Laurel,'" Anna Shannon Elfenbein has argued that "like Walt Whitman, Emily Dickinson crossed the gender barrier in some remarkable poems," such as "We learned to like the Fire / By playing Glaciers — when a Boy —" (215).

It is also possible, in the view of most gender critics, for women to read as men, men as women. The view that women can, and indeed have been forced to, read as men has been fairly noncontroversial. Everyone agrees that the literary canon is largely "androcentric" and that writings by men have tended to "immasculate" women, forcing them to see the world from a masculine viewpoint. But the question of whether men can read as women has proved to be yet another issue dividing feminist and gender critics. Some feminists suggest that men and women have some essentially different reading strategies and outcomes, while gender critics maintain that such differences arise entirely out of social training and cultural norms. One interesting outcome of recent attention to gender and reading is Elizabeth A. Flynn's argument that women in fact make the best interpreters of imaginative literature. Based on a study of how male and female students read works of fiction, she concludes that women come up with more imaginative, open-ended readings of stories. Quite possibly the imputed hedging and tentativeness of women's speech, often seen by men as disadvantages, are transformed into useful interpretive strategies — receptivity combined with critical assessment of the text — in the act of reading (Flynn and Schweickart 286).

In singling out a catalyst of gender studies, many historians of criticism have pointed to Michel Foucault. In his *History of Sexuality* (1976, trans. 1978), Foucault distinguished sexuality from sex, calling the former a "technology of sex." De Lauretis, who has deliberately developed her theory of gender "along the lines of . . . Foucault's theory of sexuality," explains his use of "technology" this way: "sexuality, commonly thought to be a natural as well as a private matter, is in fact completely constructed in culture according to the political aims of the society's dominant class" (*Technologies* 2, 12).

Foucault suggests that homosexuality as we now think of it was to a great extent an invention of the nineteenth century. In earlier periods there had been "acts of sodomy" and individuals who committed them, but the "sodomite" was, according to Foucault, "a temporary aberration," not the "species" he became with the advent of the modern concept of homosexuality (42–43). According to Foucault, in other words, sodomitic acts did not define people so markedly as the word *homosexual* tags and marks people now. Sodomitic *acts* have been replaced by homosexual *persons,* and in the process the range of acceptable relationships between individuals of the same gender has been restrictively altered. As Sedgwick writes, "to specify someone's sexuality [today] is not to locate her or him on a map teeming with zoophiles, gyneco masts, sexoesthetic inverts, and so forth. . . . In the late twentieth century, if I ask you what your sexual orientation or sexual preference is, you will understand me to be asking precisely one thing: whether you are homosexual or heterosexual" ("Gender" 282).

By historicizing sexuality, Foucault made it possible for his successors to consider the possibility that all of the categories and assumptions that currently come to mind when we think about sex, sexual difference, gender, and sexuality are social artifacts, the products of cultural discourses. Following Foucault's lead, some gay and lesbian critics have argued that the heterosexual/homosexual distinction is as much a cultural construct as is the masculine/feminine dichotomy. And practitioners of so-called queer theory, a more theoretical and less text-oriented approach to literature and culture that critiques gender and sexuality as they are commonly conceived, go even further. They emphasize that sexuality is not restricted to homo- and heterosexuality — which are usually seen as mutually exclusive, binary opposites — but, rather, manifests itself across a broad continuum of behaviors and practices not restricted to either category (e.g., anal sex, autoeroticism, fetishes, sadomasochism, transvestism).

Arguing that sexuality is a continuum, not a fixed and static set of binary oppositions, gay and lesbian critics and queer theorists have critiqued heterosexuality, arguing that it has been an enforced corollary and consequence of what Gayle Rubin has referred to as the "sex/

gender system" ("Traffic"). According to this system, persons of the male sex are assumed to be masculine, masculine men are assumed to be attracted to women, and therefore it is supposedly natural for men to be attracted to women and unnatural for them to be attracted to men. Lesbian critics have also taken issue with some feminists on the grounds that they proceed from fundamentally heterosexual and even hetero-sexist assumptions. Particularly offensive to lesbians have been those feminists who, following Doris Lessing, have implied that to affirm a les-bian identity is to act out feminist hostility against men. According to poet-critic Adrienne Rich:

> The fact is that women in every culture throughout history have undertaken the task of independent, nonheterosexual, women-centered existence, to the extent made possible by their context, often in the belief that they were the "only ones" ever to have done so. They have undertaken it even though few women have been in an economic position to resist marriage altogether; and even though attacks against [them] have ranged from aspersions and mockery to deliberate gynocide. ("Compulsory" 141)

Rich goes on to suggest, in her essay entitled "Compulsory Heterosex-uality and Lesbian Existence," that "heterosexuality [is] a beachhead of male dominance," and that, "like motherhood, [it] needs to be recog-nized and studied as a political institution" (143, 145).

If there is such a thing as reading like a woman and such a thing as reading like a man, how then do lesbians read? Are there gay, lesbian, and/or queer ways of reading? Many would say that there are. Rich, by reading Emily Dickinson's poetry as a lesbian — by not assuming that "heterosexual romance is the key to a woman's life and work"— has introduced us to a poet somewhat different from the one hetero-sexual critics have made familiar (*Lies* 158). As for gay reading, Wayne Koestenbaum has defined "the (male twentieth-century first world) gay reader" as one who "reads resistantly for inscriptions of his condition, for texts that will confirm a social and private identity founded on a desire for other men. . . . Reading becomes a hunt for histories that deliberately foreknow or unwittingly trace a desire felt not by author but by reader, who is most acute when searching for signs of him-self" (176–77).

Lesbian critics have produced a number of compelling reinterpreta-tions, or inscriptions, of works by authors as diverse as Emily Dickinson, Virginia Woolf, and Toni Morrison. As a result of these provocative readings, significant disagreements have arisen between straight and lesbian critics and among lesbian critics as well. Perhaps the most famous and interesting example of this kind of interpretive controversy involves the claim by Barbara Smith and Adrienne Rich that Morrison's novel *Sula* can be read as a lesbian text — and author Toni Morrison's counterclaim that it cannot.

Gay male critics have produced a body of readings no less revisionist and controversial, focusing on writers as staidly classic as Henry James and Wallace Stevens. In 1986, Robert K. Martin suggested that Herman Melville's *Billy Budd* and *Moby-Dick* represent a triangle of homosexual desire. In the latter novel, the hero must choose between a captain who represents "the imposition of the male on the female" and a "Dark Stranger" (Queequeg) who "offers the possibility of an alternate sexuality, one that is less dependent upon performance and conquest" (5). Richard Bozorth, a contemporary gay critic associated with queer theory, argued in his book *Auden's Games of Knowledge: Poetry and the Meanings of Homosexuality* (2001) that the modernist poetry of W. H. Auden addresses and reflects the psychological and political meanings of same-sex desire.

Masculinity as a complex construct producing and reproducing a constellation of behaviors and goals, many of them destructive (like performance and conquest) and most of them injurious to women, has become the object of an unprecedented number of gender studies. A 1983 issue of *Feminist Review* contained an essay entitled "Anti-Porn: Soft Issue, Hard World," in which B. Ruby Rich suggested that the "legions of feminist men" who examine and deplore the effects of pornography on women might better "undertake the analysis that can tell us why men like porn (not, piously, why this or that exceptional man does *not*)" (Clark 185). The advent of gender criticism makes precisely that kind of analysis possible. Stephen H. Clark, who alludes to Ruby Rich's challenge, reads T. S. Eliot "as a man." Responding to "Eliot's implicit appeal to a specifically masculine audience — 'You! hypocrite lecteur! — mon semblable, — mon *frère!*' "— Clark concludes that poems such as "Sweeney among the Nightingales" and "Gerontion," rather than offering what they are usually said to offer — "a social critique into which a misogynistic language accidentally seeps"— instead articulate a masculine "psychology of sexual fear and desired retaliation" (Clark 173).

Some gender critics focusing on masculinity have analyzed "the anthropology of boyhood," a phrase coined by Mark Seltzer in an article in which he comparatively reads, among other things, Stephen

Crane's *Red Badge of Courage,* Jack London's *White Fang,* and the first
Boy Scouts of America handbook (150). Others have examined the fear
men have that artistry is unmasculine, a guilty worry that surfaces perhaps most obviously in "The Custom-House," Hawthorne's lengthy
preface to *The Scarlet Letter.* Still others have studied the representation
in literature of subtly erotic disciple-patron relationships, relationships
like the ones between Nick Carraway and Jay Gatsby, Charlie Marlow
and Lord Jim, Doctor Watson and Sherlock Holmes, and any number
of characters in Henry James's stories. Not all of these studies have
focused on literary texts. Because the movies have played a primary role
in gender construction during our lifetimes, gender critics have analyzed the dynamics of masculinity (vis-à-vis femininity and androgyny)
in films from *Rebel without a Cause* to *Tootsie* to last year's Best Picture.
One of the "social technologies" most influential in (re)constructing
gender, film is one of the media in which today's sexual politics is most
evident.

Necessary as it is, in an introduction such as this one, to define the
difference between feminist and gender criticism, it is equally necessary
to conclude by unmaking the distinction, at least partially. The two
topics just discussed (film theory and so-called queer theory) give us
grounds for undertaking that necessary deconstruction. The alliance I
have been creating between gay and lesbian criticism on the one hand
and gender criticism on the other is complicated greatly by the fact that
not all gay and lesbian critics are constructionists. Indeed, a number of
them (Robert K. Martin included) share with many feminists the *essentialist* point of view; that is, they believe homosexuals and heterosexuals
to be essentially different, different by nature, just as a number of feminists believe men and women to be different.

In film theory and criticism, feminist and gender critics have so
influenced one another that their differences would be difficult to
define based on any available criteria, including the ones just outlined.
Cinema has been of special interest to contemporary feminists like
Trinh T. Minh-ha (herself a filmmaker) and Gayatri Chakravorty Spivak
(whose critical eye has focused on movies including *My Beautiful
Laundrette* and *Sammie and Rosie Get Laid*). Teresa de Lauretis, whose
Technologies of Gender (1987) has proved influential in the area of gender studies, continues to publish film criticism consistent with earlier,
unambiguously feminist works in which she argued that "the representation of woman as spectacle — body to be looked at, place of sexuality,

and object of desire — so pervasive in our culture, finds in narrative cinema its most complex expression and widest circulation" (*Alice* 4).

Feminist film theory has developed alongside a feminist performance theory grounded in Joan Riviere's recently rediscovered essay "Womanliness as a Masquerade" (1929), in which the author argues that there is no femininity that is *not* masquerade. Marjorie Garber, a contemporary cultural critic with an interest in gender, has analyzed the constructed nature of femininity by focusing on men who have apparently achieved it — through the transvestism, transsexualism, and other forms of "cross-dressing" evident in cultural productions from Shakespeare to Elvis, from "Little Red Riding Hood" to *La Cage aux Folles*. The future of feminist and gender criticism, it would seem, is not one of further bifurcation but one involving a refocusing on femininity, masculinity, and related sexualities, not only as represented in poems, novels, and films but also as manifested and developed in video, on television, and along the almost infinite number of waystations rapidly being developed on the information highways running through an exponentially expanding cyberspace.

The first Bedford *Case Studies in Contemporary Criticism* edition of *The Turn of the Screw* contained a feminist reading of James's story by Priscilla Walton. In this, the second edition of the volume, Walton takes the approach of gender criticism. She addresses "gender complexities" reflected by *The Turn of the Screw*, seeing them in light of the "gender experimentations" that had become more common toward the end of the nineteenth century and the resulting "backlash" that led to the criminalization of male homosexual acts in 1885 and, in 1895, the trial and imprisonment of the homosexual poet and playwright Oscar Wilde.

Implicitly reminding us that gender criticism includes the feminist approach, Walton begins by discussing the plight of nineteenth-century governesses — women she calls "servants" who "were a source of controversy due to the problematic nature of single women and of their sexuality" (p. 306 in this volume). In the prologue to the story, the character Douglas admits to having "liked . . . extremely" the governess whose story he is about to read to his fellow houseguests. When he goes on to admit that "she was in love," or "*had* been," presumably with the master of the house, he effectively "diminish[es] her credibility" by conjuring prejudicial suspicions about the motives and proclivities of young working women.

But there is in Walton's view another "covert attraction" implied by

the prologue, namely the "special bond" between Douglas an the prologue's narrator — that is, the fellow male houseguest who has produced a prose narrative account of Douglas's telling of the governess's
story. Citing subtle ("closeted") evidence that Douglas and the narrator were attracted to one another, Walton argues that the " 'astute'
reader . . . is alerted to the potential of a sexually doubled narrative to
come, one that has both hetero- and homosexual overtones" (p. 309).

Walton begins to elucidate James's narrative by discussing the governess's fantasy of suddenly encountering the master on a walk and
becoming the object of his smiling and approving gaze, as well as her
subsequent sighting of Peter Quint, standing "very erect" on a phallic
tower and "peeping" at her. Walton suggests that visual acts — such as
sighting, gazing, and peeping — serve as "marker[s] of sexuality and
control" (p. 310). Thus, "mastering" or "appropriating" Quint's gaze,
as the governess attempts to do on several occasions, would involve
"assuming a position of male authority." But the assumption of such
authority, Walton points out, is not tantamount to the development of
a positive *female* identity or "subjectivity," however much it involves
the rejection of patriarchal culture's definition of proper womanhood.

According to Walton, Mrs. Grose, the housekeeper, warns the governess of the "dangers inherent in rejecting a patriarchally inscribed
role" by telling the story of Miss Jessel, Bly's last governess. Described
by Walton as a "sexually fraught whore figure," the previous governess
may also have had lesbian leanings, according to Walton, tendencies
possibly shared by the present governess. "It is possible," Walton
writes, "that while the governess believes she is engaged in a battle with
the ghosts for the children's souls, she is struggling with her own sexual
proclivities" (p. 312).

The concluding pages of Walton's essay concentrate on the two
children. Flora is seen as being torn between her new governess and her
former governess, Miss Jessel — both of whom are gender-confused
victims of "patriarchally defined womanhood." Ultimately, Walton
maintains, "the matronly Mrs. Grose provides Flora with a 'safe' if limited role model" embodying the conventional, patriarchal definitions
(p. 314). Miles, by contrast, is torn between the governess and Peter
Quint, whose "sentinel" gaze, according to Walton, represents homoerotic sexuality. The governess ultimately wins the battle for Miles, but
her victory leads to his death.

It is impossible to summarize in this short space the complexities of
Walton's emerging argument. Suffice it to say that this gender perspective on *The Turn of the Screw* — which shows how "alternative" and

"competing" sexualities play out within and between James's characters — exemplifies gender criticism by caring about masculinity as well as femininity, treating gender and sexuality as shifting modalities, and at the same time recognizing the degree to which gender and sexuality may be culturally determined.

Ross C Murfin

GENDER CRITICISM: A SELECTED BIBLIOGRAPHY

Studies of Gender and Sexuality

Berg, Temma F., ed., and Anna Shannon Elfenbein, Jeanne Larsen, and Elisa K. Sparks, co-eds. *Engendering the Word: Feminist Essays in Psychosexual Poetics.* Urbana: U of Illinois P, 1989.

Boone, Joseph A., and Michael Cadden, eds *Engondering Men: The Question of Male Feminist Criticism.* New York: Routledge, 1990.

Butler, Judith. *Gender Trouble: Feminism and the Subversion of Identity.* New York: Routledge, 1990.

Chodorow, Nancy. *The Reproduction of Mothering: Psychoanalysis and the Sociology of Gender.* Berkeley: U of California P, 1978.

Claridge, Laura, and Elizabeth Langland, eds. *Out of Bounds: Male Writing and Gender(ed) Criticism.* Amherst: U of Massachusetts P, 1990.

de Lauretis, Teresa. *Technologies of Gender: Essays on Theory, Film, and Fiction.* Bloomington: Indiana UP, 1987.

Doane, Mary Ann. "Masquerade Reconsidered: Further Thoughts on the Female Spectator." *Discourse* 11 (1988–89): 42–54.

Eisenstein, Hester, and Alice Jardine, eds. *The Future of Difference.* Boston: G. K. Hall, 1980.

Flynn, Elizabeth A., and Patrocinio P. Schweickart, eds. *Gender and Reading: Essays on Readers, Texts, and Contexts.* Baltimore: Johns Hopkins UP, 1986.

Foucault, Michel. *The History of Sexuality.* Vol. 1. Trans. Robert Hurley. New York: Random, 1978.

Kamuf, Peggy. "Writing Like a Woman." *Women and Language in Literature and Society.* Ed. Sally McConnell-Ginet et al. New York: Praeger, 1980. 284–99.

Laqueur, Thomas. *Making Sex: Body and Gender from the Greeks to Freud*. Cambridge: Harvard UP, 1990.

Riviere, Joan. "Womanliness as a Masquerade." 1929. Rpt. in *Formations of Fantasy*. Ed. Victor Burgin, James Donald, and Cora Kaplan. London: Methuen, 1986. 35–44.

Rubin, Gayle. "Thinking Sex: Notes for a Radical Theory of the Politics of Sexuality." Abelove et al. 3–44.

———. "The Traffic in Women: Notes on the 'Political Economy' of Sex." *Toward an Anthropology of Women*. Ed. Rayna R. Reiter. New York: Monthly Review, 1975. 157–210.

Schor, Naomi. "Feminist and Gender Studies." *Introduction to Scholarship in Modern Languages and Literatures*. Ed. Joseph Gibaldi. New York: MLA, 1992. 262–87.

Sedgwick, Eve Kosofsky. *Between Men: English Literature and Male Homosocial Desire*. New York: Columbia UP, 1985.

———. "Gender Criticism." *Redrawing the Boundaries: The Transformation of English and American Literary Studies*. Ed. Stephen Greenblatt and Giles Gunn. New York: MLA, 1992. 271–302.

Lesbian and Gay Criticism

Abelove, Henry, Michèle Aina Barale, and David Halperin, eds. *The Lesbian and Gay Studies Reader*. New York: Routledge, 1993.

Bozorth, Richard. *Auden's Games of Knowledge: Poetry and the Meanings of Homosexuality*. New York: Columbia UP, 2001.

Butters, Ronald, John M. Clum, and Michael Moon, eds. *Displacing Homophobia: Gay Male Perspectives in Literature and Culture*. Durham: Duke UP, 1989.

Clark, Stephen H. "Testing the Razor: T. S. Eliot's Poems." Berg et al. 167–89.

Craft, Christopher. *Another Kind of Love: Male Homosexual Desire in English Discourse, 1850–1920*. Berkeley: U of California P, 1994.

de Lauretis, Teresa. *The Practice of Love: Lesbian Sexuality and Perverse Desire*. Bloomington: Indiana UP, 1994.

Dollimore, Jonathan. *Sexual Dissidence: Augustine to Wilde, Freud to Foucault*. Oxford: Clarendon, 1991.

Elfenbein, Anna Shannon. "Unsexing Language: Pronomial Protest in Emily Dickenson's 'Lay This Laurel.'" Berg et al. 208–23.

Fuss, Diana, ed. *Inside/Out: Lesbian Theories, Gay Theories*. New York: Routledge, 1991.

Garber, Marjorie. *Vested Interests: Cross-Dressing and Cultural Anxiety.* New York: Routledge, 1992.

Halperin, David M. *One Hundred Years of Homosexuality and Other Essays on Greek Love.* New York: Routledge, 1990.

Koestenbaum, Wayne. "Wilde's Hard Labour and the Birth of Gay Reading." Boone and Cadden 176–89.

The Lesbian Issue. Spec. issue of *Signs* 9 (1984).

Martin, Robert K. *Hero, Captain, and Stranger: Male Friendship, Social Critique, and Literary Form in the Sea Novels of Herman Melville.* Chapel Hill: U of North Carolina P, 1986.

Munt, Sally, ed. *New Lesbian Criticism: Literary and Cultural Readings.* New York: Harvester Wheatsheaf, 1992.

Rich, Adrienne. "Compulsory Heterosexuality and Lesbian Existence." *The "Signs" Reader: Women, Gender, and Scholarship.* Ed. Elizabeth Abel and Emily K. Abel. Chicago: U of Chicago P, 1983. 139–68.

Seltzer, Mark. "The Love Master." Boone and Cadden 140–58.

Smith, Barbara. "Toward a Black Feminist Criticism." *The New Feminist Criticism.* Ed. Elaine Showalter. New York: Pantheon, 1985. 168–85.

Stimpson, Catherine R. "Zero Degree Deviancy: The Lesbian Novel in English." *Critical Inquiry* 8 (1981): 363–79.

Weeks, Jeffrey. *Sexuality and Its Discontents: Meanings, Myths, and Modern Sexualities.* London: Routledge, 1985.

Wittig, Monique. "The Mark of Gender." *The Poetics of Gender.* Ed. Nancy K. Miller. New York: Columbia UP, 1986. 63–73.

———. "One Is Not Born a Woman." *Feminist Issues* 1.2 (1981): 47–54.

———. *The Straight Mind and Other Essays.* Boston: Beacon, 1992.

Queer Theory

Butler, Judith. *Bodies That Matter: On the Discursive Limits of "Sex."* New York: Routledge, 1993.

Cohen, Ed. *Talk on the Wilde Side: Towards a Genealogy of Discourse on Male Sexualities.* New York: Routledge, 1993.

de Lauretis, Teresa, ed. Spec. issue on queer theory, *Differences* 3.2 (1991).

Halperin, David. *Saint Foucault: Toward a Gay Hagiography.* New York: Oxford UP, 1995.

Jagose, Annmarie. *Queer Theory: An Introduction*. New York: New York UP, 1996.

Sedgwick, Eve Kosofsky. *Epistemology of the Closet*. Berkeley: U of California P, 1991.

———. *Tendencies*. Durham: Duke UP, 1993.

Sinfield, Alan. *Cultural Politics — Queer Reading*. Philadelphia: U of Pennsylvania P, 1994.

———. *The Wilde Century: Effeminacy, Oscar Wilde, and the Queer Moment*. New York: Columbia UP, 1994.

Other Works Referred to in "What Is Gender Criticism?"

Benstock, Shari. *Textualizing the Feminine: On the Limits of Genre*. Norman: U of Oklahoma P, 1991.

de Beauvoir, Simone. *The Second Sex*. 1949. Ed. and trans. H. M. Parshley. New York: Modern Library, 1952.

de Lauretis, Teresa. *Alice Doesn't: Feminism, Semiotics, Cinema*. Bloomington: Indiana UP, 1989.

Gallop, Jane. *Around 1981: Academic Feminist Literary Theory*. New York: Routledge, 1992.

Miller, D. A. *The Novel and the Police*. Berkeley: U of California P, 1988.

Miller, Nancy K. *Subject to Change: Reading Feminist Writing*. New York: Columbia UP, 1988.

Rich, Adrienne. *On Lies, Secrets, and Silence: Selected Prose, 1966–1979*. New York: Norton, 1979.

Tate, Claudia. *Black Women Writers at Work*. New York: Continuum, 1983.

Gender Criticism of *The Turn of the Screw*

Cannon, Kelly. *Henry James and Masculinity: The Man at the Margins*. New York: St. Martin's, 1994.

Cappello, Mary, "Governing the Master('s) Plot: Frames of Desire in Demuth and James." *Word and Image* 8 (1992): 154–70.

Killoran, Helen. "The Governess, Mrs. Grose, and 'the poison of an influence' in *The Turn of the Screw*." *Modern Language Studies* 23 (1993): 13–24.

Knowles, Ronald. "'The hideous obscure': *The Turn of the Screw* and Oscar Wilde." *"The Turn of the Screw" and "What Maisie Knew."*

Ed. Neil Cornwell and Maggie Malone. New York: St. Martin's, 1998. 164–78.

Matheson, Neill. "Talking Horrors: James, Euphemism, and the Specter of Wilde." *American Literature* 71 (1999): 709–50.

Newman, Beth. "Getting Fixed: Feminine Identity and Scopic Crisis in *The Turn of the Screw.*" *Novel* 26 (1992): 43–63.

Pearson, John H. "Repetition and Subversion in Henry James's *The Turn of the Screw.*" *Henry James Review* 13 (1992): 276–91.

Schwarz, Daniel R. "Manet, James's *The Turn of the Screw*, and the Voyeuristic Imagination." *Henry James Review* 18 (1997): 1-21.

Smith, Allan Lloyd. "A Word Kept Back in *The Turn of the Screw.*" *Victorian Literature and Culture* 24 (1998): 139–58.

Wagenknecht, David. "Here's Looking at You, Peter Quint: *The Turn of the Screw*, Freud's *Dora*, and the Aesthetics of Hysteria." *American Imago* 55 (1988): 423–58.

Walton, Priscilla L. *The Disruption of the Feminine in Henry James.* Toronto: U of Toronto P, 1992.

A GENDER STUDIES PERSPECTIVE

PRISCILLA L. WALTON

"He took no notice of her; he looked at me": Subjectivities and Sexualities in *The Turn of the Screw*

The Turn of the Screw is one of James's more enigmatic tales. Although it was written over a century ago, it continues to intrigue readers and attract critical and creative attention. It has been transformed into an opera by Benjamin Britten (first performed in 1954), and has inspired a number of films, such as *The Innocents* (1961). This ostensible ghost story raises many concerns relevant to contemporary readers, not the least of which is the issue of visibility. Indeed, much of the story revolves around questions of seeing and not seeing, gazing and appropriating the gaze, and the invisible rendered visible. A number of primary concerns of gender criticism are at play within the text, which itself was written in a period noted for its "gender panic." As a result, I will address in this essay the ways in which *The Turn of the*

Screw speaks to gender complexities, complexities that, in turn, shed light on James's text.

The late nineteenth century saw a rise in gender experimentations. More and more, sexual boundaries were tested and alternative sexualites explored, to such an extent that authorities grew concerned and passed the 1885 Criminal Law Amendment Act, which criminalized "same-sex practices between men" (Cohen 92–93). The first person charged under the new law was the acclaimed poet and playwright Oscar Wilde, who lived an overtly gay lifestyle, and was convicted of engaging in an "act of gross indecency with another male person" (see the reference to this law in Beidler's introduction, p. 9 in this volume). Wilde was indicted in 1895, three years before *The Turn of the Screw* was published, and sentenced to two years imprisonment with hard labor. The Wilde trials incited the fury of the populace, culminating in the palpable delight that greeted the author's incarceration, all of which pointed to the commencement of a period of backlash and conformity. At the same time, suffragettes rallied to fight for the right of women to vote, a move that signaled the first wave of feminism and intensified cultural anxieties about women's roles. *The Turn of the Screw,* produced within this turbulent climate, reflects and draws upon cultural fears for its ghostly effects.

I

James's narrative begins with a prologue in which the reader is introduced to a group of country house guests seated around a fire, telling and listening to ghost stories. The prologue itself was written by an unnamed narrator and placed in front of a narrative that is read by Douglas, one of the guests. Douglas had known the author of that narrative as a youth, when she was a governess to his sister. Rendering the governess "visible" to his audience, Douglas's endorsement of her also serves as an effort to subdue the fears that governesses evoked in the Victorian era.

Governesses were single women employed to act as mother substitutes. Frequently lower class, or at least lower than the class of their employers, these servants were a source of controversy due to the problematic nature of single women and their sexuality. As Mary Poovey discusses in relation to *Jane Eyre,* governesses were caught in a sexual double bind:

> That representations of the governess in the 1840s brought to her contemporaries' minds not just the middle-class ideal she was

meant to reproduce, but the sexualized and often working-class women against whom she was expected to defend, reveals the mid-Victorian fear that the governess could not protect middle-class values because she could not be trusted to regulate her own sexuality. (Poovey 131)

Poovey's argument demonstrates the sexually fraught significations of governesses, a situation that would necessitate the character reference Douglas, as the governess's supporter, supplies for her in the prologue.

Although Douglas tries to mitigate the sexual connotations of the governess's position or, in my terms, reduce their visibility, in fact, he draws attention to her attractions by admitting to his own infatuation with her. Douglas introduces the governess with the observation that " 'She was the most agreeable woman I've ever known in her position; she'd have been worthy of any whatever' " (p. 24). Clearly, his audience picks up on the sexual implications of his statement, for Douglas goes on to add: " 'Oh yes; don't grin: I liked her extremely and am glad to this day to think she liked me too' " (p. 24). Douglas's infatuation with the governess leads the fireside group to speculate on his relationship with her, which now becomes more noticeable than anything else about the story:

> "Well, if I don't know who she was in love with I know who *he* was."
> "She was ten years older," said her husband.
> "*Raison de plus* — at that age! But it's rather nice, his long ret-icence." . . .
> "The outbreak," I returned, "will make a tremendous occasion of Thursday night"; and every one so agreed with me that in the light of it we lost all attention for everything else. (p. 25)

Interestingly, Douglas's ostensible attraction to the governess works not to his disadvantage but to hers. If he is in love with the governess, then he is not a "reliable" judge of her character, an inference that would invalidate the character reference he provides for her.

Once Douglas has opened the discussion by highlighting the governess's appeal for him, her own potential as a sexual being becomes the focus of discussion. The narrator suggests: " 'She was in love' " (p. 24), to which Douglas responds: " 'Yes, she was in love. That is she *had* been. That came out — she could n't tell her story without its coming out. I saw it, and she saw I saw it; but neither of us spoke of it' " (p. 24). What was invisible in Douglas's conversation with the governess (literally, here, the governess's unspoken love interest), becomes visible when Douglas relates that conversation to the fireside group, and the mention of the governess's desire works to diminish her credibility.

Further, when Douglas characterizes the governess for his audience, he emphasizes her inexperience and sexual susceptibility. He describes her as "a fluttered anxious girl out of a Hampshire vicarage" (p. 26) applying for her first position. According to Douglas, the governess was impressed with her prospective employer who "was handsome and bold and pleasant, off-hand and gay and kind. He struck her, inevitably, as gallant and splendid" (p. 26). Moreover, "she figured him as rich, but as fearfully extravagant — saw him all in a glow of high fashion, of good looks, of expensive habits, of charming ways with women" (pp. 26–27). The governess's predilection for the master is clear, and, again, the attention of the fireside group focusses on the amorous connotations of Douglas's narrative:

> "The moral of which was of course the seduction exercised by the splendid young man. She succumbed to it."
> He [Douglas] got up and, as he had done the night before, went to the fire, gave a stir to a log with his foot, then stood a moment with his back to us. "She saw him only twice."
> "Yes, but that's just the beauty of her passion."
> A little to my surprise, on this, Douglas turned round to me. "It *was* the beauty of it." (p. 28)

Douglas attempts to establish the governess's love as pure and beautiful (hence, asexual), but his listeners receive a different impression, as their responses to Douglas's story indicate. Similarly, the ways in which the governess is characterized by Douglas — "young, untried, nervous" (p. 28) — renders her suspect and undermines the authority of her narrative.

Also rendered visible in Douglas's account is the covert attraction between him and the narrator, with whom he seems to share a special bond. In the prologue, Douglas frequently comments upon the narrator's acuity: " 'You'll easily judge,' he repeated: '*you* will' " (p. 24), or, more directly, " 'You *are* acute' " (p. 24). He also ignores others in his concentration on the narrator: "He took no notice of her; he looked at me" (p. 23). In addition, the narrator and Douglas stay in touch, as is clear when the narrator reveals that Douglas "before his death — when it was in sight — committed to me the manuscript" (p. 26).

Indeed, since the story appears in an era that demands the concealment and obfuscation of homosexuality, the relationship between

Douglas and the narrator is closeted, or, like the governess's story, hidden "in a locked drawer" (p. 23), requiring a key (or inside knowledge?) for elucidation. When Douglas announces the location of the material, the narrator observes: "It was to me in particular that he appeared to propound this — appeared almost to appeal for aid not to hesitate. He had broken a thickness of ice, the formation of many a winter; had had his reasons for a long silence. The others resented postponement, but it was just his scruples that charmed me" (pp. 23–24). The "astute" reader, therefore, is alerted to the potential of a sexually doubled narrative to come, one that has both hetero- and homosexual undertones.

II

In the governess's narrative of her life at Bly, she recalls walking in the grounds and constructing a fictive male gaze. Since her sexuality has become noticeable as a result of Douglas's introduction, her construction has been read as an indication of her desire for a male companion, presumably the master in Harley Street:

> One of the thoughts that, as I don't in the least shrink now from noting, used to be with me in these wanderings was that it would be as charming as a charming story suddenly to meet some one. Some one would appear there at the turn of a path and would stand before me and smile and approve. I did n't ask more than that — I only asked that he should *know;* and the only way to be sure he knew would be to see it, and the kind light of it, in his handsome face. That was exactly present to me — by which I mean the face was — when, on the first of these occasions, at the end of a long June day, I stopped short on emerging from one of the plantations and coming into view of the house. (p. 39)

The governess does not encounter the master on a pathway, but rather another male figure atop a tower. The man, whom readers later learn is Peter Quint, is standing on one of two phallic towers that "were probably architectural absurdities, redeemed in a measure indeed by not being wholly disengaged nor of a height too pretentious, dating, in their gingerbread antiquity, from a romantic revival that was already a respectable past" (p. 39). Quint's figure, "very erect, as it struck me" (pp. 40–41), highlights the sexual implications of the governess's sighting and emphasizes her possession of a potentially dangerous sexuality.

Alternatively, Quint's appearance on the tower can be construed as an indication of the sexuality that he, himself, possesses and that becomes noticeable to her.

Initially, the governess fantasizes herself as the object of the gaze of the master in Harley Street. Accordingly, Quint assumes the master's place when he peeps at her, and he reconstructs her as the object of his gaze, a situation that is exemplified in her next meeting with him, when she is inside the house and he is on the outside, looking in:

> He was the same — he was the same, and seen, this time, as he had been seen before, from the waist up, the window, though the dining-room was on the ground floor, not going down to the terrace on which he stood. His face was close to the glass, yet the effect of this better view was, strangely, just to show me how intense the former had been. He remained but a few seconds — long enough to convince me he also saw and recognized; but it was as if I had been looking at him for years and had known him always. Something, however, happened this time that had not happened before; his stare into my face, through the glass and across the room, was as deep and hard as then, but it quitted me for a moment during which I could still watch it, see it fix successively several other things. (p. 44)

Although Quint is posited as the gazer in this scene, the gaze shifts, first when the governess finds herself able to "watch" him watching (and note that his gaze fixes on "other things" besides herself), next when she steps outside the house — usurping his position by becoming the gazer — and peers through the window herself. This moment is significant, since the gaze serves as a marker of sexuality and control. From that moment on, the two will struggle to dominate the children.

III

From a gender perspective, the governess's assumption of the gaze is significant, as I have been suggesting. Film theorists have argued that when a woman "sees" clearly, her transformation from spectacle (object) into spectator (subject) is highlighted.[1] As a result, when the gov-

---

[1]Mary Ann Doane stresses the importance of the female gaze in relation to cinematic representation:

> The woman with glasses signifies simultaneously intellectuality and undesirability; but the moment she removes her glasses . . . she is transformed into spectacle, the

erness (who is posited as the object of Quint's gaze twice) appropriates Quint's gaze, her action serves to indicate her intention to appropriate his place. The governess is in the process of assuming a position of (male) authority, and the difficulties of her endeavor are figured when her view is impeded. The governess tries to master the gaze by looking through the window as Quint has done, but her gaze is arrested by Mrs. Grose, the housekeeper, a representation of maternal respectability.

The other women the governess encounters at Bly signify the traditional spaces inhabited by women. The governess is confronted with the responsible mother figure in Mrs. Grose, and the sexually fraught whore figure in Miss Jessel, the previous governess. Not surprisingly, it is Mrs. Grose, the "proper" feminine character, who alerts the governess to the dangers inherent in rejecting a patriarchally inscribed role by telling the story of Miss Jessel. In response to the governess's query about her predecessor — " 'What was the lady who was here before?' " — Mrs. Grose explains:

> "The last governess? She was also young and pretty — almost as young and almost as pretty, Miss, even as you."
> "Ah then I hope her youth and her beauty helped her! . . . Was she careful — particular?"
> Mrs. Grose appeared to try to be conscientious. "About some things — yes."
> "But not about all?"
> Again she considered. "Well, Miss — she's gone. I won't tell tales." (pp. 35–36)

Miss Jessel, whose story is not quite told, constitutes a portrait of a woman fallen. Mrs. Grose confirms that Miss Jessel "*was* infamous" (p. 58) and had dealings with the valet, Quint:

> "He did what he wished."
> "With *her*?"
> "With them all." (p. 58)

---

very picture of desire. Now, it must be remembered that the cliche is a heavily loaded moment of signification, a social knot of meaning. It is characterized by an effect of ease and naturalness. Yet the cliche has a binding power so strong that it indicates a precise moment of ideological danger or threat — in this case, the woman's appropriation of the gaze. Glasses worn by a woman in the cinema do not signify a deficiency in seeing but an active looking, or even simply the fact of seeing as opposed to being seen. The intellectual woman looks and analyzes, and in usurping the gaze she poses a threat to an entire system of representation. (27)

Doane's contention highlights the significance of the governess's assumption of the male gaze in *The Turn of the Screw*.

A moment later Mrs. Grose adds, "'Poor woman — she paid for it!'" (p. 59). If Miss Jessel's acquiescence to Quint has wrought her downfall, such is not the fate that threatens the governess, who is performing as a subject, a position traditionally allotted to men. Yet, if Miss Jessel's fall is due not to Quint himself, but to her own sexuality, that fact would generate a different reading.

Terry Castle has argued that lesbians are often depicted as ghosts: "The lesbian is never with us, it seems, but always somewhere else, in the shadows, in the margins, hidden from history, out of sight, out of mind, a wanderer in the dusk, a lost soul, a tragic mistake, a pale denizen of the night. She is far away and she is dire" (Castle 2). Since this passage could have been written about Miss Jessel, it leads the reader to wonder whether the former governess's sexual orientation is in question. And if so, is the present governess's? James knew about women's love for each other, since his sister Alice was involved in a "Boston marriage" — that is, a close friendship between women who usually lived together and loved each other, yet whose sexual relationship was unclear. It is possible that while the governess believes she is engaged in a battle with the ghosts for the children's souls, she is struggling with her own sexual proclivities. Her condemnation of Miss Jessel — "'You terrible miserable woman!'" (p. 88) — may be a signal that she protests too much; certainly, she and Mrs. Grose kiss and touch frequently (pp. 37, 46, 51, 76, 110). Whatever her sexual orientation, the governess is caught in a catch-22 as she attempts to define herself against the sexualized whore figure Miss Jessel, while trying to supplant the male-authority figure Peter Quint. Neither of these roles can help her in her struggle, however, since she cannot replace Miss Jessel for Flora, nor Quint for Miles. The governess does not want to assume Miss Jessel's place, and she resists the negative connotations of feminine sexuality represented in the previous governess's characterization; but, her attempt to perform like Quint is also doomed to failure, since she is not male and cannot usurp his position. She must perform as a *female* subject, even though she has no model of female subjectivity to follow.

IV

Flora becomes the battleground on which the story's three female characters struggle, since Flora, as the girl child, is being schooled into womanhood. In an important passage, the governess sees Miss Jessel while she is supervising Flora. As the governess watches Miss Jessel, and thus assumes the position of the gazer, Flora indulges in what Edmund Wilson has flagged (see Beidler's "Critical History," p. 193) as sexual behavior: "She had picked up a small flat piece of wood which happened to have in it a little hole that had evidently suggested to her the idea of sticking in another fragment that might figure as a mast and make the thing a boat" (p. 55). Flora's endeavor in this passage signals both the need for female subjectivity and the patriarchal fear of a woman's sexuality. Is Flora's budding desire figured here as a reaction to the lesbian sexuality Miss Jessel may be viewed as embodying? If so, her actions conversely assume a male form, that is, her masculine effort to penetrate a piece of wood with a stick. Alternatively, is she unable to express her budding desire in anything other than male terms? Whatever the reason, the importance of the governess's project is foregrounded because she is trying to open a space (or a subject position) that would allow for the formulation and articulation of a positive female sexuality. Yet Flora's knowledge of sexuality, a knowledge that is denied to Victorian women, points to the dangers impassioned female role models pose to girls growing into patriarchally defined womanhood, which has no place for constructive female sexuality. Neither of Flora's female teachers can help her, for Miss Jessel, who is desirous, has become a whore figure, and the present governess is at this point a sexualized but undefinable figure. While Flora would not think in these terms, the confusion the two governesses engender in her is apparent in her sexually suggestive behavior.

Later in the story, Flora escapes to the lake, and all of the female characters meet in one scene. The governess confronts Miss Jessel in an effort to vanquish her, and, on one level, to reject the whore (lesbian?) role in which Miss Jessel is cast. In so doing, she is attempting to create a place for herself apart from the asexual mother role played by Mrs. Grose and the sexual whore role played by Miss Jessel. The repercussions of the slippage in gender roles are dramatized when Flora — who combines the traits of both traditional female characterizations — shifts her status from innocent child to experienced woman. The governess perceives Flora as "a vulgarly pert little girl in the street" (p. 103) whose "incomparable childish beauty had suddenly failed, had quite vanished. I've said it already — she was literally, she was hideously hard; she had turned common and almost ugly" (p. 103). The governess cannot offer Flora a model different from those offered by Miss Jessel or Mrs. Grose because she has not yet forged such a place for herself. As a result, Flora rejects the governess and returns to the safety of the roles she knows. Flora cries to Mrs. Grose, " 'Take me away, take me away —

oh take me away from *her!*'"(p. 103), and reverts to a child-innocent status that is less fraught with genderbending tension. The matronly Mrs. Grose provides Flora with a "safe" if limited role model that the governess, who has refused to conform to patriarchal definitions of womanhood, cannot offer her.

Because the governess cannot reassume the position of the mother, Flora casts her in the only other female position with which she has become familiar by associating the governess with the sexualized whore figure. Flora complains of the governess to Mrs. Grose, and while Mrs. Grose does not repeat directly what Flora has told her, she does indicate clearly enough in a conversation she has with the governess Flora's negative assessment:

> "I've *heard* — ! . . . From that child — horrors. There!"
> she sighed with tragic relief. "On my honour, Miss, she says things — !" . . .
> "She's so horrible?"
> I saw my colleague scarce knew how to put it. "Really shocking."
> "And about me?"
> "About you, Miss — since you must have it. It's beyond everything, for a young lady; and I can't think wherever she must have picked up — "
> "The appalling language she applies to me? I can then!"
> (p. 108)

The governess's inability to offer Flora a role model leads to Flora's indictment of her as a whore figure. (Of course, there are other readings available here, including one that casts the governess as the seductress figure who attempts to corrupt Flora.) Steering between the roles of the good mother and the whore, the governess's own place in the narrative is indeterminate. Although her sexuality situates her in the whore space, the governess continues to perform as a subject. This effort leads to her battle of wills with Quint, as the male subject, for control over Miles.

V

Left alone with Miles after Mrs. Grose takes Flora from Bly, the governess tries to extract a confession from the little boy about why he was expelled from school. Finally, she discovers that Miles "said things" (p. 118) to "those I liked" (p. 119). Miles's statement has sometimes been construed as an admission of lying. But as Miles is watched through the window by Quint, the man to whom he was initially attracted, his words take on a potentially different reading, for he may well be confessing to homoerotic attachments. When the governess presses him for more information, he must choose between her and Quint (or between alternative sexualities), under Quint's sentinel-like gaze: "Peter Quint had come into view like a sentinel before a prison. The next thing I saw was that, from outside, he had reached the window, and then I knew that, close to the glass and glaring in through it, he offered once more to the room his white face of damnation" (p. 116). The governess once again seeks to wrest the gaze from Quint, just as she attempts to wrest Miles from him. As she confronts Miles, she is aware of the man staring through the window:

> For there again, against the glass, as if to blight his confession and stay his answer, was the hideous author of our woe — the white face of damnation. I felt a sick swim at the drop of my victory and all the return of my battle, so that the wildness of my veritable leap only served as a great betrayal. I saw him, from the midst of my act, meet it with a divination, and on the perception that even now he only guessed, and that the window was still to his own eyes free, I let the impulse flame up to convert the climax of his dismay into the very proof of his liberation. "No more, no more, no more!" I shrieked to my visitant as I tried to press him against me. (pp. 119–20)

The governess does displace Quint because Miles had already "jerked straight round, stared, glared again, and seen but the quiet day" (p. 120). She has succeeded in mastering the gaze, but her mastery cannot be positive for her since she cannot assume Quint's place. She does not yet understand that her subjectivity must be established and cannot be appropriated, that female subjectivity involves more than a mimicry of male subjectivity. The governess's victory over Quint, therefore, is only a Pyrrhic victory, which leads to the death of Miles: "We were alone with the quiet day, and his little heart, dispossessed, had stopped" (p. 120). Perhaps the decision facing Miles is too overwhelming, and he cannot choose between sexualities. Torn, his heart stops, and so too does the paternal lineage at Bly, for the governess's ineffectual attempt to usurp Quint's position results in the death of the male heir. This conclusion, then, embodies male anxieties ensuing from a woman's refusal to play her patriarchally inscribed role, at the same time that it illustrates the difficulties and dangers of "coming out," or becoming visible as a gay man.

Consequently, whether or not James intended to write a tale that depicted the problems inherent in a woman's assumption of a subject position, or to produce a story that demonstrated the threat posed by alternative sexualities, his story effectively draws attention to the heterosexual and patriarchal boundaries that work to confine sexuality and subjectivity. Miles's death highlights the ways in which sexual and gender transgressions jeopardize the status quo. As Robert K. Martin has suggested, "Oscar [Wilde], or his creation, Dorian [Gray], is one of the most ominous of the ghosts that haunt Bly" (406). The governess, throughout, has performed as a sexual boundary-keeper and as a woman who appropriates a place not accorded to her within Victorian discourse. She is left, defeated, having failed at her job of caring for the children. The children, who are either dead or damaged, are the victims of the conflicting forces within the narrative. What the text dramatizes, therefore, are the difficulties an independent woman faces at the turn of the century, as well as the near-impossibility of a gay lifestyle in this period. Visibility, whether that of "coming out" or that of being recognized as a subject, focuses these issues within *The Turn of the Screw,* and becomes a prism through which to view the sexualities competing in the text.

WORKS CITED

Castle, Terry. *The Apparitional Lesbian: Female Homosexuality and Modern Culture.* New York: Columbia UP, 1993.

Cohen, Ed. *Talk on the Wilde Side.* New York: Routledge, 1993.

Doane, Mary Ann. *Femme Fatales: Feminism, Film Theory, Psychoanalysis.* New York: Routledge, 1991.

Martin, Robert K. "The Children's Hour: A Postcolonial *Turn of the Screw.*" *The Canadian Review of American Studies* 31 (2001): 401–08.

Poovey, Mary. *Uneven Developments: The Ideological Work of Gender in Mid-Victorian England.* Chicago: U of Chicago P, 1988.

Wilson, Edmund. "The Ambiguity of Henry James." 1938. *The Question of Henry James: A Collection of Critical Essays.* Ed. F. W. Dupee. London: Allan Wingate, 1947.

Marxist Criticism and
The Turn of the Screw

WHAT IS MARXIST CRITICISM?

To the question "What is Marxist criticism?" it may be tempting to respond with another question: "What does it matter?" In light of the rapid and largely unanticipated demise of Soviet-style communism in the former USSR and throughout Eastern Europe, it is understandable to suppose that Marxist literary analysis would disappear too, quickly becoming an anachronism in a world enamored with full-market capitalism.

In fact, however, there is no reason why Marxist criticism should weaken, let alone disappear. It is, after all, a phenomenon distinct from Soviet and Eastern European communism, having had its beginnings nearly eighty years before the Bolshevik revolution and having thrived since the 1940s, mainly in the West — not as a form of communist propaganda but rather as a form of critique, a discourse for interrogating *all* societies and their texts in terms of certain specific issues. Those issues — including race, class, and the attitudes shared within a given culture — are as much with us as ever, not only in contemporary Russia but also in the United States.

The argument could even be made that Marxist criticism has been strengthened by the collapse of Soviet-style communism. There was a time, after all, when few self-respecting Anglo-American journals would use Marxist terms or models, however illuminating, to analyze Western issues or problems. It smacked of sleeping with the enemy. With the collapse of the Kremlin, however, old taboos began to give way. Even the staid *Wall Street Journal* now seems comfortable using phrases like "worker alienation" to discuss the problems plaguing the American business world.

The assumption that Marxist criticism will die on the vine of a moribund political system rests in part on another mistaken assumption, namely, that Marxist literary analysis is practiced only by people who would like to see society transformed into a Marxist-communist state, one created through land reform, the redistribution of wealth, a tightly and centrally managed economy, the abolition of institutionalized religion, and so on. In fact, it has never been necessary to be a communist political revolutionary to be classified as a Marxist literary critic. (Many of the critics discussed in this introduction actually *fled* communist societies to live in the West.) Nor is it necessary to like only those literary works with a radical social vision or to dislike books that represent or even reinforce a middle-class, capitalist worldview. It is necessary, however, to adopt what most students of literature would consider a radical definition of the purpose and function of literary criticism.

More traditional forms of criticism, according to the Marxist critic Pierre Macherey, "set . . . out to deliver the text from its own silences by coaxing it into giving up its true, latent, or hidden meaning." Inevitably, however, non-Marxist criticism "intrude[s] its own discourse between the reader and the text" (qtd. in Bennett 107). Marxist critics, by contrast, do not attempt to discover hidden meanings in texts. Or if they do, they do so only after seeing the text, first and foremost, as a material product to be understood in broadly historical terms. That is to say, a literary work is first viewed as a product *of* work (and hence of the realm of production and consumption we call economics). Second, it may be looked upon as a work that *does* identifiable work of its own. At one level, that work is usually to enforce and reinforce the prevailing ideology, that is, the network of conventions, values, and opinions to which the majority of people uncritically subscribe.

This does not mean that Marxist critics merely describe the obvious. Quite the contrary: the relationship that the Marxist critic Terry Eagleton outlines in *Criticism and Ideology* (1978) among the soaring cost of books in the nineteenth century, the growth of lending libraries, the practice of publishing "three-decker" novels (so that three borrowers could be reading the same book at the same time), and the changing *content* of those novels is highly complex in its own way. But the complexity Eagleton finds is not that of the deeply buried meaning of the text. Rather, it is that of the complex web of social and economic relationships that were prerequisite to the work's production. Marxist criticism does not seek to be, in Eagleton's words, "a passage from text to reader." Indeed, "its task is to show the text as it cannot know itself, to manifest those conditions of its making (inscribed in its very letter) about which it is necessarily silent" (43).

As everyone knows, Marxism began with Karl Marx, the nineteenth-century German philosopher best known for writing *Das Kapital,* the seminal work of the communist movement. What everyone doesn't know is that Marx was also the first Marxist literary critic (much as Sigmund Freud, who psychoanalyzed E. T. A. Hoffmann's supernatural tale "The Sandman," was the first Freudian literary critic). During the 1830s Marx wrote critical essays on writers such as Goethe and Shakespeare (whose tragic vision of Elizabethan disintegration he praised).

The fact that Marxist literary criticism began with Marx himself is hardly surprising, given Marx's education and early interests. Trained in the classics at the University of Bonn, Marx wrote literary imitations, his own poetry, a failed novel, and a fragment of a tragic drama *(Oulanem)* before turning to contemplative and political philosophy. Even after he met Friedrich Engels in 1843 and began collaborating on works such as *The German Ideology* and *The Communist Manifesto,* Marx maintained a keen interest in literary writers and their works. He and Engels argued about the poetry of Heinrich Heine, admired Hermann Freiligrath (a poet critical of the German aristocracy), and faulted the playwright Ferdinand Lassalle for writing about a reactionary knight in the Peasants' War rather than about more progressive aspects of German history.

As these examples suggest, Marx and Engels would not — indeed, could not — think of aesthetic matters as being distinct and independent from such things as politics, economics, and history. Not surprisingly, they viewed the alienation of the worker in industrialized, capitalist societies as having grave consequences for the arts. How can people mechanically stamping out things that bear no mark of their producer's individuality (people thereby "reified," turned into things themselves) be expected to recognize, produce, or even consume things of beauty? And if there is no one to consume something, there will soon be no one to produce it, especially in an age in which production (even of something like literature) has come to mean *mass* (and therefore profitable) production.

In *The German Ideology* (1846), Marx and Engels expressed their sense of the relationship between the arts, politics, and basic economic reality in terms of a general social theory. Economics, they argued, provides the "base" or "infrastructure" of society, but from that base emerges a "superstructure" consisting of law, politics, philosophy, religion, and art.

Marx later admitted that the relationship between base and superstructure may be indirect and fluid: every change in economics may not be reflected by an immediate change in ethics or literature. In *The Eighteenth Brumaire of Louis Bonaparte* (1852), he came up with the word *homology* to describe the sometimes unbalanced, often delayed, and almost always loose correspondence between base and superstructure. And later in that same decade, while working on an introduction to his *Political Economy,* Marx further relaxed the base–superstructure relationship. Writing on the excellence of ancient Greek art (versus the primitive nature of ancient Greek economics), he conceded that a gap sometimes opens up between base and superstructure — between economic forms and those produced by the creative mind.

Nonetheless, *at* base the old formula was maintained. Economics remained basic and the connection between economics and superstructural elements of society was reaffirmed. Central to Marxism and Marxist literary criticism was and is the following "materialist" insight: consciousness, without which such things as art cannot be produced, is not the source of social forms and economic conditions. It is, rather, their most important product.

Marx and Engels, drawing upon the philosopher G. W. F. Hegel's theories about the dialectical synthesis of ideas out of theses and antitheses, believed that a revolutionary class war (pitting the capitalist class against a proletarian, antithetical class) would lead eventually to the synthesis of a new social and economic order. Placing their faith not in the idealist Hegelian dialectic but, rather, in what they called "dialectical materialism," they looked for a secular and material salvation of humanity — one in, not beyond, history — via revolution and not via divine intervention. And they believed that the communist society eventually established would be one capable of producing new forms of consciousness and belief and therefore, ultimately, great art.

The revolution anticipated by Marx and Engels did not occur in their century, let alone lifetime. When it finally did take place, it didn't happen in places where Marx and Engels had thought it might be successful: the United States, Great Britain, and Germany. It happened, rather, in 1917 Russia, a country long ruled by despotic czars but also enlightened by the works of powerful novelists and playwrights, including Chekhov, Pushkin, Tolstoy, and Dostoyevsky.

Perhaps because of its significant literary tradition, Russia produced revolutionaries like V. I. Lenin, who shared not only Marx's interest in literature but also his belief in literature's ultimate importance. But it was not without some hesitation that Lenin endorsed the significance of texts written during the reign of the czars. Well before 1917 he had questioned what the relationship should be between a society undergoing a revolution and the great old literature of its bourgeois past.

Lenin attempted to answer that question in a series of essays on Tolstoy that he wrote between 1908 and 1911. Tolstoy — the author of *War and Peace* and *Anna Karenina* — was an important nineteenth-century Russian writer whose views did not accord with all of those of young Marxist revolutionaries. Continuing interest in a writer like Tolstoy may be justified, Lenin reasoned, given the primitive and unenlightened economic order of the society that produced him. Since superstructure usually lags behind base (and is therefore usually *more* primitive), the attitudes of a Tolstoy were relatively progressive when viewed in light of the monarchical and precapitalist society out of which they arose.

Moreover, Lenin also reasoned, the writings of the great Russian realists would *have* to suffice, at least in the short run. Lenin looked forward, in essays like "Party Organization and Party Literature," to the day in which new artistic forms would be produced by progressive writers with revolutionary political views and agendas. But he also knew that a great proletarian literature was unlikely to evolve until a thoroughly literate proletariat had been produced by the educational system.

Lenin was hardly the only revolutionary leader involved in setting up the new Soviet state who took a strong interest in literary matters. In 1924 Leon Trotsky published a book called *Literature and Revolution,* which is still acknowledged as a classic of Marxist literary criticism.

Trotsky worried about the direction in which Marxist aesthetic theory seemed to be going. He responded skeptically to groups like Proletkult, which opposed tolerance toward pre- and nonrevolutionary

writers, and which called for the establishment of a new, proletarian culture. Trotsky warned of the danger of cultural sterility and risked unpop-
ularity by pointing out that there is no necessary connection between
the quality of a literary work and the quality of its author's politics.

In 1927 Trotsky lost a power struggle with Josef Stalin, a man who
believed, among other things, that writers should be "engineers" of
"human souls." After Trotsky's expulsion from the Soviet Union, views
held by groups like Proletkult and the Left Front of Art (LEF), and by
theorists such as Nikolai Bukharin and A. A. Zhdanov, became more
prevalent. Speaking at the First Congress of the Union of Soviet Writers
in 1934, the Soviet author Maxim Gorky called for writing that would
"make labor the principal hero of our books." It was at the same writers' congress that "socialist realism," an art form glorifying workers and
the revolutionary State, was made Communist party policy and the official literary form of the USSR.

Of the writers active in the USSR after the expulsion of Trotsky and
the unfortunate triumph of Stalin, two critics stand out. One, Mikhail
Bakhtin, was a Russian, later a Soviet, critic who spent much of his life
in a kind of internal exile. Many of his essays were written in the 1930s
and not published in the West or translated until the late 1960s. His
work comes out of an engagement with the Marxist intellectual tradition as well as out of an indirect, even hidden, resistance to the Soviet
government. It has been important to Marxist critics writing in the
West because his theories provide a means to decode submerged social
critique, especially in early modern texts. He viewed language — especially literary texts — in terms of discourses and dialogues. Within a
novel written in a society in flux, for instance, the narrative may include
an official, legitimate discourse, plus another infiltrated by challenging
comments and even retorts. In a 1929 book on Dostoyevsky and a
1940 study titled *Rabelais and His World*, Bakhtin examined what he
calls "polyphonic" novels, each characterized by a multiplicity of voices
or discourses. In Dostoyevsky the independent status of a given character is marked by the difference of his or her language from that of the
narrator. (The narrator's voice, too, can in fact be a dialogue.) In works
by Rabelais, Bakhtin finds that the (profane) language of the carnival
and of other popular festivals plays against and parodies the more official discourses, that is, of the king, church, or even socially powerful
intellectuals. Bakhtin influenced modern cultural criticism by showing,
in a sense, that the conflict between "high" and "low" culture takes
place not only between classic and popular texts but also between

the "dialogic" voices that exist within many books — whether "high" or "low."

The other subtle Marxist critic who managed to survive Stalin's dictatorship and his repressive policies was Georg Lukács. A Hungarian who had begun his career as an "idealist" critic, Lukács had converted to Marxism in 1919; renounced his earlier, Hegelian work shortly thereafter; visited Moscow in 1930–31; and finally emigrated to the USSR in 1933, just one year before the First Congress of the Union of Soviet Writers met. Lukács was far less narrow in his views than the most strident Stalinist Soviet critics of the 1930s and 1940s. He disliked much socialist realism and appreciated prerevolutionary, realistic novels that broadly reflected cultural "totalities"— and were populated with characters representing human "types" of the author's place and time. (Lukács was particularly fond of the historical canvasses painted by the early-nineteenth-century novelist Sir Walter Scott.) But like his more rigid and censorious contemporaries, he drew the line at accepting nonrevolutionary, modernist works like James Joyce's *Ulysses*. He condemned movements like expressionism and symbolism, preferring works with "content" over more decadent, experimental works characterized mainly by "form."

With Lukács its most liberal and tolerant critic from the early 1930s until well into the 1960s, the Soviet literary scene degenerated to the point that the works of great writers like Franz Kafka were no longer read, either because they were viewed as decadent, formal experiments or because they "engineered souls" in "nonprogressive" directions. Officially sanctioned works were generally ones in which artistry lagged far behind the politics (no matter how bad the politics were).

Fortunately for the Marxist critical movement, politically radical critics *outside* the Soviet Union were free of its narrow, constricting policies and, consequently, able fruitfully to develop the thinking of Marx, Engels, and Trotsky. It was these non-Soviet Marxists who kept Marxist critical theory alive and useful in discussing all *kinds* of literature, written across the entire historical spectrum.

Perhaps because Lukács was the best of the Soviet communists writing Marxist criticism in the 1930s and 1940s, non-Soviet Marxists tended to develop their ideas by publicly opposing those of Lukács. German dramatist and critic Bertolt Brecht countered Lukács by arguing that art ought to be viewed as a field of production, not as a container of "content." Brecht also criticized Lukács for his attempt to enshrine realism at the expense not only of other "isms" but also of poetry and drama, both of which had been largely ignored by Lukács.

Even more outspoken was Brecht's critical champion Walter Benjamin, a German Marxist who, in the 1930s, attacked those conventional and traditional literary forms conveying a stultifying "aura" of culture. Benjamin praised dadaism and, more important, new forms of art ushered in by the age of mechanical reproduction. Those forms — including radio and film — offered hope, he felt, for liberation from capitalist culture, for they were too new to be part of its stultifyingly ritualistic traditions.

But of all the anti-Lukácsians outside the USSR who made a contribution to the development of Marxist literary criticism, the most important was probably Theodor Adorno. Leader since the early 1950s of the Frankfurt school of Marxist criticism, Adorno attacked Lukács for his dogmatic rejection of nonrealist modern literature and for his belief in the primacy of content over form. Art does not equal science, Adorno insisted. He went on to argue for art's autonomy from empirical forms of knowledge and to suggest that the interior monologues of modernist works (by Beckett and Proust) reflect the fact of modern alienation in a way that Marxist criticism ought to find compelling.

In addition to turning against Lukács and his overly constrictive canon, Marxists outside the Soviet Union were able to take advantage of insights generated by non-Marxist critical theories being developed in post–World War II Europe. One of the movements that came to be of interest to non-Soviet Marxists was structuralism, a scientific approach to the study of humankind whose proponents believed that all elements of culture, including literature, could be understood as parts of a system of signs. Using modern linguistics as a model, structuralists like Claude Lévi-Strauss broke down the myths of various cultures into "mythemes" in an attempt to show that there are structural correspondences, or homologies, between the mythical elements produced by various human communities across time.

Of the European structuralist Marxists, one of the most influential was Lucien Goldmann, a Rumanian critic living in Paris. Goldmann combined structuralist principles with Marx's base–superstructure model in order to show how economics determines the mental structures of social groups, which are reflected in literary texts. Goldmann rejected the idea of individual human genius, choosing to see works, instead, as the "collective" products of "trans-individual" mental structures. In early studies, such as *The Hidden God* (1955), he related seventeenth-century French texts (such as Racine's *Phèdre*) to the ideology of Jansenism. In later works, he applied Marx's base–superstructure model even more strictly, describing a relationship between economic conditions and texts unmediated by an intervening, collective consciousness.

In spite of his rigidity and perhaps because of his affinities with structuralism, Goldmann came to be seen in the 1960s as the proponent of a kind of watered-down, "humanist" Marxism. He was certainly viewed that way by the French Marxist Louis Althusser, a disciple not of Lévi-Strauss and structuralism but rather of the psychoanalytic theorist Jacques Lacan and of the Italian communist Antonio Gramsci, famous for his writings about ideology and "hegemony." (Gramsci used the latter word to refer to the pervasive, weblike system of assumptions and values that shapes the way things look, what they mean, and therefore what reality *is* for the majority of people within a culture.)

Like Gramsci, Althusser viewed literary works primarily in terms of their relationship to ideology, the function of which, he argued, is to (re)produce the existing relations of production in a given society. Dave Laing, in *The Marxist Theory of Art* (1978), has attempted to explain this particular insight of Althusser by saying that ideologies, through the "ensemble of habits, moralities, and opinions" that can be found in any literary text, "ensure that the work-force (and those responsible for re-producing them in the family, school, etc.) are maintained in their position of subordination to the dominant class" (91). This is not to say that Althusser thought of the masses as a brainless multitude following only the dictates of the prevailing ideology: Althusser followed Gramsci in suggesting that even working-class people have some freedom to struggle against ideology and to change history. Nor is it to say that Althusser saw ideology as being a coherent, consistent force. In fact, he saw it as being riven with contradictions that works of literature sometimes expose and even widen. Thus Althusser followed Marx and Gramsci in believing that although literature must be seen in *relation* to ideology, it — like all social forms — has some degree of autonomy.

Althusser's followers included Pierre Macherey, who in *A Theory of Literary Production* (1978) developed Althusser's concept of the relationship between literature and ideology. A realistic novelist, he argued, attempts to produce a unified, coherent text, but instead ends up producing a work containing lapses, omissions, gaps. This happens because within ideology there are subjects that cannot be covered, things that cannot be said, contradictory views that aren't recognized as contradictory. (The critic's challenge, in this case, is to supply what the text cannot say, thereby making sense of gaps and contradictions.)

But there is another reason why gaps open up and contradictions become evident in texts. Works don't just reflect ideology (which Goldmann had referred to as "myth" and which Macherey refers to as a system of "illusory social beliefs"); they are also "fictions," works of art, *products* of ideology that have what Goldmann would call a "world-view" to offer. What kind of product, Macherey implicitly asks, is identical to the thing that produced it? It is hardly surprising, then, that Balzac's fiction shows French peasants in two different lights, only one of which is critical and judgmental, only one of which is baldly ideological. Writing approvingly on Macherey and Macherey's mentor Althusser in *Marxism and Literary Criticism* (1976), Terry Eagleton says: "It is by giving ideology a determinate form, fixing it within certain fictional limits, that art is able to distance itself from [ideology], thus revealing . . . [its] limits" (19).

A follower of Althusser, Macherey is sometimes referred to as a "post-Althusserian Marxist." Eagleton, too, is often described that way, as is his American contemporary Fredric Jameson. Jameson and Eagleton, as well as being post-Althusserians, are also among the few Anglo-American critics who have closely followed and significantly developed Marxist thought.

Before them, Marxist interpretation in English was limited to the work of a handful of critics: Christopher Caudwell, Christopher Hill, Arnold Kettle, E. P. Thompson, and Raymond Williams. Of these, Williams was perhaps least Marxist in orientation: he felt that Marxist critics, ironically, tended too much to isolate economics from culture; that they overlooked the individualism of people, opting instead to see them as "masses"; and that even more ironically, they had become an elitist group. But if the least Marxist of the British Marxists, Williams was also by far the most influential. Preferring to talk about "culture" instead of ideology, Williams argued in works such as *Culture and Society 1780–1950* (1958) that culture is "lived experience" and, as such, an interconnected set of social properties, each and all grounded in and influencing history.

Terry Eagleton's *Criticism and Ideology* is in many ways a response to the work of Williams. Responding to Williams's statement in *Culture and Society* that "there are in fact no masses; there are only ways of seeing people as masses" (289), Eagleton writes:

> That men and women really are now unique individuals was
> Williams's (unexceptionable) insistence; but it was a proposition
> bought at the expense of perceiving the fact that they must mass

and fight to achieve their full individual humanity. One has only to adapt Williams's statement to "There are in fact no classes; there are only ways of seeing people as classes" to expose its theoretical paucity. (*Criticism* 29)

Eagleton goes on, in *Criticism and Ideology,* to propose an elaborate theory about how history — in the form of "general," "authorial," and "aesthetic" ideology — enters texts, which in turn may revivify, open up, or critique those same ideologies, thereby setting in motion a process that may alter history. He shows how texts by Jane Austen, Matthew Arnold, Charles Dickens, George Eliot, Joseph Conrad, and T. S. Eliot deal with and transmute conflicts at the heart of the general and authorial ideologies behind them: conflicts between morality and individualism, and between individualism and social organicism and utilitarianism.

As all this emphasis on ideology and conflict suggests, a modern British Marxist like Eagleton, even while acknowledging the work of a British Marxist predecessor like Williams, is more nearly developing the ideas of Continental Marxists like Althusser and Macherey. That holds, as well, for modern American Marxists like Fredric Jameson. For although he makes occasional, sympathetic references to the works of Williams, Thompson, and Hill, Jameson makes far more *use* of Lukács, Adorno, and Althusser as well as non-Marxist structuralist, psychoanalytic, and poststructuralist critics.

In the first of several influential works, *Marxism and Form* (1971), Jameson takes up the question of form and content, arguing that the former is "but the working out" of the latter "in the realm of superstructure" (329). (In making such a statement Jameson opposes not only the tenets of Russian formalists, for whom content had merely been the fleshing out of form, but also those of so-called vulgar Marxists, who tended to define form as mere ornamentation or window dressing.) In his later work *The Political Unconscious* (1981), Jameson uses what in *Marxism and Form* he had called "dialectical criticism" to synthesize out of structuralism and poststructuralism, Freud and Lacan, Althusser and Adorno, a set of complex arguments that can only be summarized reductively.

The fractured state of societies and the isolated condition of individuals, he argues, may be seen as indications that there originally existed an unfallen state of something that may be called "primitive communism." History — which records the subsequent divisions and alienations — limits awareness of its own contradictions and of that lost, Better State, via ideologies and their manifestation in texts whose strategies essentially contain and repress desire, especially revolutionary desire, into the collective unconscious. (In Conrad's *Lord Jim,* Jameson shows, the knowledge that governing classes don't *deserve* their power is contained and repressed by an ending that metaphysically blames Nature for the tragedy and that melodramatically blames wicked Gentleman Brown.)

As demonstrated by Jameson in analyses like the one mentioned above, textual strategies of containment and concealment may be discovered by the critic, but only by the critic practicing dialectical criticism, that is to say, a criticism aware, among other things, of its *own* status as ideology. All thought, Jameson concludes, is ideological; only through ideological thought that knows itself as such can ideologies be seen through and eventually transcended.

Bruce Robbins begins the essay that follows by reminding us that "the many varieties of Marxist criticism have two things in common. First they put texts into historical context. [Then] they try to change that context — to have an effect on history" (p. 333 in this volume). To place *The Turn of the Screw* in its historical context, Robbins looks at the story in relation to the history of English governesses and house servants.

Focusing on the relationship between the narrating governess and two ghosts — ghosts whose very ghostliness keeps us from thinking about them as real people, as house servants who led real lives and had real histories — Robbins suggests that James attempted to "resist" the kind of "historical interpretation" that would bring to bear a "knowledge of social groups and ideologies" (p. 335). The ghosts, he suggests, are among the means James used to effect that resistance. "How can a critic talk about ideology," Robbins asks, "when the major characters are not social beings, but supernatural ones?" (p. 335).

The fact that the governess's lower-class associates are ghosts is not surprising, Robbins's subsequent analysis of Douglas's narrative reveals, in that working-class people were *like* ghosts to their social superiors, who neither needed nor wanted to deal with them as real people and who usually only thought about them when the noises of their work drifted up from downstairs. Ironically, the same attitude toward the lower classes that made the death of the former governess a mere "awkwardness" for the master is replicated in the attitude of the governess-narrator toward her social inferiors, for although governesses were not free to associate with their masters, they also thought of themselves (and were thought of as being) several notches above house servants in the Victorian social hierarchy.

Focusing on passages and scenes in the story, Robbins goes on to show that what individuals were willing to say to one another, what they saw when they looked at one another, what they knew about themselves, and what they were willing to *admit* they knew about themselves were all functions of class and class consciousness. James's governess, for instance, will not allow herself to see the analogy between her own situation and the tragic story of Miss Jessel and Peter Quint, because to do so she would have to see that her own love for the master "is a sort of inverted parallel" (p. 338) to Miss Jessel's love for a man of even lower social station.

Having shown, in the early pages of his essay, how James sought to resist historical readings of his story, Robbins turns his attentions to a consideration of the ways in which *The Turn of the Screw* "questions the society it describes more searchingly than [the governess] does" (p. 341). To do so, he places a great deal of interpretive weight on a conversation between the governess and Miles, who seems to be able to see through the unfairness of the society that surrounds him because of the fact that he has been raised by servants in "bizarre isolation." "[W]ithout interference from the upper classes," Robbins contends, "the children have become little democrats, unable to see the sin in transgressing those class divisions that the adult world takes for granted" (p. 343). Through the children, whom Robbins views as "innocent" in a "challenging sense," James — and perhaps even the governess — can see "what [the children] see," namely, "the absurdity of believing that 'the others' [i.e., members of the servant class] don't 'count'" (p. 343).

Robbins proceeds by engaging in a fruitful discussion of the story's ending, which he places in the context of the romance tradition as understood by Fredric Jameson. And he ends his essay by bringing it full circle, by helping us see that it has that second feature all Marxist readings have in common, namely, the attempt to change the historical context in which we read, to have an actual *effect* on history. What he doesn't discuss is a less obvious feature his analysis has in common with other Marxist analyses — the tendency both to show that the text reinforces the prevailing ideology and, at the same time, to reveal those gaps that occasionally allow the author to show, and us to see, the tragic contradictions implicit in such an ideology.

Ross C Murfin

MARXIST CRITICISM:
A SELECTED BIBLIOGRAPHY

Marx, Engels, Lenin, and Trotsky

Engels, Friedrich. *The Condition of the Working Class in England.* Ed. and trans. W. O. Henderson and W. H. Chaloner. Stanford: Stanford UP, 1968.

Lenin, V. I. *On Literature and Art.* Moscow: Progress, 1967.

Marx, Karl. *Selected Writings.* Ed. David McLellan. Oxford: Oxford UP, 1977.

Trotsky, Leon. *Literature and Revolution.* 1924. New York: Russell, 1967.

General Introductions to and
Reflections on Marxist Criticism

Bennett, Tony. *Formalism and Marxism.* London: Methuen, 1979.

Demetz, Peter. *Marx, Engels, and the Poets.* Chicago: U of Chicago P, 1967.

Eagleton, Terry. *Literary Theory: An Introduction.* Minneapolis: U of Minnesota P, 1983.

———. *Marxism and Literary Criticism.* Berkeley: U of California P, 1976.

Elster, Jon. *An Introduction to Karl Marx.* Cambridge: Cambridge UP, 1985.

———. *Nuts and Bolts for the Social Sciences.* Cambridge: Cambridge UP, 1989.

Fokkema, D. W., and Elrud Kunne-Ibsch. *Theories of Literature in the Twentieth Century: Structuralism, Marxism, Aesthetics of Reception, Semiotics.* New York: St. Martin's, 1977. See ch. 4, "Marxist Theories of Literature."

Frow, John. *Marxism and Literary History.* Cambridge: Harvard UP, 1986.

Jefferson, Ann, and David Robey. *Modern Literary Theory: A Critical Introduction.* Totowa, NJ: Barnes, 1982. See the essay "Marxist Literary Theories," by David Forgacs.

Laing, Dave. *The Marxist Theory of Art.* Brighton: Harvester, 1978.

Selden, Raman, Peter Widdowson, and Peter Brooker. *A Readers' Guide to Contemporary Literary Theory.* 4th ed. Lexington: U of Kentucky P, 1997. See ch. 5, "Marxist Theories."

Slaughter, Cliff. *Marxism, Ideology, and Literature*. Atlantic Highlands: Humanities, 1980.

Some Classic Marxist Studies and Statements

Adorno, Théodor. *Prisms: Cultural Criticism and Society*. Trans. Samuel Weber and Sherry Weber. Cambridge: MIT P, 1982.

Althusser, Louis. *For Marx*. Trans. Ben Brewster. New York: Pantheon, 1969.

Althusser, Louis, and Étienne Balibar. *Reading Capital*. Trans. Ben Brewster. New York: Pantheon, 1971.

Bakhtin, Mikhail. *The Dialogic Imagination: Four Essays*. Ed. Michael Holquist. Trans. Caryl Emerson. Austin: U of Texas P, 1981.

———. *Rabelais and His World*. Trans. Hélène Iswolsky. Cambridge: MIT P, 1968.

Benjamin, Walter. *Illuminations*. Ed. with introd. by Hannah Arendt. Trans. H. Zohn. New York: Harcourt, 1968.

Brecht, Bertolt. *Brecht on Theatre: The Development of an Aesthetic*. Ed. and trans. John Willett. New York: Hill, 1964.

———. *William Morris: Romantic to Revolutionary*. New York: Pantheon, 1977.

Caudwell, Christopher. *Illusion and Reality*. 1935. New York: Russell, 1955.

———. *Studies in a Dying Culture*. London: Lawrence, 1938.

Goldmann, Lucien. *The Hidden God*. New York: Humanities, 1964.

———. *Towards a Sociology of the Novel*. London: Tavistock, 1975.

Gramsci, Antonio. *Selections from the Prison Notebooks*. Ed. Quintin Hoare and Geoffrey Nowell Smith. New York: International UP, 1971.

Kettle, Arnold. *An Introduction to the English Novel*. New York: Harper, 1960.

Lukács, Georg. *The Historical Novel*. Trans. H. Mitchell and S. Mitchell. Boston: Beacon, 1963.

———. *Studies in European Realism*. New York: Grosset, 1964.

———. *The Theory of the Novel*. Cambridge: MIT P, 1971.

Marcuse, Herbert. *One-Dimensional Man*. Boston: Beacon, 1964.

Thompson, E. P. *The Making of the English Working Class*. New York: Pantheon, 1964.

Williams, Raymond. *Culture and Society 1780–1950*. New York: Harper, 1958.

————. *The Long Revolution*. New York: Columbia UP, 1961.

————. *Marxism and Literature*. Oxford: Oxford UP, 1977.

Wilson, Edmund. *To the Finland Station*. Garden City: Doubleday, 1953.

Studies by and of Post-Althusserian Marxists

Dowling, William C. *Jameson, Althusser, Marx: An Introduction to "The Political Unconscious."* Ithaca: Cornell UP, 1984.

Eagleton, Terry. *Criticism and Ideology: A Study in Marxist Literary Theory*. London: Verso, 1978.

————. *Exiles and Émigrés*. New York: Schocken, 1970.

Goux, Jean-Joseph. *Symbolic Economies after Marx and Freud*. Trans. Jennifer Gage. Ithaca: Cornell UP, 1990.

Jameson, Fredric. *Marxism and Form: Twentieth-Century Dialectical Theories of Literature*. Princeton: Princeton UP, 1971.

————. *The Political Unconscious: Narrative as a Socially Symbolic Act*. Ithaca: Cornell UP, 1981.

Macherey, Pierre. *A Theory of Literary Production*. Trans. G. Wall. London: Routledge, 1978.

Marxist Approaches to *The Turn of the Screw*

Fussell, Edwin. "The Ontology of *The Turn of the Screw*." *Journal of Modern Literature* 8 (1980): 118–28.

Killoran, Helen. "The Governess, Mrs. Grose, and 'the poison of an influence' in *The Turn of the Screw*." *Modern Language Studies* 23 (1993): 13–24.

McMaster, Graham. "Henry James and India: A Historical Reading of *The Turn of the Screw*." *Clio* 18 (1988): 23–40.

Pearson, John H. "Repetition and Subversion in Henry James's *The Turn of the Screw*." *Henry James Review* 13 (1992): 276–91.

Robbins, Bruce. "Shooting off James's Blanks: Theory, Politics, and *The Turn of the Screw*." *Henry James Review* 5 (1984): 192–99.

A MARXIST PERSPECTIVE

BRUCE ROBBINS

"They don't much count, do they?": The Unfinished History of *The Turn of the Screw*

The many varieties of Marxist criticism have two things in common. First, they put texts into historical context. But unlike certain other styles of historical criticism, they also do something else. They try to change that context — to have an effect on history.

The number of possible contexts into which any text could be placed may not be infinite, but it is certainly large. Setting out to interpret *The Turn of the Screw* historically, one might look for example at the England of the 1890s, in which Henry James was writing, or at the America of the 1840s and 1850s, in which he was growing up, or again at the America of the early twenty-first century, in which we read him now. And within each of these periods, we might examine the story in its relation to very different histories. There is the history (or *her*story, as some feminists have begun to say) of women, which might urge us to see the governess, in a somewhat heroic light, as making a challenging entry into a wider world of employment. Or, on the contrary, we might see her as a male fantasy of the *femme fatale*. There is the history of education, which might encourage us to ask different questions, say, about the governess's desire to "possess" her pupils or about how serious the offense would have to be for a child like Miles to get expelled from boarding school. More obviously, there is the history of class; the unique discomforts of being a governess, who belongs neither with the masters far above her nor, quite, with the servants immediately below her, are inexplicable without it. The meaning of Quint's being "too free" (p. 51 in this volume) with the other servants is similarly inexplicable without the history of sexuality. The history of childhood might divert our attention from the controversy about the reality of the ghosts and focus it instead on taboos against speaking to children about topics like sex and death, taboos that from a child's point of view turn sex and death into ghostly half-realities. Perhaps James's story asks what it might mean for anyone, whether ghost or not, to "corrupt" children. The ghost-story genre has its own (literary) history. And then there is the social history of the literary marketplace, where ghost stories "sell" better than more "serious" fiction.

Marxist criticism can and does talk about any and all of these contexts. But for Marxist critics — and it is their politics I am talking about, not the far more diverse politics of the authors they analyze — the decision to say more about one and less about another in any given interpretation, and about what to look for within it, depends on a premise that Marx expressed in his famous "Theses on Feuerbach": "The philosophers have only *interpreted* the world differently, the point is, to *change* it" (Marx 199). The second and perhaps definitive assumption that Marxist criticism makes, in other words, is that history is unfinished, and that, however modestly, our interpretations should and will help push it in one direction or another, slow it down or speed it up.

I

In interpreting *The Turn of the Screw*, it may help to know that, since the beginnings of the English novel in the eighteenth century, the point of view of fictional servants and governesses has often been closely associated with those energies that have been pushing hardest to change the world. From Samuel Richardson's *Pamela* (1740) to Charlotte Brontë's *Jane Eyre* (1847) — which James's governess clearly has in mind when she alludes to "an unmentionable relative kept in unsuspected confinement" (p. 41) — the servant or governess who is in love with a master far above her in wealth and rank, yet who somehow manages to marry him in the end, has carried with her the aspirations of generations of women and men who are discontented with the limited possibilities offered them by their society. Through such figures, the novel has refashioned the folktale of Cinderella into sophisticated allegories of collective upward mobility in which all those who did not own mansions like Bly could imaginatively participate.

What does all this imply about *The Turn of the Screw*? Like Pamela and Jane Eyre, James's governess does most of the narrating of her text, thus forcing us to identify, at least provisionally, with her perspective and her hopes. And like the other protagonists, she too is clearly in love with her distant master. Yet her version of the Cinderella story is frustrated, truncated, unfinished. She doesn't get the guy; indeed, she never even sees him again. In her own eyes, as she admits, she is trying her best to win his love by heroically protecting his niece and nephew from the ghosts. But heroic or not, she manages only to alienate Flora and to kill Miles — an outcome that doesn't become more pleasant to contemplate if one judges, as many readers do, that the ghosts are her own inventions or hallucinations. What happens, then, to the aspirations that the reader invests in her? Has James written a sort of counterargument to the Cinderella narrative, the darker allegory of a society in which hopes of upward mobility have come to seem misguided, doomed to failure, and horribly destructive?

Even if we agree to consider *The Turn of the Screw* as a class allegory, this is clearly not the whole truth about it. For one thing, the story has little to say about the governess's relations with the master. It has a great deal to say, on the other hand, about her relations with the ghosts. And odd as this may seem, it is her relations with the ghosts that lead us to the very heart of the story's reflections on social hierarchy and its refashioning of social allegory.

In the Preface to the 1908 edition of *The Turn of the Screw* (pp. 179–86), James states his intention not to specify the evil of the ghosts, but to leave it to the imagination of the reader. "I cast my lot with pure romance," he says (p. 184). "There is not only from beginning to end of the matter not an inch of expatiation, but my values are positively all blanks" (p. 186). James clearly resists historical interpretation, which would fill in these blanks with knowledge of social groups and ideologies, and he uses the ghosts in his resistance. How can a critic talk about ideology when the major characters are not social beings, but supernatural ones? On the other hand, whether or not the ghosts are real, they are definitely and unmistakably the ghosts *of a former servant* and *a former governess.* There is some doubt about what they *are,* but there is no doubt at all about what they *were.* And if one looks at the text with class in mind, one sees that *The Turn of the Screw* is systematic, indeed almost obsessive, in its confusion of ghosts and servants. Both categories are impalpable, alien, and threatening — at least, to their masters. Both seem (to their masters) to fill the house with unexplained noises, mysteries, signs of some other, unimaginable life. When the governess describes "the faint sense I had had, the first night, of . . . something undefinably astir in the house" (p. 67), she sounds as if, instead of setting the mood for a ghost story, she were unconsciously describing a house where people live who don't count as people, people who are not supposed to be "present" in the full sense, who are there only for the convenience of the "real" inhabitants.

After all, it is intriguing how much the ghosts have in common, looked at from above, with servants who are *not* ghosts, who are very much alive. In Douglas's narrative at the opening of the story, we are

given a paraphrase of the master's account of Miss Jessel, while inter-
viewing the governess for her job: "She had done for them quite beautifully — she was a most respectable person — till her death, the great
awkwardness of which had, precisely, left no alternative but the school
for little Miles" (pp. 27–28). Think about the syntax of this sentence —
"the great awkwardness of which" — and the choice of the word "awkwardness." Not only is there no expression of sympathy or other comment on the death, as one might have expected, but the speaker does
not even consider the death important enough to bring the sentence to
a close, thereby leaving a decent interval before returning to his business. Instead, the sentence rushes immediately on to another subordinate clause. (Significantly, the death itself is in a subordinate clause;
dying doesn't even rate an independent clause of its own.) The sentence hastens on to the word "awkwardness," which of course refers
exclusively and ostentatiously to the effect of the death on the master's
arrangements, its *inconvenience* for *him*. Douglas's listeners do not miss
the casual brutality of this; they ask whether the governess's position
brought with it "[n]ecessary danger to life" (p. 28). In a sense, this is
just James's point: from the perspective of the master — though not, it
seems, from the perspective of Douglas or his listeners — a governess's
life doesn't matter. For him and his kind, Miss Jessel never *was* real. She
was already a sort of ghost.

Douglas's narrative hammers this home: "there were, further, a
cook, a housemaid, a dairywoman, an old pony, an old groom and an
old gardener, all likewise thoroughly respectable" (p. 28). The point is
made, of course, with the pony. Cooks, ponies, and gardeners are equal,
leveled out as items on a list of Bly's possessions; none of these servants
counts more than an animal. Servants, like ghosts, are something less
than human beings.

This idea must be suggested in *Douglas's* narrative, however, because
the governess herself, in spite of her own in-between class position,
shares much of the same hierarchical attitude as her master. If her master turns his subordinates into ghosts, so too in a sense does the governess. Consider the scene in which the governess gets the story of Quint
and Jessel out of Mrs. Grose, the housekeeper: " 'Come, there was
something between them,' " the governess insists. Mrs. Grose replies,

> "There was everything."
> "In spite of the difference — ?"
> "Oh of their rank, their condition" — she brought it woefully
> out. "*She* was a lady."

> I turned it over; I again saw. "Yes — she was a lady."
> "And he so dreadfully below," said Mrs. Grose.
> I felt that I doubtless need n't press too hard, in such company, on the place of a servant in the scale; but there was nothing to prevent an acceptance of my companion's own measure of my predecessor's abasement. (p. 58)

The governess cannot agree openly with Mrs. Grose that Quint was "so dreadfully below" Miss Jessel without seeming to imply, impolitely, that Mrs. Grose is "dreadfully below" herself. When the social station of the person you are addressing is at stake, there are severe limits on what can be said. But everything the governess says about the ghosts is subject to such limits. And so is everything she hears. For if there are things that the governess cannot say to Mrs. Grose because of the class difference between them, the story invites us to see that there are also things Mrs. Grose will not be able to say to the governess, and for the same reason. Mrs. Grose's supposed belief in the reality of the ghosts (though she never actually sees them) is the only support the governess has when she fears that she herself may be "cruel" or "mad" (p. 101). But could an inferior like Mrs. Grose ever tell her superior, "in supreme authority" at Bly (p. 27), that she *was* cruel or mad? Aren't the housekeeper's "plunges of submission" (p. 99) to the governess's view of things exactly that, moments of "submission" to the governess's authority?

Power and hierarchy interrupt what can be said, forcing communication into "obscure and roundabout allusions" (p. 31). They even determine what can be *seen*. Arriving at the great house of Bly from a poor country parsonage, the governess notes that she has never before had the luxury of seeing her entire body, for she has never had access to such large mirrors: "the long glasses in which, for the first time, I could see myself from head to foot" (p. 30). Even self-knowledge seems to depend, for James, on one's place and power in the social hierarchy. The hierarchical microcosm that James displays in *The Turn of the Screw* is therefore full of socially produced gaps, lapses, ambiguities. And it is in these spaces of necessary obscurity that the ghosts emerge and operate. To the extent that the story is about the ghosts, it is not merely (as everyone knows) about ambiguity; it is also about the *social production* of ambiguity.

Another reason for turning our attention to the ghosts after considering the governess's love for the master is that the forbidden love between Peter Quint and Miss Jessel (the fact that we are told his first name but not hers is another reminder of their class difference) is a sort of inverted parallel to it. The former governess, like the present governess, has allowed her erotic desires to stray across class lines; the only difference is that the object of Miss Jessel's feelings is someone below her on the social scale (Quint) rather than someone above her (the master in Harley Street). One might imagine, therefore, that the governess would recognize in the story of those tragic lovers something of her own longings. Of course she does not. On the contrary, their class transgression immediately brands them in her eyes as *evil* spirits rather than *good* spirits, which Henry James showed some interest in. (In James's notebook entry of January 22, 1888, for example, the ghost desires to "interpose, redeem, protect" [*Notebooks* 9].) Indeed, it seems at times as if the fact that Quint and Jessel appear to her as ghosts is less important and even less horrifying to the governess than the social violation they committed while they were alive.

Consider for example the conversation with Mrs. Grose in which the governess describes her first sighting of Quint. The man she saw on the tower was not a gentleman, the governess says. Mrs. Grose responds in an incomplete sentence: "But if he is n't a gentleman — " As so often, the governess fills in the blank herself: "What *is* he? He's a horror" (p. 47). In order to be a horror, it appears, there is no need of supernatural props or special effects, no need to be a ghost at all. It is enough to occupy a gentleman's place, or to wear his clothes, without being a gentleman. Here the governess as much as admits that in her mind, supernatural evil cannot be readily distinguished from the "unnaturalness" of servants stepping out of their designated place.

The story's willingness to consider the ghosts less as supernatural phenomena than as social phenomena, and more particularly as a servant and a governess who refuse to be bound by their station, can also be deduced from the circumstances in which the ghosts are made to appear. Each makes a carefully staged entry "below" the governess on the staircase. In a society which routinely referred to class difference in terms of "upstairs" (the domain of the masters) and "downstairs" (the domain of the servants), these staircase scenes are heavily charged with the symbolism of hierarchy: "I knew that there was a figure on the stair. . . . The apparition had reached the landing halfway up and was therefore on the spot nearest the window, where, at sight of me, it stopped short and fixed me exactly as it had fixed me from the tower and from the garden." Then "I saw the figure disappear; . . . I definitely saw it turn, as I might have seen the low wretch to which it had once belonged turn on receipt of an order, and pass . . . straight down the staircase and into the darkness" (pp. 67–68). The adjective "low" makes a connection between their physical positions, higher and lower on the staircase, and their moral or class positions. Quint has been trying to rise, but the governess sends him back down where he belongs. It seems clear that, in class terms, this is a tiny allegory of frustrated upward mobility. And as we shall see, there is some reason to ask whether it might not be a moral allegory as well.

The next sighting is also on the staircase:

> Looking down it from the top I once recognised the presence of a woman seated on one of the lower steps with her back presented to me, her body half-bowed and her head, in an attitude of woe, in her hands. I had been there but an instant, however, when she vanished without looking round at me. . . . I wondered whether, if instead of being above I had been below, I should have had the same nerve for going up that I had lately shown Quint. (p. 70)

Here the ghost is not rising. Sitting on "one of the lower steps" and with a body "half-bowed," she suggests on the contrary someone who has descended. All of this would correspond to how the governess sees her predecessor's social transgression: Miss Jessel has "lowered" herself by falling in love with a servant. Even more interesting, though, is the final speculation: the governess's willingness to imagine *herself,* like Miss Jessel, "below" rather than "above" and seeking the "nerve for going up."

The comparison of herself to Miss Jessel is fragmentary but telling. And it becomes stronger and more visible in the scene where the governess decides not to run away from Bly. Having "made up my mind to cynical flight," she says,

> I remember sinking down at the foot of the staircase — suddenly collapsing there on the lowest step and then, with a revulsion, recalling that it was exactly where, more than a month before, in the darkness of night and just so bowed with evil things, I had seen the spectre of the most horrible of women. At this I was able to straighten myself; I went the rest of the way up; I made, in my turmoil, for the schoolroom, where there were objects belonging to me that I should have to take. (pp. 87–88)

There she finds herself again in "the presence" of Miss Jessel's ghost:

> Seated at my own table in the clear noonday light I saw a person whom, without my previous experience, I should have taken at the

first blush for some housemaid who might have stayed at home to
look after the place and who, availing herself of rare relief from
observation and of the schoolroom table and my pens, ink, and
paper, had applied herself to the considerable effort of a letter to
her sweetheart. (p. 88)

If the governess at first places herself in the exact spot where she has
seen Miss Jessel, she then sees Miss Jessel sitting at her own official
spot, "at my own table." Some force — perhaps her unconscious, perhaps only James's text — is evidently pushing her to ask what points of
similarity there might be between her and the ghost. As if offering a
slightly displaced answer to this question, the governess then imagines a
servant who is borrowing her writing materials. The governess's eagerness to insist on how different she herself is from such a servant, to
insist on her own superiority, is odd, given that this servant is a figment
of her imagination. (Thanks to her "previous experience," she implies,
she has instantly recognized that this is *not* a servant, but Miss Jessel.)
But her sense of superiority is nonetheless manifest: the phrase "considerable effort" reminds us that writing letters may be difficult for maids,
but it is easy for governesses. This is the same mockery of the uneducated servants that we can hear in the phrase "perturbation of scullions"
(p. 51), a phrase that "scullions" — that is, those lowest of kitchen servants who wash the dishes — could not be expected to pronounce with
assurance. But if the governess is making such a considerable effort to
distance herself, it is clearly because she is finding it difficult not to *recognize* herself in Miss Jessel and her situation. Why does she imagine a
"sweetheart" as the recipient of the letter? Much of the story has come
to focus on the question of whether she herself can now communicate
with the master: a man she has been forbidden to write to and is forbidden to think of as a possible sweetheart, just as the maid is forbidden to
have a sweetheart.

After this unconscious alignment with her made-up maid, the governess experiences an extraordinary moment of self-questioning, a
moment of moral leveling. Her assumption of moral superiority to Miss
Jessel, her "vile predecessor," this "most horrible of women," suddenly
slips: "she had looked at me long enough to appear to say that her right
to sit at my table was as good as mine to sit at hers. While these instants
lasted indeed I had the extraordinary chill of a feeling that it was I who
was the intruder" (p. 88). This identification of her interests with
the lovelorn, tragic Miss Jessel becomes still more intense in the last
scene of confrontation between them. At the lake, the governess no-

tices Miss Jessel's ghost not with horror but with a "thrill of joy": "she was there, so I was justified; she was there, so I was neither cruel nor mad." Thus she sends the other governess "an inarticulate message of gratitude" (p. 101)

II

Further than this gratitude the governess does not seem to go. Yet there is reason to think that Henry James has pushed his story further — that *The Turn of the Screw* questions the society it describes more searchingly than its protagonist does. The evidence in favor of this claim comes not from the governess but from the children. Miles has been accused, remember, of excessive intimacy with a "base menial." In his final, fatal confrontation with the governess, when the subject of his expulsion from school is at last brought up, it is this theme of intimacy with servants that James dramatically returns to: "We continued silent while the maid was with us — as silent, it whimsically occurred to me, as some young couple who, on their wedding-journey, at the inn, feel shy in the presence of the waiter. He turned round only when the waiter had left us. 'Well — so we're alone!'" (p. 113).

This is the end of the eleventh weekly installment in the original *Collier's Weekly* serialization of the story. The next and last installment begins by opening up the ironies of Miles's statement: the various senses in which they are not, after all, "alone." In my interpretation, the brief conversation that follows is the very heart of the story:

> "Oh more or less." I imagine my smile was pale. "Not absolutely. We should n't like that!" I went on.
> "No — I suppose we should n't. Of course we've the others."
> "We've the others — we've indeed the others," I concurred.
> "Yet even though we have them," he returned, still with his hands in his pockets and planted there in front of me, "they don't much count, do they?"
> I made the best of it, but I felt wan. "It depends on what you call 'much'!" (p. 113).

On one level, of course, Miles and the governess are simply trying to fill up an uncomfortable silence, and that purpose can be served by words that are not especially meaningful. But the subject of "the others" is in fact quite meaningful for them. Who are these "others"? If Miles is not admitting here to the existence of the ghosts, as seems unlikely in light of what follows, then he can only be talking about the servants. And when he says that they "don't much count, do they?" he is not giving his *own* opinion; rather, he is provocatively questioning the *governess's* opinion. We have seen multiple proofs that to her, indeed, the servants "don't much count." And we have also seen evidence that to him they *do* count to a rather extraordinary if also understandable degree. An orphan whose guardian is absent and indifferent, Miles has spent months "perpetually together" (p. 61) with a servant, and he has lived through that servant's death — an event, along with Miss Jessel's death, that might well explain a great deal of mysterious behavior on the part of the children. He has been reprimanded for this unbecoming friendship by Mrs. Grose — "*she* liked to see young gentlemen not forget their station" (p. 62) — and he has snapped back at her with a response that the governess takes as a sign of his corruption. Miles's answer, we are told, is "bad": bad because it rudely reminds Mrs. Grose that she too is a "base menial," no doubt, but also bad, we may surmise, in a larger or more ideological sense: as an expression of Miles's rejection of class hierarchy. This is after all just what we might expect him to be learning in those instructive months when, "quite as if Quint were his tutor" (p. 62), he was "perpetually together" with a servant who was engaged in a forbidden relation with a woman above him in rank. Perhaps — this we cannot know for sure — it is even the message contained in those things he said at school that caused him to be thrown out, things we recall he said only to those he liked. In Victorian England, to assert that "the others" do "count" might well have been enough to earn expulsion from a respectable school.

Aside from Peter Quint and Mrs. Grose, the only one of the other servants who is named in *The Turn of the Screw* is "Luke," the servant who was supposed to mail the governess's letter to the master. It seems significant that Miles's last request (p. 116) is to speak to him. Even if it is only to protect the secret of who took the letter — and we don't know that this is in fact his motive — it is clear that Luke does "count" for Miles. In short, Miles is well placed to wonder how it happens that Luke and the other servants "don't much count" for the governess, or for the society she uncomfortably represents. Miles has refused to play along with the willful blindness of his class that consigns the servants to willed, organized invisibility — that makes them all ghostly. He is not "corrupted" by the ghosts, in other words, but is still more charming and extraordinary than he at first seems to be.

One virtue of this interpretation is that it preserves and indeed deepens the charming innocence of the children. Interpretations that judge the ghosts and the children to be joined with each other in the pursuit of evil are obliged to conclude that the children are secretly corrupted, an idea that many readers will find hard to take. The alternative I propose is to take them as innocent in a real if also a challenging sense. Thanks to their bizarre isolation, raised by servants alone, without interference from the upper classes, the children have become little democrats, unable to see the sin in transgressing those class divisions that the adult world takes for granted. What they do see, therefore, as the governess cannot, is the absurdity of believing that "the others" don't "count."

III

If this reading has its virtues, it also has at least one major problem: it makes Miles's death into a tragedy that is even worse, if possible, than one might otherwise feel. The governess does precisely what she accuses the servant-ghosts of wanting to do. We have no evidence of her assertion that the ghosts want to "possess" the children. We have a great deal of evidence, on the other hand, of her own desire to possess them. She who, *as* an upper servant, possesses almost nothing else but her responsibility to the children — little time of her own, no love, and hardly any life — comes back to "the chance of possessing" the children (p. 95) with fierce repetitiveness: " 'They're not mine — they're not ours. They're his and they're hers!' " (p. 76). The ending is of course the most painful: " 'What does he matter now, my own? -- what will he *ever* matter? I have you,' I launched at the beast, 'but he has lost you for ever!' " Her desire for possession is fulfilled in Miles's death: "his little heart, dispossessed, had stopped" (p. 120). And what is sacrificed by the governess's misplaced protective zeal, in this view, is not the boy's life alone, but also the extraordinary beauty of the alternative social vision he embodied — a vision of social equality to which she is utterly blind.

Or is she? There is no question that *The Turn of the Screw* ends in a moment of loss and desolation. Whether we imagine that the governess has frightened Miles to death or embraced him to the point of suffocation, the scaring and the caring leave us with a bitter image of democratic innocence slain, ironically, not by the absolute might of the governing class but by the relative weakness of its indoctrinated underlings, the "governessing" class. Yet this view of the ending does not neatly resolve all the meanings the story has so energetically unleashed. Some of them spill over, and for a criticism which insists that history is unfinished, these excess meanings may well be crucial. A few pages before the end, the governess notices something new in the servants. Or rather, she makes an unprecedented connection between the servants and her own concerns: "[F]or the first time, I could see in the aspect of others a confused reflexion of the crisis" (p. 110). Significantly, the servants take on or take over, as she sees them now, just that word that James was to use in the Preface for his own "values" in writing the ghost story, and for the ghosts themselves: "The maids and the men looked blank" (p. 110). Blankness, which had seemed to mark an avoidance of history, both on the part of James and on the part of the governess, now appears as the mark of historical "crisis," a sign rich in suppressed or at any rate unexpressed inner feelings. This is the "perturbation of scullions" that the governess could not see before. She can see more of it now. She has perhaps made some progress.

The governess may not learn all of her lesson, but James puts it there to be learned, if only by the discerning reader. In the New York Preface, as I said, James in effect calls *The Turn of the Screw* a romance, a genre in which the malignity of the ghosts can remain blank, motiveless, unspecified. But if this choice of genre protects some secrets, it gives away others. In particular, it hints at the secret identity of the "others," the villains or enemies — that is, their identity with the protagonist. In *The Political Unconscious* Fredric Jameson describes romance as a

> symbolic answer to the perplexing question of how my enemy can be thought of as being *evil* (that is, as other than myself and marked by some absolute difference), when what is responsible for his being so characterized is simply the *identity* of his own conduct with mine, the which — challenges, points of honor, tests of strength — he reflects as in a mirror image. Romance "solves" this conceptual dilemma by producing a new narrative. . . . The hostile knight, in armor, exudes that insolence which marks a fundamental refusal of recognition and stamps him as the bearer of the category of evil, up to the moment in which, defeated and unmasked, he asks for mercy and *tells his name* . . . at which point . . . he becomes one knight among others and loses all his sinister unfamiliarity. (Jameson 118–19; emphases in original)

There is of course no moment in *The Turn of the Screw* when "the antagonist *ceases to* be a villain" (119), as Jameson says, when the mask of otherness is lifted and evil evaporates from the world. But to judge from the critical controversy surrounding this text, much of it might be said to build toward just such a missing scene. The sightings of the ghosts, along with scenes I have not discussed, all suggest that in some sense the ghosts are mirror images, duplications, reenactments of the governess and her situation. These connections between governess and ghosts have been assembled as evidence, mainly by the antighost party, in order to undermine the governess's narrative credibility. Yet in the light of Jameson's description of romance, these parallels could also be interpreted in another way. They could be seen as continual, unanswered beckonings to a recognition that, like the unmasking of the "villain" in medieval romance, would convert these threatening aliens into mere versions of herself.

Here we must remember that, for the governess, the collapse of class otherness is erotically charged with pleasure as well as negatively charged with threat. What the governess herself desires is, as we set out by saying, nothing but the erotic transgression of class. Her love for the master, which is reaffirmed in the narrative frame at the start of the story, requires that at some future point she herself will repeat the ghosts' transgression and indulge a love prohibited by the social hierarchy. Of course, the text does not actually follow her romance script. But its unrealized happy end — victory over the ghosts and union with the master — is present in a sense from the outset.

Recall how far the text goes not only to show that evil is defined in class terms but also to remind us that the governess herself is, after all, nothing but an upper servant. The crowning example, perhaps, is her cross-examination of Mrs. Grose concerning Miles and his intimacy with Quint. Again she puts words in Mrs. Grose's mouth:

> "If Quint — on your remonstrance at the time you speak of — was a base menial, one of the things Miles said to you, I find myself guessing, was that you were another." Again her admission was so adequate that I continued: "And you forgave him that?"
> "Wouldn't *you?*"
> "Oh yes!" And we exchanged there, in the stillness, a sound of the oddest amusement. (p. 63)

What is both odd and amusing here is the double meaning. Mrs. Grose's "Would n't *you?*" could of course be taken as meaning simply, "Wouldn't you forgive him if he said something equally outrageous to you, knowing what a wonderful child he is?" But it can also be taken to mean, "Wouldn't you forgive him for saying that *you* are a base menial — since you are just as much a menial as I am?" Mrs. Grose's "Would n't *you?*" suggests to the governess, in a style approaching that of stage comedy, what so many critics of *The Turn of the Screw* have suggested in a more scholarly mode: her resemblance to the servant-ghosts. From this resemblance we can deduce the fragility of an "evil" that depends for its existence on nothing more than the illusion of otherness. In this sense it can be maintained that *The Turn of the Screw* projects an unrealized "happy ending": the return of Bly to the classless Edenic state in which the governess first found it, the ghostlike evaporation from her world of the "evil" that she added to it. These happy events would result from her recognition of what so many voices are trying to tell her: her identity with "the others."

And what of critics, who like the governess are teachers of the young? The Marxist critic who constructs this implicit sequel to the story is not simply trying (like the governess) to soften the cruel knowledge of social reality. Rather, the critic is trying to learn from the governess's pupils how to change social reality, trying to edge history in the direction that James's children have pointed out to us. The point of this piece of criticism is to help ensure that children in the future will know that the others *do* count.

WORKS CITED

James, Henry. *The Notebooks of Henry James.* Ed. F. O. Matthiessen and Kenneth B. Murdock. New York: Oxford UP, 1947.

Jameson, Fredric. *The Political Unconscious.* Ithaca: Cornell UP, 1947.

Marx, Karl. "Theses on Feuerbach" in Karl Marx and Friedrich Engels, *The German Ideology.* Ed. R. Pascal. New York: International, 1947.

Combining Perspectives
on *The Turn of the Screw*

So far, the emphasis in this volume has been on mapping the boundaries of particular contemporary approaches and traditions. In presenting this final essay by Sheila Teahan, the emphasis is reversed, for the intention is to demonstrate the permeability of such approaches, traditions, and boundaries. The goal is to suggest how supposedly disparate assumptions can be held simultaneously — and how supposedly diverse rhetorical traditions can mix, merge, and metamorphose. To put it more plainly, Teahan's essay allows us to see how a critic can draw on the insights of several critical traditions — in effect, combining perspectives — to present a view of a work unavailable from any one window, any single critical perspective.

Toward the beginning of the essay that follows, Teahan sounds like a reader-response critic (though one whose approach differs decisively from Wayne Booth's reader-response approach to *The Turn of the Screw* printed earlier in this volume). Turning her attention to the frame narrator, who at once "models our own reading" and yet seems, himself, an unreliable reader and narrator, she suggests that "James's story dramatizes the problem of reading" and even develops "a thematics of reading" (p. 350 in this volume).

But as she shifts her focus from the readerly frame narrator to the governess, a more "inside" narrator, Teahan also avails herself of the psychoanalytic approach to literature. She uses Jacques Lacan's concept of the "mirror stage" to analyze a rare "moment of psychic wholeness" experienced by a woman whose "identity" is largely "divided." She also treats, implicitly, the full-length mirror at Bly as what Freudians would call an "overdetermined" image, serving simultaneously as a symbolic or "allegorical" marker suggesting the governess's psychic state and as a realistic detail, "a marker of verisimilitude" reminding us that the governess's poor parson father "could not have afforded such a luxury" (p. 351).

Teahan proceeds by considering the social and class history of governesses in nineteenth-century England. In analyzing the "ambiguous class status" of governesses and the strong "prejudice" against them, she effectively makes use of the cultural documents found in this edition. She also quotes from scholarly commentaries by Nancy Armstrong and Mary Poovey, whose writings exemplify an approach commonly referred to as cultural criticism, insofar as they place literary texts in their social and economic contexts. She even incorporates a labor-oriented, class-based, Marxist analysis of the "artificial" and "anomalous" position of the governess by building on the writings of Anna Jameson. In the 1840s, Jameson had argued that, during an era in which a woman's only proper sphere was the home, "the occupation of governess [was] sought merely through necessity" — by women "not born in the servile classes" but who either had "no home" or, for whatever reason, felt "exiled" from it (pp. 353–54).

By seeing James's text in light of Marxist and cultural criticism, and through her implied awareness that historical criticism must, in Stephen Greenblatt's words, be "conscious of its status as interpretation," Teahan takes positions not unlike those associated with the so-called new historicism. Like cultural criticism — and unlike Marxist, psychoanalytic, and reader-response criticism — the new historicism is an approach to literature that is not represented by the previous essays in this volume but that is defined at some length in the Glossary of Critical and Theoretical Terms at the back of this book (pp. 376–77).

The distrust of governesses documented in various historical materials was often grounded in sexual suspicions, as both Armstrong and Poovey have pointed out. Teahan's eventual consideration of the governess's sexual nature leads her back to a psychoanalytic approach to the woman's (mis)reading of various situations. These involve her tendency to project onto "ambiguous evidence" insupportable conclusions, particularly ones involving the "displacement of her own distressing sexual feelings" (p. 355). But in reading a series of scenes in which ambiguous evidence leads to conclusions on the governess's part that may be fictitious, Teahan also borrows the tenets and tendencies of narratology and deconstruction, two text-based approaches to literature that, like cultural criticism and the new historicism, are described in the Glossary.

Particularly with regard to deconstruction, Teahan uses a close reading of James's text to note Miles's status as a text to be read, Quint's as a text to be written: "I saw him as I see the letters I form on this page" (p. 41). Even more deconstructively, she expands on a suggestion made by Shoshana Felman by seeing that Miles's death "literalizes a series of metaphors of grasping, seizing, embracing, gripping, taking hold, and the like — locutions that play on the etymological meaning of 'comprehend.' " Teahan then shows that the Latin root for the word "comprehend" implies that "to comprehend is metaphorically to seize hold" of it (p. 358). Furthermore, having stated that the governess "reads [Miles] to death" (p. 359), Teahan goes on to argue that "James has constructed his story so as to make possible multiple readings that appear incompatible but are equally supported by textual evidence" (p. 359).

Combining as she does Lacanian psychoanalytic theory with cultural criticism, deconstruction, Marxist criticism, narratology, the new historicism, and an analysis oriented toward readers and narrators, Teahan mixes approaches in a way that is typical of much contemporary scholarship. In doing so, she creates a critical whole that is greater than the sum of its parts.

Ross C Murfin

COMBINING PERSPECTIVES

SHEILA TEAHAN

"I caught him, yes, I held him": The Ghostly Effects of Reading (in) *The Turn of the Screw*

One of the most striking features of *The Turn of the Screw* is the sheer volume of scholarly commentary it has generated. In the last four decades, more than three hundred books, articles, and doctoral dissertations have been devoted to *The Turn of the Screw*. Even by the standards of the prolific Henry James scholarly industry, this is an astounding amount of critical debate, and it shows no signs of waning. Clearly, we don't stand a ghost of a chance of getting this text out of our system anytime soon. It is worth asking why James's story has inspired so much, and such sharply divided, critical commentary.

In this essay I will suggest that James's story dramatizes the problem of reading as such, in ways that readers have found so provocative that they have felt compelled to put their responses into words, and often into print. The story dramatizes the theme of reading at several levels: in its open-ended frame narrative, in the notorious question of the governess's reliability, and in James's rereading of the tale in his retrospective preface. *The Turn of the Screw*'s thematics of reading — its sustained dramatization of acts of reading that raises questions about what it means to read — mirrors our own confrontation with this elusive story. James's representation of the governess suggests that she consciously or unconsciously manipulates evidence in support of her thesis that Miles and Flora have been corrupted by the ghosts. The climax of the story coincides with the governess's fatal "reading" of Miles: unable to tolerate the ambiguity of his failure to conform to her polarized stereotypes of the sexually innocent "angel" and corrupt "fiend" (pp. 43, 63 in this volume), she fixes his meaning by strangling him in a deadly literalization of the recurring metaphors of "seizing" and "grasping" that track her struggle to understand the mysterious events at Bly.

I

The frame narrative that introduces *The Turn of the Screw* is a source of ambiguity as well as important background information. As Paul G. Beidler has observed, "Douglas's 'prologue' has the odd effect of making it unclear to the reader exactly where the story starts; the first sentences of the governess's narrative seem to imply that others once came before them. . . . The word 'beginning' [in the first sentence of the governess's narrative] emphasizes not the beginning itself but the fact that the beginning is absent and must remain so" (51, 52–53). The governess's narrative is thrice mediated: by Douglas's comments to his circle of listeners, by the narrator's transcription of the governess's narrative, and by the narrator's introductory remarks. Each of these mediations is itself a preemptive "reading" of the governess's narrative. Because the frame narrator both introduces and inherits her story from Douglas, he is an unmistakable figure for the reader. But if the frame narrator models our own reading, we should take pause. Douglas appears, although on the basis of no evidence, to single him out as an ideal reader, indeed as the most intuitive and perceptive listener present: " 'You'll easily judge,' he repeated: '*you* will' " (p. 24). But we should be suspicious of the frame narrator's complacency about his ability to supply a title for a narrative he has not yet heard. When asked by one of the auditors, "What's your title?" Douglas responds, "I have n't one," and the narrator breaks in, "Oh *I* have!" (p. 29). Is this title *The Turn of the Screw*? If not, has the title been supplied by what Wayne Booth would call the implied author, or perhaps by the governess? There is no way to know, and this ambiguity is frustrating, since the title is an important part of the text. Both Douglas ("If the child gives the effect another turn of the screw, what do you say to *two* chil-dren — ?" [p. 23]) and the governess ("I could only get on at all by . . . demanding after all, for a fair front, only another turn of the screw of ordinary human virtue" [p. 111]) play on the metaphor of turning a screw. Is that metaphor potentially sexual in its implications? Is James suggesting that the governess "has a screw loose"? All of these ques-tions must be kept in mind as we pass from the frame narrative to the governess's narrative, even if (or perhaps because) they are impossible to answer.

In the second paragraph of her narrative, the governess mentions that her bedroom at Bly contains a full-length mirror, "the long glasses in which, for the first time, I could see myself from head to foot" (p. 30). The detail of the mirror indicates the relative poverty of the governess's father, and so contributes to the text's verisimilitude: a poor parson could not have afforded such a luxury. But the mirror also lends itself to a psychoanalytic reading. We should heed Douglas's promise that the "story *won't* tell, . . . not in any literal vulgar way" (p. 25). His prediction both comments on the text's representational procedures and warns the reader that it may "tell" in ways that are counterintuitive. In particular, the governess's vision of herself "from head to foot" is evocative of Lacan's theory of the mirror stage. In the mirror stage, infants first recognize that they are autonomous beings, separate both from their mother and from others. This recognition occurs when they are able to identify a literal or figurative reflection of themselves, for example in a mirror or in another infant. (Lacan specifies that the mir-ror is merely a metaphor for this process; an actual mirror need not be involved.) Because the reflection is external and discontinuous with us, we experience it as alienated, literally and figuratively Other. This fun-damental (mis)recognition is repeated throughout life: in the words of

Ellie Ragland-Sullivan, although the mirror stage "signals the beginning of a sense of identity, this unity has been found *outside* and, accordingly, the destiny of humans is to (re-)experience ourselves only in relationship to others" (27). The governess thus repeats the infant's illusory experience of autonomy and wholeness — an illusion that covers over the fundamentally divided nature of subjectivity. Before Miles confesses to having intercepted her letter, she refers to the "fierce split of my attention" (p. 116), and she spends the entire narrative trying to repair this split.

Throughout this essay, I assume that a narrative or narrative sequence can be both realistic and allegorical. "Allegory" etymologically means an other-speaking; to suggest that a text is allegorical is to suggest that it can say something other than what it appears or means to say. Here, the mirror can be read realistically as a marker of verisimilitude, or allegorically as a marker of the governess's divided identity. To be sure, Henry James had not read Lacan; but one need not have recourse to Lacanian theory to think about the mirror as a metaphor for identity. Recall Snow White: "mirror, mirror, on the wall, who's the fairest of them all?" When a mirror appears in a literary work, questions of identity are at stake. (After hearing the mysterious sobs and moans in the night, Mrs. G. "looked in the glass to see if my hair had turned white from the awful night I had spent," as if seeking reassurance that she is still the same person she was the night before [see p. 158 in Cultural Documents and Illustrations]).

The governess spends the rest of her narrative trying to recapture this fleeting and phantasmal moment of psychic wholeness. It is ironic that she experiences an illusion of autonomy at this particular point, for when she arrives at Bly she steps into a complex weave of expectations and assumptions about the gender and class status of governesses. On this view, the governess sees in the glass an alienated gender- and class-inflected identity that has been constructed for her. Indeed, because of his interest in the ways in which subjectivity is discursively constructed, Lacan's work has been important to a number of feminist and other politically oriented literary critics.

II

The constructedness of the identity of governesses in nineteenth-century England is the concern of a number of the cultural documents in this edition. As those documents reflect, the class position of the governess was "artificial" and "anomalous," in the words of Anna Jameson (p. 129). Maria Edgeworth and Mary Maurice both express anxiety about the governess's ambiguous class status and her potentially delete-rious influence on children. Edgeworth expresses the common ambiva-lence toward governesses on the part of their employers: she concedes that those "who desire to treat the person who educates their children as their equal, act with perfect propriety" (p. 126), presumably because the governess would be improved by contact with her social superiors. But Edgeworth warns that if parents spend too much time in the gov-erness's company, the children will be exposed to the undesirable in-fluence of servants: "if they make her their companion in all their amusements they go a step too far, and they defeat their own purposes" (p. 126). Note that when James's governess learns from Mrs. Grose that "for a period of several months Quint and the boy had been per-petually together" (p. 61), she believes that she has discovered a key to the improper behavior that has resulted in Miles's expulsion from his school. Maurice's comments on the "strong prejudice against gov-ernesses" (p. 134) reflect an anxiety that a governess might engage in sexual intrigue either with children or with the master — issues that clearly resonate with James's story.

The inclusion of cultural documents in this edition suggests that novels about governesses, such as Thackeray's *Vanity Fair* (1847), Brontë's *Jane Eyre* (1847), and James's *The Turn of the Screw*, both reflected and shaped contemporary discourse about the social status of the governess. Much current scholarship on the nineteenth-century novel investigates the ways in which both literary and so-called nonlit-erary texts contribute to the construction of such conceptual categories as class, gender, sexuality, and race. Both Nancy Armstrong and Mary Poovey, for example, analyze what Jameson terms the "artificial" and "anomalous" status of governesses. For Armstrong and Poovey, the governess is a disruptive figure who challenges some major tenets of nineteenth-century gender and class ideology. She "was commonly rep-resented as a threat to the well-being of the household" because, since she performed for money many of the duties of the mother, she blurred what was thought to be a stable distinction between domestic duty and labor for money (Armstrong 78–79). According to the ideology of the separate spheres, men occupied the public sphere of labor and money, whereas women belonged in the domestic sphere of the home: Jameson observes that "with the woman, 'whose proper sphere is home,' — the woman who either has no home, or is exiled from that which she has, — the occupation of governess is sought merely through necessity, as the *only* means by which a woman not born in the servile classes *can* earn the means of subsistence" (p. 130). Because the public and domestic spheres were gendered, the governess thus destabilized a distinction "on which the very notion of gender appeared to depend" (Armstrong 79). Indeed, the distinction between domestic duty and labor performed for money was so deeply ingrained that "the figure of the prostitute could be freely invoked to describe any woman who dared to labor for money" (Armstrong 79). Armstrong's claim is not that governesses were prostitutes, but that in the mind of the public, a working woman was only steps away from the status of the prostitute. (Frederic W. H. Myers seems to register this association in his reference to the "partially-materialized ghost of a harlot-governess" [p. 175]).

James's highly literate governess would have been aware of the ambivalence toward governesses as reflected in the work of writers like Edgeworth, Jameson, and Maurice. She would have been conscious of the concern expressed by Maurice that "she, to whom the care of the young has been entrusted, instead of guarding their minds in innocence and purity, has become their corrupter — she has been the first to lead and to initiate into sin, to suggest and carry on intrigues, and finally to be the instrument of destroying the peace of families" (pp. 134–35). It is this corruption from which the governess wishes to protect the children, and of which she suspects the ghosts of Jessel and Quint. The tainted aura surrounding Jessel reflects the new governess's awareness of the sexually suspect status of governesses in general. In perceiving her predecessor as sexually corrupt, the governess both recognizes her own ambiguous status as a paid laborer who is expected to reproduce the "domestic ideal" by inculcating virtue in the children she teaches (Poovey 128) and displaces onto Jessel her anxiety about the precarious discursive slippage between the working woman and the prostitute.

The mirror passage discussed above is crucially related to Quint's appearances, which give "material" form to the governess's anxieties about her social status. Before Quint first appears, she is thinking about the absent uncle and reflecting that he would approve of her work with the children, were he to observe her: "by my discretion, my quiet good sense and general high propriety, I was giving pleasure — if he ever thought of it! — to the person to whose pressure I had yielded" (p. 38). There is a distinct sexual overtone to this "yielding," and we know that the governess is attracted to the uncle; she confides to Mrs. Grose that "I was carried away in London!" (p. 31) — another erotically charged turn of phrase. When her thoughts turn to the uncle, she imagines that "it would be as charming as a charming story suddenly to meet some one. Some one would appear there at the turn of a path and would stand before me and smile and approve" (p. 39). In a moment of wish fulfillment, the governess's desire "had, in a flash, turned real. He did stand there!" (p. 39). Not until the next paragraph does she reveal that "the man who met my eyes was not the person I had precipitately supposed" (p. 39). The man who appears is not the uncle, but another sexualized man who is differentiated from him, in the governess's mind, by his inferior class and sinister appearance. The governess thus disavows her attraction toward the uncle by conjuring a figure who is both repulsive and beneath her in class terms. In an echo of the mirror image, Quint appears to her "as definite as a picture in a frame" (p. 40). The connection to the mirror is reinforced in Quint's second appearance, when the governess sees him looking in through the window. James underlines the connection by referring to the window as a "glass" (p. 44), which means both mirror and window; so too, when Quint appears for the third time, "with a glimmer in the high glass and another on the polish of the oak stair below, we faced each other in our common intensity" (p. 67). The governess's arresting comment that "it was as if I had been looking at him for years and had known him always" (p. 44) suggests that Quint's dangerous sexuality may be a displacement of her own distressing sexual feelings, which appear in an externalized and uncanny form. Her identification with Quint is reinforced when she takes his place at the window in an attempt to "govern," through repetition, his uncanny appearance. Through this disavowal of her desire for the uncle, she preserves the illusory sexlessness of the ideal governess, who was expected to "police the emergence of undue assertiveness or sexuality in her maturing charges" and "expected not to display willfulness or desires herself" (Poovey 128).

III

The governess's construction of the sexually charged image of Quint is only one episode of her troubled career as a reader. In her reaction to the letter from Miles's school, she reads into ambiguous evidence conclusions that it may not support. Although the school authorities "go into no particulars" of the reason for his dismissal, she dogmatically insists that the letter's lack of particularity "can have but one meaning" (p. 34): that Miles has behaved improperly toward his classmates. He later confesses to having "said things" (p. 118), but we never learn what these were.

In the following five passages, James similarly invites us to question the governess's credibility as a reader:

1. The more I've watched and waited the more I've felt that if there were nothing else to make it sure it would be made so by the systematic silence of each. *Never,* by a slip of the tongue, have they so much as alluded to either of their old friends, any more than Miles has alluded to his expulsion. (p. 76)

The governess interprets the children's silence as signifying their refusal to acknowledge that they have been meeting with the ghosts of Quint and Jessel. On this logic, anything the children say or don't say is grist for her interpretive mill. Her suspicion, however, is in keeping with Edgeworth's warning against the "awkward and vulgar tricks which children learn in the society of servants": "the habits of cunning, falsehood, envy, which lurk in the temper, are not instantly visible to strangers, they do not appear the moment children are reviewed by parents; they may remain for years without notice or without cure" (p. 124). Edgeworth claims that the capacity for cunning learned from servants will by its nature be cunningly concealed; children who have suffered harm from exposure to servants may remain symptom-free indefinitely. In assuming that Flora and Miles have something to hide, James's governess could be heeding contemporary advice that children who have been so influenced would naturally be secretive and must be carefully watched. Again, this passage can be read either realistically or allegorically: the governess may be heeding the advice of didactic writers like Edgeworth or may be reading into the situation meaning for which there is questionable textual evidence.

2. I only sat there on my tomb and read into what our young friend had said to me the fulness of its meaning; by the time I had grasped the whole of which I had also embraced, for absence, the pretext that I was ashamed to offer my pupils and the rest of the congregation such an example of delay. What I said to myself above all was that Miles had got something out of me and that the gage of it for him would be just this awkward collapse. (p. 86)

Referring to Miles's promise that he will summon his uncle, the governess determines that he means to use her discomfort to his own advantage. The "grasping" and "embracing," and especially the detail of the tomb, foreshadow Miles's death. Mrs. Grose's previous urging that the uncle should be called back suggests that she may be worried not about the ghosts, as the governess assumes, but about the governess's own psychological stability.

3. His clear listening face, framed in its smooth whiteness, made him for the minute as appealing as some wistful patient in a children's hospital. (p. 92)

This description of Miles both echoes the appearance of Quint, "as definite as a picture in a frame" (p. 40), and likens his face to a sheet of paper, as if he were a text to be read — as, in a sense, he is, since the governess is a watchful and suspicious reader of both children. This chapter opens with her sitting before the "blank sheet of paper" (p. 91) on which she intends to write to the uncle, and the lake is later described as a "sheet of water" (p. 98), another readable text. This metaphor of reading is also applied to Quint. When he first appears, she writes, "I saw him as I see the letters I form on this page" (p. 41), a formulation that suggests she actually "writes" or constructs him.

4. I've said it already — she was literally, she was hideously hard; she had turned common and almost ugly. "I don't know what you mean. I see nobody. I see nothing. I never *have*. I think you're cruel. I don't like you!" Then, after this deliverance, which might have been that of a vulgarly pert little girl in the street, she hugged Mrs. Grose more closely and buried in her skirts the dreadful little face. (p. 103)

Flora's refusal to confirm that she has seen Jessel's ghost transforms her in the governess's eyes. Her initial "angelic beauty" (p. 30) disappears, in keeping with the fairy tale motif in which an evil person is revealed in the previously concealed ugliness that metaphorically manifests the person's true nature. The governess now perceives Flora as tainted by the sexual impurity associated with Quint and Jessel; she determines that if the children are not the innocent and asexual "angels" she initially took them to be, they must be corrupt "fiends." The revelation of Flora's vulgarity recalls Edgeworth's concern about children's exposure by servants to "vulgar tricks" (p. 124) and "high vulgarity" (p. 126). The comparison of Flora to a "pert little girl in the street" alludes to the danger, as analyzed by Poovey, that the identity of the governess as paid laborer could spill over into that of the streetwalker. I am not suggesting that the governess believes Flora might become a prostitute. But because she feels betrayed by Flora's assertion that she does not see Jessel's ghost, she perceives Flora as an embodiment of the sexual and class anxieties that preoccupy her: poor little Flora suddenly appears lower class ("vulgar") and sexualized.

5. I suppose I now read into our situation a clearness it could n't have had at the time. . . . "I'll tell you everything," Miles said — "I mean I'll tell you anything you like." (pp. 115–16)

The governess acknowledges that she is reading back retrospectively onto the evidence, finding in it only after the fact an unambiguous clearness. If she were to listen attentively, she might detect the significant slippage between "tell you everything" and "tell you anything you like," which suggests that Miles is desperate to placate her by telling her what she wants to hear. Indeed, she has discerned in him "the approach of immediate fear" (p. 115).

When the governess confronts Miles with Quint's reappearance, she "caught him, yes, I held him — it may be imagined with what a passion; but at the end of a minute I began to feel what it truly was that I held" (p. 120). Miles's "little heart, dispossessed, had stopped" because the governess's overzealous "grasp" has strangled him (p. 120). His death literalizes a series of metaphors of grasping, seizing, embracing, gripping, taking hold, and the like — locutions that play on the etymological meaning of "comprehend," which contains a dead metaphor of seizing hold. In the word's Latin etymology, to comprehend is metaphorically to seize hold. (I am indebted here to Felman's challenging and influential analysis of the problematics of mastery in the story.) The governess's reading of the events at Bly is repeatedly figured in these terms: she claims to have found "horrible proofs. Proofs, I say, yes — from the moment I really took hold" (p. 53); struggles to keep Mrs. Grose "thoroughly in the grip" of the conviction that Jessel's ghost has appeared (p. 59); gets "hold of still other things" from the children's "systematic silence" (p. 76); and when she asks Miles what happened at school, she discerns "a small faint quaver of consenting consciousness — it made me drop on my knees beside the bed and seize once more the chance of possessing him" (pp. 94–95). The text even more specifically anticipates Miles's death: the governess "then and there took him to my heart" (p. 37); acknowledges her desire to "catch [the children] up by an irresistible impulse and press them to my heart" (p. 64); and when Miles confesses to having taken her letter, "I held him to my breast, where I could feel in the sudden fever of his little body the tremendous pulse of his little heart" (p. 117). She finds "heartbreaking" her suspicion that Miles may be toying with her (p. 84), but it is her own interpretive "act of violence" (p. 115) that stops his heart. The governess stabilizes Miles's meaning by "catching" him with a vengeance: she breaks his fall, but also fixes his meaning as a readable text by detecting his alleged relation with Quint. In short, she reads him to death.

Many readers, myself included, believe that the governess is sincere in her desire to "save" the children (p. 51). How can we reconcile her good intentions with the idea that she reads Miles to death? I would suggest that James has constructed his story so as to make possible multiple readings that appear incompatible but are equally supported by textual evidence. My thesis about *The Turn of the Screw* as an allegory of reading by no means contradicts the historicist analysis of the contradictions surrounding the figure of the governess in nineteenth-century England. In fact, I showed these readings to be interconnected in my discussion of the mirror passage, above. Any conscientious reader feels compelled to find a coherent meaning in James's story, much as the governess seeks to impose a coherent meaning on Miles. But as the sheer volume and diversity of critical commentary on the text suggests, it may be impossible to do so. The story's accommodation of heterogeneous readings has consistently transfixed its readers and helps to explain why it has produced so much commentary.

IV

Readers should also be aware that James was familiar with the conventions of the ghost "sighting" narrative. Interest in psychical phenomena was an important element of James's intellectual milieu, and *The Turn of the Screw* bears the imprint of this interest. The modern reader may find it curious that Edmund Gurney appeals to the values of "reason" and "common-sense" (p. 148) in asserting their belief in the existence of ghosts. But as reflected by the history of the Society for Psychical Research, with which Henry James was familiar and in which his brother William James was centrally involved, many people of the time — including intellectuals like the Jameses — believed that psychic phenomena were a valid feature of human experience. Henry James realized that many readers would take what Booth calls the "straight" approach to his story and would understand it primarily as a ghost tale (p. 245). Indeed, James's Preface explicitly endorses this reading.

Like the narrators of many of the personal statements collected by
the Society for Psychical Research, the governess does not provide us
with her name, and James's readers would have recognized this omission as a feature of the ghost narrative. The narratives of Mrs. Vatas-
Simpson, Miss C., and Mrs. G. display more specific parallels to that of
the governess. The appearance in James's story of such motifs as a
woman with two small children, the appearance of a male and female
ghost, and the presence of servants, suggests that James may have intended to emulate the genre of the ghost narrative. Further, the ghost
narratives are highly literary in their representation of the uncanny
experiences they record. By this I mean not that they are fictional or
inauthentic, but that they are metaphorically constructed. As in *The
Turn of the Screw,* the appearance of ghosts is associated with windows,
doors, gates, and staircases. In Mrs. Vatas-Simpson's narrative, strange
noises issue from the window grating, the ghost of an old woman
appears in the doorway (p. 152) and a man's face is "clearly seen above
the balustrade" (p. 153). Windows, doors, gates and staircases are transitional and liminal (pertaining to limits, boundaries, and thresholds)
spaces suggestive of in-betweenness, of the condition of being between
one place and another place — inside and outside, up and down — or
between one state and another state of being. Figurative space is a
major resource of literature, and liminal spaces are peculiarly appropriate to narratives about ghosts, since a ghost is both present and absent,
and therefore the ultimate emblem of in-betweenness. The governess
makes explicit the text's association of Quint and Jessel with liminal and
theshhold spaces: "They're seen only across, as it were, and beyond —
in strange places and on high places, the top of towers, the roof of
houses, the outside of windows, the further edge of pools" (p. 77). At
two climactic moments, when she questions Miles about the past and
when she asks Flora where Jessel is, the governess compares her sense of
crisis to the smashing of a window (pp. 95, 101), a metaphor that suggests both a shattering of the glass in which she earlier studies her
reflection and a disorienting collapse of the distinction between inside
and outside. This distinction is germane to the theme of ghostly possession, which is an invasion of the self by an outside being.

James may or may not have borrowed the threshold imagery of *The
Turn of the Screw* from Mrs.Vatas-Simpson, but it is clear that her narrative either consciously or instinctively draws upon a long literary tradition of using metaphorical space. Far from rendering it less authentic or
credible, this feature is part of what makes her narrative compelling. So
too, L.'s request that Mrs. Vatas-Simpson give orders to the servants to

lock "the iron gate that shuts in the private portion of the house from that which is below" (pp. 152–53) can be read either realistically or allegorically. Barring entrance from the cellar seems a sensible precaution if ghosts have been seen, but the phrase "that which is below" also evokes the unconscious. The house is a common metaphor of mind — the governess laments that the "house [at Bly] is poisoned" (p. 77) — and in the words of Gaston Bachelard, the cellar "is first and foremost the *dark entity* of the house, the one that partakes of subterranean forces" (Bachelard 18). If the ghosts represent the subterranean forces of our unconscious fears and desires, this level of implication is suggestive for ghost narratives in general and *The Turn of the Screw* in particular.

Finally, no discussion of reading (in) *The Turn of the Screw* would be complete without a consideration of James's rereading of the text in his 1908 Preface. One purpose of a preface is to direct the reader's response to what follows. To the extent that it seeks to master the text it introduces, James's Preface may be complicitous in the will to interpretation dramatized and critiqued in *The Turn of the Screw* itself. For this reason, the reader should look for signs of tension between the text and the Preface. Rather than assume that the Preface is a transparent explanation of the text, we should read it "against" the text, especially because many of the prefaces James wrote for his New York Edition contain figurative language that is as dense as that of his novels themselves. The Preface to *The Turn of the Screw* is one of James's most accessible, but it contains moments that do not tell in any literal, vulgar way, to recall Douglas's warning. What, for example, are we to make of James's assertion that his tale "rejoices" in its "prompt retort to the sharpest question that may be addressed to it," and that its "perfect homogeneity" is such that it is "least apt to be baited by earnest criticism" (p. 179)? He seems to claim that *The Turn of the Screw* speaks so fully for itself that it preempts critical commentary. This statement is potentially ironic, given the enormous volume of criticism that his story has inspired. Perhaps James is enjoying a joke at his readers' expense, or perhaps he earnestly believed that he had written a "shameless potboiler" (p. 178) — that is, a work of literature written for money, to "keep the soup pot boiling" — that would be of no interest to literary critics. If so, we have here a striking illustration of the impossibility of predicting how a literary work will be received by its readers.

In another sense, James is correct to claim that his story escapes being "baited by earnest criticism": in its uncanny accommodation of multiple readings, *The Turn of the Screw* ultimately resists our critical grasp. In developing our own readings of the story, as the contributors to this volume have done, we defy this resistance by imposing a coherent critical narrative on a text that famously eludes its readers. If I have argued that James's governess kills Miles by imposing on him a unified meaning that suits her own purposes, it should be clear that I have repeated her crime. Even if one believes, as I do, that the governess misreads the events at Bly, one has no way of verifying what "really" happened. Like the letters in *The Turn of the Screw*, to which the reader is never given access, what happened at Bly remains forever concealed by the narrative that reveals it.

And if the governess is a flawed reader, it is nonetheless true that all reading is necessarily misreading — not because all readings are equally valid or invalid, which is demonstrably not the case, but because any reading is partial and incomplete, since it privileges some textual evidence while ignoring other evidence in the interest of advancing a particular theory about the text. James's story is an allegory of (mis)reading because every reader, including the present one, is condemned to repeat the governess's impossible but necessary effort to master a text that can never be mastered. It should come as no surprise that James turns out to have been way ahead of his readers from the start. Jacques Derrida has written that a "masterpiece always moves, by definition, in the manner of a ghost" (Derrida 18). If ghostliness may be understood as a metaphor for the mysterious elusiveness of a masterpiece that at once baffles and beckons us, *The Turn of the Screw* may well be our exemplary narrative about the ghostly effects of reading and writing alike.

WORKS CITED

Armstrong, Nancy. *Desire and Domestic Fiction: A Political History of the Novel*. New York and Oxford: Oxford UP, 1987.

Bachelard, Gaston. *The Poetics of Space*. Trans. Maria Jolas. Boston: Beacon, 1964.

Beidler, Paul G. *Frames in James: "The Tragic Muse," "The Turn of the Screw," "What Maisie Knew," and "The Ambassadors."* Victoria, BC: U of Victoria English Literary Studies, 1993.

Derrida, Jacques. *Specters of Marx: The State of the Debt, the Work of Mourning, and the New International*. Trans. Peggy Kamuf. New York and London: Routledge, 1994.

Felman, Shoshana. "Turning the Screw of Interpretation." *Literature and Psychoanalysis: The Question of Reading: Otherwise*. Ed.

Shoshana Felman. Baltimore and London: Johns Hopkins UP, 1982. 94–207.

Poovey, Mary. *Uneven Developments: The Ideological Work of Gender in Mid-Victorian England.* Chicago: U of Chicago P, 1988.

Ragland-Sullivan, Ellie. *Jacques Lacan and the Philosophy of Psychoanalysis.* Urbana and Chicago: U of Illinois P, 1986.

Glossary of Critical
and Theoretical Terms

ABSENCE The idea, advanced by French theorist Jacques Derrida, that authors are not present in texts and that meaning arises in the absence of any authority guaranteeing the correctness of any one interpretation.

See **Presence and Absence** for a more complete discussion of the concepts of presence and absence.

AFFECTIVE FALLACY *See* **New Criticism**; **Reader-Response Criticism**.

BASE *See* **Marxist Criticism**.

CANON A term used since the fourth century to refer to those books of the Bible that the Christian church accepts as being Holy Scripture — that is, divinely inspired. Books outside the canon (noncanonical books) are referred to as *apocryphal*. *Canon* has also been used to refer to the Saints Canon, the group of people officially recognized by the Catholic Church as saints. More recently, it has been employed to refer to the body of works generally attributed by scholars to a particular author (for example, the Shakespearean canon is currently believed to consist of thirty-seven plays that scholars feel can be definitively attributed to him). Works sometimes attributed to an author, but whose authorship is disputed or otherwise uncertain, are called apocryphal. *Canon* may also refer more generally to those literary works that are "privileged," or given special status, by a culture. Works we tend to think of as classics or as "Great Books" — texts that are repeatedly reprinted in anthologies of literature — may be said to constitute the canon.

Note: The following definitions are adapted and/or abridged versions of ones found in the second edition of *The Bedford Glossary of Critical and Literary Terms*, by Ross Murfin and Supryia M. Ray (© Bedford Books 2003).

Contemporary **Marxist** and **feminist** critics, as well as scholars of **post-colonial literature and postcolonial theory**, have argued that, for political reasons, many excellent works never enter the canon. Canonized works, they claim, are those that reflect — and respect — the culture's dominant ideology or perform some socially acceptable or even necessary form of "cultural work." Attempts have been made to broaden or redefine the canon by discovering valuable texts, or versions of texts, that were repressed or ignored for political reasons. These have been published both in traditional and in nontraditional anthologies. The most outspoken critics of the canon, especially certain critics practicing **cultural criticism**, have called into question the whole concept of canon or "canonicity." Privileging no form of artistic expression, these critics treat cartoons, comics, and soap operas with the same cogency and respect they accord novels, poems, and plays.

CULTURAL CRITICISM, CULTURAL STUDIES Critical approaches with roots in the British cultural studies movement of the 1960s. A movement that reflected and contributed to the unrest of that decade, it both fueled and was fueled by the challenges to tradition and authority apparent in everything from the antiwar movement to the emergence of "hard rock" music. Birmingham University's Centre for Contemporary Cultural Studies, founded by Stuart Hall and Richard Hoggart in 1964, quickly became the locus of the movement, which both critiqued elitist definitions of culture and drew upon a wide variety of disciplines and perspectives.

In Great Britain, the terms *cultural criticism* and *cultural studies* have been used more or less interchangeably, and, to add to the confusion, both terms have been used to refer to two different things. On one hand, they have been used to refer to the analysis of literature (including popular literature) and other art forms in their social, political, or economic contexts; on the other hand, they have been used to refer to the much broader interdisciplinary study of the interrelationships between a variety of cultural **discourses** and practices (such as advertising, gift giving, and racial categorization). In North America, the term *cultural studies* is usually reserved for this broader type of analysis, whereas *cultural criticism* typically refers to work with a predominantly literary or artistic focus.

Cultural critics examine how literature emerges from, influences, and competes with other forms of discourse (such as religion, science, or advertising) within a given culture. They analyze the social contexts in which a given text was written, and under what conditions it was — and is — produced, disseminated, and read. Like practitioners of cultural studies, they oppose the view that culture refers exclusively to high culture, culture with a capital C, seeking to make the term refer to popular, folk, urban, and mass (mass-produced, -disseminated, -mediated, and -consumed) culture, as well as to that culture we associate with so-called great literature. In other words, cultural critics argue that what we refer to as a culture is in fact a set of interactive *cultures*, alive and changing, rather than static or monolithic. They favor analyzing literary works not as aesthetic objects complete in themselves but as works to be seen in terms of their relationships to other works, to economic conditions, or to broad social discourses (about childbirth, women's education, rural decay, etc.). Cultural critics have emphasized what Michel de Certeau, a French theorist, has called "the practice of everyday life," approaching literature more as an anthropologist than as a traditional "elitist" literary critic.

Several thinkers influenced by **Marxist** theory have powerfully affected the development of cultural criticism and cultural studies. The French philosophical historian Michel Foucault has perhaps had the strongest influence on cultural criticism and **the new historicism,** a type of literary criticism whose evolution has often paralleled that of North American cultural criticism. In works such as *Discipline and Punish* (1975) and *The History of Sexuality* (1976), Foucault studies cultures in terms of power relationships, a focus typical of Marxist thought. Unlike Marxists, however, Foucault did not see power as something exerted by a dominant class over a subservient one. For Foucault, power was more than repressive power: it was a complex of forces generated by the confluence — or conflict — of discourses; it was that which produces what happens. British critic Raymond Williams, best known for his book *Culture and Society: 1780–1950* (1958), influenced the development of cultural studies by arguing that culture is living and evolving rather than fixed and finished, further stating in *The Long Revolution* (1961) that "art and culture are ordinary." Although Williams did not define himself as a Marxist throughout his entire career, he always followed the Marxist practice of viewing culture in relation to **ideologies,** which he defined as the "residual," "dominant," or "emerging" ways in which individuals or social classes view the world.

Recent practitioners of cultural criticism and cultural studies have focused on issues of nationality, race, gender, and sexuality, in addition to those of power, ideology, and class. As a result, there is a significant overlap between cultural criticism and **feminist criticism,** and between cultural studies and African American studies. This overlap can be seen in the work of contemporary feminists such as Gayatri Chakravorty Spivak, Trinh T. Minh-ha, and Gloria Anzaldua, who stress that although all women are female, they are something else as well (working-class, lesbian, Native American), a facet that must be considered in analyzing their writings. It can also be seen in the writings of Henry Louis Gates, who has shown how black American writers, to avoid being culturally marginalized, have produced texts that fuse the language and traditions of the white Western **canon** with a black vernacular and tradition derived from African and Caribbean cultures.

Interest in race and ethnicity has accompanied a new, interdisciplinary focus on colonial and postcolonial societies, in which issues of race, class, and ethnicity loom large. Scholars of **postcolonial literature and postcolonial theory,** branches of cultural studies inaugurated by Edward Said's book *Orientalism* (1978), have, according to Homi K. Bhabha, revealed the way in which certain cultures (mis)represent others in order to achieve and extend political and social domination in the modern world order. Thanks to the work of scholars like Bhabha and Said, education in general and literary study in particular is becoming more democratic, multicultural, and "decentered" (less patriarchal and Eurocentric) in its interests and emphases.

DECONSTRUCTION Deconstruction involves the close reading of **texts** in order to demonstrate that any given text has irreconcilably contradictory meanings, rather than being a unified, logical whole. As J. Hillis Miller, the preeminent American deconstructor, has explained in an essay entitled

"Stevens' Rock and Criticism as Cure" (1976), "Deconstruction is not a dismantling of the structure of a text, but a demonstration that it has already dismantled itself. Its apparently solid ground is no rock but thin air."

Deconstruction was both created and has been profoundly influenced by the French philosopher of language Jacques Derrida. Derrida, who coined the term *deconstruction,* argues that in Western culture, people tend to think and express their thoughts in terms of *binary oppositions.* Something is white but not black, masculine and therefore not feminine, a cause rather than an effect. Other common and mutually exclusive pairs include beginning/end, conscious/unconscious, **presence/absence**, and speech/writing. Derrida suggests these oppositions are hierarchies in miniature, containing one term that Western culture views as positive or superior and another considered negative or inferior, even if only slightly so. Through deconstruction, Derrida aims to erase the boundary between binary oppositions — and to do so in such a way that the hierarchy implied by the oppositions is thrown into question.

Although its ultimate aim may be to criticize Western logic, deconstruction arose as a response to **structuralism** and to **formalism**. Structuralists believed that all elements of human culture, including literature, may be understood as parts of a system of signs. Derrida did not believe that structuralists could explain the laws governing human signification and thus provide the key to understanding the form and meaning of everything from an African village to Greek myth to a literary text. He also rejected the structuralist belief that texts have identifiable "centers" of meaning, a belief structuralists shared with formalists.

Formalist critics, such as the **New Critics**, assume that a work of literature is a freestanding, self-contained object whose meaning can be found in the complex network of relations between its parts (allusions, images, rhythms, sounds, etc.). Deconstructors, by contrast, see works in terms of their *undecidability.* They reject the formalist view that a work of literary art is demonstrably unified from beginning to end, in one certain way, or that it is organized around a single center that ultimately can be identified. As a result, deconstructors see texts as more radically heterogeneous than do formalists. Formalists ultimately make sense of the ambiguities they find in a given text, arguing that every ambiguity serves a definite, meaningful — and demonstrable — literary function. Undecidability, by contrast, is never reduced, let alone mastered. Though a deconstructive reading can reveal the incompatible possibilities generated by the text, it is impossible for the reader to decide among them.

DIALECTIC Originally developed by Greek philosophers, mainly Socrates and Plato (in *The Republic* and *Phaedrus* [c. 360 B.C.]), a form and method of logical argumentation that typically addresses conflicting ideas or positions. When used in the plural, dialectics refers to any mode of argumentation that attempts to resolve the contradictions between opposing ideas.

The German philosopher G. W. F. Hegel described dialectic as a process whereby a *thesis,* when countered by an *antithesis,* leads to the *synthesis* of a new idea. Karl Marx and Friedrich Engels, adapting Hegel's idealist theory, used the phrase *dialectical materialism* to discuss the way in which a revolutionary class war might lead to the synthesis of a new socioeconomic order.

In literary criticism, *dialectic* typically refers to the oppositional ideas and/or mediatory reasoning that pervade and unify a given work or group of works. Critics may thus speak of the dialectic of head and heart (reason and passion) in William Shakespeare's plays. The American **Marxist critic** Fredric Jameson has coined the phrase "dialectical criticism" to refer to a Marxist critical approach that synthesizes **structuralist** and **poststructuralist** methodologies.

DIALOGIC *See* **Discourse.**

DISCOURSE Used specifically, (1) the thoughts, statements, or dialogue of individuals, especially of characters in a literary work; (2) the words in, or text of, a **narrative** as opposed to its story line; or (3) a "strand" within a given narrative that argues a certain point or defends a given value system. Discourse of the first type is sometimes categorized as *direct* or *indirect*. Direct discourse relates the thoughts and utterances of individuals and literary characters to the reader unfiltered by a third-person narrator. ("Take me home this instant!" she insisted.) Indirect discourse (also referred to as free indirect discourse) is more impersonal, involving the reportage of thoughts, statements, or dialogue by a third-person narrator. (She told him to take her home immediately.)

More generally, *discourse* refers to the language in which a subject or area of knowledge is discussed or a certain kind of business is transacted. Human knowledge is collected and structured in discourses. Theology and medicine are defined by their discourses, as are politics, sexuality, and literary criticism.

Contemporary literary critics have maintained that society is generally made up of a number of different discourses or *discourse communities,* one or more of which may be dominant or serve the dominant ideology. Each discourse has its own vocabulary, concepts, and rules — knowledge of which constitutes power. The psychoanalyst and **psychoanalytic critic** Jacques Lacan has treated the unconscious as a form of discourse, the patterns of which are repeated in literature. **Cultural critics,** following Soviet critic Mikhail Bakhtin, use the word *dialogic* to discuss the dialogue between discourses that takes place within language or, more specifically, a literary text. Some **poststructuralists** have used *discourse* in lieu of text to refer to any verbal structure, whether literary or not.

FEMINIST CRITICISM A type of literary criticism that became a dominant force in Western literary studies in the late 1970s, when feminist theory more broadly conceived was applied to linguistic and literary matters. Since the early 1980s, feminist literary criticism has developed and diversified in a number of ways and is now characterized by a global perspective.

French feminist criticism garnered much of its inspiration from Simone de Beauvoir's seminal book *Le Deuxième Sexe (The Second Sex)* (1949). Beauvoir argued that associating men with humanity more generally (as many cultures do) relegates women to an inferior position in society. Subsequent French feminist critics writing during the 1970s acknowledged Beauvoir's critique but focused on language as a tool of male domination, analyzing the ways in which it represents the world from the male point of view and arguing for the development of a feminine language and writing.

Though interested in the subject of feminine language and writing, North American feminist critics of the 1970s and early 1980s began by analyzing literary texts — not by abstractly discussing language — via close textual reading and historical scholarship. One group practiced "feminist critique," examining how women characters are portrayed, exposing the patriarchal **ideology** implicit in the so-called classics, and demonstrating that attitudes and traditions reinforcing systematic masculine dominance are inscribed in the literary canon. Another group practiced what came to be called "gynocriticism," studying writings by women and examining the female literary tradition to find out how women writers across the ages have perceived themselves and imagined reality.

While it gradually became customary to refer to an Anglo-American tradition of feminist criticism, British feminist critics of the 1970s and early 1980s criticized the tendency of some North American critics to find universal or "essential" feminine attributes, arguing that differences of race, class, and culture gave rise to crucial differences among women across space and time. British feminist critics regarded their own critical practice as more political than that of North American feminists, emphasizing an engagement with historical process in order to promote social change.

By the early 1990s, the French, American, and British approaches had so thoroughly critiqued, influenced, and assimilated one another that nationality no longer automatically signaled a practitioner's approach. Today's critics seldom focus on "woman" as a relatively monolithic category; rather, they view "women" as members of different societies with different concerns. Feminists of color, Third World (preferably called **postcolonial**) feminists, and lesbian feminists stressed that women are not defined solely by the fact that they are female; other attributes (such as religion, class, and sexual orientation) are also important, making the problems and goals of one group of women different from those of another.

Many commentators have argued that feminist criticism is by definition **gender criticism** because of its focus on the feminine gender. But the relationship between feminist and gender criticism is, in fact, complex; the two approaches are certainly not polar opposites but, rather, exist along a continuum of attitudes toward sex, sexuality, gender, and language.

FIGURE, FIGURE OF SPEECH *See* **Trope.**

FORMALISM A general term covering several similar types of literary criticism that arose in the 1920s and 1930s, flourished during the 1940s and 1950s, and are still in evidence today. Formalists see the literary work as an object in its own right. Thus, they tend to devote their attention to its intrinsic nature, concentrating their analyses on the interplay and relationships between the text's essential verbal elements. They study the form of the work (as opposed to its content), although form to a formalist can connote anything from **genre** (for example, one may speak of "the sonnet form") to grammatical or rhetorical structure to the "emotional imperative" that engenders the work's (more mechanical) structure. No matter which connotation of form pertains, however, formalists seek to be objective in their analysis, focusing on the work itself and eschewing external considerations. They pay particular attention to literary devices used in the work and to the patterns these devices establish.

Formalism developed largely in reaction to the practice of interpreting literary **texts** by relating them to "extrinsic" issues, such as the historical circumstances and politics of the era in which the work was written, its philosophical or theological milieu, or the experiences and frame of mind of its author. Although the term formalism was coined by critics to disparage the movement, it is now used simply as a descriptive term.

Formalists have generally suggested that everyday language, which serves simply to communicate information, is stale and unimaginative. They argue that "literariness" has the capacity to overturn common and expected patterns (of grammar, of story line), thereby rejuvenating language. Such novel uses of language supposedly enable readers to experience not only language but also the world in an entirely new way.

A number of schools of literary criticism have adopted a formalist orientation, or at least make use of formalist concepts. **The New Criticism**, an American approach to literature that reached its height in the 1940s and 1950s, is perhaps the most famous type of formalism. But Russian formalism was the first major formalist movement; after the Stalinist regime suppressed it in the early 1930s, the Prague Linguistic Circle adopted its analytical methods. The Chicago School has also been classified as formalist insofar as the Chicago Critics examined and analyzed works on an individual basis; their interest in historical material, on the other hand, was clearly not formalist.

GAPS When used by **reader-response critics** familiar with the theories of Wolfgang Iser, the term refers to "blanks" in **texts** that must be filled in by readers. A gap may be said to exist whenever and wherever a reader perceives something to be missing between words, sentences, paragraphs, stanzas, or chapters. Readers respond to gaps actively and creatively, explaining apparent inconsistencies in point of view, accounting for jumps in chronology, speculatively supplying information missing from plots, and resolving problems or issues left ambiguous or "indeterminate" in the text.

Reader-response critics sometimes speak as if a gap actually exists in a text; a gap, of course, is to some extent a product of readers' perceptions. One reader may find a given text to be riddled with gaps while another reader may view that text as comparatively consistent and complete; different readers may find different gaps in the same text. Furthermore, they may fill in the gaps they find in different ways, which is why, a reader-response critic might argue, works are interpreted in different ways.

Although the concept of the gap has been used mainly by reader-response critics, it has also been used by critics taking other theoretical approaches. Practitioners of **deconstruction** might use *gap* when explaining that every text contains opposing and even contradictory **discourses** that cannot be reconciled. **Marxist critics** have used the term gap to speak of everything from the gap that opens up between economic **base** and cultural **superstructure** to two kinds of conflicts or contradictions found in literary texts. The first of these conflicts or contradictions, they would argue, results from the fact that even realistic texts reflect an **ideology**, within which there are inevitably subjects and attitudes that cannot be represented or even recognized. As a result, readers at the edge or outside of that ideology perceive that something is missing. The second kind of conflict or contradiction within a text results from the fact that works do more than reflect ideology; they are also fictions that, consciously or unconsciously, distance themselves from that ideology.

GAY AND LESBIAN CRITICISM sometimes referred to as *queer theory,* an approach to literature currently viewed as a form of **gender criticism**. *See* **Gender Criticism**.

GENDER CRITICISM *See* "What Is Gender Criticism?" pp. 290–301.

GENRE From the French *genre* for "kind" or "type," the classification of literary works on the basis of their content, form, or technique. The term also refers to individual classifications. For centuries works have been grouped and associated according to a number of classificatory schemes and distinctions, such as prose/poem/fiction/drama/lyric, and the traditional classical divisions: comedy/tragedy/lyric/pastoral/epic/satire. More recently, Northrop Frye has suggested that all literary works may be grouped with one of four sets of archetypal myths that are in turn associated with the four seasons; for Frye, the four main genre classifications are comedy (spring), romance (summer), tragedy (fall), and satire (winter). Many more specific genre categories exist as well, such as autobiography, the essay, the gothic novel, the picaresque novel, the sentimental novel. Current usage is thus broad enough to permit varieties of a given genre (such as the novel) as well as the novel in general to be legitimately denoted by the term *genre*.

Traditional thinking about genre has been revised and even roundly criticized by contemporary critics. For example, the prose/poem dichotomy has been largely discarded in favor of a lyric/drama/fiction (or narrative) scheme. The more general idea that works of imaginative literature can be solidly and satisfactorily classified according to set, specific categories has also come under attack in recent times.

HEGEMONY Most commonly, one nation's dominance or dominant influence over another. The term was adopted (and adapted) by the Italian **Marxist critic** Antonio Gramsci to refer to the process of consensus formation and to the pervasive system of assumptions, meanings, and values — the web of **ideologies**, in other words — that shapes the way things look, what they mean, and therefore what reality is for the majority of people within a given culture. Although Gramsci viewed hegemony as being powerful and persuasive, he did not believe that extant systems were immune to change; rather, he encouraged people to resist prevailing ideologies, to form a new consensus, and thereby to alter hegemony.

Hegemony is a term commonly used by **cultural critics** as well as by Marxist critics.

IDEOLOGY A set of beliefs underlying the customs, habits, and practices common to a given social group. To members of that group, the beliefs seem obviously true, natural, and even universally applicable. They may seem just as obviously arbitrary, idiosyncratic, and even false to those who adhere to another ideology. Within a society, several ideologies may coexist; one or more of these may be dominant.

Ideologies may be forcefully imposed or willingly subscribed to. Their component beliefs may be held consciously or unconsciously. In either case, they come to form what Johanna M. Smith has called "the unexamined ground of our experience." Ideology governs our perceptions, judgments, and prejudices — our sense of what is acceptable, normal, and deviant. Ideology may cause a revolution; it may also allow discrimination and even exploitation.

Ideologies are of special interest to politically oriented critics of literature because of the way in which authors reflect or resist prevailing views in their texts. Some **Marxist critics** have argued that literary texts reflect and reproduce the ideologies that produced them; most, however, have shown how ideologies are riven with contradictions that works of literature manage to expose and widen. Other Marxist critics have focused on the way in which texts themselves are characterized by gaps, conflicts, and contradictions between their ideological and anti-ideological functions.

Fredric Jameson, an American Marxist critic, argues that all thought is ideological, but that ideological thought that knows itself as such stands the chance of seeing through and transcending ideology.

Not all of the politically oriented critics interested in ideology have been Marxists. Certain non-Marxist **feminist critics** have addressed the question of ideology by seeking to expose (and thereby call into question) the patriarchal ideology mirrored or inscribed in works written by men — even men who have sought to counter sexism and break down sexual stereotypes. **New historicists** have been interested in demonstrating the ideological underpinnings not only of literary representations but also of our interpretations of them.

IMAGINARY ORDER *See* **Psychological Criticism and Psychoanalytic Criticism.**

IMPLIED READER *See* **Reader-Response Criticism.**

INTENTIONAL FALLACY *See* **New Criticism.**

INTERTEXTUALITY The condition of interconnectedness among *texts,* or the concept that any text is an amalgam of others, either because it exhibits signs of influence or because its language inevitably contains common points of reference with other texts through such things as allusion, quotation, genre, stylistic features, and even revisions. The critic Julia Kristeva, who popularized and is often credited with coining this term, views any given work as part of a larger fabric of literary **discourse,** part of a continuum including the future as well as the past. Other critics have argued for an even broader use and understanding of the term *intertextuality,* maintaining that literary history per se is too narrow a context within which to read and understand a literary text. When understood this way, *intertextuality* could be used by a **new historicist** or **cultural critic** to refer to the significant interconnectedness between a literary text and contemporary, nonliterary discussions of the issues represented in the literary text. Or it could be used by a **poststructuralist** to suggest that a work of literature can only be recognized and read within a vast field of signs and tropes that is like a text and that makes any single text self-contradictory and **undecidable.**

MARXIST CRITICISM *See* "What Is Marxist Criticism?" pp. 317–29.

METAPHOR A **figure of speech** (more specifically a **trope**) that associates two unlike things; the representation of one thing by another. The image (or activity or concept) used to represent or "figure" something else is the **vehicle** of the figure of speech; the thing represented is called the **tenor.** For instance, in the sentence "That child is a mouse," the child is the tenor, whereas the mouse is the vehicle. The image of a mouse is being used to represent the child, perhaps to emphasize his or her timidity.

Metaphor should be distinguished from **simile,** another figure of speech with which it is sometimes confused. Similes compare two unlike things by using a connective word such as *like* or *as.* Metaphors use no connective word to make their comparison. Furthermore, critics ranging from Aristotle to I. A. Richards have argued that metaphors equate the vehicle with the tenor instead of simply comparing the two.

This identification of vehicle and tenor can provide much additional meaning. For instance, instead of saying, "Last night I read a book," we might say, "Last night I plowed through a book." "Plowed through" (or the activity of plowing) is the vehicle of our metaphor; "read" (or the act of reading) is the tenor, the thing being figured. (As this example shows, neither vehicle nor tenor need be a noun; metaphors may employ other parts of speech.) The increment in meaning through metaphor is fairly obvious. Our audience knows not only *that* we read but also *how* we read, because to read a book in the way that a plow rips through earth is surely to read in a relentless, unreflective way. Note that in the sentence above, a new metaphor — "rips through" — has been used to explain an old one. This serves (which is a metaphor) as an example of just how thick (another metaphor) language is with metaphors!

Metaphors may be classified as *direct* or *implied*. A direct metaphor, such as "That child is a mouse" (or "He is such a doormat!"), specifies both tenor and vehicle. An implied metaphor, by contrast, mentions only the vehicle; the tenor is implied by the context of the sentence or passage. For instance, in the sentence "Last night I plowed through a book" (or "She sliced through traffic"), the tenor — the act of reading (or driving) — can be inferred.

Traditionally, metaphor has been viewed as the principal trope. Other figures of speech include simile, **symbol**, personification, allegory, **metonymy**, synecdoche, and conceit. **Deconstructors** have questioned the distinction between metaphor and metonymy.

METONYMY A **figure of speech** (more specifically a **trope**), in which one thing is represented by another that is commonly and often physically associated with it. To refer to a writer's handwriting as his or her "hand" is to use a metonymic figure.

Like other figures of speech (such as **metaphor**), metonymy involves the replacement of one word or phrase by another; thus, a monarch might be referred to as "the crown." As narrowly defined by certain contemporary critics, particularly those associated with **deconstruction**, the **vehicle** of a metonym is arbitrarily, not intrinsically, associated with the **tenor**. (There is no special, intrinsic likeness between a crown and a monarch; it's just that crowns traditionally sit on monarchs' heads and not on the heads of university professors.)

More broadly, metonym and metonymy have been used by recent critics to refer to a wide range of figures. **Structuralists** such as Roman Jakobson, who emphasized the difference between metonymy and metaphor, have recently been challenged by deconstructors, who have further argued that *all* figuration is arbitrary. Deconstructors such as Paul de Man and J. Hillis Miller have questioned the "privilege" granted to metaphor and the metaphor/metonymy distinction or "opposition," suggesting instead that all metaphors are really metonyms.

MODERNISM *See* **Postmodernism**.

NARRATIVE A story or a telling of a story, or an account of a situation or events. Narratives may be fictional or true; they may be written in prose or verse. Some critics use the term even more generally; Brook Thomas, a **new historicist**, has critiqued "narratives of human history that neglect the role human labor has played."

NARRATOLOGY The analysis of the **structural** components of a **narrative**, the way in which those components interrelate, and the relationship between this complex of elements and the narrative's basic story line. Narratology incorporates techniques developed by other critics, most notably Russian **formalists** and French **structuralists**, applying in addition numerous traditional methods of analyzing narrative fiction (for instance, those methods outlined in the "Showing as Telling" chapter of Wayne Booth's *The Rhetoric of Fiction* [1961]). Narratologists treat narratives as explicitly, intentionally, and meticulously constructed systems rather than as simple or natural vehicles for an author's representation of life. They seek to analyze and explain how authors transforms a chronologically organized story line into a literary plot. (Story is the raw material from which plot is selectively arranged and constructed.)

Narratologists pay particular attention to such elements as point of view; the relations among story, teller, and audience; and the levels and types of **discourse** used in narratives. Certain narratologists concentrate on the question of whether any narrative can actually be neutral (like a clear pane of glass through which some subject is objectively seen) and on how the practices of a given culture influence the shape, content, and impact of "historical" narratives. Mieke Bal's *Narratology: Introduction to the Theory of Narrative* (1980) is a standard introduction to the narratological approach.

NEW CRITICISM, THE A type of **formalist** literary criticism that reached its height during the 1940s and 1950s, and that received its name from John Crowe Ransom's 1941 book *The New Criticism*. New Critics treat a work of literary art as if it were a self-contained, self-referential object. Rather than basing their interpretations of a **text** on the reader's response, the author's stated intentions, or parallels between the text and historical contexts (such as the author's life), New Critics perform a close reading of the text, concentrating on the internal relationships that give it its own distinctive character or form. New Critics emphasize that the structure of a work should not be divorced from meaning, viewing the two as constituting a quasi-organic unity. Special attention is paid to repetition, particularly of images or symbols, but also of sound effects and rhythms in poetry. New Critics especially appreciate the use of literary devices, such as irony and paradox, to achieve a balance or reconciliation between dissimilar, even conflicting, elements in a text.

Because of the importance placed on close textual analysis and the stress on the text as a carefully crafted, orderly object containing observable formal patterns, the New Criticism sometimes been called an "objective" approach to literature. New Critics are more likely than certain other critics to believe and say that the meaning of a text can be known objectively. For instance, **reader-response critics** see meaning as a function either of each reader's experience or of the norms that govern a particular interpretive community, and **deconstructors** argue that texts mean opposite things at the same time.

The foundations of the New Criticism were laid in books and essays written during the 1920s and 1930s by I. A. Richards (*Practical Criticism* [1929]), William Empson (*Seven Types of* Ambiguity [1930]), and T. S. Eliot ("The Function of Criticism" [1933]). The approach was significantly developed later, however, by a group of American poets and critics, including R. P. Blackmur, Cleanth Brooks, John Crowe Ransom, Allen Tate, Robert Penn Warren, and

William K. Wimsatt. Although we associate the New Criticism with certain principles and terms (such as the *affective fallacy* — the notion that the reader's response is relevant to the meaning of a work — and the *intentional fallacy* — the notion that the author's intention determines the work's meaning) the New Critics were trying to make a cultural statement rather than to establish a critical dogma. Generally Southern, religious, and culturally conservative, they advocated the inherent value of literary works (particularly of literary works regarded as beautiful art objects) because they were sick of the growing ugliness of modern life and contemporary events. Some recent theorists even link the rising popularity after World War II of the New Criticism (and other types of formalist literary criticism such as the Chicago School) to American isolationism. These critics tend to view the formalist tendency to isolate literature from biography and history as symptomatic of American fatigue with wider involvements. Whatever the source of the New Criticism's popularity (or the reason for its eventual decline), its practitioners and the textbooks they wrote were so influential in American academia that the approach became standard in college and even high school curricula through the 1960s and well into the 1970s.

NEW HISTORICISM, THE A type of literary criticism that developed during the 1980s, largely in reaction to the text-only approach pursued by **formalist New Critics** and the critics who challenged the New Criticism in the 1970s. New historicists, like formalists and their critics, acknowledge the importance of the literary **text**, but they also analyze the text with an eye to history. In this respect, the new historicism is not "new"; the majority of critics between 1920 and 1950 focused on a work's historical content and based their interpretations on the interplay between the text and historical contexts (such as the author's life or intentions in writing the work).

In other respects, however, the new historicism differs from the historical criticism of the 1930s and 1940s. It is informed by the **poststructuralist** and **reader-response** theory of the 1970s, as well as by the thinking of **feminist, cultural**, and **Marxist critics** whose work was also "new" in the 1980s. They are less fact- and event-oriented than historical critics used to be, perhaps because they have come to wonder whether the truth about what really happened can ever be purely and objectively known. They are less likely to see history as linear and progressive, as something developing toward the present, and they are also less likely to think of it in terms of specific eras, each with a definite, persistent, and consistent *Zeitgeist* (spirit of the times). Hence, they are unlikely to suggest that a literary text has a single or easily identifiable historical context.

New historicist critics also tend to define the discipline of history more broadly than did their predecessors. They view history as a social science like anthropology and sociology, whereas older historicists tended to view history as literature's "background" and the social sciences as being properly historical. They have erased the line dividing historical and literary materials, showing not only that the production of one of William Shakespeare's historical plays was both a political act and a historical event, but also that the coronation of Elizabeth I was carried out with the same care for staging and **symbol** lavished on works of dramatic art.

New historicists remind us that it is treacherous to reconstruct the past as it really was — rather than as we have been conditioned by our own place and time to believe that it was. And they know that the job is impossible for those who are unaware of that difficulty, insensitive to the bent or bias of their own historical vantage point. Hence, when new historicist critics describe a historical change, they are highly conscious of (and even likely to discuss) the theory of historical change that informs their account.

Many new historicists have acknowledged a profound indebtedness to the writings of Michel Foucault. A French philosophical historian, Foucault brought together incidents and phenomena from areas normally seen as unconnected, encouraging new historicists and new cultural historicists to redefine the boundaries of historical inquiry. Like the philosopher Friedrich Nietzsche, Foucault refused to see history as an evolutionary process, a continuous development from cause to effect, from past to present toward *the end,* a moment of definite closure, a day of judgment. No historical event, according to Foucault, has a single cause; rather, each event is tied into a vast web of economic, social, and political factors. Like Karl Marx, Foucault saw history in terms of power, but, unlike Marx, he viewed power not simply as a repressive force or a tool of conspiracy but rather as a complex of forces that produces what happens. Not even a tyrannical aristocrat simply wields power, for the aristocrat is himself empowered by discourses and practices that constitute power.

Not all new historicist critics owe their greatest debt to Foucault. Some, like Stephen Greenblatt, have been most nearly influenced by the British cultural critic Raymond Williams, and others, like Brook Thomas, have been more influenced by German Marxist Walter Benjamin. Still others — Jerome McGann, for example — have followed the lead of Soviet critic Mikhail Bakhtin, who viewed literary works in terms of polyphonic **discourses** and dialogues between the official, legitimate voices of a society and other, more challenging or critical voices echoing popular culture.

POSTCOLONIAL LITERATURE AND POSTCOLONIAL THE-ORY *Postcolonial literature* refers to a body of literature written by authors with roots in countries that were once colonies established by European nations, whereas *postcolonial theory* refers to a field of intellectual inquiry that explores and interrogates the situation of colonized peoples both during and after colonization.

Postcolonial literature includes works by authors with cultural roots in South Asia, Africa, the Caribbean, and other places in which colonial independence movements arose and colonized peoples achieved autonomy in the past hundred years. Works by authors from so-called settler colonies with large white populations of European ancestry — such as Australia, New Zealand, Canada, and Ireland — are sometimes also included. Critical readings of postcolonial literature regularly proceed under the overt influence of *postcolonial theory,* which raises and explores historical, cultural, political, and moral issues surrounding the establishment and disintegration of colonies and the empires they fueled.

The most influential postcolonial theorists are Edward Said, Gayatri Chakravorty Spivak, and Homi K. Bhabha. Said laid the groundwork for the development of postcolonial theory in his book *Orientalism* (1978). In this study, Said, who was influenced by French philosophical historian Michel Foucault, analyzed European **discourses** concerning the exotic, arguing that stereotypes systematically projected on peoples of the East contributed to establishing European domination and exploitation through colonization. Spivak, an Indian scholar, highlighted the ways in which factors such as gender and class complicate our understanding of colonial and postcolonial situations. Bhabha, another Indian scholar, has shown how colonized peoples have co-opted and transformed various elements of the colonizing culture, a process he refers to as "hybridity."

POSTMODERNISM A term referring to certain radically experimental works of literature and art produced after World War II. *Postmodernism* is distinguished from *modernism,* which generally refers to the revolution in art and literature that occurred during the period 1910–1930, particularly following the disillusioning experience of World War I. The postmodern era, with its potential for mass destruction and its shocking history of genocide, has evoked a continuing disillusionment similar to that widely experienced during the modern period. Much of postmodernist writing reveals and highlights the alienation of individuals and the meaninglessness of human existence. Postmodernists frequently stress that humans desperately (and ultimately unsuccessfully) cling to illusions of security to conceal and forget the void over which their lives are perched.

Not surprisingly, postmodernists have shared with their modernist precursors the goal of breaking away from traditions (including certain modernist traditions, which, over time, had become institutionalized and conventional to some degree) through experimentation with new literary devices, forms, and styles. While preserving the spirit and even some of the themes of modernist literature (the alienation of humanity, historical discontinuity, etc.), postmodernists have rejected the order that a number of modernists attempted to instill in their work through patterns of allusion, symbol, and myth. They have also taken some of the meanings and methods found in modernist works to extremes that most modernists would have deplored. For instance, whereas modernists such as T. S. Eliot perceived the world as fragmented and represented that fragmentation through poetic language, many also viewed art as a potentially integrating, restorative force, a hedge against the cacophony and chaos that postmodernist works often imitate (or even celebrate) but do not attempt to counter or correct.

Because postmodernist works frequently combine aspects of diverse **genres**, they can be difficult to classify — at least according to traditional schemes of classification. Postmodernists, revolting against a certain modernist tendency toward elitist "high art," have also generally made a concerted effort to appeal to popular culture. Cartoons, music, "pop art," and television have thus become acceptable and even common media for postmodernist artistic expression. Postmodernist literary developments include such genres as the Absurd, the antinovel, concrete poetry, and other forms of avant-garde poetry written in free verse and challenging the **ideological** assumptions of contemporary society. What postmodernist theater, fiction, and poetry have in common is the view (explicit or implicit) that literary language is its own reality, not a means of representing reality.

Postmodernist critical schools include **deconstruction**, whose practitioners explore the **undecidability** of texts, and **cultural criticism**, which erases the boundary between "high" and "low" culture. The foremost theorist of postmodernism is Francois Lyotard, best known for his book *La Condition post-moderne* (*The Postmodern Condition*) (1979).

POSTSTRUCTURALISM The general attempt to contest and subvert **structuralism** and to formulate new theories regarding interpretation and meaning, initiated particularly by **deconstructors** but also associated with certain aspects and practitioners of **psychoanalytic, Marxist, cultural, feminist,** and **gender criticism.** Poststructuralism, which arose in the late 1960s, includes such a wide variety of perspectives that no unified poststructuralist theory can be identified. Rather, poststructuralists are distinguished from other contemporary critics by their opposition to structuralism and by certain concepts they embrace.

Structuralists typically believe that meaning(s) in a text, as well as the meaning of a text, can be determined with reference to the system of signification – – the "codes" and conventions that governed the text's production and that operate in its reception. Poststructuralists reject the possibility of such "determinate" knowledge. They believe that signification is an interminable and intricate web of associations that continually defers a determinate assessment of meaning. The numerous possible meanings of any word lead to contradictions and ultimately to the dissemination of meaning itself. Thus, poststructuralists contend that texts contradict not only structuralist accounts of them but also themselves.

To elaborate, poststructuralists have suggested that structuralism rests on a number of distinctions — between signifier and signified, self and language (or **text**), texts and other texts, and text and world — that are overly simplistic, if not patently inaccurate, and they have made a concerted effort to discredit these oppositions. For instance, poststructuralists have viewed the self as the subject, as well as the user, of language, claiming that although we may speak through and shape language, it also shapes and speaks through us. In addition, poststructuralists have demonstrated that in the grand scheme of signification, all "signifieds" are also signifiers, for each word exists in a complex web of language and has such a variety of denotations and connotations that no one meaning can be said to be final, stable, and invulnerable to reconsideration and substitution. Signification is unstable and indeterminate, and thus so is meaning. Poststructuralists, who have generally followed their structuralist predecessors in rejecting the traditional concept of the literary "work" (as the work of an individual and purposeful author) in favor of the impersonal "text," have gone structuralists one better by treating texts as "intertexts": crisscrossed strands within the infinitely larger text called language, that weblike system of denotation, connotation, and signification in which the individual text is inscribed and read and through which its myriad possible meanings are ascribed and assigned. (Poststructuralist **psychoanalytic critic** Julia Kristeva coined the term **inter-textuality** to refer to the fact that a text is a "mosaic" of preexisting texts whose meanings it reworks and transforms.)

Although poststructuralism has drawn from numerous critical perspectives developed in Europe and in North America, it relies most heavily on the work of French theorists, especially Jacques Derrida, Kristeva, Jacques Lacan, Michel Foucault, and Roland Barthes. Derrida's 1966 paper "Structure, Sign and Play in the Discourse of the Human Sciences" inaugurated poststructuralism as a coherent challenge to structuralism. Derrida rejected the structuralist presupposition that texts (or other structures) have self-referential centers that govern their language (or signifying system) without being in any way determined, governed, co-opted, or problematized by that language (or signifying system). Having rejected the structuralist concept of a self-referential center, Derrida also rejected its corollary: that a text's meaning is thereby rendered determinable (capable of being determined) as well as determinate (fixed and reliably correct). Lacan, Kristeva, Foucault, and Barthes have all, in diverse ways, arrived at similarly "antifoundational" conclusions, positing that no foundation or "center" exists that can ensure correct interpretation.

Poststructuralism continues to flourish today. In fact, one might reasonably say that poststructuralism serves as the overall paradigm for many of the most prominent contemporary critical perspectives. Approaches ranging from **reader-response criticism** to **the new historicism** assume the "antifoundationalist" bias of poststructuralism. Many approaches also incorporate the poststructuralist position that texts do not have clear and definite meanings, an argument pushed to the extreme by those poststructuralists identified with deconstruction. But unlike deconstructors, who argue that the process of signification itself produces irreconcilable contradictions, contemporary critics oriented toward other poststructuralist approaches (**discourse** analysis or Lacanian psychoanalytic theory, for instance) maintain that texts do have real meanings underlying their apparent or "manifest" meanings (which often contradict or cancel out one another). These underlying meanings have been distorted, disguised, or repressed for psychological or **ideological** reasons but can be discovered through poststructuralist ways of reading.

PRESENCE AND ABSENCE Words given a special literary application by French theorist of **deconstruction** Jacques Derrida when he used them to make a distinction between speech and writing. An individual speaking words must actually be present at the time they are heard, Derrida pointed out, whereas an individual writing words is absent at the time they are read. Derrida, who associates presence with logos (the creating spoken Word of a present God who "In the beginning" said, "Let there be light"), argued that the Western concept of language is *logocentric*. That is, it is grounded in "the metaphysics of presence," the belief that any linguistic system has a basic foundation (what Derrida terms an "ultimate referent"), making possible an identifiable and correct meaning or meanings for any potential statement that can be made within that system. Far from supporting this common Western view of language as logocentric, however, Derrida in fact argues that presence is not an ultimate referent" and that it does not guarantee determinable (capable of being determined) — much less determinate (fixed and reliably correct) — meaning. Derrida thus calls into question the "privileging" of speech and presence over writing and absence in Western thought.

PSYCHOLOGICAL CRITICISM AND PSYCHOANALYTIC CRITICISM *See* "What Is Psychoanalytic Criticism?" pp. 254–65.

QUEER THEORY *See* **Gay and Lesbian Criticism; Gender Criticism**.

READER-RESPONSE CRITICISM *See* "What Is Reader-Response Criticism?" pp. 223–34.

REAL, THE *See* **Psychological Criticism and Psychoanalytic Criticism**.

SEMIOLOGY Another word for **semiotics**, created by Swiss linguist Ferdinand de Saussure in his 1915 book *Course in General Linguistics*. *See* **Semiotics**.

SEMIOTICS A term coined by Charles Sanders Peirce to refer to the study of signs, sign systems, and the way meaning is derived from them. **Structuralist** anthropologists, psychoanalysts, and literary critics developed semiotics during the decades following 1950, but much of the pioneering work had been done at the turn of the century by Pierce and by the founder of modern linguistics, Ferdinand de Saussure.

To a semiotician, a sign is not simply a direct means of communication, such as a stop sign or a restaurant sign or language itself. Rather, signs encompass body language (crossed arms, slouching), ways of greeting and parting (handshakes, hugs, waves), artifacts, and even articles of clothing. A sign is anything that conveys information to others who understand it based upon a system of codes and conventions that they have consciously learned or unconsciously internalized as members of a certain culture. Semioticians have often used concepts derived specifically from linguistics, which focuses on language, to analyze all types of signs.

Although Saussure viewed linguistics as a division of semiotics (semiotics, after all, involves the study of all signs, not just linguistic ones), much semiotic theory rests on Saussure's linguistic terms, concepts, and distinctions. Semioticians subscribe to Saussure's basic concept of the linguistic sign as containing a *signifier* (a linguistic "sound image" used to represent some more abstract concept) and *signified* (the abstract concept being represented). They have also found generally useful his notion that the relationship between signifiers and signified is arbitrary; that is, no intrinsic or natural relationship exists between them, and meanings we derive from signifiers are grounded in the differences among signifiers themselves. Particularly useful are Saussure's concept of the *phoneme* (the smallest basic speech sound or unit of pronunciation) and his idea that phonemes exist in two kinds of relationships: diachronic and synchronic.

A phoneme has a diachronic, or "horizontal," relationship with those other phonemes that precede and follow it (as the words appear, left to right, on this page) in a particular usage, utterance, or **narrative** — what Saussure called *parole* (French for "word"). A phoneme has a synchronic, or "vertical," relationship with the entire system of language within which individual usages, utterances, or narratives have meaning — what Saussure called *langue* (French for "tongue," as in "native tongue," meaning language). *Up* means what it means in English because those of us who speak the language are plugged into the same system (think of it as a computer network where different individuals access the same information in the same way at a given time). A principal tenet of semiotics is that signs, like words, are not significant in themselves, but instead have meaning only in relation to other signs and the entire system of signs, or *langue*. Meaning is not inherent in the signs themselves, but is derived from the differences among signs.

Given that semiotic theory underlies structuralism, it is not surprising that many semioticians have taken a broad, structuralist approach to signs, studying a variety of phenomena ranging from rites of passage to methods of preparing and consuming food to understand the cultural codes and conventions they reveal. Because of the broad-based applicability of semiotics, furthermore, structuralist anthropologists such as Claude Lévi-Strauss, literary critics such as Roland Barthes, and **psychoanalytic theorists** such as Jacques Lacan and Julia Kristeva, have made use of sermotic theories and practices. The affinity between sermotics and structuralist literary criticism derives from the emphasis placed on *langue,* or system. Structuralist critics were reacting against **formalists** and their method of focusing on individual words as if meanings did not depend on anything external to the text.

See also **Structuralism**; **Symbolic Order**.

SIMILE *See* **Metaphor**; **Trope**.

STRUCTURALISM A theory of humankind whose proponents attempted to show systematically, even scientifically, that all elements of human culture, including literature, may be understood as parts of a system of signs. Critic Robert Scholes has described structuralism as a reaction to "'modernist' alienation and despair."

European structuralists such as Roman Jakobson, Claude Lévi-Strauss, and Roland Barthes (before his shift toward poststructuralism) attempted to develop a **semiology**, or **semiotics** (science of signs). Barthes, among others, sought to recover literature and even language from the isolation in which they had been studied and to show that the laws that govern them govern all signs, from road signs to articles of clothing. Structuralism was heavily influenced by linguistics, especially by the pioneering work of linguist Ferdinand de Saussure. For a discussion of Saussure's ideas, and particularly of his use of the concept of the *phoneme,* see **semiotics**.

Following Saussure, Lévi-Strauss, an anthropologist, studied hundreds of myths, breaking them into their smallest meaningful units, which he called "mythemes." Removing each from its diachronic relations with other mythemes in a single myth (such as the myth of Oedipus and his mother), he vertically aligned those mythemes that he found to be homologous (structurally correspondent). He then studied the relationships within as well as between vertically aligned columns, in an attempt to understand scientifically, through ratios and proportions, those thoughts and processes that humankind has shared, both at one particular time and across time. Whether Lévi-Strauss was studying the structure of myths or the structure of villages, he looked for recurring, common elements that transcended the differences within and among cultures.

Structuralists followed Saussure in preferring to think about the overriding *langue,* or language, of myth, in which each mytheme and mytheme-constituted myth fits meaningfully, rather than about isolated individual *paroles,* or narratives. Structuralists also followed Saussure's lead in believing that sign systems must be understood in terms of binary oppositions (a proposition later disputed by poststructuralist Jacques Derrida). In analyzing myths and texts to find basic structures, structuralists found that opposite terms modulate until they are finally resolved or reconciled by some intermediary third term. Thus a structuralist reading of Milton's *Paradise Lost* (1667) might show that the war between God and the rebellious angels becomes a rift between God and sinful, fallen man, a rift that is healed by the Son of God, the mediating third term.

Although structuralism was largely a European phenomenon in its origin and development, it was influenced by American thinkers as well. Noam Chomsky, for instance, who powerfully influenced structuralism through works such as *Reflections on Language* (1975), identified and distinguished between "surface structures" and "deep structures" in language and linguistic litera- tures, including **texts**.

SYMBOL Something that, although it is of interest in its own right, stands for or suggests something larger and more complex — often an idea or a range of interrelated ideas, attitudes, and practices.

Within a given culture, some things are understood to be symbols: the flag of the United States is an obvious example, as are the five intertwined Olympic rings. More subtle cultural symbols might be the river as a symbol of time and the journey as a symbol of life and its manifold experiences. Instead of appropri- ating symbols generally used and understood within their culture, writers often create their own symbols by setting up a complex but identifiable web of associ- ations in their works. As a result, one object, image, person, place, or action suggests others, and may ultimately suggest a range of ideas.

A symbol may thus be defined as a **metaphor** in which the **vehicle** — the image, activity, or concept used to represent something else — represents many related things (or **tenors**), or is broadly suggestive. The urn in John Keats's "Ode on a Grecian Urn" (1820) suggests interrelated concepts, including art, truth, beauty, and timelessness.

Symbols have been of particular interest to **formalists**, who study how meanings emerge from the complex, patterned relationships among images in a work, and **psychoanalytic critics**, who are interested in how individual authors and the larger culture both disguise and reveal unconscious fears and desires through symbols. Recently, French **feminist critics** have also focused on the symbolic, suggesting that, as wide-ranging as it seems, symbolic language is ultimately rigid and restrictive. They have favored **semiotic** language and writ- ing — writing that neither opposes nor hierarchically ranks qualities or ele- ments of reality nor symbolizes one thing but not another in terms of a third — contending that semiotic language is at once more fluid, rhythmic, unifying, and feminine.

SYMBOLIC ORDER *See* **Psychological Criticism and Psychoanalytic Criticism**; **Symbol**.

TENOR *See* **Metaphor**; **Metonymy**; **Symbol**.

TEXT From the Latin *texere,* meaning "to weave," a term that may be defined in a number of ways. Some critics restrict its use to the written word, although they may apply the term to objects ranging from a poem to the words in a book to a book itself to a biblical passage used in a sermon to a written tran- script of an oral statement or interview. Other critics include nonwritten mate- rial in the designation text, as long as that material has been isolated for analysis.

French **structuralist** critics took issue with the traditional view of literary compositions as "works" with a form intentionally imposed by the author and a meaning identifiable through analysis of the author's use of language. These critics argued that literary compositions are texts rather than works, texts being the product of a social institution they called *écriture* (writing). By identifying compositions as texts rather than works, structuralists denied them the personalized character attributed to works wrought by a particular, unique author. Structuralists believed not only that a text was essentially impersonal, the confluence of certain preexisting attributes of the social institution of writing, but that any interpretation of the text should result from an impersonal *lecture* (reading). This *lecture* included reading with an active awareness of how the linguistic system functions.

The French writer and theorist Roland Barthes, a structuralist who later turned toward **poststructuralism**, distinguished text from *work* in a different way, characterizing a text as open and a work as closed. According to Barthes, works are bounded entities, conventionally classified in the **canon**, whereas texts engage readers in an ongoing relationship of interpretation and reinterpretation. Barthes further divided texts into two categories: *lisible* (readerly) and *scriptible* (writerly). Texts that are *lisible* depend more heavily on convention, making their interpretation easier and more predictable. Texts that are *scriptible* are generally experimental, flouting or seriously modifying traditional rules. Such texts cannot be interpreted according to standard conventions.

TROPE One of the two major divisions of **figures of speech** (the other being *rhetorical figures*). Trope comes from a word that literally means "turning"; to trope (with figures of speech) is, figuratively speaking, to turn or twist some word or phrase to make it mean something else. **Metaphor, metonymy, simile,** personification, and synecdoche are sometimes referred to as the principal tropes.

UNDECIDABILITY *See* **Deconstruction**.

VEHICLE *See* **Metaphor; Metonymy; Symbol**.

About the Contributors

THE VOLUME EDITOR

Peter G. Beidler is the Lucy G. Moses Distinguished Professor of English at Lehigh University in Bethlehem, PA. He has published more than one hundred articles on Chaucer, Native American fiction, and American literature. Among his dozen books is *Ghosts, Demons, and Henry James: "The Turn of the Screw" at the Turn of the Century* (1989). More recently he coauthored *A Reader's Guide to the Novels of Louise Erdrich* (1999, with Gay Barton). He taught as a Fulbright professor in China in 1987–88. In 1983 he was named National Professor of the Year by the Council for Advancement and Support of Education and the Carnegie Foundation. He spent the 1995–96 academic year as the Robert Foster Cherry Visiting Distinguished Teaching Professor at Baylor University, and has won a number of teaching awards.

THE CRITICS

Wayne C. Booth is emeritus professor at the University of Chicago. His many books include several classics of literary theory and criticism, among the *The Rhetoric of Fiction* (1961, revised edition 1983), *A Rhetoric of Irony* (1974), and *The Company We Keep: An Ethics of Fiction* (1988). A distinguished teacher, he has published *The Vocation of a*

Teacher (1988). His most recent books are *The Art of Growing Older* (1992), an anthology of poems and meditations with extended commentary, *The Craft of Research* (1992, with Williams and Colomb), and *For the Love of It: Amateuring and Its Rivals* (1999).

Stanley Renner is emeritus professor of English at Illinois State University. He has published articles on Joseph Conrad, D. H. Lawrence, T. S. Eliot, and others, as well as on Henry James.

Bruce Robbins is professor of English and comparative literature at Columbia University. He is the author of *The Servant's Hand: English Fiction from Below* (1986) and *Secular Vocations: Intellectuals, Professionalism, Culture* (1993). He has edited *Intellectuals, Aesthetics, Politics, Academics* (1990) and *The Phantom Sphere* (1993).

Sheila Teahan, associate professor of English at Michigan State University, is the author of *The Rhetorical Logic of Henry James* (1995) and of articles in *Arizona Quarterly, The Henry James Review,* and elsewhere. She was president of the Henry James Society in 2001.

Priscilla L. Walton is professor of English at Carleton University in Canada. She published *The Disruption of the Feminine in Henry James* (1992) and recently edited the Everyman paperback edition of James's *The Portrait of a Lady*. She is the coauthor of *Patriarchal Desire and Victorian Discourse: A Lacanian Reading of Anthony Trollope's Palliser Novels* (1995, with Manina Jones). She has published numerous articles and is current editor of the *Canadian Review of American Studies*. She has recently coedited *Pop Can: Popular Culture in Canada* (1999) and *Detective Agency: Women Rewriting the Hardboiled Tradition* (1999). Her current project is entitled *Our Cannibals Ourselves: The Body Politic*.

THE SERIES EDITOR

Ross C Murfin, general editor of the series, is provost of Southern Methodist University. He has taught literature at Yale University and the University of Virginia and has published scholarly articles on Joseph Conrad, Thomas Hardy, and D. H. Lawrence. With Supryia M. Ray, he is the author of *The Bedford Glossary of Critical and Literary Terms*.